STONE SKY

STONE & SKY

Z.S. DIAMANTI

GOLDEN
GRIFFIN

To Brittany,
To our future hope.

MAP of TARRINE

A CONTINENT OF FINLESTIA

CHARTOK TUNDRA

ICE LAKE

BOROKA · DAK TAHN

D R E L E K

RENJAK

PORAK · LAKJO

RUK

EANT SEA

SEA

CROSSDIN

ELUN-RA

BLK · RIVER

CALROK

STRANDED COAST

EALIUM

LORALITH

ELDERWOOD FOREST

HILL STOP

WHITESTONE

WHITESTONE FOREST

EANT SEA NARROWS

PALORI RUINS

DAHRENPORT

TANDAL

TELRO

TAMARIA

EANT

BASTIAN RIVER

MARON

BLACKMAR FOREST

LAKERUN

PEARL LAKE

PALORI RIVER

RIVER

STALFORD

WILDLANDS

LASTTOWN

LAST LAKE

KANDOR

KALIMANDIR

MOON BAY

SEA

N

NARI DESERT

LIAMORT

CHAPTER ONE

THE LONE GUARDIAN

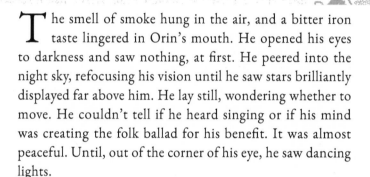

T he smell of smoke hung in the air, and a bitter iron taste lingered in Orin's mouth. He opened his eyes to darkness and saw nothing, at first. He peered into the night sky, refocusing his vision until he saw stars brilliantly displayed far above him. He lay still, wondering whether to move. He couldn't tell if he heard singing or if his mind was creating the folk ballad for his benefit. It was almost peaceful. Until, out of the corner of his eye, he saw dancing lights.

Torches!

Reality sliced through his grogginess, and he realized the peril that might follow those torches. He must move.

A jagged rock under his back stabbed him. He made a quick heft to roll over, but sharp pains along his rib cage halted his progress. He fell flat. He assessed his situation and realized it was difficult to breathe. Orin lifted a hand to his ribcage and found a throwing axe lodged in his side.

For a brief second, he wondered how he was still alive. He navigated his fingers around the axe blade to analyze the damage. The throwing axe had hit him with enough force to pierce his armor and crack a few ribs. Fortunately, however, the axe had not continued to collapse his lung. He would not have survived any deeper wound.

As he pondered his predicament, Orin nearly lost consciousness.

No. Must stay ... awake.

He started turning his head toward the torches but stopped after only a budge. The pain seared up his neck. Even breathing shot lightning bolts through his body. If he moved too much and passed out, he would be unable to defend himself from the torchbearers. Gingerly, he turned his face toward the dancing lights.

Orin saw moving figures, but his pain impaired his vision. He wondered if he also suffered a head wound. The blurry figures made their way systematically toward him. Were they looking for him? He did not know.

Since he couldn't make out the figures, he adjusted his position in an attempt to focus his vision.

"Aghh!" Orin blurted.

He froze.

One of the figures stopped its pattern and turned toward him. There were several large objects between them, and the figure climbed tenderly over them and walked around them when possible, almost reverently.

Orin's breathing quickened. The pain increased with every breath. He eased his curved dagger from its sheath and waited.

Stay ... awake...

Orin could hardly keep his eyes open, but the flame of the torch grew nearer, along with its bearer.

He continued to encourage himself to stay lucid but was quickly losing that battle. When the figure was within striking distance, or so Orin thought, he attempted a lunge in the torchbearer's direction.

"Raghh!"

2

Almost immediately, Orin lost the battle to himself. The pain was so unbearable, he dropped his dagger and slumped in a heap on the ground.

The bearer thrust the torch into the ground nearby and moved quickly to Orin's side. The bearer shifted Orin, who wailed in agony. The darkness closed in on his mind and vision.

This is it, he thought. *This is the end.*

As the pain overwhelmed him, he strained his eyes open to see the creature that would end his life.

Orin beheld a face, beautiful and fair. Her eyes were brilliantly green, and her hair was an emblazoned red. A small green stone hung from her neck and brushed against his chin. The girl looked desperately into his eyes and said something, but he heard only muffled sounds. As unconsciousness swallowed him, he smiled at the beauty he was granted in his final moment.

Orin woke in a small room, colorful in the evening sunlight. The bed in which he lay was comfortable and warm. He stared at the ceiling, hoping if he focused enough, the fog that clouded his mind would lift. He studied the knots in the wooden crossbeams that held the ceiling high. If he could remain focused, he might be able to figure out where he was. And that was the question.

Where am I?

He turned his attention to a small wooden bowl on a table beside him. It was a finely crafted bowl that had been carved and painted with care. After admiring its craftsmanship, Orin realized it was steaming. Next to it, an old, well-used round candle was unlit, and a shallow bowl of incense offered a pleasant aroma.

Agarwood? he guessed.

The room was small, but cozy. There was something peaceful about the place. Something so caring, so warm. For a moment, Orin thought maybe he didn't want to know where he was. Perhaps that was where his journey ended; not such a bad end, if that were the case. But the thought faded as the fog lifted. He truly had no idea where he was.

Suddenly, a sound came from the next room.

Orin closed his eyes and mimicked a statue. Someone entered the room, and Orin's heart beat so hard he thought it might tear right out of his chest. He squinted to peek at the incomer. When his mind put together the image of the person, his mouth gaped..

The young woman with red hair turned toward him and paused. He knew her face. She moved toward the bedside and lowered herself into a wooden chair. Her emerald eyes beamed at him, and a smile eased across her face.

"Hello, you," she said quietly. "Have you decided to wake up today?"

Her accent was slightly different from his, and he knew he was a long way from home. He stared at her as she stared back with her enchanting smile.

Orin's mouth moved, but his voice only croaked. The girl laughed. She turned to the table beside the bed and lifted the steaming bowl.

"Are you going to sit up on your own today, or am I going to have to lift that big head of yours again?"

Orin was speechless. *Who was this girl?*

As he pressed himself upright, the soreness of his ribs thrummed through his body, and his head throbbed. Every second, his eyes remained on her. He studied her, trying to learn anything he could about the young woman. She must be about his age, no more than two years his younger, he thought.

"Good, Orin! Very good!" She said excitedly, lifting the bowl to him.

He stopped. She had said his name.

How did she know his name?

"Khmh," he rasped. Orin cleared his throat so he might ask any of the myriad of questions he had.

He lifted his hands to the bowl and cringed slightly at the pain in his ribs. With delicate care, she helped him sip the hot liquid. It was some sort of tea. He had never tasted a tea quite like it, but it had a pleasant flavor.

Maybe some type of lemon flower tea, he thought.

"Who are you?" Orin croaked out. He gently took the bowl from her, nodding his thanks, and sipped again.

"Me name's Ellaria. You don't remember?" She asked, with a dip of her head.

Orin racked his brain. The fog had lifted, but his head pounded. He searched for any memory of the girl, but the only one he found was the image of her face. In fact, that vision seemed the only thing he remembered seeing for a long time.

"I don't know," he said evenly. "You are familiar, but I don't remember you. How do you know my name?"

"Well, you woke up a few days ago. All I could get out of you was your name. I spent weeks calling you 'Kallon' because I didn't know your true name." She smiled and again turned to the table next to the bed. She grabbed a small piece of bread and tore it into bite-sized morsels.

"Kallon? What does that mean?" Orin asked between sips, his voice strengthening.

"It means 'mysterious one,'" Ellaria explained. She handed him a piece of the bread she had torn. "Eat this. You need to regain your strength."

Orin took the food graciously, realizing how hungry he was. The two sat in silence for a few minutes while he deliberately ingested the tea and pieces of bread into his system. It was hard work merely sitting upright, let alone holding a conversation, while eating.

Finally, he let the questions in his mind defeat the challenge.

"So, where are we?" He asked, surprised at the trust he already felt toward her. He supposed if she or anyone with her had wanted him dead, he never would have awakened to begin with.

"We're in me home, you bump." She smiled again. When the confusion didn't erase from his face, she continued. "We're in Tamaria."

"Tamaria? The plains city?" Orin was even more confused.

"Well, we may not have a lot of hills, but we do have one," Ellaria continued to tease.

"How did I come to be in this place?"

"I brought you here. Do you remember nothing?"

Orin strained his mind to remember. Everything was fuzzy, and he wasn't sure what he could count on as dream or fact.

"I remember leaving Whitestone with a squadron of some of the finest in the Griffin Guard. We had twenty guardians in all."

"Aye, that was our count." Ellaria nodded solemnly.

"What do you mean?" Orin looked at her anxiously.

"I ..." Ellaria reached for Orin's hand, seemingly more for her own comfort than his. "You are one of the brave Griffin Guardians of Whitestone. As children, we are told stories of the brave men who serve. We are told tales of the valor and victory of the lords of the sky, fighting off the dreadful goblin kings of

6

the Drelek Mountains in the north. But yet ... we almost never see them and never get to thank them for what they do for us."

Orin stared at Ellaria. He couldn't bear the sight of her sadness. Her eyes welled with tears, and he squeezed her hand firmly.

"Ellaria, please," he whispered, begging her to go on.

"I am ..." She hesitated. "I was one of the people that went into the battlefield to collect the riders and their griffins to give them proper honor in death. I found you as we scoured the field. This was the closest battle we've ever witnessed. All the slain we collected were just on the other side of Lady Bird Hill.

"People in the city dropped everything to look up into the sky and watch the battle as the sun began to set. Each guardian fought off handfuls of goblin wyvern riders. We were actually witnessing what the sky lords could do. It was an amazing display of the skill of your Griffin Guard. Then ... I don't know how many, but it must have been nearly twenty more wyvern riders came from the northwest .... The battle ended quickly after that. People screamed in horror; the entire city was on the brink of panic. Once the battle was over, the wyvern riders flew off in the direction from whence they came. That's when we made our way toward the battlefield."

"I ..." Orin paused for a long moment, trying to find his words. "Thank you."

"For what?" Ellaria enveloped Orin's hand with both of hers, trying to smile through her tears.

"For many reasons. Thank you for honoring our guardians. Thank you for finding me. Thank you for tending my wounds. I don't think I can thank you enough, actually."

"Consider us even for all the battles you've fought that the people of Tamaria don't even know about," Ellaria replied. "Now, get yourself some rest. That's enough talking for today.

When you wake up tomorrow, if you're able to stand, I have something that may raise your spirits. And high spirits are good for healing!"

Orin looked at Ellaria and shook his head slowly. "I don't suppose you'd let me try to stand up now?"

"No, Sir Guardian, I would not. Get some rest. I will return in the morning."

Ellaria fixed his blankets and retrieved the ornate bowl from the small table next to him. His body ached all over, but he guessed Ellaria had made him as comfortable as he could be. She opened the door, turned to him, and bowed her head slightly before she exited the room.

Orin stared at the ceiling for a few moments before sleep and exhaustion overtook him. He studied the same knots in the ceiling he had focused on earlier to help him wake up. This time, however, he had information to digest. Eventually, he closed his eyes, and Ellaria's sweet face appeared before he was swept into slumber.

"Good morning, you bump! You've been sleeping like a log for weeks. It's time to try and get up."

Orin sat up with a start. "Aghh!" The pain in his ribs felt like someone had thrust their hand in his side and pulled a couple out.

"Oh, I'm sorry. I shouldn't have burst in like that. Didn't mean to startle you so. It's still going to take work to get you feeling all better."

Orin looked at Ellaria with pain and pleading on his face. A grin crawled across hers. Orin couldn't help but grin in return.

"Well, before we get you up and walking around, I'm going to change that wrapping on your side."

Ellaria approached him and grabbed wrapping material from next to the bed. She unraveled the bandaging that snaked around Orin's body. He peered down at his ribs to see the damage. A long scar ran down his rib cage, barely closed up and covered in greenish goo.

"Have I got rot?"

"Oh, no. That's me own special recipe. It seems to be healing you up quite well, if I do say so, meself."

"It's ... impressive," Orin admitted. "Where did you learn the art of healing?"

"I've been learning it all me life, actually. Been caring for the animals and me brothers. Though, they are just as bad as the animals," Ellaria laughed. She finished wrapping Orin's wounds and helped him to the edge of the bed. "Alright, are you ready?"

"I suppose I don't really have a choice, do I?"

"No, Sir Guardian, you do not."

Orin grunted as he made his way to his feet.

"There you go. See, I knew you could do it. You'll be a little stiff for a while, but I think you're healing nicely."

"Yeah, it felt great." Orin shook his head, grimacing. "You spoke about something to raise my spirits?"

"Well, you're going to have to walk to get it. I'll give you a little help, though."

They made their way out the door of the cozy room and into a hallway. The hallway was lined with more doors, and Orin guessed they all contained similar small rooms. Each room had wooden walls, but the outermost walls of the building were stone.

Each step Orin took came easier and with more confidence. He clearly had been bedridden for a while. His stiff muscles tightened and loosened uncomfortably as they walked. He looked at the young woman helping him through the hallway, and a deep gratitude for her welled within him. He may have stared too long, as she turned and met his gaze.

"Ellaria, I, um ..." He stumbled over his words and then said genuinely, "I must thank you again."

"Nonsense! I told you we're even," she smirked.

They reached the end of the hallway, where it opened into a larger room. The ceiling was higher there. Several wooden support beams ran from the floor to the ceiling in two rows, leading to a large door on the opposite end of the room. Ornate carvings of beasts of the land, sky, and sea adorned the beams. Each beam seemed to record a story. The large door at the end was similarly carved, but Orin couldn't quite make out the images from where they stood. On the left side of the room were a cooking area and an older, but also fair, woman. Judging by her features, Orin guessed she was Ellaria's mother.

"Good morning." He nodded his greeting and thanks to her.

"Kallon! Yer alive!" A gruff voice came from the other side of the room.

The right side held a long wooden table with a dozen chairs around it. Men, ranging in age from 12 to 50, occupied half of those chairs. The exclamation came from the eldest.

"Good morning." Orin nodded to them with a smile.

"Ella said you'd woken up a few days ago, but we weren't convinced that ye were ever going to join the land of the living again! Come! Join us for breakfast, Kallon!" The older man was broad shouldered with red and silver hair. His beard cascaded thickly over his chest.

"Da! His name is Orin. I told you that," Ellaria corrected him.

"I'm sorry, me dear. Orin, please join us for breakfast," he replied, scolded.

"I'd be honored," Orin said, as Ellaria helped him to the table.

"Marie, me dearest, would ye please bring Kallon a plate?" Ellaria's father turned to Orin. "Marie is the most amazing wife a man can have. Beauty beyond measure, gave me a whole horde of strong boys, cooks like an angel, and gave me me beautiful baby girl, Ella. Yep, I tell ye, she's the finest woman from here to Kalimandir."

"Alright, alright. Stop buttering me up, you. Breakfast is ready," Ellaria's mother said, as she brought plates to the table.

"No buttering, me dear. It's all true," he said, grabbing her in his massive arms and stealing a kiss.

The breakfast was good. The eggs were fresh, and the meat was cooked just right. Orin wondered what his last real meal was. If he had been here for weeks, he couldn't say for sure. He was, however, grateful to have some substantial food in his stomach. He was regaining strength already, as a result. He could feel it. He turned to Ellaria's father.

"Sir, I must thank you for your hospitality."

"Sir? I'm no knight. That's what ye are, Sir Guardian," he replied. "Me name is Grell, son of Grellario. I'm merely a hunter."

"Please, call me Orin. Or, I suppose, Kallon will do as well. I am at your mercy. Sincerely, you have shown me great kindness. I will see to it that you are repaid for your goodness."

"Well, me boy, ye need not thank me. That baby girl o' mine ... well, she's not such a baby girl anymore," he trailed off momentarily, furrowing his brow. "The truth is, we didn't think ye were ever going to wake up. But Ellaria wouldn't let us give up on ye. I am glad to see ye well."

Grell placed a giant hand on Orin's shoulder, showing his approval at the young Guardian's recovery.

"I see." Orin nodded again to Ellaria with an even deeper gratitude in his eyes. "She's taken great care of me. She's a skilled healer."

"Aye, she is at that," Grell noted. "Ella, did ye show him his armor?"

"No, Da. I haven't yet. Shall I?"

"Fetch it for him, darling." Grell grinned and raised an eyebrow toward Orin. Ellaria gracefully stepped away from the table and headed down the hallway with the many doors. "Son, I don't know how much good yer armor will be for ye after this. It looks like it was good armor, but the throwing axe Ellaria pulled out of ye did a lot of damage. I've never seen armor take a hit like that!"

Ellaria reentered the room, carrying what was left of Orin's armor. The silver polish on it was not quite as shiny as it was before the battle. It bore smears of blood and other indistinguishable stains. He examined it and rubbed at the stains over the griffin-garnished crest of Whitestone. As Orin looked over the chest piece, he found himself drawn to the mangled, gaping hole where the throwing axe had slammed through his armor and into his side.

"It was good armor. Strong, but light," Ellaria said. "If not for the armor, the axe would have killed you instead of breaking your ribs."

"I'm sure you're right," Orin agreed, not taking his eyes away from the blood-stained crest. The crest was small and located on the chest of the armor just over the heart, as it was on every guardian's armor.

"It's a beautiful crest," Ellaria said, noticing Orin's gaze.

"Whitestone's crest was established in the same year as Whitestone itself, just after the Second Great Black War. Men, elves, and dwarves banded together to ward off the conquering goblin king, Larek. King Larek grew up on tales of the First Great Black War told to him by his uncle," Orin said.

"The first war was led by Larek's great-great-grandfather, the goblin king, Torak the Terrible. If me memory serves," Ellaria recalled.

"That's right," Orin replied. "Torak the Terrible believed goblins, orcs, and trolls were the dominant species of the world and, therefore, should rule it entirely. It was at that time the orcs and trolls first joined forces with the goblin king and took up arms against all those who lived in the lands south of the great northern forests, Elderwood Forest and Whitestone Forest.

"That first war ended poorly for Torak and his forces. He was a gifted motivator and was able to gather mass forces for his disposal, but he was a weak strategist. After sustaining heavy losses for nearly twenty years, Torak the Terrible was assassinated by one of his own generals. His son, Jorak, took his place on the throne."

"Whoa," one of Ellaria's little brothers said, leaning on the table as he listened in awe.

"Many years later, King Larek renewed the spirit of conquest in the goblins, orcs, and trolls. He, however, was a much better tactician. The Second Great Black War saw the rise of aerial warfare. The goblins and orcs had trained the wyverns of their native lands in the Drelek Mountains of the north; but more importantly, they had domesticated dragons. Or at least, they domesticated them as well as one can such savage monsters.

"Small towns and villages south of the great northern forests were annihilated, and no trace remained of many of those towns and villages. They had had no chance to defend themselves from the new aerial threat of the goblins."

"Except the Griffin Guard!" the boy piped.

"Well, not quite yet," Orin corrected him. "Larek and his forces were so powerful they felled the great elven city of Palori, leaving ruins in their wake. It was only when the elves, men, and dwarves banded together that they were able to thwart the tide of King Larek's army. The elves had already been domesticating the Pegasi for various tasks, but never had they been used for war. The dwarves had domesticated griffins to defend their homelands in the hills of Garome, so close to the Drelek Mountains that they were always vigilant. The dwarves partnered with men to teach them how to raise griffins themselves and even gifted one hundred adult griffins to men for the war effort. After that, the battles waged high in the sky for another thirteen years, until Larek and his army were finally defeated.

"The power of Larek's dragons was difficult to overcome. The dragons were the largest and most powerful of all the flying beasts and proved to be such in battle after battle. However, they were also the hardest to breed. Eventually, the combined forces of the south killed enough of the dragons that the goblin king could no longer breed them, and, without their might, the Second Great Black War came to an end."

"And then the Griffin Guard became the heroes of the north!" the boy exclaimed.

"That's right. After the success of the united army, the leaders of the individual groups met to establish two cities of the north: one in Elderwood Forest and the other in Whitestone Forest. These two cities would become the first lines of defense against any future threats from the forces of the Drelek Mountains. The elves built their city in the middle of Elderwood Forest, and it came to be known as Loralith, 'The Green City.'

"The kingdom of men built their city at the edge of Whitestone Forest, in the hills between the forest and the mountains. The picturesque land was covered in great white stones that jutted out of the green landscape. Enormous white stones were interspersed throughout the great forest as well. The monoliths inspired such awe, the men adopted their name for the city, and thus, it was called Whitestone.

"All those present at the dedication for the city celebrated with a festival and feast. Those who died in the Second Great Black War were honored, and the new crest of Whitestone was established. The Grand Leader of the Griffin Guard, Koraal the Wise, became the first king of Whitestone and the first to bear its crest. The blue shield flanked by white wings and a silver griffin in the center is a reminder to all in Whitestone of who built the city, who live in the city, and who defend the city. The lords of the sky."

When he'd finished the tale, Orin gazed at the crest and the blood splatter that dirtied it. He was staring at the crest so intently that he was startled when Grell spoke.

"So, Kallon—er, uh—Orin." Grell corrected himself, glancing sheepishly at his only daughter.

"Kallon is fine," Orin laughed at the large man's fear of scolding from his daughter.

"Great." Grell sighed with relief. "We've been calling ye Kallon for so long, it's hard to call ye anything else. But tell me, what's it like to ride a griffin into battle against the orcs of the north?"

"Da! Let that alone for another day," Ellaria scolded.

"No. It's alright," Orin suggested. "Riding a griffin is like ... life itself. Flying on his back, high into the clouds above the hills and the forests, is something I can't even begin to describe. It's like seeing a map come to life below you. And the bond .... Guardians and their griffins choose each other. A guardian comes to a point in his training when he is ready to choose his griffin. You see, it isn't like a horse and his rider, where the rider chooses the horse for its strength or its courage; a griffin and his guardian are partners. They work together in the throes of war. We have griffin raisers who care for the griffins and train them as they grow. But when both are ready, the guardian and the griffin become partners and train together from then on. You see, we fight with swords, bows, and axes. They fight alongside us with their beaks and dagger-like talons. They are extremely strong and do a fair share of the fighting themselves."

"Aye. I can see how they would be worthy allies." Grell nodded, stroking his beard thoughtfully. "What about the wyverns those dirty rotten orcs ride?"

"They're dangerous in their own right." Orin reasoned, "Wyverns are often looked at as 'weaker' dragons. Even without front arms, they can still be dangerous. While they can't grab you as well mid-flight, they are called 'weaker dragons' because they retain the scaly armor and powerful jaws, like their ancestral cousins. You can imagine how dangerous that would be. Their riders are skilled warriors as well."

"Aye. We know many stories about their boldness, but the Guardians always win!" another of Ellaria's brothers exclaimed.

"I wish that were so ..." Orin looked down. For a moment, they all sat quietly, giving Orin a second to process whatever heavy burden spread through his mind. "Ellaria, was I the only survivor?"

Ellaria glanced down at the table and then to her father. Grell nodded for her to go ahead. She turned to Orin.

"I'm sorry, Orin," she said, her eyes glossing with tears. "You were the only guardian we found alive."

Orin's jaws clenched tightly, and he rose a fist in front of his chin.

The only one ...

Ellaria placed a comforting hand on the guardian's shoulder.

Orin shook his head, attempting to shake the grief away. There was a mournful silence in the room. None spoke. What could they say?

Orin looked around to the others sitting at the table. All of their eyes bored into the table, not making eye contact with the guardian. Except Ellaria.

"I don't know what to say," he whispered.

"That's alright," she said comfortingly. "You don't have to say anything at all."

"My brothers and sisters ..." Orin trailed off.

For a long time, everyone remained in silent remembrance. Though the house of Grell knew none of the guardians, they held a deep respect for the fallen who had sacrificed themselves to keep their town safe. When Orin finally started picking at the scraps of breakfast left before him, everyone else took it as permission to stand and attend to their daily chores.

Ellaria grabbed Orin by the arm and squeezed. "I think some sunshine would do you some good," Ellaria said with a half-smile. "And I have something to show you."

Orin lifted himself from his chair, and Ellaria helped him toward the door at the end of the large room. He wasn't sure he needed her help anymore, but he accepted it graciously. She reached for the door ring and hefted it open. Sunlight poured into the large room, bathing Orin's face with rejuvenating warmth.

He guessed he hadn't experienced the sun on his face since the last battle, and that's why he welcomed it like an old friend. Or maybe, feeling the sun on his face reminded him he was alive.

CHAPTER TWO

A FINAL RITE

Whitestone Castle shimmered in the morning sun as the dew rolled down the great white stone walls. Prince Garron stood at a north window of the castle, staring across the rolling hills at the mountain range. If not for its convenient location and obviously man-made angles, the castle would have appeared as part of the landscape. It sat atop an imposing cliff on the northern edge of Whitestone Forest and offered spectacular views from any of its precipices. To the south, sights included the ancient forest and great white stones standing tall and sprawled among the trees, gigantic monoliths breaking the deep green shadows. To the east and the west, views shifted to emerald rolling hills, peppered with more stone monuments of nature. To the north, where the prince gazed, the grand Drelek Mountains would invoke awe, were they not tainted by the knowledge of what lingered beyond.

The Griffin Guard had been highly active due to increased activity of the goblins and orcs, whose homes lay beyond the range. Regular patrols were increased and new routes were planned, but their missions came with a cost. More guardians and griffins were being lost than in many of the previous years combined. The increased boldness and volume of goblin activity was unsettling. It was as if someone had laid logs on the long-dwindling coals of their desire to fight.

King Farrin, the prince's father, whose health was already failing, had taken a deeper plunge toward death with the overwhelming news that he had lost two of his sons. Both of Garron's younger brothers had been lost in a skirmish with goblin wyvern riders a few weeks earlier.

The Griffin Guard of Whitestone tried to keep themselves apprised of goblin and orc politics, but goblin politics were confusing, to say the least, and their informants were of questionable integrity at best. Goblins are goblins, after all.

Skirmishes with the goblins had been more and more frequent of late, and more and more bloody. Even the elders of Whitestone couldn't remember a time in all of their lives in which the goblins had been so aggressive and bloodthirsty.

The cold stone of the window ledge made Garron shudder. He was the only one of his brothers left. Both of his brothers had been lost in skirmishes only weeks prior. Garron himself had narrowly survived a battle near the Drelek Mountains. He had been the only survivor of his twenty-man troop. It had taken him weeks to make his way home. Most thought he had perished because he had been gone so long. But one morning, he walked up to the castle gates looking as though death had spit him out and he'd crawled through mire to return home.

King Farrin had been overjoyed and wanted to have a feast for his son's return, but his health would not cooperate. And with his health waning, he and Garron had had important matters to discuss. After days of long discussions behind closed doors, just father and son, king and prince, Garron had emerged from the king's chamber looking no less weary than when he'd returned to Whitestone.

Garron's gaze shifted from the grandeur of the mountains, the weight of his memories heavy on his shoulders. He rubbed his stiff neck as he looked to the floor. The white stone from which the castle had been built hosted beautiful ribbons of peppered black stone that flitted to and fro within.

He smiled in recognition of a specific spot on the floor. He had found it many years ago as a child when he sat in that very hallway outside his father's chambers, waiting to receive discipline. His father had forgotten his son was waiting, and by the time he emerged for supper, he couldn't remember why Garron was in trouble. Garron recalled thinking the spot looked like an eagle and concocting all sorts of stories in his head while waiting for his father. Again, he waited to enter his father's chamber, but not for discipline .... As reality crept back into his mind, the simple joy in his memory faded.

The door to King Farrin's chamber opened slowly, and a small man came out silently. The man's shoulders stooped low, bearing the weight of years of battle and the waning fire that blazed so furiously in younger men. Melkis was an elder of Whitestone and had seen more seasons than most. Garron held an immense respect for the man. Not only had he been a guardian for many years, but he had also been King Farrin's closest adviser and friend. He had always been around while the boys were growing up. Melkis had personally tutored Garron and his brothers in their training to become guardians. Garron did not know a more loyal and honorable man in all of Whitestone.

Garron waited respectfully for the old man's weary eyes to turn toward him. Melkis's familiar eyes penetrated the prince's own, and Garron feared his face might betray him. Certainly, Melkis would see his sorrow, but what else would those wise old eyes see? With great effort, the corner of Melkis's lip raised ever so slightly.

"It is time," Melkis said softly. "He needs to see you now."

The prince sat in a chair next to his father's bed for most of the day. The sun had shifted from its throne high above to begin its plodding westward march, and Garron could smell the feast preparations.

Thank you, Melkis, he thought, bowing his head in gratitude.

Garron was sure Melkis had taken care of preparing the castle staff to accomplish their various tasks for the evening. Garron, on the other hand, had been sitting in the same spot all day waiting for anything to happen. When he had finally entered his father's chambers, he found the king in a deep sleep. His breathing was strained, but still there. So, Garron had decided to sit next to him until he woke.

Throughout the day, King Farrin made different noises and short movements, but never once did he open his eyes. Sometimes he would appear to stop breathing, and Garron feared it was over. A moment later, however, he would resume his strenuous rasping, and the wait would begin anew.

The taxing cycle would have shattered a weaker man, but how can a broken man be broken again? Ever since his return, Garron seemed broken already. He no longer took pleasure in the activities he had before, and he often spent noticeable time in isolation.

He felt especially alone in his father's chambers. He hated the questions that filled his mind. The more time he spent with himself, the more he hated himself.

Garron tried to distract himself by taking inventory inside the chamber. It was a chamber fit for a king. The massive bed sat in the center of the room. Its wooden structure was carved with images of griffins spiraling to the top. The furs were well worn and smelled of the sickly king. Banners and weapons adorned the stone walls; their vibrancy accentuated by the bold white stone. To one side of the room was a large bathing basin and not far from that a knotty old table with eight chairs highlighted by the rose sunset beams that peaked in through the windows. The other side of the chamber opened to a balcony facing west. It was well chronicled that the kings of old would say their morning prayers on the balcony, keeping a vigilant watch for would-be invaders.

"Father," Garron broke the silence. "Please, let this end. Either talk to me, or let it be finished."

He stared at his father's near-motionless form, waiting, praying for a response to his plea. None came.

Garron threw his head back, his arms up, and yelled at the top of his lungs. After a long moment, he looked back to his father and quietly asked, "Why?"

King Farrin made a soft, gruntled noise and wearily opened his eyes.

"Father? Father, I'm here. It's Garron."

The king slowly focused on the prince and took a long look at his only remaining son. His eyes welled with tears, but his face betrayed a smile.

"Garron, my son ..., I have been waiting for you."

"Well, I'm here, Father," Garron replied with a chuckle, shaking his head. "I'm here. What can I do for you, Father?"

"When you were young ..." the king started. He took a hard swallow and tried again. "When you were young, you were a very happy child. You used to say that every day was the best day of your life. Every father wishes their children will have such a life. If every day is the new best day of your life ... I think it would be a very good life, indeed."

Garron squeezed his father's hand in his own as tears ran into his thick golden-brown beard. He stared hard into his father's face, attempting to capture his every word and stow them away in his memory. The wrinkles on the king's face drove deep shadowy crevices into his pale skin. The sickness had taken all of his color. His eyes were bloodshot, and involuntary tears escaped their control.

"I have seen many things," the king continued. "But the saddest thing I have seen is my son's loss of joy in life. You ... you are to be the king of Whitestone. You will bear this crest as your own name. You will be the one to lead Whitestone in these trying times. A heavy burden, no doubt. But a king without joy has a hard heart ... and a hard heart leads to a cruel hand. You must find that joy once more. You must find your joy for them."

The earnestness in the king's voice was too much to bear.

"How can I find joy in a world that has taken so much, Father? How? I am drowning in loss!" Garron sounded more desperate than he had intended, but the time was desperate.

"My boy ...," Farrin said, furrowing his brow. He pulled Garron close in an embrace shared only between father and son. He whispered, "There is joy all around you. You just have to see it."

The king held his prince against his chest for a long while. Soon, the king fell asleep again, and Garron lay as still as possible in his father's arms. He listened to the faint pounding of his father's heart and the slow winds that filled his lungs. It sounded like the march of an army headed to war, fading away over a distant hill. It was not long before the king gave one last exhale and both noises ceased.

And so was the death of Farrin the Just, King of Whitestone.

The evening sky's pinks, reds, and yellows poked through the windows in the hallway when Garron finally exited the king's chamber. Melkis was sitting on a stool outside the chamber doors. He was prepared to help in any way, but his eyes were far away. His gaze cast through the windows toward the north but seemed to travel further to some distant realm.

Garron placed his hand on the old man's shoulder.

"Melkis," he said softly. "It is over. He has joined into the halls of Kerathane."

Melkis looked up and nodded, a silent storm welling in his grey eyes. Garron extended his arm and helped the old man to his feet. With his fist Melkis covered the crest on his chest and bowed low, saying, "The loss of your father is painful, but the hope for our future with you brings me great joy, my King."

Garron winced at the words. There it was. He was king.

"I have taken the liberty of preparing the castle staff for their various tasks for the funeral feast. The feast itself is nearly prepared, and I have seen to it that the rite stand is ready. I will have the hands retrieve King Farrin's body, and they will deliver him to the rite stand. The murmurs have been loud today, and I believe all of Whitestone is waiting for the bells to toll. You give the word, my King, and I will ring the bells myself."

Garron squeezed the shoulder of his mentor and looked at him with thankful eyes.

"You have done enough, Melkis. I could not have asked for more. But if I might extend you further, might I ask that you stand by my side while I address the people?"

"King Garron," Melkis paused. Looking down, he searched for the right words to say. When he had found them, he looked resolutely toward the new king. "As I have stood by your father's side all of my life, I shall be glad to finish it standing by yours."

Soon thereafter, the bells in the high towers of Whitestone Castle rang out across the kingdom. As Melkis had predicted, many of the people had been waiting for the resounding tolls. The people piled in through the gates and made their way into the square that lay at the base of the keep. The square, however, was surprisingly quiet. Painfully quiet. There had been too many funerals in Whitestone of late, but this one seemed to hurt more.

King Farrin was loved by his people. He was a just man and larger than life in many ways. He was not an isolated king, and his sons, while they were young, were often seen playing in the fields while he visited with the people. His openness, generosity, and sense of justice made him well-loved. His death was a sad passing, indeed.

The crowd remained silent, save for a few muffled sobs, as they looked expectantly upon the rite stand at the top of the stairs that led to the main entrance of the castle's keep. The stand was woven in an intricate fashion out of wood from the southerly forest and stood as high as the average man. The king's body, wrapped in rite cloth, lay atop the stand, awaiting its final release. Inside the keep doors, the new king readied himself for what must be done.

Garron stood hunched over with his hands on the cold stone wall murmuring something to himself. Melkis stood next to the younger man and prayed. He was a faithful man; he always had been. But such times, he found, required more prayer than usual. An aide came to his side and whispered in his ear. He nodded in response and turned to the new king.

"King Garron," he said, placing his hand on the younger man's back, startling him.

"What?"

"I've been informed that everything is ready, and all the people seem to be here. It's time."

Garron's hands slowly slid off the wall in front of him as he arched himself upright. He turned toward his mentor and barely raised his eyes to see his face. Without a word, Melkis gave him a nod that said all he needed to hear. He put one foot in front of the other and made his way to the doors. Melkis followed close behind. Two guards opened the doors before them, and they exited under the colorful evening sky.

Before him, on the rite stand, lay his father. Garron paused for a long moment and one last look. He took solace knowing the people in the square could not see him behind the rite stand from their vantage point. He knew as soon as he stepped forward, it would be a different kingdom. He took a few steps forward and placed his hand on his father's chest and said, "I'm sorry."

Melkis's face contorted when he heard the words. Surely, Garron couldn't think King Farrin's death was his fault. His health had been waning for some time, and death had been waiting around the corner. Before Melkis could say anything to the new king, the younger man retrieved his hand, took a step back, glanced at his father once more, and moved around the rite stand to the front of the steps.

For a moment, time slowed. As Garron approached the edge of the top step, the entire population of the square lowered to one knee, crossed their chests with one fist, and bowed low to the ground. The people were as one rolling wave of the sea. The reverence and care with which they did so surprised him. He was not sure whether they had some sense of sympathy, heartbreak, or respect for him, but he knew they were with him. At that moment, he realized he was responsible for all of them, and he loved them.

He stood silently, seeking the words to start. He had been deeply moved, but a dark reality loomed in his mind. Weakness lurked, and he could not ignore it. He looked at the precipices surrounding the square. The Griffin Guard squadrons that were currently at the castle lined the tops bearing crest flags. Man and griffin stood in reverent salute to old king and new.

Garron looked down at the stone beneath his feet, and a dark whisper on the air scraped his ear, *Go on ...*

"People of Whitestone! This is a sad day. My father, King Farrin, was a great man. He loved you all, and you loved him. And I ... I can see why."

He paused. Thousands of dependent eyes stared at him.

"He is gone now, and I have taken up his charge. We face an enemy we have fought for a very long time. But they are different now .... We face an enemy that has lost its civility. We face an enemy that has taken from us that which we cannot get back. They hurt for the sake of hurting. They take for the sake of taking ..."

Melkis looked toward his new king from the corner of his eye. He could sense a rage building within the younger man.

"Yet we have fought them. People elsewhere call us the lords of the sky, and our Griffin Guard are matched by none. But those people do not fight beside us. Those people do not send their sons to die. Their brothers ... their fathers ..."

Garron stole a glance back toward his father's body, at first with sadness, but he turned back with a determined rage.

"We are Whitestone! And Whitestone will stand! We have experienced a great tragedy; to overcome this tragedy, we must come together and take care of our own!"

At his words, the people cheered. Melkis, however, did not. He knew the king well, and he had never heard him speak like that. King Garron raised a hand to silence the raging sea of people. When they had settled down, Garron grabbed the torch from the torch bearer and raised it high.

"With a new king comes change, and we will have change."

He dropped the torch on the rite stand and strode into the keep. Melkis stood motionless as the crowd chanted, "GARRON! GARRON!"

When he composed himself, Melkis took a final look at his old friend on the rite stand and set off in pursuit of his new king.

The south forest wood caught quickly, and the flames grew high. King Farrin's final rite was complete.

CHAPTER THREE

SILVERWING

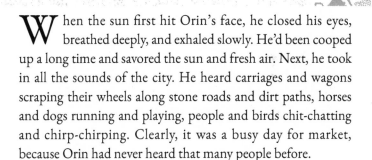

When the sun first hit Orin's face, he closed his eyes, breathed deeply, and exhaled slowly. He'd been cooped up a long time and savored the sun and fresh air. Next, he took in all the sounds of the city. He heard carriages and wagons scraping their wheels along stone roads and dirt paths, horses and dogs running and playing, people and birds chit-chatting and chirp-chirping. Clearly, it was a busy day for market, because Orin had never heard that many people before.

Tamaria was abuzz in the light of the day. The Plains City, as Orin knew it, was of particular significance, and rightly so. It was built around a calm section of the great Palori River, named after the great city of old that had once stood proudly to the north where the river ran adjacent to Elderwood Forest. The river ran from the ice caps somewhere in the Drelek Mountains in the north, all the way to Last Lake in the south. Tamaria's centralized location in the land of Tarrine made it a hub for trade and commerce. It was not uncommon for one to see men, elves, and dwarves from across Tarrine within the city limits. With such prosperity, the city had grown quickly to become one of the largest cities in all the land.

Orin opened his eyes and turned to the young woman holding his arm. Ellaria patiently waited, watching him as he had his moment. His gaze wandered over the vast city.

Tamaria's diversity was not limited to its people but extended to its structures. Many people groups had influenced its construction. The view from Lady Bird Hill, on the outskirts of the Karos district in the north end of the city, better revealed to the beholder how varied Tamaria truly was. Watchtowers of men and elvish design were scattered throughout the city. Over time, the city had grown past its original watchtowers, and the builders erected new ones. The city's rapid growth resulted in dozens of such towers throughout Tamaria. The city, while nonuniform, was a marvelous sight that inspired wonder at the greatness people could achieve when they worked together.

After a while, Ellaria squeezed the guardian's arm. "How does the sun feel on your face?"

Though he hardly heard her, he replied, "Better than I can say."

He was mesmerized by the view. From just outside Ellaria's home, he could see much of the Karos district. Towers jutted toward the sky in all directions, and their size seemed titanic in relation to the endless sea of homes around them. Down one street, he glimpsed the edge of the Karos market square where people were trading, bartering, and going about their business. To his right, Orin saw the slope of Lady Bird Hill, on top of which stood a single tower. He wondered if it was the highest tower in Tamaria or if his vantage point was playing tricks on him.

And the noise!

"This is amazing. I don't think I've ever heard so many noises in my life."

Ellaria laughed. "You get used to it. Whitestone must be similar on good market days, aye?"

Orin shrugged his shoulders and shook his head. "Not like this. I'd certainly like to see more of the city one of these days."

"Well, maybe I can take you to the market afterward."

"After?" Orin asked.

"You'll see." She gave him a wry grin.

Ellaria led Orin toward Lady Bird Hill. They walked down the dirt street and, after a short stint, found themselves next to a field that rested at the bottom of the hill. Horses grazed on the wild green grass, and flowers painted the field with color. Hundreds of butterflies flitted about like a beautiful storm. Off to the right was a small stable. They walked to the stable, and Ellaria led Orin inside.

"The horses are all outside, but I've been bringing this fella in at night. Good morning, you!" She almost sang as she left Orin's side to greet the young griffin.

Orin's heart leapt. "Silverwing!"

"Silverwing? Ah, so you do have a name then. That's much better than Silly Boy now, isn't it?" She teased the young griffin as she stroked him around the neck. Silverwing nudged her red hair affectionately with his beak and head.

Orin stood to the side in awe. He had never seen a griffin get along with anyone who was not its guardian. He understood that after the last battle Ellaria must have become the griffin's only caretaker. The notion made him uneasy, and his head swirled. He slumped against a wooden railing and tried to hold back his devastation.

"Orin!" Ellaria said, startled. She raced to his side. "Are you alright? What is it?"

He raised his face toward Ellaria while his eyes welled with tears. "He ... he was my brother's."

Ellaria's heart broke for him. She didn't know what to say. Words cannot bring back a man's brother. She held him. For a long time, they stood in a silent embrace.

31

"I am so very sorry, Orin," she said with all the sincerity in the world. "I ... what was his name?"

Orin took a deep breath. "Rayin. He was my younger brother. The youngest of us."

Ellaria looked at her feet, then back to Orin. "We lost me oldest brother, two years back. Greggo. Plains bear got him. It had been a tough season, and Greggo decided we needed to go out for one more hunt. One more. We were out for four days, and on that fourth night, the bear found us. We weren't sure how long he had been tracking us, but his intentions were clear.

"I shot that bear with three arrows, but they were like bee stings to him. Greggo grabbed a large log from the fire and yelled over his shoulder at us. 'Run! Run!' he said. Me other brother, Merrick, grabbed me hand, and we fled. The last time I saw me brother, Greggo, he was standing his ground with flame in his hand, as he stared that beast down.

"The next day, when Merrick and I returned to the camp site, Greggo and the bear were both gone. My brother died a hero, Orin. He died to save Merrick and me. I have often wondered if my aim had been better, would I have been able to save him? I don't know, but what I do know is that my brother joined the heroes in the gardens of Kerathane. A hero's death granted him that. There is no love greater than that of one willing to lay down his life for his brothers—or in this case, his sister. I believe your brother and my brother are there together, toasting and feasting, right now."

As Ellaria told her tale, she twiddled a necklace in her hand.

"What's that?" Orin asked.

"Greggo gave it to me after he found it on one of his hunts. Said it was caught on a rock, wagging in the current of Bron's Creek," she said, holding it up for the guardian to see.

At the end of the leather necklace was tied a small green stone. The stone was smooth, and when it caught the light just right, it glimmered like an emerald. Ellaria's similarly emerald eyes were lost in the distance, and Orin couldn't help noticing a glow of sadness, and yet, a glow of pride in them. He knew she really believed their brothers were together in Kerathane.

"Thank you, Ellaria," Orin said softly. "I believe you may be right."

She wiped the tears from her face and helped him upright again.

"Let's get Silverwing some fresh air." She smiled broadly and produced some reins from a hook around the corner and prepared Silverwing to go outside.

The griffin's feathers bristled, and the beast began an excited dance. Apparently, he knew what was happening. As they exited the stable, Ellaria picked up a small saddle. Orin was still in awe at the respect Silverwing showed her. Griffins were notoriously ornery creatures with anyone other than their guardians. Yet he watched as Ellaria meticulously saddled the young griffin.

"His wing was damaged in the battle, but I've been mending him for as long as I've been mending you. He was very ornery at first; that's why I called him Silly Boy. Eventually he came around to liking me ..." She paused, looked over her shoulder at Orin, and shrugged. "I think."

She laughed and rubbed the top of Silverwing's head. The griffin riled with joy and cooed.

"I can see that," Orin laughed.

"Well, he's ready. Would you like to take him for a flight?"

Orin looked at Ellaria as if she had lost her mind.

"What? I can't."

"Oh, you'll be fine. He hasn't gone very fast or high while on the mend. I would like to push him a little harder to see what he can really do. Your injuries should be fine, as well."

Orin stared at her, dumbfounded. He walked closer to the pair and looked hard at Silverwing. He was a young griffin, lean and strong. He had always been one of the faster griffins in the Guard. Many griffins had white feathers peppering their heads and chest. But most griffins had predominantly brown feathers on their wings and down their backs to where the fur took over. Silverwing, however, had beautiful white and grey wings that shone like silver in the moonlight. As Orin approached, the griffin's back paws stamped the wild grass, and he raised one of his front talons uneasily.

"Whoa! Easy there, Silly Boy," Ellaria said, trying to settle him down.

"Have you been able to ride him?" Orin asked as he backed away to give the griffin space.

"I have, but I'm sure a guardian like you could show me how it's really done. And again, we haven't flown much at all as we have been repairing that wing of his. But surely, you'd be able to get him really going?"

"No, really I can't."

"What?" Ellaria studied the guardian for a moment. She didn't understand. "What is it?"

"It's just ...," he paused, trying to figure out where to begin. "Griffins are loyal creatures, but they are only loyal to certain people. That's why, in the Griffin Guard, we are carefully matched. I don't know what it is about you, but you seem to have some sort of connection with Silverwing. One that he and I could never share because I'm not Rayin ..."

"I never meant to ..."

"No. No, really. It's alright. I've never seen this before. My brother was kind. Rayin cared deeply for people. You must have that same spirit in you." Ellaria's green eyes never left his as the guardian shook his head, trying to process all the morning's news. "I am truly grateful, you know. You have done more for me than I can ever repay. You honor my brother's memory with Silverwing. I know he will be well cared for. Thank you."

With some prompting and a few tips, Orin convinced Ellaria to show him what she had learned with Silverwing. He watched the two of them fly in spurts around the tower atop Lady Bird Hill. Silverwing did not have the speed he did before his injury, but it looked as though his recovery was going well. Ellaria explained that most of the damage Silverwing took was to his left wing, and even with all her experience at healing, she wasn't sure he would ever be back to full strength. All the same, her brilliant red hair blew wildly in the wind as Ellaria and Silverwing worked in tandem. All Orin could do was smile.

After many hours at the field beneath Lady Bird Hill, Ellaria prepared Silverwing for an afternoon of shade in the stable while she took Orin to the Karos market square. The square itself was impressive, but not wholly unlike that of Whitestone. The difference between there and Whitestone, however, was Karos market square was one of many in Tamaria. Orin also noticed many more colors in the market. Common colors in Whitestone's market square were greens, blues, and, of course, white, lots of white. But here, the array of blues and oranges, reds and purples, greens and yellows made it hard to focus on any single thing.

Pitched tent stands were strewn across the square. Vendors of cloth, breads, meats, grains, toys, tools, and everything else were set up in crooked rows. People from all over filled the walking paths, bartering and trading with vendors, looking to get the best deals on what they needed.

"Oh, Ella!" an elderly woman cried from a small stand under a bright yellow rain cloth. "Hi, deary! Have ya come to git some bread?"

"Aye, that I have, Gabby!" She replied, a giant grin on her face. "I'll have the usual."

"Of course, deary."

The old woman began to separate some loaves into a new pile. She had half a dozen baskets filled with a dozen types of bread. She was clearly a skilled baker. Orin smelled all the breads in front of him and realized he was hungry again. He watched the old woman doing what she did best and studied the breads she had. Some were familiar, but others looked completely foreign.

The baker's eyes noticed Orin, and a wry smile crept across her wrinkled and sun-spotted face. She turned to look at Ellaria, brought a hand up to her face as if to block Orin from hearing, and said, "Ella, deary, who's the handsome fella?"

"Gabby! Don't let that name of yours turn you into a gab, now!" Ellaria scolded her.

"No, no. Not me," she replied, shaking her hands in front of her innocently and donning the most heartbreaking face she could muster. "But all a poor ole' woman like meself has nowadays is stories from ya young'uns."

Ellaria tried to hide her amusement and shook her head at the elder woman. When she had feigned her disapproval long enough, she conceded. "This is the Kallon I was telling you about. Meet Orin."

"Oh! Ya didn't tell me he was so handsome!" Gabby replied with wide eyes and a larger-than-life grin.

Orin shook his head and chuckled quietly.

"Pleased to meet you, Miss Gabby."

"Oh, and such a gentleman," Gabby gushed.

When the pair pried themselves away from Gabby's conversation, they returned to the house of Grell, laughing the whole way. When they walked through the door, Marie had already begun dinner preparations, and Ellaria's brothers and father were sitting in the front room.

Orin noted one brother he had not seen that morning when he shared breakfast with the family. There was something different about him. He seemed older than the others, his shoulder length mess of hair was more brown than red, and his face revealed moments of sorrow when he wasn't laughing with his father and brothers. His brothers seemed to look up to him, and Orin learned the man was Merrick.

They sat around the table and enjoyed a savory rabbit stew. Merrick and his falcon, Rora, had caught a dozen rabbits earlier in the week and half a dozen ducks the other day. Marie had prepared the stew with local herbs and vegetables, and the aroma was almost as good as the taste. They passed a loaf of fresh bread around the table and tore off pieces as they shared stories and laughs. Eventually, the small feast ended, and Grell invited Merrick and Orin to join him on the outside steps. Orin glanced at Ellaria, who returned his gaze with an impressed look and nod of approval.

Once outside, the three men sat on the top step and observed the night sky. From there, Orin saw several of Tamaria's watchtowers. Inside the top of each, small fires signified a man was posted within. The night was clear, and the stars had begun their slow invasion of the sky. Night in the Karos district was much different from the day. It was, in fact, peaceful and quiet.

Grell produced a long pipe from a pocket inside his tunic and chewed the tip. Orin stared longer than he intended, wondering if Grell was going to light it. The older man caught him out of the corner of his eye.

He laughed a hearty laugh, slapped his knee, and held up the pipe.

"I am an old man with old habits. I don't smoke no more. Marie doesn't like the smoke, see. Or the smell. Well, she doesn't like anything about it, actually."

He twirled the pipe between his fingers and then placed it back between his teeth.

The three men sat silent for a long time. Orin glanced at Merrick's unmoving shape. The man seemed to be somewhere else entirely. He couldn't have been more than a couple years Orin's elder, but there seemed to be an ancient determination in him that Orin couldn't quite figure out. Eventually, Grell adjusted, cleared his throat, and was about to break the silence when the door swung open behind them. Grell quickly concealed the pipe beneath his tunic.

"Gentlemen, Ma wanted me to bring you all some lemon flower tea," Ellaria said, handing a bowl to Grell, who took it with the most innocent face he could muster.

"Thank ye, me dear," he said, as sweet as gravel covered in honey.

She gave him a suspicious look and glanced at Orin out of the corner of her eye.

"You just came to snoop," Merrick accused with a smirk.

Ellaria crinkled her nose at him and went back inside. Grell blew the steam off the top of the bowl and took a careful sip. He slowly passed the bowl to Orin, who took a sip as well and passed it on to Merrick. They passed the bowl and shared the tea as Grell spoke to the younger men.

"Ye haven't had any contact with your folks in several weeks. I suppose they will probably be thinking ye're dead," he said somberly.

Orin nodded. "For a while, I wasn't sure myself."

"I imagine ye'll be heading back to Whitestone now that yer up and about?"

"I will. Your hospitality has been more than I can repay, and I can't stay longer. I've imposed long enough."

"It's been no imposition, Sir Guardian." Grell waved one of his big hands dismissively.

"I am grateful. But if I have been gone so long, no doubt, my brother would think himself all that's left of our family. Unfortunately, I will bear the news of the death of our youngest brother, Rayin, but I hope my survival will bring him some small comfort."

Grell nodded and stroked his beard while he listened. "So, ye'll be heading back, then?"

"Yes, sir."

"Again, with the 'sir.'" Grell laughed and shook his head. "I have a request."

"Anything," Orin assured him.

"I want ye to take Merrick with ye."

CHAPTER FOUR

JAERNOK TUR

O nly the highest peaks of the Drelek Mountains were capped with snow that time of year. They were hardened, rugged mountains, and their rocky faces proved fatal to outsiders with little experience. Bones were found at the bottom of many crevasses, where unwary wanderers had lost their footing or grip and plummeted to their demise. From the air, none of those problems were a concern. Karnak always thought the mountains looked like a sea of teeth from his current altitude. He patted his wyvern on the back of the neck and began his descent.

Karnak had always been more comfortable in the sky. It seemed to him he was able to do more from there; certainly, height was an advantage. As his steed adjusted its wide membranous wingspan to shift downward, Karnak grabbed the hilt of his throwing axe, Dalkeri. The double-edged axe had been passed down his family line for generations. Ancient runes from a long dead language ran along the sides of the blades and down the large handle. A small stone glinting sunset orange accented the center of the powerful weapon. The axe was larger than most, but then again, Karnak was larger than most orcs. Perhaps that is why he had been given his position. Others seemed to respond to his size. He had also been a good soldier and had proven himself in battle again and again. So, maybe that was it.

Whatever the reason for his advancement, Karnak was not entirely comfortable with his new position. He did not doubt his abilities in battle, nor did he doubt his ability to lead soldiers. His discomfort arose from the fact that those who worked in close proximity to the king tended to disappear.

His wyvern, Ker, leveled out as they approached the castle of Ruk. The castle was not conventional to those outside the area, but it was similar in design to all the other forts in the Drelek Mountains. Ruk was the largest of all their steads, and rightly so. It was the king's castle, and many of the joint goblin, orc, and troll operations were planned, prepared, and launched there.

The castle itself was carved directly into the side of the mountain Ruk. All orc castles and forts received their names from the mountains that housed them. Great stone archways and windows peppered the face of the mountain. Many of the archways had small landing areas for wyvern-riding orcs and goblins to enter. Most of them were guarded by armed goblins, but one large archway was guarded by two massive, heavily armed trolls and a whole troop of goblins. That was the king's personal entryway. Having been summoned by the king, Karnak was to use his entry.

Only two ground paths to the castle of Ruk existed, the road to the north and the road to the south, both of which wrapped around the mountain on the western face where the castle resided. As Ker glided past the south side of the mountain, Karnak raised a massive orc finger to his brow and bowed his head slightly. He gazed upon the ruins of the original castle of the mountain. Almost no archways of the old castle remained unbroken. Charred stone and rubble covered the mountain face, results of the Second Great Black War. Many goblins and orcs had been lost in the castle as a result of cave-ins, having been buried in their eternal tombs in mere moments within the mountain. Many of the archways on the western face got their beginnings from goblins and orcs who dug themselves out through walls at the ends of tunnels during that time.

The goblins and orcs had learned, however, and reinforced many secret tunnels out of the castle in case of emergencies or attacks. In fact, they had implemented similar tunnel systems in all their forts and castles throughout the Drelek Mountains. Goblins were crafty engineers and made quick work of the maze-like tunnels. Karnak grunted and shook his head in amusement. *Goblins.* He didn't care much for them.

Not many goblins traveled to his home fort. Goblins preferred the dark, but Karnak's home, Calrok, was on the eastern edge of the Drelek Mountains on the coast. It was nestled in a valley cove with mountains surrounding it to the north, south, and west and the Gant Sea to the east. Occasionally, a goblin troop would visit the orc fort and city for various business purposes. Most often for the fish supply. The sun shone often there, and his people, a predominately fishing community, lived heartily in the light of day.

The journey to Calrok was not a particularly easy one. There was only one mountain road by which to get there, the road that followed the Irk River through the mountains to the Gant Sea Narrows. Calrok had developed a somewhat peculiar culture of its own because of its isolation from the rest of the kingdom. Growing up on the sea made the women tough and the men strong and dependable soldiers; not to mention, they were orcs who had a certain affinity for the sun and the sea. The Scar Cliffs to the north of the port city made great flight training grounds for wyverns and their riders. As a result, Calrok wyvern warriors were among the best in the kingdom.

Ker methodically lifted her wings to slow their approach and gently brought them to a landing on the stone pad of the King's

Archway. Karnak hoisted himself out of his saddle and brushed his hand along her elongated and scaly neck as he made his way toward the large corridor. "Good girl," he thanked her as he reached her head and patted her snout, easily avoiding the myriad of small horns on her head. After a moment, he turned to his greeters.

The trolls towered above him, each about twice his height. Their armor was light, as trolls had extremely tough hides and any armor they did wear lay awkwardly limp upon their shoulders. One of the trolls was the obvious elder. His skin was more wrinkled and grey, and he had creases on his face so thick his eyes were barely visible. The long, crazy, white hairs of his brow and his beard blew sideways in the wind.

He took one giant step forward and addressed Karnak. "Who be goin' thar?" His bushy brows wrinkled and crawled curiously like a giant white caterpillar; his large nose scrunched; and his mouth twitched as he inspected the orc.

"Greetings," Karnak started, trying to be cordial.

"Gratins?" the old troll barked back, astonished. His eyebrows raised just high enough for Karnak to see his old, silver eyes. "The king ain't spectin' no Gratins tis day! What be yer? Liar? Teef? Sassin?"

The old troll raised a shaky spear to Karnak, suspicion dripping from his overly hairy pointed ears. At that, Ker made an audible warning, riling up to protect her master. Karnak took a step backward, placed one hand on the throwing axe in his belt, and extended the other to quiet Ker.

"My name is Karnak, Gar of Calrok! I'm no liar, thief, nor assassin. I'm here at the beckon of King Sahr!"

"Karnak?" the old troll spat back. He chewed the words, mumbling to himself. "Why dincha say dat, young Gar?" The large old troll's demeanor relaxed, and he turned to the younger troll, who hadn't moved the entire time, and said, "Stand ye dowrn."

The younger troll shook his head in embarrassment and apologetically motioned for the orc gar to proceed. Karnak reached over and patted his trusty wyvern on the head one more time and moved past the two trolls into the corridor. As he did, he heard the old troll mumbling to the younger, who listened indifferently.

"I ain't ever heerd no bodies called Gratins afore ..."

Karnak surveyed the scene as he advanced. At least four dozen goblins lined the corridor, running its length to the large door at the end. They stood two deep, and each was heavily armored and bore a long spear and sheathed straight swords. Karnak didn't like swords; he preferred his axe, Dalkeri. Its magic had served him well in many battles and struck down many foes. He wouldn't trade it for anything. But goblins were goblins, and they had their preferences, too.

Goblins were inherently smaller than orcs, but being a bigger orc, Karnak stood a good two heads above even the tallest of goblins. They were also paler. Spending a majority of their time in darkness or underground, they had little exposure to the sun. Karnak's deep green, sun-exposed skin contrasted noticeably as he walked between the goblin ranks.

Behind the rows of goblins on either side of the corridor were stables. On one side he saw a couple of stable hands cautiously attempting to feed a particularly difficult wyvern. The goblins struggled to raise the bucket to the feeding hook as the wyvern toyed with them. When they almost had it, the wyvern rocked the gate, knocking one goblin off balance and sending him to the floor. The other goblin couldn't hook the bucket by himself and lost his grip. The bucket fell on the head of his partner, and chum splattered all over him, spilling onto the floor. Karnak chuckled softly and shook his head.

Goblins ...

Two armored goblins worked together to heave the enormous entry door open before him, and another guided him through the tunnels toward the throne room. The tunnels were surprisingly well lit by numerous torches that lined the walls. Between the torches on small stands, obscure stone-sculpted gargoyles stared at the passing pair. The gargoyle's eyes seemed to watch them as they walked by. Karnak took a deep breath in the stuffy tunnels and pressed onward.

"The throne room is just past 'ere," the goblin guide explained, pointing to a door at the end of the hallway. "Don't be makin' a fool of yerself in front o' the king now, orc," he snarled with a slurp and a laugh.

Karnak stopped in his tracks. He looked down at the goblin and stared. He said nothing, only stared. The disconcerted goblin slowly slinked away, back down the hallway, never able to look away from the enrapturing stare of the mighty orc.

Karnak turned toward the door with a smirk on his face, shaking his head again.

Goblins ...

The throne room in the castle of Ruk was enormous. The cavern ceilings stood high enough that several trolls standing on each other's shoulders would barely be able to touch the stalactites that clung there. Time had finely crafted the stalactites into sharp teeth pointed menacingly toward the floor far below. The goblin engineers gouged holes high on one side of the great cavern to allow indirect sunlight to illuminate the large open space. These light windows were so well disguised it was nearly impossible to see them outside the mountain. The great cavern sloped slightly, and stairs had been carved into the bedrock that led to the highest area in the cavern where the throne was perched. The lower level held long tables. That was the Great Hall of Ruk, where celebrations and feasts were held, something the king was known for. The hall's splendor did not disappoint the stories of its grandeur.

King Sahr, a particularly ugly orc, sat on his cold stone throne. His one good eye danced around the large cavern as though he were pondering something intensely. He muttered to himself as a small, sniveling goblin attendant stood next to the throne. The goblin's knees knocked together, and he was visibly shaking.

"Sire—," the attendant squeaked out.

"Raghh!" The king whirled in his seat and grabbed the small goblin by the throat. The two guards suddenly stood straighter and tried to avoid eye contact. The attendant wept and struggled with all his might to catch his breath, groping at the far more muscular arms of the king.

The king stared crazily at the attendant's pleading eyes until the door to the left of the throne creaked open. He turned his gaze to the door to see the large orc gar slip through the doorway. The king dropped the helpless attendant to the floor and turned to greet the orc.

"Gar Karnak! Welcome! Welcome!" he hacked, raising his hands wide open. "Please do come forward!"

A whimper escaped the attendant, who was trying to stand and regain his composure. King Sahr angrily swiped a backhand at the goblin's face, sending him sprawling to the floor again. "Leave us!"

The attendant hurriedly scampered out of the throne room through the door opposite Karnak. The orc approached the king, placed a large finger to his brow, and bowed low. "Karnak, Gar of Calrok, Son of Plak, at your request, High King Sahr!"

"All the formalities," the king snorted with a dismissive wave of his hand, coughing again. "Come, friend. Let's talk."

Karnak lifted his eyes and marveled at the cavern's enormity. The echo of the king's words settled far on the other side of the great hall. The windows made the cavern glow eerily. Normally, dozens of torches lit the great hall, but the only ones ablaze were the few around the throne.

The king stood and walked around Karnak, looking him up and down. He mumbled to himself and, when he had finished his inspection, murmured, "Very good." He straightened himself in front of the large orc and placed a grubby hand up on the orc's thick shoulder. "I trust you know why you're here?" He rasped, staring intently into the orc's eyes.

"Your herald has informed me you wish me to join in the war council as one of your commanding generals," Karnak replied directly.

"Yes, yes!"

King Sahr blinked crazily in anticipation of Karnak's response to the promotion. As Karnak drew in a breath to reply, a chill crept across the room. While goblin homes in the caves are normally cool, Karnak was used to living in the sun in Calrok. This chill, however, was unusual; Karnak felt its ice in his bones.

As if forming from pure darkness, a figure slithered out of the shadows. The figure pulled back the hood of his cloak as he strolled toward Karnak and the king. As he approached, the darkness followed in his wake. Instinctually, Karnak gripped the belted axe in his right hand, prepared for anything.

"Ah, Jaernok Tur!" the king noted excitedly. "I am glad you're here!"

Jaernok Tur acknowledged the king with a slight bend at the waist in the direction of the king, never taking his scrutinizing eyes off Karnak. A strange hue shimmered about him, almost like the black sheen of a raven. When he spoke, whispered echoes seemed to follow his words. "Gar Karnak, it is good you have come."

Unsettled and still undecided as to what kind of sorcery he was witnessing, Karnak relinquished a greeting. "Jaernok Tur. Forgive me, I do not know your family."

"Oh," King Sahr interjected. "Our friend Jaernok Tur is from the lands beyond the Gant Sea Narrows. He has pledged his service and that of his people to us."

"Aye, but does he bear the right and responsibility to pledge such loyalties?" Karnak questioned, not letting his gaze afford the sorcerer a moment's respite.

"His family is quite prosperous in his lands, and they rule over nearly the entire continent," the king stated with a longing in his eyes.

"I am quite capable of explaining myself to the young gar, my good King," the sorcerer said, placing a large stone claw on the king's shoulder.

Karnak didn't like the familiarity and comfort Jaernok Tur showed in the presence of the king but was more struck by the sorcerer's stone arm. He was no ordinary orc. As Karnak studied him, he noted that the sorcerer's skin had a scaly texture to it, something he hadn't noticed at first due to the strange hue. His dark robes shrouded him exceptionally, and his eyes seemed to exude the same dark hue as the obsidian black stone at the pinnacle of the sorcerer's staff. Jaernok Tur turned his back to Karnak and walked to a table a few feet away.

"My family is quite powerful, indeed," Jaernok Tur began, pouring glorb, a putrid beverage and the goblin alternative to ale, into a goblet on the table. "In fact, our influence spans the entire continent of Kelvur, 'the lands beyond the Gant Sea Narrows,' as the good king called it."

He handed the king the goblet, who took it and continued to stare into space, seemingly entranced by the story he already knew. Jaernok Tur approached Karnak and motioned with his stone hand toward a clear area on the floor. With his right hand, which appeared to be entirely normal to Karnak, the sorcerer did a flick twist and conjured a shadowy green smoke from the air. Karnak instinctively stepped backward. The sorcerer painted moving images on the floor as he continued his tale.

"A long time ago, our people were all one race. At that time, we lived peacefully in the dark of our caves. We grew as a race and flourished as new generations rose. We were a contented people, with great underground cities, and we enjoyed a lively culture. But the greed of dwarves knows no bounds. Our halls were filled with raw materials, gems, and metals the dwarves coveted for crafting.

"Our people knew nothing of the outside world, and the dwarves offered unique treasures to rob us of our birthright. While the young generations were intrigued by the treasures and peoples of the outside world, the elders and shaman of the day warned against them. Eventually, their worried prophecies became reality. A group of young orcs was slaughtered, and in rightful outrage, our people rose against the dwarven intruders. Our ancestors attacked several of their mining cities that were built far too close to our home. But the alliances of the dwarves extended farther than we knew.

"More surface dwellers came to the aid of the dwarves, and within weeks many of our underground cities were overrun.

Our race was on the verge of extinction. But then, as if remembering something long forgotten, the elders and shaman reached out to the magics within the stone that surrounded them and called upon the ancient high dragon Kilretheon the Red. He answered their cries and rose from the fiery pits of Malkra to rescue his people. He led our people to victory over the surface dwellers and drove them back out into the light. The safety of the darkness was ours once more.

"But Kilretheon warned our elders that it was not over. The surface dwellers would not soon forget their defeat, and they would return for vengeance. So, he sent troops comprised of the three races (goblins, orcs, and trolls) to build upon and conquer the lands across the seas. Thus, your direct lineages began here on this continent."

Karnak was kneeling, watching the smoke show. He sat quietly, digesting the information. Nothing about the mode of the revelations sat well with him, but he had not witnessed a magic such as it. As the images faded, he slowly stood and turned toward Jaernok Tur. The sorcerer stared at him with a wicked grin scrawled across his face.

"Over the last centuries, our people have made a complete recovery, and our might has grown to all the reaches of Kelvur. We eliminated all who opposed us, and the time has come for us to aid our brothers beyond the reaches of Kelvur. Tarrine is next. And then perhaps, all Finlestia!" Jaernok Tur said jovially. "And you, Karnak, Gar of Calrok, Son of Plak, will have the honor of helping us lead this inquisition!"

CHAPTER FIVE

A SHOW IN REIMALD SQUARE

After much debate under the moonlight, Orin was forced to concede that Grell made several valid points. Grell insisted, because of Orin's injuries, he would not only need aid in defending himself on the long journey back to Whitestone, but also he would need continued care. For this purpose, Ellaria would accompany Orin and Merrick as well.

"A party of three is stronger than a pair," Grell had rationalized. "Ye will all be able to take care of each other. And Merrick's bird will be able to provide ye all with food on the road. Or maybe ye forgot the road to Whitestone is longer when ye can't fly through the air."

"Your family has done so much for me already," Orin argued. "I couldn't impose further by taking away a daughter and a son."

"Ha! Ye'd be doing me a favor!" Grell joked. "But really, where do ye think Ella learned her healing? Marie is quite skilled herself. And I have buckets o' other sons who will help with the hunting and field work. They go with ye. That's how ye can repay me."

With that definitive statement, Orin could hardly argue. However, he realized Merrick had been completely silent during the debate and hadn't even moved in reaction to anything that was said. He'd sat, listening intently, stroking Rora's feathered head, and treating her with scraps of some sort from a pouch on his belt. The spotted falcon gobbled up the treats without complaint, well trained and loyal to Merrick. Orin looked over at him, not sure what thoughts might be running through his head. "So, I suppose you'll be joining me on my journey home, then?"

"Aye, that I will," Merrick responded, not taking his eyes off the vastness of the stars.

Orin turned back to Grell, who extended a hand with a great grin. Orin returned the gesture and embraced the large man's arm in agreement.

"I will tell Marie, and she will prepare for yer departure. Tomorrow eve, we shall discuss plans for the journey, and ye all can begin the trek the following morn."

"Now that I am up and about again, I'd be glad to help with preparations," Orin replied.

"No. Yer day tomorrow is already planned. Ye'll be going to Reimald Square at the keep. The King has requested an audience with ye before ye leave."

At the puzzled look on Orin's face, Grell continued. "It's not every day we have a knight of the Griffin Guard in Tamaria. I'm sure the good King Hugen wouldn't want to miss an opportunity to make himself look good."

Orin did not miss the large man's dripping sarcasm.

Merrick released an unintentional laugh. Rora's feathers ruffled at the sudden start. Merrick stood, turned to the other two men, and said, "Good evening," laughing to himself as he left them. The other two followed suit and made their way inside to rest for the next day's events.

The following morning, the birds sang their pleasure with the day's beauty from every precipice in the city. The myriad towers no longer looked like giant torches but rather returned to the daytime intrigue of their distinct craftsmanship, standing stark against the early morning orange in the sky. The stir of the Karos market square was audible once more as people bartered and traded goods and services. After a quick breakfast, Orin, Ellaria, and Merrick left the house of Grell for the Reimald Square. The square, located outside the keep in the center of Tamaria, was the largest in the city and was used for market like all the other squares. It was also used for special events of the king's choosing. The companions strolled through the city, and Orin tried to take in all the sights. The buildings and towers seemed to get bigger the closer they got to the city center.

At one point, they passed a particularly busy market square adjacent to the Palori River, the main river that ran through the city. Merrick took his leave of them. He told Orin and Ellaria to go ahead, that he needed to stop in that particular market for something. Before either could reply, he had vanished into the crowd. As the pair continued, Ellaria noticed the concerned look on Orin's face. She took a deep breath and put a hand on his shoulder.

"Merrick blames himself."

"What?" Orin asked, surprised out of his thoughts.

"He blames himself for what happened to Greggo," she specified.

"Oh. I see …"

"He has wondered, ever since that day, what he could have done different. I told him that he saved me, but the loss of Greggo was especially hard on him. He and Greggo had been hunting together long before I was old enough to go with them. His hunts are longer now. Sometimes he's gone for two weeks at a time." She paused. "He always makes sure there's enough food at home for his extended hunts, but I think he is out there looking for that bear. He goes out alone, now. He won't take me anymore. I'm just thankful for that falcon of his. Rora has given him a small sense of companionship on his hunts, and since having her, he's laughed again. I pray that bird lives forever ... or at least until he finds himself a good wife," Ellaria teased with a wink.

Orin dipped his chin with a half-smile. "And what about you? How are you?"

"It's been two years. I've come to believe all of life is precious. I don't want to live it in sorrow. That's why I love to heal. It gives someone the chance to overcome adversity and live again."

"And what an adept healer you are!" Orin proclaimed. "I know one man who is very grateful."

They continued winding their way through the city for some time before the noise of Reimald Square was too loud to ignore. As they passed between two buildings, they came upon the enormous square. Orin's mouth gaped at the immense keep at the other end. Innumerable flags waved in the wind from the tops of the buildings on all sides of the square. The keep itself was covered in them, and many of them were attached at odd angles as more flags were added with no discernible organization.

Reimald Square, made with an abundance of ancient stone, buzzed with activity. Though it was the first square built in Tamaria, its engineers had designed it with grand intentions.

Merchants, artisans, and craftsmen were buying, selling, and trading wildly. Armored guards equipped with spears engaged in purchasing, eating, and idle conversations. Children ran around the square playing games.

The scene thrummed with life and diversity and mirrored the myriad of colors Orin had already seen in the Karos section of the massive city. Elvish merchants were scattered throughout the square, selling various wares. Several dwarven craftsmen negotiated with sellers looking for finely crafted tools, weapons, and the like. In front of a tavern at one of the corners of the square, a halfling jovially encouraged guests to come in and enjoy a pint at his fine establishment. The exterior of the place was littered with flags, showing only the wooden sign that said The Flagkeep Tavern and the door below. The smell of roasted meat hit Orin's nose, and he couldn't tell if it was coming from the tavern. If it was, the smell alone convinced him to stop in the next time he found himself in Tamaria.

A small sack of beans hit Orin's leg, and he reached down to pick it up. An elvish boy looked at him and motioned for Orin to toss it back. The boy caught the sack with his knee, made a quick twist, and flipped the bag to one of his friends to begin their game anew.

Orin and Ellaria waded through the crowds to the bottom of the keep's steps. The keep loomed even larger up close, and the plethora of flags gave it a sort of organic illusion, waving like colorful, scraggly hair. As they were about to continue up the steps, a loud call of trumpets sounded, resonating throughout the square. The initially startled crowds fell silent and gathered near the steps. Orin turned to Ellaria with questions on his face, but she returned his questions with the same puzzled look and shrugged her shoulders.

The large entryway to the keep was already open, but a troop of guards came out, marching to the trumpets' rhythm. Some carried spears; others carried more flags. The troop split and formed two lines, one on either side of the entryway. They turned toward the center and raised their spears and flags high. Out of the entryway came a large elf in rather splendid armor. He made his way to the front of the stairs, stepped to one side, and turned. The trumpets stopped, and all was quiet. Some of the children could be heard murmuring in the back. A woman scolded them, and the murmuring was replaced by muffled chuckling that rolled through the rest of the crowd. The elf knight at the top of the stairs rolled his eyes in obvious displeasure. The crowd settled down again and stared at the top of the stairs, waiting. The quiet ended as abruptly as it had begun.

"Tamaria! Your Highness, the King! The comforter of the weak. Your champion for freedom. Your pursuer of justice ..."

The elf knight mustered as much enthusiasm as he could, but the compliments and titles droned on far too long before, finally, "The keeper of wisdoms. King Hugen!"

At that, the trumpets sounded again, and cheers and applause erupted from the crowds. Orin laughed at the spectacle but joined in the clapping to not make a scene.

King Hugen was an enormously fat man. He waddled out, waving to all his loyal subjects. The fat on his face was pushed oddly by his wide grin, and his eyes were almost invisible as the skin folds wrinkled around them. His robes were of the finest materials, but the extreme colors were so overwhelming that Orin thought he looked like a shorter, stouter version of the flag-adorned keep. His crown was made with the finest gold, but every inch was covered with different colored gems. When King Hugen finally reached the front of the steps, Orin made out a thin mustache that accompanied the king's beady eyes on his engorged face.

Regardless of who the king really was, it was easy to tell, he enjoyed being the king.

The gathering was released to continue business as King Hugen waddled through the square, interacting with his people. Deep belly laughs rolled often from the rotund king. He stopped here and there at different stands while the elf knight stayed close behind.

Orin and Ellaria wandered nearby, waiting for the right moment to engage the king.

The king stopped at a cluster of merchant stands where some elves were selling pastries and treats. The sweet aroma was enticing, to say the least. Ellaria thought King Hugen might be a while, so she signaled for Orin to wait and went to speak to the elf knight. Orin couldn't hear what the two were saying, but as she spoke with him, the elf knight looked over at him in recognition. Orin continued to take it all in: the colors, the smells, the noises. It was overwhelming. So much so, he started feeling cramped. He stepped to the side, trying to focus on anything in order to ground himself.

His eyes fell upon a man, his clothing browned with dirt, his hair matted. The man's eyes, the only part of him that wasn't brown, were piercingly blue. Streaks in the dirt on his face betrayed his tears as he walked, his blue eyes determined. Orin felt the man's sorrow, even from where he stood. Something didn't feel right. The whole world slowed down.

Orin's experience in battles had taught him to follow his instincts. They often meant the difference between life and death. The man's face was grim with death. As Orin watched, the man pulled a jagged dagger from underneath his cloak, his hands shaking with uncontrollable rage. The tears on his face streaked the dirt even more. Orin followed the man's gaze. He was going for the king!

No longer thinking, but letting his muscle memory take over, Orin bolted from his position near a stand, startling the surrounding crowd. Seeing Orin out of the corner of his eye, the man charged forward, hoping to reach the king before he was intercepted. Orin had read his motives quickly and cut him off.

The man lunged at Orin, knifepoint first, swinging wildly at anything he might hit. Orin dodged the blade as each swipe came. He twisted around the assailant, grabbed his arm, and hit the man's elbow until the dagger clanged to the ground. With one swift move, Orin wrapped around the man's back, throwing him into a choke hold. The man savagely fought to get free, to no avail, as the elf knight came to assist Orin. The elf knight slammed the man to the ground and pinned him for apprehension.

"Why did you have to find yourself a dagger? Did you mean to stick the king?" the elf knight asked, sounding disappointed by the whole thing, as he held the man down.

The farmer spit and screamed. All the people around the king watched in horror.

"Ye fat, ugly king! Ye done nothin' fer us! Nothin'!" His rage burst out with all sincerity. He coughed under the weight of the elf knight. "We been tellin' ye that thar's somethin' goin' on out thar. And ye did nothin'!"

The farmer sobbed violent, heaving tears. The crowd was stunned by the spectacle. Orin stood, unable to move, wondering what the farmer meant. King Hugen looked around at the appalled witnesses, not knowing whether they were disgusted with him or the wretched farmer. He took a step forward to address the farmer.

"I hav—"

"Raghh!" the farmer wailed wildly, interrupting the king. "Ye what? Ye what? Ye dinnit lissen! Ye dinnit!" He tried to compose himself, but the despair had boiled over and would not be contained easily.

"And then ... I brunged me crop to market. And then ... I goed home. They killt her ... They killt her!" His sobs were low, deep, and fitful.

King Hugen looked around at his people, recognizing the pity they took on the farmer. For a moment, he was at a loss, until he looked at Orin, and a glint of recognition appeared on his face. He found his victory.

"My friend," the king said, showing as much feigned compassion as he could muster. "I *have* done something. I heard your cry." He stood taller, extended his arm fully toward Orin, and raised his voice for all to hear. "For here! Before us, in your very midst, one of the valiant Griffin Guard. A true Guardian of Whitestone!"

Excited whispers rippled through the crowd. The king, seeing his plan was working, continued, "Tamaria, your king loves you! It breaks my heart that any should feel unheard. Why, this very day, I had planned to meet with our young Guardian to discuss this very matter. Surely, we have heard the disconcerting rumblings of the peculiar strangeties in our northern farmlands."

Ellaria rolled her eyes at the king's wordplay, not deluded by his game.

Now, having the crowd's complete attention, the king stepped over the head of the farmer, walked over to Orin, and draped an arm around his shoulder in a sideways hug, bringing him close before continuing.

"And look! Our Guardian's first act in Tamaria is to save your beloved king! The heart of a true Guardian, this one! He will not let our northern farmlands be dismayed any longer! Surely, as he has shown us victory today, he will not let us down! Your king loves you! I commission this Guardian today, and all will be well!"

He grabbed Orin's hand and heaved it high as the crowd erupted into applause. He waved with his other hand, the fat on his arm waggling.

He turned a beady eye to Orin and said out of the corner of his mouth, without losing his smile, "Wave to them, Guardian. They love you."

Chapter Six

A Whisper On The Wind

King Garron stood in the dark corner of his chamber, not having worked himself up to moving into the king's chamber. It had been a couple of days since his father passed, and no one had seen him since the final rite ceremony. Daily operations around the kingdom continued unimpeded, save for the increasing lot of items that required the king's overview. Garron had been mumbling to himself for hours without realizing. A sudden, resounding knock banged at his chamber door.

"Your Highness, it's Melkis. Please let me in."

Melkis' loud knocks and pleas snapped Garron from his daze. He hesitated and then strolled to the door to open it.

"Melkis, what is it?" Garron asked, looking as though he hadn't slept for a month.

"Sire," Melkis started, but at the sight of his forlorn young king, the duty in his voice turned to concern. "Have you not slept at all?"

"No. I ..." Garron trailed off. He wasn't sure if he had slept or not. Certainly, he was exhausted, but he couldn't remember much of the past few days.

His bloodshot eyes turned to his old teacher and friend as Melkis grabbed his arm.

"Let's get you some food, my king."

The old guardian led his young king through the castle to the kitchen, where he gathered some bread, a hunk of cured meat, and wine. He led the younger man through an anterior hallway that opened to a balcony, which overlooked the rolling hills peppered with monumental stones to the west. He set the plate of meat and bread on the wide balcony railing and poured wine for each of them. Garron broke the bread and ripped the meat, a half for each of them. He stared over the hills. One large white stone in the distance caught his eye. He had camped under that very stone on his return journey home.

Melkis had seen that distant look in others' eyes. He was an old veteran and had seen much in his years in the Griffin Guard, but King Garron's look was different somehow. He was a new, but broken king. Melkis released a heavy sigh, but it was covered by the wind. He stood beside his king, pulling apart pieces of meat and drinking wine.

After a long while, he spoke.

"I remember when your father became king."

The remark startled Garron back to the present. He took a swig of wine and turned to listen to the old guardian.

"He was so afraid. He had just lost his father, your grandfather, and thought he would never be able to live up to his father's standard." He laughed at the notion. "He always saw the best in others, but sometimes it's hard to see anything good in yourself.

"Your father was like a brother to me. I can't count how many times we fought side by side during our time together in the Griffin Guard. He saved my life; I saved his. We were unstoppable. I saw him accomplish amazing things. He led us to victory in battles we thought we'd lost. He gave his all for those around him. I had no doubts he would make an excellent king. And when he became king, he proved me right."

Melkis took a bite of bread and looked at the silent king, considering the younger man's needs.

"Though, as many times as your father surprised me with his goodness …" A lump grew in the old Guardian's throat. "All of his best, he saved for you and your brothers."

Garron flinched. He was the only one left. His two brothers had died in a recent incident against an orc wyvern troop a few weeks prior.

How much loss can one heart bear? Garron wondered.

Melkis turned toward the king and spoke with certainty. "I have watched you grow your entire life. You are strong. You have a heart for others. I've seen it. You've sacrificed yourself for your brothers a hundred times."

The guardian laughed as he sipped his wine.

"I remember one morning getting an unexpected shower coming to retrieve you and your brothers for training. The bucket fell right off the chamber door and hit me in the head. I was a little less patient in my younger years, and even though you weren't the sole culprit, you took the punishment on yourself to save your brothers. Your sacrifice moved me, and I took it easy on your punishment."

"Ha!" Garron laughed. Relief spread across the old man's face, and his grin widened as Garron continued. "As I recall, Danella's wooden bread paddle did not spare me any punishment."

"You were little. You don't remember right," Melkis winked at him. He took a long last swig of his wine and said, "Come, let's finish this and go visit the training field."

The two men finished their meal, reminiscing about fond memories and enjoying the westward view. There was work to do, but they could finish lunch first.

The residents of Whitestone milled about busily, accomplishing their business as usual. Their just king had died only a few days prior, but life went on within the white stoned city. A woman rolled her cart down the street toward the market square. A gust of wind caught up the fine linen on the top of the cart and unfurled it onto the ground. She cursed her luck and began rolling it back up when suddenly she stopped to witness what everyone else had paused to see—the new king, Garron. The people were glad to see him out and about.

Though there were many things to take care of, Melkis thought it would be good for Garron to get his blood pumping on the training field with the Griffin Guard. Along the way, people stopped to gawk and smile at their new king. The young ladies were particularly interested in him, as he hadn't yet taken a wife.

Melkis laughed at their enamored interactions. "You'll have a lot more time for a wife and family, fulfilling the responsibility of king rather than on mission with the Guard," he said, nodding toward a pretty, young woman with golden hair.

"One thing at a time, Melkis," Garron teased back.

They rounded a street corner and stood before the griffin training complex, the Grand Corral. Aside from the castle, it was the largest structure in Whitestone. The white stone walls rose high and were adorned with large blue banners with silver griffins embroidered on them. Just the sight of the complex raised Garron's spirits.

The men walked to the massive front doors, and without words, two guards heaved them open. An immense field area in the center of the complex was ornamented with various training dummies and obstacles. The entire field was confined within the walls of the structure, which had no roof over the central area. Of course, there were guardians and griffins throughout. Some worked on different battle strategies; others practiced ground attacks. A few on the top of the far veranda practiced diving techniques.

Griffin stables lined the outside walls, opening inward under the terraces. The barracks rooms were all on the second floor and ran around the complex, except for the front side. A large training room, where instructors would teach the trainees, occupied the space above them. Most of the tactical operations were planned in the rooms above.

Garron had spent many years in the place, and in a lot of ways, the Grand Corral was more home than the castle. As they continued forward, they stepped out of the shadows of the entryway and into the sun of the field. All activity in the Grand Corral halted with one horn blast, all eyes on King Garron. Remembering his responsibility to return them to work, he waved them off. The buzz of training continued.

A large griffin flew from above the main terrace behind them and landed hard before the king. The guardian riding it swung his legs over and hopped off in one fluid motion. The large griffin stood statuesque, well trained. Its muscles were taut, ready for any command.

"My King," the guardian placed a fist over the Whitestone crest painted on his chest armor. "It pleases me to see you."

The two stared at each other for a moment. Garron breathed a heavy sigh and hugged the guardian with everything he had, glad to see his cousin.

Clanging swords rang out through the complex. Melkis had requested a sword that they might get a round of sparring in, hoping the physical exertion would help Garron release some frustrations. Pernden, Garron's cousin, was happy to oblige, lending his own sword to the king.

Many of the guardians, who had been resting in their barracks rooms, made their way to the balconies around the training ground to watch the spectacle. Watching Master Melkis in sword combat was a special treat on its own, but seeing him spar the new king could not be missed.

A wide swing from Garron nearly touched the old master. With surprising agility for his age, Melkis sidestepped the attack and countered with his own swipe. Garron deflected with a well-practiced parry, stepping away from his opponent. The move required him to play the defensive, parrying a short flurry from the old master. And then Garron took up the offense.

He launched into a hard and heavy attack routine, hoping to use brute force to defeat the master's old muscles. Melkis smiled as he parried the first, then the second, recognizing the routine.

Smart, he thought.

He had taught that very routine to the young king. On just the right jab, Melkis rolled out to the side, swiping his thin, slightly curved sword into the armored shin of the young king. Because of his position in the jab, Garron's weight carried him straight to the ground at the sweeping move of the master. He lifted his head from the dirt and turned toward the grinning old man.

This fool ... the wind whispered in his ear. *He's trying to kill you.*

Rage overcame Garron, and he bolted at Melkis, striking furious blows. His movements paired with a wild-eyed frenzy. The old master parried and dodged, surprised at the younger man's fury. Cuts flew far too close to his throat. Melkis mumbled a magical command through gritted teeth to his sword, Wintertide. The clangs became crashes like lightning as the swords met. The white crystalline stone in the hilt of his sword glowed, and chips of ice flew with each parry.

Finally, Melkis saw an opportunity in Garron's tiring rampage and took it. He dove past the throttling king, sending him wildly off balance to the side. Melkis rolled, popped, and spun, swiping Wintertide through the air.

A blade of chilled air blasted the young king. Garron pressed forward in slow motion, barely able to move as the freeze covered him. Icicles formed on his sword, cloak, and hair. He stopped a few feet from his old master, the point of the magical sword inches from the king's throat.

"Well, do it then!" Garron screamed. "If you mean to kill me, get it over with!"

The stunned master wavered with his sword.

"Garron ... What ..."

"It would be better this way!"

Silence. Not yet ...

Tears streamed down Garron's face, as if he had snapped back to the present from some distant plane. Melkis stared, as did many of the guardians who had been watching the sparring session. Pernden stepped forward toward the old master, laying his hand on Melkis's arm to lower Wintertide's deadly stance. He looked to his cousin with empathetic eyes.

"Garron, I'm going to take my sword back now." He cautiously reached for his sword and grabbed his cousin's hand.

"I'm sorry," Garron whimpered. "I'm so sorry."

After they had sent all the spectators back to training, they brought Garron inside the officers' dining hall. There, they grabbed some tea and retreated into an adjacent sitting room. The room was nicely furnished with large chairs for comfort and a fireplace that was already burning. Pernden sat the king in one of the comfortable chairs next to the hearth. Melkis grabbed a large fur blanket, made from the pelt of a plains bear. He wrapped it around Garron and rubbed the younger man's shoulders as Pernden pressed the hot tea into Garron's hands.

"Thank-k y-you." Garron shivered but smiled at his friends' concerned faces.

"You just warm up here, my King," Melkis said, trying to hide his worries. "Pernden and I will get some food from the kitchen, and we will all have something to eat."

They left the anteroom and headed through the dining hall toward the kitchen, easily navigating the tables. The concern on Pernden's contorted face was not lost on the old master.

"I'm not sure," Melkis said, guessing at the guardian's question.

"That did not seem like my cousin," Pernden replied. "I have rarely seen him with that kind of rage, even in the midst of battle. What was that?"

Melkis shook his head and stroked his white beard thoughtfully. "I cannot say, but it is not the first strange outburst of late. I have seen men come back from battles changed, but his extended exile after the battle he survived may have done more damage than I thought."

"He was out there for a long time. I haven't had much time to talk to him about it. Come to think of it, he's hardly spoken to me since his return," Pernden realized aloud.

"He's been rather distant, even at the castle," Melkis agreed. "I thought it more about King Farrin's death, but now I'm not so sure."

By the time they had eaten and Garron had warmed up, the hour was late. They stayed in the guest rooms at the Grand Corral, thinking it better to rest and return to the castle in the morning. Long after Melkis and Pernden left him in his room, Garron stared at the stone ceiling in the dark, seeing only what the lights in the blued night sky could illuminate from the small window.

Blankly, he stood from his bed, opened the creaky old door, and made his way to the stairs. The trainees on interior guard duty were surprised to see the king stroll up to the mighty front doors. The two straightened themselves quickly in their oversized armor.

"Your Highness."

Garron put a finger to his lips and a hand out to settle the young guards, not wanting to draw any attention. "I'll be making my way back to the castle this evening, instead," he whispered with a polite smile and nod.

"Oh, sure. Suppose kings' quarters are much more comfortable than our accommo-, accommodations here," one of the trainees said with a chuckle, proud of his broad vocabulary.

Garron winced at the mention of the king's chamber. He still hadn't slept there. "I'll take my leave now, thank you," he directed.

They opened the large front doors of the Grand Corral, and Garron stepped through, into the night of the city. The two exterior guards watched him curiously as he made his way down the street and around a corner.

He walked quietly under the night sky through the city toward the castle. Everything around him seemed peaceful, but inside, a war waged.

When he finally arrived at the door to his chamber, Garron paused.

Not here ... you know where you belong, the whisper guided.

He looked at his old chamber door with a blank stare, uncertain. An impulse roared from deep within his core. He did not belong there. Not anymore.

Yes ...

King Garron strode down the hall of the king's chamber at an even pace. He did not pause at the door but walked right in. He turned around and watched the hallway, as he closed the creaking door, and disappeared into the dark chamber.

CHAPTER SEVEN

THE FLAGKEEP TAVERN

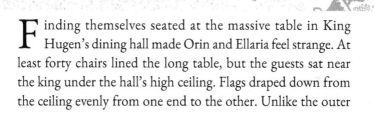

Finding themselves seated at the massive table in King Hugen's dining hall made Orin and Ellaria feel strange. At least forty chairs lined the long table, but the guests sat near the king under the hall's high ceiling. Flags draped down from the ceiling evenly from one end to the other. Unlike the outer adornments, these flags appeared to be hung with organization and order. With no other people in the room, the noise of the fat king eating echoed.

The elf knight stood nearby, clearly annoyed by King Hugen's attempt at a power play. Ellaria inhaled as if she were about to break the silence, but a greasy sausage of a finger from the king shot up to stay her. He licked the last morsels off the large turkey leg he had inhaled and dropped the gnarled bone on the platter in front of him. He rubbed his greasy hands together and wiped them on his shirt.

"Now ..." he mumbled, finishing the last bite. "Now, Kallon."

"Orin," Ellaria corrected.

The king shot her a callous glare.

"Orin," he corrected himself. "I am glad to see your recovery has gone well. Honestly, we didn't think you were going to make it. You looked awful—that axe all stuck in your side." He chuckled at the memory.

"Well, Ellaria is quite the skilled healer," Orin said, giving all the credit away.

"Yes ... I suppose she is."

King Hugen slid the platter away. Before kicking back, he motioned, as an afterthought, to Orin to sample the remaining scraps. Orin brought his hand up to reject the offer, and the massive king shrugged back into his chair.

He laughed again. "The way you tackled that farmer today! Even Kaelor didn't see that guy coming! Maybe I should hire you to take his place."

The elf knight, Kaelor, rolled his eyes behind the king's back.

Orin shook his head. "I appreciate the offer, but I must be getting home to Whitestone. Goblin activity has been increasing. I hit my head hard, so the battle's details are fuzzy in my memory, but if the battle went as Ellaria told me, they are getting bolder."

King Hugen leaned forward expecting a grand story.

"Orin'll be accompanied by me brother and me," Ellaria cut in. "He is still recovering. Though, I admit I was impressed at his actions today. He lost his griffin in the battle, so the journey will be more difficult."

The king waved her off, cutting her from the conversation, and leaned toward Orin.

"Listen, Orin. It appears that the house of Grell has taken good care of you. And again, we thought you weren't going to make it. But I can set you up with a small troop of guards that would gladly help you get home. No need to travel with the huntsman's children."

Ellaria's eyes widened at the king's derisive tone. Orin quickly tried to diffuse the situation.

"No, no. I have been quite happy in the care of the huntsman. His family has been good to me, and I believe Ellaria and Merrick to be quite capable."

"Walk with me," the king said, shoving away from the table.

King Hugen's fat arm held Orin close as they walked through a corridor while Ellaria and Kaelor followed closely. Ellaria appeared as annoyed with the king as his elvish aide. The corridor's ceiling was also draped with flags, and the walls were adorned with valuable items: finely smithed tools and weapons, shields and armor pieces, instruments and utensils.

"Listen, Orin. I've got a little predicament. You've got a little predicament. Let's help each other. You see, Kaelor and I have had run-ins with that stupid farmer before. Whining and crying about his crops being stolen. Blubbering about strange noises and lights in the northern farmlands. He's been a real thorn in my side, you see. But other people have started complaining about the same things now. And you saw that wretched display today. Half the square saw it! Luckily for us, I was able to turn it so the people adored us once more. You heard their chanting.

"So, here's what I need you to do. On your journey back to Whitestone, take a small detour to the northern farmlands near the old Palori Ruins for me and take a loo—"

"We can't do that! The Palori Ruins are far out of the way!" Ellaria butted in.

"Now, now. It's still north," the king retorted.

As the two began to argue, Orin no longer heard them. His focus had been drawn by a single item hanging on the wall. The thin curved sword was well crafted by dwarven hands, as many of the oldest Griffin Guard weapons were, but there could be no doubt which sword hung before him. Orin knew the runic symbols on it well, for it had been his brother's. Clearly, King Hugen had recovered many fine items from that battle.

"We'll do it."

Ellaria and King Hugen went silent. Ellaria's face scrunched in confusion. King Hugen smirked smugly.

"We'll look into your strangeties in the northern farmlands on our way to Whitestone, but I'll be needing this sword."

The king had readily agreed to let Orin take the Griffin Guard sword. He had found several swords that seemed very much the same to his untrained eyes. At Kaelor's insistence, the king offered to send them with supplies for the journey.

"A generous offer from such a generous king, of course."

Orin agreed to accept, despite Ellaria's disapproval. The two were shown to the exit, and the doors were promptly shut behind them. Orin gripped the hilt of his brother's sword, belted to him, with satisfaction.

Ellaria was less than pleased.

"Now, what'd you go and do that for?" She scolded him.

"I know this sword." He patted it. "It was Rayin's."

Ellaria's mouth softened, and she didn't reply. If she had been in his place, she would have made a deal for the sword as well. Her scolding on the matter ended. She touched his shoulder with understanding, and the two started back through Reimald Square.

They stopped at a nearby merchant tent run by a strange elf in regal attire. He had all the wares they needed and included a few extras he suggested would be good to have on the journey. Each time he added a supply, he mentioned his sacrifice of profit for them and aimed a coy wink and self-righteous laugh at Orin, an attempt to solicit favor with the guardian. Orin guessed the elf's charisma had gained the king's recommendation, and the merchant hadn't hesitated when the king's letter for supplies had been presented to him.

Once their supplies were loaded on a cart, the elvish merchant snapped his fingers and called a young human boy. He gave him specific instructions to deliver the cart to Grell's house in the Karos district in the north end of Tamaria. Before Orin could protest, as he was more than capable of rolling the supplies himself, the stout young man hopped to the cart and took off through the sea of people in the market square. They thanked the elvish merchant, who insisted it was actually his pleasure and honor, and headed to the square exit.

Before they reached the exit, they saw Merrick shaking hands and laughing with the halfling owner of The Flagkeep Tavern. He caught up to Orin and Ellaria and fell in step with them. His sister's discontented look made it apparent to him that their time with the king had been as fun as he had expected it would be.

"So, how was King Hugen?" Merrick asked, a tinge of teasing in his voice.

"Well, we'll be taking a rather long detour on our journey." Ellaria sighed. "Orin has agreed to help the 'good king' by looking into the stirrings in the northern farmlands."

"Oh, up by the Palori Ruins?"

"Aye, that'd be the way."

"That is a detour. Quickest way to get there is the Palori River route." Merrick chuckled and looked back at The Flagkeep Tavern. "I suppose we'll be needing a boat, then."

The Flagkeep Tavern bustled with patrons from the Reimald Square market. All kinds of folk filled the place, and the music of the tavern bard was drowned out by boisterous laughter and general merriment. A jovial elf spun around Orin, Ellaria, and Merrick, using some light magic to carry eight tankards of ale to his companions at a nearby table. Cheers rang out at the elf's feat.

Orin noticed the tavern was larger than it had appeared from the outside. He counted four hearths within sight and wouldn't have been surprised to see another one or two farther in. Merrick led the way, weaving between excited patrons. One of the tavern maids caught Merrick by the arm and whispered something in his ear. He let out a slight chuckle and joked back with her. He signaled to Orin and Ellaria that he'd be back in a moment and hastened away with the tavern maid.

A raggedy man in a booth next to Ellaria stood. "Well, ain't yer a perty un, eh?" He hiccupped, and the rancid smell of his breath burned Ellaria's nostrils. "Let's av a kiss, wunt we?"

Ellaria recoiled at the thought. "I'd rather not, thank you."

"Ahhh, com'on now, just a itty bitty un?"

Right as Orin was about to step in, a heavy *clunk* sent the man's face into a confused panic. Before he could even cry out, his eyes rolled into the back of his head, and he seemed to float back into his seat at the booth. Revealed behind him was a skinny gnome, holding out his hands in the midst of some magical conjuration. His eyes glowed with an eerie blue fire, as did one of the tattooed runes on his hands. Once the raggedy man was back in his booth, the hairless little gnome's lights went out. He shrugged at them with a cheeky grin.

A sturdy dwarf with slate black hair and a long beard, braided in the middle, lifted the culprit of the loud *clunk*.

"Excuse me, Miss. I seem to have dropped my hammer." The hearty dwarf winked as he waved his mighty war hammer in his hand. "She has a tendency to do that around fools." He glanced over to the raggedy man who was snoring, drool rolling down his cheek.

"Me hero," Ellaria feigned.

Though her tone was clear, the dwarf puffed up, enjoying the game.

"Join me and my compatriot for an ale?" He gestured to a table in the corner by a hearth, before suddenly stopping. Someone caught the corner of his eye. "You! I told you, if I ever saw your face again, I'd be having to put my hammer through your nose holes!"

Merrick had returned, three tankards in his hands. Stubbornly, he replied, "And I thought I told you if I ever saw you again, I'd rip off that braid of yours and use it to tie you to a tree!"

The crowd around them fell silent.

The dwarf pawed at the bottom of his slate black braid. He looked to the scrawny gnome standing next to him and handed him his hammer. Without words, the two slowly walked toward Merrick. The dwarf tightened the linen wrappings around his hands and wrists, forming fists as though preparing for a fight. Orin's hand instinctively reached for the hilt of his sword.

Merrick set two of the tankards down on the table next to him. The dwarf grabbed one, passed it to the gnome, and then grabbed the other. The three stared at each other, until the dwarf broke the silence.

"Didn't I tell you that like ten minutes ago?" The dwarf asked.

"You did. But then again, you tell me that every time I see you," Merrick replied with a wry smile.

"And you never learn."

They let out hearty laughs, clanked their tankards, downed their drinks, and raised them high with a cheer. The surrounding tables cheered along, and the merriment recommenced. Orin turned to Ellaria, who also had no idea what was happening.

"I thought you were going on a trip to Whitestone with that guardian. Did you forget something?" the dwarf asked.

"No, no," Merrick assured him, placing a hand on the short dwarf's shoulder. "Actually, we'll be taking a detour. And we may need your services."

Coal, a son of Kalimandir, the great dwarven city of the south, didn't need much debate or deliberation. He ordered several rounds for them as they ate and drank together. He was generous; a trait Orin had not often seen in his limited dealings with dwarves. From what the guardian gathered, Coal and Merrick had a solid friendship built on past shared experiences, which would make their journey easier.

In partnership with Ezel, the scrawny hairless gnome, Coal had a boat they used for the transport of goods along the Palori River. Coal explained they had hauled everything from farm produce to mining equipment. He laughed as he recalled for his captive audience the time he and Ezel had transported a strange man that Coal swore was a wizard. Ezel had not been so convinced. They still couldn't agree.

After much mirth and storytelling, the party went their separate ways. Coal agreed to meet them the next morning at his vessel, which was tied up at one of the docks. Merrick knew the one.

Orin, Merrick, and Ellaria headed back to the house of Grell for the evening. Grell was not excited about their newly planned detour but understood Orin accepted the charge to acquire his brother's sword. Orin and Merrick spent the rest of the evening preparing supplies for their travels, while Ellaria walked through all the care instructions her mother would need for Silverwing's continued recovery. They enjoyed one last family meal and slept cozily in their beds, excited about what the dawn would bring.

CHAPTER EIGHT

THE SCAR SQUADRON

Ker glided easily over the Drelek Mountain range. The wyvern always loved solo missions. Karnak cared for her well, and she never wanted for anything. As she stole glances back at him, she noticed a heaviness in his face. Ker bent her long neck back, nuzzling Karnak's foot with her chin and clicking affectionately.

"Okay, okay," Karnak laughed, forced into a momentary reprieve from his worries by his trusted companion. He took in a full breath and let out a long, heavy sigh that floated away on the mountain winds.

The big green orc stretched his mighty shoulders, reaching his arms up and back. He gazed over the mountains and saw alpine lakes nestled high among the peaks. Below, he saw the Irk River. He knew its turns well. They were almost home to Calrok. How he had missed it.

His meeting with King Sahr had not gone as expected. Truly, he had not known what to expect, but the appearance of Jaernok Tur unsettled him. They hadn't seen a Kelvurian in many years. Little was written about them and their lands in the tomes at the library of Calrok. The Gant Sea, of course, was full of treacherous waters on the best of days, so the foreigners' absence was understandable. Though Jaernok Tur did not seem to Karnak as one who needed sea transport. Dark magic surrounded him.

Karnak didn't care for most magic, as it was. Even his own mages in Calrok used it sparingly. His best friend Smarlo used magic occasionally, usually to prank Karnak.

Once, Smarlo levitated Karnak's glorb right out of his tankard while he wasn't looking. When Karnak turned back to drink, he lifted the empty tankard to his lips, tipped his head back, and witnessed the levitating liquid for a split second before it splashed into his face. A raucous laugh had risen from the orcs all around, and Smarlo, wisely, had taken his leave—though he flashed a toothy grin as he departed.

Karnak shook his head at the memory and patted Ker's neck, thankful for the wyvern's companionship. His other hand thumbed at the handle of his axe, Dalkeri.

A little magic is okay, he thought.

Dalkeri, meaning "Fire Storm," had more than proven its worth in combat. Though Karnak did not fully understand why, the axe had the habit of bursting into mystical flame. Strangely, the fire had never burned Karnak but scorched every enemy it cleaved.

A little magic was okay.

As they crested a ridge of particularly jagged mountains, the smell of sea vapors hit Karnak's nose, and he joyously inhaled. There it was: Calrok.

The Scar Cliffs peninsula on the north side of the bay curved out into the Gant Sea. The small city was settled and quiet in the late evening. Radiant pinks and oranges from the sky reflected off the bay. Karnak always loved that time of day, with its last light as the sun slowly descended, peeking over the mountains for one last glimpse at their bay.

The reminder of what he must do struck Karnak again. Their task would be hard. His wyvern squadron had not deployed in some time, but his orcs had trained on the Scar Cliffs. He would stand with one of his orcs over a hundred from elsewhere.

Ker smoothly swooped into a dive, bringing them in for a soft landing at their home on a hill at the northern slope. Karnak unloaded Ker's saddle. He grabbed a tasty fish from a barrel nearby and tossed it to her. She reared up, catching it easily, her long neck bobbing as she swallowed. She rattled off a series of happy clicks, and Karnak gave her another loving pat on the snout. Ker flew to a nearby rocky perch with easy access and a view of the modest house.

Karnak nodded to her and turned to his house of stone and wood. Among the gars of the Drelek Mountains, his home was the least palatial. Karnak didn't care. He walked toward the house, his outstretched hands feeling the long stems of grain that grew from the ground. He knew what awaited him.

This place was home.

The morning sun softly spilled into the room. Karnak held his wife's hand on his chest, happy to be home in his own bed. He looked upon the orc woman, who truly, by all accounts, was beautiful. Her deep green skin always got a little rosy in her cheeks when she slept.

A sudden rustling and clinking in the other room grabbed his attention.

The steps moved toward the door of their room, and the old wooden beams of the house creaked under each step. The door's hinges whined as they slowly swung open.

In the doorway stood a groggy little orc. He rubbed his eyes with one hand and hugged a small blanket in the other. As he crossed to the side of the bed, the young orc yawned widely. He looked at his father with a delirious, surprised smile, and Karnak scooped him up into the bed between him and his wife. The little one was asleep again before hitting the pillow.

"When do you leave again?" Tanessa whispered. Oh, how he loved the way she looked at him.

"I'll talk to Smarlo this morning and have him gather the squadron on the cliffs this eve. But we won't leave for a few days."

"Good," she replied. "He missed you."

"Only him?"

"And I think he mostly missed Ker," Tanessa teased. She stroked the black hair on the sleeping orc's head. "He kept looking to the sky over the western ridges, hoping to spot you."

Karnak beamed at his young son. "I missed him, too."

Tanessa placed a warm hand on Karnak's shoulder.

"So, husband, what is it that King Sahr wanted with the mighty Gar Karnak?"

He breathed a heavy sigh, saddened at the prospect of ending the tender moment with his family.

"The king has called Calrok to stand and fight."

"Where will you go?"

"I'm to bring the squadron to Ghun-Ra. From there, Smarlo and I are to meet with Gar Nargoh. He is apparently working on something important, but very secret, for the king." Concern etched his face.

"You seem displeased, husband."

"I ... hmm ..." He paused, seeking the right words. "Not displeased ..."

"Well, I, for one, am glad you won't be working closely with the king."

Karnak's look scolded her.

"You know, as well as I do, that gars who work closely with the king don't tend to do so for many seasons," she continued, unapologetically. "I'd rather my husband fight droves of ravaging men than be found with a dagger in his back at Castle Ruk."

He grabbed her hand with urgency. "Tanessa, you must not say such things about the king."

"I am not afraid to be heard. Who will hear? I whisper only for the sake of our sleeping son."

Karnak's face turned as stone, and for the first time in years, Tanessa could not read her husband. The large orc had always been fierce. He worked fiercely, battled fiercely, and loved fiercely. His look concerned her. She pinched his large hand to summon him back from the mystery of his thoughts. The intensity in his eyes stilled her.

"The king has a new ally," Karnak spoke seriously. "A sorcerer from Kelvur across the Gant Sea. He calls himself Jaernok Tur. His magic is unlike anything I have ever seen. I do not know his true intentions."

They sat quietly, each lost in thought, until Tanessa once more broke the silence.

"Well, husband, I suppose you will have to keep a wary eye on this Jaernok Tur."

Smarlo had gathered the Calrok wyvern squadron to the Scar Cliffs as Gar Karnak had instructed. On that section of cliff, the stone formed a natural amphitheater where they met often for briefings. Wyverns dropped their riders at the top of the amphitheater and flew to various perches on the side of the cliffs to await their calls.

Smarlo stood at the back, rechecking his list to ensure every orc had arrived. Finding some still missing, he observed the squadron, which was abuzz with conversation and excitement.

They knew Karnak had visited King Sahr, and the theories about what that might mean for their squadron were many. They hadn't deployed in some time. Some of the younger orcs had never deployed, so nervous laughter and unproven boasts bobbed in great waves.

A large wyvern and its rider descended. The wind wafted at Smarlo from the beast's mighty wings. The wyvern landed with surprising delicacy, and the large orc on its saddle helped a passenger down before slipping off himself. Belguv, the large orc, signaled to his wyvern to take off and join the others. Without looking back, Belguv grunted past Smarlo, who checked him in. That was everyone.

The passenger, a slender green goblin, tugged at his tunic, reorienting himself. Dissatisfied with the results, he peered helplessly up at Smarlo, who only gave him an incredulous look. He hadn't expected the goblin.

Reglese hurried over to Smarlo. "Do you know what all this 'ere is about, then?" The goblin snarled more than he intended.

"I know what *this* is about," Smarlo replied, waving a hand over the crowded amphitheater. "But this ..." He looked the goblin up and down, shaking his head. "This, I know nothing about."

Confusion lined the goblin's big eyes. It was hard enough being a goblin in the eastern Drelek Mountains, but here in Calrok, he was one of very few goblins who dared live under the sun. As the local tavern owner, however, he had built a prosperous business on the back of his "proprietary" glorb wine. It was a local favorite, and he dared believe it to be the best in all of Drelek.

He pulled again at his tunic, readjusting his belt. Apparently, his ride upon Belguv's steed was not to his liking. Just as he was about to inquire further, a hush came over the crowd. Someone had spotted the majestic wyvern, high above them.

The creature hurtled herself toward them in a dizzying dive. Faster and faster, she barreled toward the amphitheater. Right before the highest seated orcs, Ker spread her wings wide, immediately thrusting upward toward the back to land in an agile move that inspired awe. Karnak hopped off Ker's back and landed dramatically to the delight of those in the rear rows, who had turned to view his entrance. Cheers and heavy orc handclapping rang out from the gathered squadron.

Smarlo turned his toothy grin to the goblin. "Hurry, sit here." He ushered him quickly to a spot nearby.

Hoots, growls, grunts, and cheers of excitement issued from the orcs. Karnak stopped his descent down the stairs to nod to Reglese. He patted the goblin on the back and continued to the front, greeting many of his orcmates along the way.

Smarlo had run ahead to wait for his gar at the front. Karnak grabbed his friend's shoulders with both giant hands and gave a hearty laugh. Then he embraced him with an exaggerated hug. The display reiterated Smarlo's command and place next to the gar.

Gar Karnak turned and raised his massive green arms into the air, receiving another roar from the gathered squadron. Reglese couldn't help but clap. He could not deny the spectacle before him. Orcs were a passionate people.

Karnak settled them down with the wave of his hand. He did not lose his grin, however.

"Brothers!" he started, a swell of pride and anticipation filling the crowd. "I have sat with the king. We have been invited to be part of the movement of our people. We have been chosen for special missions that only the best wyvern riders in Drelek can accomplish."

"Yeeaaahhh!" a rambunctious young orc burst out. A raucous reverb joined in. The commotion that the young orc started amused Karnak.

Good. He will need that passion in battle, he thought.

"And yes, you are the best!" Karnak continued. "You have trained on the Scar Cliffs. Though wave after wave comes crashing against them, they do not fall. They do not waver. They are strong. Like these cliffs, you are hardened and razor sharp.

"We make for Ghun-Ra, where we will post for our missions. The first night, Smarlo and I will accompany Gar Nargoh for a night flight. Belguv will be in charge of camp setup at Ghun-Ra."

Excited grunts rose as orcs nudged Belguv in congratulations for the honor.

Karnak paused, allowing the tension of his next words to build.

"Riders of Calrok! We have been called. And the Scar Squadron will answer!"

The last of the squadron had left, after much uproarious celebration. Reglese stood at the top of the amphitheater, alone. Belguv had walked by him, called to his wyvern, and taken off without even looking at the goblin. Reglese looked down at the gar and his commander, unsure of his part in the evening. The two whispered quickly and deliberately. Smarlo glanced up at the goblin with a less than confident look on his face, and the whispering recommenced. Finally, Smarlo gave a resigned shrug, and the two ascended to the lonely goblin.

As the two approached, Reglese placed a long, pointed finger to his dipped brow. "My Gar."

Karnak's big hand rested heavily on the goblin's shoulder. "My friend, there is no need for the formalities."

Reglese relaxed, the gar's kindness putting him at ease. "Well, then ... uh ... if your Gar doesn't mind my asking, what am I doing 'ere?"

Karnak laughed at the goblin's bluntness, but Reglese saw the concern that crinkled Smarlo's countenance. Karnak got right to it.

"I need you to go to Ruk."

"What?" The goblin was stunned.

"I need someone in Ruk who can be my eyes and ears, reporting anything suspicious or out of the ordinary."

"I would stand out like a sore, warted toe. I 'ave lived in the sun far too long. My skin is almost as green as yours!" Reglese's confusion at the request was evident.

"Reglese, we need you for this."

"But I 'ave my tavern 'ere."

"And a wonderful tavern it is. Lox will manage it well in your stead. I need your help."

The appeal to the goblin's sense of honor was not strong enough. Karnak had always been good to Reglese and was a loyal patron at his tavern. These had always been helpful reminders as to why Reglese had chosen to live under the sun rather than in the safety of darkness under a mountain stead. Nonwarrior goblins were not known for bravery, though, and he could not understand why Karnak would choose him for such a task.

"I cannot. I will not. Lox would run it into the ground."

"Lox is good at his job, and with your proprietary glorb wine, the tavern will practically run itself."

The goblin swelled with pride. Karnak had found his in with Reglese.

"You make the finest glorb wine in all of Drelek—no, all of Tarrine!" Karnak continued, shaking the goblin's whole body with his fervor. "Think of it as an expansion opportunity. We know the king has a taste for glorb. Certainly, he has never tasted anything quite so glorious as your glorb wine! Yours could be the official glorb wine of all Drelek by year's end. The best glorb wine in all of Tarrine! Probably all Finlestia."

Reglese's eyes swam with his own imaginings.

Say what you want about goblins, but they dream big, Karnak thought. He knew his plan was in motion.

"I have already arranged for the training master to assign a student to fly you to Ruk, and you have your first investor," Karnak said, pulling a pouch of coins from his belt.

The goblin hesitated for a moment. His eyes bounced back and forth between the pouch and Karnak's friendly eyes. He reached out and grabbed the bag, but Karnak gripped it tightly and pulled him in close. His eyes narrowed as he said, "Can I count on you?"

"You will never 'ave 'ad a more trusted ally," the goblin grinned. His grin was short-lived when he noticed the scowl on Smarlo's face. He backtracked quickly, giggling nervously. "Ex-except for ma-maybe 'im, that is."

CHAPTER NINE

STRANGETIES OF PALORI RUINS

"He was a wizard!" Coal argued, louder than he intended.

Ezel glanced at him, his face showing pity for his dwarven friend's delusion, as he loaded another supply bag. The gnome remained unconvinced.

A boy helped load more supplies from the cart he had rolled to the huntsman's house the night before. He was a local boy who had previously worked for the dwarf and gnome. He found their argument to be quite entertaining. With Tamaria's vast diversity, stories were told of lush elven woods, magnificent dwarven caverns, mysterious vanishing islands, and even more outlandish oddities. But stories of wizards of old were few and far between. Admittedly, it was unlikely the dwarf and gnome had actually met a wizard, even with their extensive travel history.

When everything was loaded, Coal patted the boy on the back and slipped him a coin, lowering his voice so his gnome companion couldn't hear. "He was a wizard, he was."

The boy graciously took the coin, nodded a less-than-convinced agreement, and happily sped through the port square with his cart, zipping past Merrick as he went. Spinning out of the way, Merrick raised his arm, holding Rora high, and the falcon ruffled her spotted feathers at the sudden jolt.

"Aye! There we are!" Coal's dwarven voice carried to them, even over the bustle of the port square. "Come on, now! Let's get you loaded!"

Ezel greeted them with a warm smile and grabbed Ellaria's bag to load it into the boat. The vessel was no ship of the seas, but it was not uncomfortably small, either. The Palori River was quite the waterway, but open sea ships did not venture upon its waters, with their treacherous sections where unwary boatmen could destroy ships on unseen rocks reaching from the bottom. Coal's was a fine boat, though, and the aft bore the finely painted name *Lady Leila*.

Merrick seemed surprised by the cargo as he set Rora on a post on the fore of the boat. She nestled in for the journey, apparently having ridden there before.

"What are you hauling today, my friend?"

"Seed," the dwarf responded. "It came in from Telro. I'm to take it to the northern farm guild. There was an accident at their seed house, and they lost it all. Fire, I think. I imagine King Hugen had to do some persuading to secure this much, though."

The dwarf patted one of the large sacks, and dust spit out. He twisted away and sheepishly brushed it from his beard.

"Thank you, Ezel," Orin said, as the gnome took his bag.

Ezel waved long skinny fingers at him to relay that his assistance was no problem. Orin watched the little creature as he sorted cargo. He had encountered dwarves before but had never met a gnome. He seemed a sad sight to Orin, with his skinny hairless body tensing as he moved sacks of seed. He stood half the man's height and his stone-grey skin was spotted by a myriad of ornate runic tattoos. Orin had already seen the magical markings in action but was curious to know what more the little gnome could do with such magic.

Orin's concerns for his well-being were fleeting as Ezel cheerfully went about his business. Whatever the gnome's story, Orin saw Ezel was happy with his life.

"Ezel, can I ask what your markings mean?" Orin inquired.

"Ha!" Coal laughed as he stacked the last bag of seed.

"Ezel doesn't talk much," Merrick chimed. "He's a mute. An accident from long ago, before I knew either Coal or Ezel."

"Aye, but if you know how to use his gnome sign, he is quite the chatterbox," the dwarf ribbed as he prepped the wooden mechanism in the aft of the boat.

Ezel's hands swirled and signed something to the dwarf, who laughed harder. The gnome turned to Orin and shrugged before untying the rope from the dock.

And just like that, they were off.

The trip north on the Palori River was the longer and more difficult route, as it traversed against the current of the mighty river. Usually, travelers would take the northeast road to Whitestone. Coal expertly maneuvered the two wooden levers on the aft of the *Lady Leila*. The vessel glided through the water with a smoothness only experience could provide. Coal's dwarven strength capably maintained their momentum as they cut through the oncoming current. Occasionally, Ezel and Coal would swap, and the little gnome's eyes would light with cerulean flame. A rune on each hand ignited, and he used his magic to continue the deliberate work on the wooden levers.

Up the river they went.

Though Ellaria was impressed at Orin's renewed fervor and healing, she monitored him during their course upriver. She insisted he rest, and while Orin felt he had done nothing but rest for weeks since the battle, he would eventually lose the fight and close his eyes to appease her worry.

"I noticed the elegant name on the back of the boat," Ellaria mentioned to Coal as he and Ezel swapped turns. The gnome rolled his eyes and shook his head before lighting up his runic magic.

"Aye," Coal replied. A dreamlike look overtook his face, and he stared off into another plane in time. "Lady Leila."

Ellaria was amused by the dwarf's reminiscent tone. "Ah, a lady friend, then?"

"Aye," Coal replied. He wiped his oversized dwarven hands on a rag, which he then used to wipe the sweat from his brow. "More than a woman ... She was fierce. Some might say savage. Her golden locks blew in the sea breeze as if the breeze existed only to behold her visage."

"More than a woman, indeed!" Merrick added with a laugh. He had heard the stories. He took a puff from his long pipe, a habit he had gotten from his father, as he awaited the dwarf's inevitable retelling.

"She must have been, to turn such a heroically tough dwarf into a poet!" Ellaria quipped.

Coal straightened, taking her words as a compliment, regardless of their intent, and began his tale. He told of his home city, the great Kalimandir. He told how, even in those great halls, he had never seen a woman like the marvelous Leila. He and

Ezel spent time on a vessel in the Gant Sea with her and her crew, which is where they learned to be boatmen. There was intrigue, laughter, and heartbreak—everything a good dwarven story needed. Ezel shook his head in amusement, and Orin couldn't tell how much of the dwarf's story was true and how much had been embellished. Merrick commented on how the dwarf's stories grew in eloquence every time he heard them.

The stories put the group in a cheerful mood, and that evening, after lighting a couple of lanterns, Coal tapped a small barrel of ale and taught the group a game with dice and cards. He and Ezel had learned it during their time on the Gant Sea.

At one point in the evening, Merrick took a turn at the aft. It was hard work, and though Merrick was strong, the boat was difficult to maneuver for his human frame. Eventually, Coal replaced him, to Merrick's relief, and Coal and the gnome took turns sleeping. That night was quiet for the companions on the *Lady Leila*, and they slept restfully for the last time in a long while.

The *Lady Leila* docked at the northern farmers guild port in the afternoon. The heat of the day was in full measure, and the portmaster met them at the end of the dock. His old, sun-cooked skin wrinkled his face, and white wisps of hair floated on his head.

"One moment! One moment!" the portmaster called. His rough hands fumbled the crinkled pages as he produced a ledger from his patchy cloak.

"Oy, Marty! It's good to see you!" Coal called, knowing Marty would shuffle for a long time if he didn't interrupt the portmaster's thoughts.

"Oh, oh," the portmaster looked up from his mess of papers. "Coal, yer back. It's good to see ye too! Have ye got the wares we been promised by King Hugen?"

"Aye, that I do, Marty."

Marty brimmed with joy as Merrick and Orin started unloading the seed bags onto the dock. Ezel guided them by sorting which bags to take and which to keep.

"Yep, twenty-three sacks of seed for you, here and accounted for."

"Twenny-three?" The old portmaster ruffled through his crumpled papers again. This time Coal was close enough to see the pages and stopped Marty when he saw the right one. "Ah, yes ... No, I mean! No! Twenny. I was only 'specting twenny!"

The dwarf laughed and gave Marty an encouraging slap on the back. "Looks like King Hugen was able to get you a few more! I'm sure he wouldn't mind everyone hearing about his great benevolence and kindness," Coal said, dripping sarcasm with his words.

Marty was unsure. He mumbled incoherently. He didn't like the numbers to be off. The numbers were the numbers, after all. If they didn't match, he didn't like it. Not one bit. He was not satisfied.

Coal signed to Ezel, who signed back his understanding and held three bags of seed on the boat.

"Marty, I have the answer," Coal started. The old portmaster looked to the dwarf, hopeful. "I'll leave twenty bags on the dock here, and I'll take the other three bags on the boat with me. Then you'll only have twenty bags of seed and no worries."

Marty nodded vigorously. That was a better plan. His numbers would match, and matching numbers were good numbers.

"Now, Marty, I need to know about the strange things happening out near the old Palori Ruins," Coal prodded, changing the subject with a serious tone.

Marty's eyes widened. "Ye mean to investergate them noises then?"

"Aye. I've got a guardian from Whitestone with me. King Hugen has charged him to investigate the situation. Anything you can tell us would aid his mission."

Marty looked past the dwarf at Orin and decided he looked well enough like a guardian as far as an old farming portmaster could tell. He turned back to Coal and lowered his voice.

"The Macintroh farm is up thataway. Macintroh's wife done died, and his barn burned up! Not just this, not just this," Marty shuddered. "Macintroh ain't been seen in days. Days!"

Coal nodded thoughtfully. He guessed the farmer in Reimald Square—the one his companions had told him about—had been Macintroh. "I believe him to be in the city," Coal encouraged the old man.

"Oh, good ... good!"

"What else can you tell me, Marty?"

Marty looked around nervously, hoping he wasn't forgetting anything. His memory wasn't what it used to be, but as long as the numbers added up, he would be fine. His eyes landed on the twenty sacks of seed, and he remembered.

"The seed house! Yes, the seed house. It was all burnt up one morn when we waked up."

"Have all these things happened at night?" Coal pushed.

"Yes, at night! At night. Macintroh says always at night."

"Thank you, my friend."

Coal hopped into the boat as Marty headed down the dock to employ the young farmer boys to return for the seed. Seeing the thoughtful demeanor on the dwarf's face, Orin asked, "So, you know where we need to go next?"

"We go to the Macintroh farm. We need to get there before nightfall. Then we'll see about these strangeties."

Coal signed something quickly to Ezel before setting up at the maneuvering levers in the aft. The gnome's eyes and a couple of runes burned with blue flame, as he levitated the three sacks of seed out of the boat and stacked them neatly on the others already on the dock. Coal knew the old portmaster would enlist aid to haul the sacks to the new seed storage facility, and Marty didn't worry about the numbers past his port. After losing their seed house, the farmers would need all the seed they could get.

The travelers shoved off the dock and back against the current of the Palori River. It would only strengthen as they approached the Palori Ruins. Many of the ruins of the old elven city had collapsed into the river and formed forced currents and rapids, making the river around there strong and treacherous. The lone river outlet, the Rolling River, that split out west from the Palori, took the majority of the river's rage, making the Palori River calmer in the south. But Coal feared he and his new companions might face more dangerous things than river rapids.

Steering the *Lady Leila* up the river against such a strong current was difficult work. Coal took to one lever and Merrick the other, while Ezel used his magic to help. They turned west onto the Rolling River, which was just south of the Macintroh farm. Seeing the family bridge, they turned hard, all three pushing mightily into the small inlet cove that gave the only reprieve for miles on the Rolling River. The natural rock barrier where the two rivers split had forced the creation of the single safe cove on the edge of the farm. Once they tied the boat to a sturdy tree in the cove, they disembarked and headed to the farmhouse.

The group walked somberly past the scorched earth and rubble that appeared to be the splintered remains of the barn. The farmhouse had charred stone on the backside and half of the roof was missing.

"What happened here?" Ellaria asked aloud, unable to keep the question to herself.

"Shh," Orin put a hand out to dissuade any of them from speaking. He drew his brother's sword from its scabbard and took the lead.

Rora teetered and ruffled uncomfortably on Merrick's shoulder. "Up," he commanded with a whisper. She flew into the air, and Merrick readied his bow.

Ellaria notched an arrow of her own, as Coal gripped his war hammer in both hands and Ezel's eyes burned cerulean once more.

They stealthily moved around the farmhouse, searching for any sign of movement. They found none. Orin entered the house and found it empty. The kitchen was open to the sky, and much of the interior was rain damaged.

"I know a good elven roofer in Tamaria," Coal said in a low voice, startling the group. Realizing he had surprised them, he finished his sincere thought. "Might have to introduce him to Macintroh when we get back."

Orin followed Merrick outside and began looking for tracks. Hearts pounding, they found the farmer's tracks, embedded in the ground from continued use of the same routes in his daily farming. Some led to the fields and some to the bridge that led south to the other side of the Rolling River. Some led to the barn, many of which were fresher. But then they found a new set of tracks.

The group followed them to see where the strange new trail might lead. Toward the end of the tracks, they saw Ezel, having beaten them to their conclusion. The gnome stood with his hand out on a large stone, his bald, rune-tattooed head bowed. The stone marked the grave of poor Macintroh's wife.

They had found nothing to give definitive answers, though Coal reminded them that Marty had told them, "Always at night!" And night was falling.

The group settled into the farmhouse, eating some food and regaining their strength from the difficult trudge upriver. As the night crept in, Orin knew, one way or another, they would soon have answers to what had happened there.

As night covered the sky and the stars came out to play, Coal led their group to the north end of the farm where the ocean of trees that was Elderwood Forest crashed into the sprawling farmlands. The forest had grown well over the years, covering many parts of Palori, the old elven city. They approached the forest with caution, as most people did, for it was an ancient forest filled with whispers and magic that held many mysteries.

Boom.

A deep resounding explosion of sound halted them before they entered the edge of the forest.

Boom, boom.

It sounded again. A large shadow sped by, covering the stars high above them.

Boom.

Again.

Merrick slid into position ahead of them and pointed above the tree line. Strange yellow and orange lights washed out the darkness beyond the trees. The companions looked at Orin for direction. He nodded to Coal, who took the lead again, that time with hammer in hand. Merrick whispered to Rora, who flew above the canopy of the great forest.

It didn't take them long to make their way through that part of Elderwood Forest to the large opening where the Palori Ruins sat on river's edge. The city had been massive in its day, and even at the edge of the city, they could not spot the source of the noise.

They climbed down an embankment that led them to street level and maneuvered around old buildings until they rounded a corner before an open square.

And then they saw it.

Old towers and buildings were ablaze. The shadow flew lower over them. The wind of the shadow's powerful wings pressed hard against them as it soared past.

Boom!

A fireball from the creature's mouth exploded against a tower, lighting it up like a massive torch. The beast landed on a tower next to a pair of perched wyvern-riding orcs.

Orin signaled in a flash of gestures for the group to take cover behind a broken wall. His heart thrummed in his chest, his whole body feeling the beat. The pain in his ribs returned momentarily with the sudden rush of adrenaline.

"A dragon?" he whispered to Coal, whose astonishment was evident even in the dark.

The dwarf whispered what they were all thinking, "I thought them all to be extinct."

Karnak and Smarlo marveled at the young dragon's capabilities. Ker bristled at the dragon as it landed on a tower next to the one where she was perched. Karnak patted her neck to calm her, unsure if he was doing it for her comfort or his own. Gar Nargoh had flown a couple of drill patterns with the young dragon and demonstrated its destructive power as it spit fire from its great maw.

Smarlo blinked at Karnak, reservation and discomfort in his eyes.

"So, Gar Karnak, what do you think of our new weapon?" Gar Nargoh asked the question with a smug arrogance, knowing neither the young gar nor his commander had ever seen the likes of its power.

"It is ... most impressive," Karnak replied, trying to keep some strength in his tone. He adjusted the bun of long black hair on the back of his head. He knew, as well as Nargoh, that the revelation shook him. "How long have you been training it?"

"We've had him here for three months, training among the ruins. And how he's grown! He's still a young spitfire, but each day he's getting better at heeding my commands."

Karnak bobbed his head, not quite sure he believed what he was seeing. He had thought dragons extinct. Smarlo couldn't contain himself.

"And where did this dragon come from?" The mage commander snarled.

"You will address me as Gar, Commander."

Smarlo reared up, but Karnak extended his large hand to stay him.

"Gar Nargoh, I too would like to know where the dragon came from," Karnak insisted.

"Kelvur," Nargoh replied, patting the young dragon proudly. And suddenly it made more sense to Karnak. King Sahr's new adviser and ally, Jaernok Tur, was a strange orc sorcerer from Kelvur, the land beyond the Gant Sea. Since they had not seen such a strange sorcerer before, perhaps Kelvur, across the sea, contained more mysteries than they knew.

"Why here at the Palori Ruins?" Karnak probed for more answers.

"King Sahr wanted us to test the capabilities of our new dragon. What better material to test against than elvish masonry? We all know they build better than men."

Karnak understood the thought but didn't relent. "And what about the location? It is dangerous to venture this far south. The Griffin Guard of Whitestone patrols often. And this close to Elderwood Forest, you must certainly have seen Loralith Riders?"

Nargoh waved a hand over the ruined city. "No one comes here. Some weeks back, a guardian unit came close on patrol, and one of our wyvern squadrons rerouted them with a perfectly executed diversion, leading them away toward Tamaria. They slew every single guardian." Nargoh snarled another chuckle, running his hand through the mohawk on his grey-green head.

"You haven't encountered the Guard since?" Smarlo pried.

"Not a one." Nargoh's wicked grin spread from ear to ear. "The king's new sorcerer said he would take care of that."

A sudden jerk from the young dragon stirred the two wyverns into a chorus of angry clicking and cawing. The young dragon smelled something it hadn't before and lurched into the evening air. Nargoh attempted to regain control of the dragon, yanking at the long reins with all his might. The dragon's nose hunted hungrily for the scent, and his eyes found his prey.

The small falcon recognized the pursuit and rapidly flew through the city, weaving and cutting in between broken buildings and leaning towers. The dragon burst through walls, hardly noticing anything else as it blindly pursued its new snack. The hunting bird raced through the ruins, faster than it had ever flown, as it became the hunted.

Nargoh raged, kicking and beating the dragon, trying to regain some restraint over the great beast. Its frenzy continued until it lost sight of the falcon. The dragon wafted its wings, lifting it higher above the city ruins so it might spot the bird again. In that momentary reprieve, Nargoh noticed a band of intruders through the billowing dust, recovering behind a wall that had fallen only moments before.

"Intruders!" He screamed violently to the ground troop of goblins below. "Get them! Kill them all!"

"Run!" Coal coughed in the flying dust as he grabbed Ellaria's arm and dragged her to her feet.

Orin hustled Merrick along while the hunter's eyes darted wildly, searching for his beloved falcon. The group turned a corner down an abandoned alley they had used coming into the ruined city but found the way blocked by rubble from a recently collapsed tower. Ezel's eyes flashed into blue fire, and runes blazed on his hands. He hastily levitated chunks of debris away from the pile, attempting to make a hole for their exit.

Goblins barreled into the alleyway.

"Here they come!" Coal yelled over his shoulder. He gripped his mighty battle hammer and charged the goblin warriors. His first swing met the unlucky front goblin in the face, smashing his jaw and felling him instantly. His next swing obliterated the knee of another goblin who was rearing up with his jagged sword. The goblin screamed as the heavy hammer splintered the bones in its leg before the dwarf lifted the weapon high and slammed it down to finish the job.

Without hesitation, Orin joined the dwarf. He smoothly unsheathed the thin curved sword. The first goblin he reached jabbed forward, attempting to stick the guardian in the gut, but Orin deftly parried the lackluster thrust, spun, and sliced his sword diagonally across the goblin's chest. The goblin's face contorted in confusion before he hit the ground.

As the pair fought the goblins, hacking and slashing away, Merrick and Ellaria provided cover fire, hurtling arrow after arrow into the goblin gang. Orin sliced down another goblin, but another came roaring behind him, ready to strike.

At that moment, the world stopped for Ellaria. Her scream was deafeningly silent in her own ears as she yelled a warning to Orin, her notched arrow pulled taut. A surge of energy ran through her body as green electricity danced around her arms and ran along the length of her arrow as she loosed it.

The arrow zipped in a flash of glowing green fury, blasting into the goblin running up behind Orin. The goblin was launched into a group of his kin, where the mystical green lightning leapt from one goblin to another, felling the remaining creatures.

Orin and Coal whipped their heads around to Ellaria, stunned. Merrick stared at his sister in shock. The loud sound of massive stone falling on other piles of rubble brought them back to the problem at hand: escape. Ezel had opened a hole to the forest.

They ran as quickly as they could into the edge of Elderwood Forest. With luck, they could get to the other side and the *Lady Leila*. If they did, the power of the waters there would easily propel them down the Rolling River. And maybe, just maybe, they would survive the night.

Gar Nargoh beat and kicked and screamed at the young dragon. Finally, recognizing the scolding, the dragon flew to a tower and roosted in remorse.

"Raghh!" Nargoh screamed helplessly.

Until then, it would have been overstepping for Karnak and Smarlo to involve themselves. Having witnessed from a distance the green and blue fireworks that overwhelmed Gar Nargoh's goblin ground troops, Karnak recognized the band of intruders to be more than thieves and scavengers. Smarlo grinned smugly to Karnak as they flew by Nargoh, still struggling with the pouting dragon.

"They ran into the forest, south!" Smarlo yelled over the wind as they flew.

"They'll be running home, no doubt," Karnak agreed. "If they escape, they'll be able to warn their people what we were doing."

"And what exactly are we doing, my Gar?" Smarlo snarled. "This is crazy!"

The large gar didn't like the situation they found themselves in, either. Nonetheless, if their enemies spread the word about the dragon, it might start a war Drelek was not ready to fight.

Gar Nargoh's unpredictable control over the young dragon was proof of that.

They flew high above the canopy of Elderwood Forest, its vastness spreading west beneath them. Their heading took them south, over the short distance where the group would have cover. As soon as they flew over the edge of the tree line, the orcs spotted the group running past a crumbling farmhouse.

Karnak took his axe Dalkeri from his side and, in an instant, it blazed with red faery fire.

"Fly true, Fire Storm," he said aloud, and he hurled the axe toward the group.

Boom!

The axe exploded into the remnants of the Macintroh farmhouse, sending the group sprawling. Coal hoisted himself quickly and turned to see the blazing axe attempting to shake itself loose from a flaming beam.

"Boehlen's beard ...," he mumbled. To his friends, he called, "We need to be going! Now!"

"You think?" Ellaria snapped as Ezel helped her to her feet and they continued running as fast as they could toward the boat.

Orin and Merrick stood to face their pursuers. Coal ran to them, keeping a wary eye on the blazing magic axe vibrating violently. "This is a battle we can't win, boys! We need to go!"

Merrick turned to the other two with an entirely different fire in his eyes. "Coal, you have to get Orin to Whitestone." Before the dwarf could retort, Merrick continued his plan. "I will hold them off so you can get the boat going down the Rolling River. It's quick and will get you into the cover of Blackmar Forest soon enough. You have to get them out of here."

Orin protested, "You'll be killed. And this is my batt—"

"I'll draw them to Elderwood Forest and escape into the cover of the canopy. You must get to Whitestone. If the Guard doesn't know about the dragon, it could be to the ruin of all Tarrine! Our whole world could end up in flames."

Merrick was right, of course, but it didn't make the situation sit any better in Orin's stomach. He was impressed by the hunter's willingness to sacrifice himself for the mission. He smacked Merrick on the back for luck and ran to catch Ellaria and Ezel. Coal hesitated. The large beam vibrated as the axe's power increased the closer its orc master came.

"Go, my friend." Merrick's eyes softened. "They need your help."

Coal banged his hammer on a stone in frustration. The rock cracked, and the fissure spread deep below the surface, all the way to the bottom of the massive stone, splitting it forever in two. The dwarf punched the hunter on the arm as he conceded and raced after the others.

Merrick stepped around the other side of the farmhouse as Fire Storm exploded into the air, free from the massive beam. The axe flew the entire distance back to its orc master. In any other circumstance, Merrick thought it might be a beautiful sight. Facing the axe's power, he readied his arrow.

Karnak grinned at the gall of the lone huntsman. "I'll take care of this one. You go! Get to the others," he commanded Smarlo, who snorted at the sight.

"If I can take one of them alive, maybe we can learn of their magic," Smarlo suggested.

Karnak didn't care for their magic, as it was difficult to know what capabilities they might possess. But he saw the wisdom in capturing one of them alive. Perhaps he would be able to find out what their mission was and who had sent them.

"Do it."

Smarlo chased the group, which was nearing the boat.

Karnak spun Dalkeri in his hand, flaunting it for the huntsman to see. The huntsman had guts, that was certain. He continued to walk in Karnak's direction, clearly attempting to get within range of the orc. Karnak led Ker lower to taunt the human hunter.

Merrick released an arrow that sped through the air and shattered against the blocking axe. Merrick had no misconceptions about the battle. The orc wyvern rider had all the advantage. But, by separating the riders, he had given his friends a better chance. He glanced toward Elderwood Forest. If he was going to survive the encounter, the dangerous forest would be his only escape.

Suddenly, the wyvern of the axe-wielding orc screeched horrifically, roiling in the air. It heaved and swayed, trying to shake the little falcon clawing and tearing at its face. Merrick's heart soared at the sight, but the orc slung his magical axe, and it hurtled toward him. Merrick dove, just in time. The axe crashed into the ground, sending displaced earth flying. Merrick didn't linger. He rolled to his feet and dashed for the forest.

Smarlo hit the dwarf with a concussive potion jar that smashed into the ground next to him. Before the dwarf hit the ground, his body floated through the air the last twenty feet to the boat.

Orin and Ellaria shoved the *Lady Leila* away from the shore as soon as Ezel got Coal safely aboard. Ezel pushed out both hands, sending a wave of air against the shore and launching the boat into the rapid current.

Smarlo grunted and rushed after them. "This little gnome is starting to annoy me."

Ezel turned his attention to their attacker as Orin and Ellaria manned the control levers to maneuver the boat in the raging waters of the Rolling River. His eyes blazed blue, and one of the runic tattoos on his forehead lit up as his hands swirled to create a mystical orb.

Smarlo reached into his satchel to grab another concussive potion jar. He needed at least one of them alive, so he couldn't blast the boat with a fireball. He lobbed the jar at the same time the little grey gnome released his magical blue orb.

Dalkeri had nicked the pesky bird on its flight back to Karnak, living up to the meaning of its name, spitting spurts of fire and forcing the falcon to retreat. Karnak roared when he saw the human hunter running into the cover of the forest.

Merrick stood just inside the forest, yelling for Rora to hurry to him. The falcon had taken some hits and was banged up. She fluttered inconsistently, frantically trying to reach Merrick in the forest.

He watched helplessly as the blazing axe flew and crashed against the falcon, severing one of her spotted wings and sending the bird reeling through the forest and crashing into a massive tree.

Merrick darted to the bird, scooped her up into his arms, and raced deeper into the forest. The crumpled bird was limp in his grasp, and tears of regret streamed down the hunter's face. The tears didn't cease for a long time, and neither did his running.

The blue orb smashed into Smarlo and his wyvern, blinding them. Smarlo held on tightly as his wyvern tumbled toward earth, trying to stabilize. They slammed hard into the ground, with the wyvern guessing its trajectory incorrectly.

Unfortunately for the occupants of the *Lady Leila*, however, Smarlo's aim had been true as well. The concussive potion shattered in the center of the vessel, knocking the friends into the sides of the boat and flipping empty crates and supplies into the Rolling River.

By the time Karnak reached Smarlo, the *Lady Leila* had floated down the Rolling River, far removed from sight. Karnak landed next to the recovering wyvern and commander.

Smarlo rubbed his eyes, trying to wipe out the magical blindness, still unable to see clearly. "They've escaped, my Gar," he breathed, his disappointment at his own failure sincere.

"As has the hunter," Karnak replied, not pleased with either result. "I think Gar Nargoh has some explaining to do."

Chapter Ten

The King's Secret Mission

S everal days had passed since King Garron announced changes to the Griffin Guard's immediate mission status. He had grounded all griffin squadrons, declaring the most necessary mission to prepare Whitestone's defenses.

Pernden, cousin of the king and captain of one of the griffin squadrons, marched into the war room on the third floor of the Grand Corral. All the other captains were there, seated around the large table, and all but one of the commanders sat in their designated places between their respective captains.

High Commander Danner Kane had called the meeting. He was a rigid man with close-cut grey hair and a neatly trimmed beard. He walked tall, and when he entered, the room fell silent, save for the old master arguing with him as they entered.

"Melkis," Commander Kane placed a thin hand on the old master's shoulder. "My old friend, we are following the king's decree to the letter. Until the time he deems necessary to give us new orders, we shall continue to do so."

"And what about my squadron?" one of the commanders piped in, overhearing the High Commander's words. "They've been barricading walls around the city. Day and night. Working like miners and masons!"

A wave of grumbling complaints resonated throughout the room, as many of the commanders agreed.

"One of my squadrons has been pulling guard duty for weeks. They were supposed to be leaving on mission two days ago!"

"One of mine has been on Corral training for weeks!"

Arguing broke out around the table. Commander Kane turned to Melkis with a sigh.

"Hey!" Pernden slammed his fist on the table.

The dissident lot quieted, and all eyes turned toward the young captain.

"Commander Hammond, can a guardian ever train too much? How much more prepared will that squadron be when the time comes to fight? 'Sweat in the Corral saves blood in the skies.' Isn't that what we have always said? I imagine all the extra training will fine-tune them into an exemplary squadron. Bards sing of the glory of battles won, but battles are won by the ones who train the most."

The captains beside Commander Hammond laughed proudly and patted the commander on the back, excited about the victories and glory they would see.

Melkis and Kane said nothing. They watched the young captain with pride as he commanded the room.

"And you, Commander Mattness," he turned to the stern face of the female commander. "Is not the Griffin Guard, in fact, a guard? Whether in the skies fighting wretched wyvern riders from Drelek to ensure they never reach the good people of Tarrine or guarding the people of Whitestone, is not the charge the same? We are protectors. We are called guardians, and on that we shall stand unwavering."

All those gathered nodded and grunted their enthusiastic agreement with the bold captain.

"Yes, but what about Tarrine? As far as I can tell, the king is only worried about Whitestone now," another younger captain blurted what many thought.

"As it should be." The words issued as a growl.

All eyes fell on Commander Jolan. The grizzled commander was a mountain of a man. When he stood to continue his sentiment, he loomed over the captains flanking him.

"The king is to whom we are loyal. We fight for Whitestone. Look at the crest on your armor. How many years have we fought the battles of others? He sees now, as well as any of us do, that Drelek is mounting. The wyvern squadrons have been more frequent. The goblin sightings on the front range of the mountains have increased. Drelek prepares for something. Where do you think they'll strike first?"

Commander Jolan didn't retake his seat. He stood with grim visage, letting the weight of his words linger. A long moment passed as they soaked in the grave reality that hung in the air. The truth was they had all seen the increased Drelek activity in recent months, and every commander in the place had felt in their bones something bigger approached.

Pernden leaned into his stance, both hands on the table, and deadlocked eyes with Commander Jolan. "You are not the only one to have lost someone recently, Commander."

His words cracked the austere commander's stoicism, and a hatred glinted in the elder's eyes. The young captain was right. Not a single commander or captain in the room had been spared from loss because far too many guardians had been lost in recent skirmishes with the enemy.

"He was my son, you little ..." Jolan's words released as a growl. "You don't know what it is to lose a son ..."

"No, I don't." Pernden's compassion was evident in his gentle response. "But I know what it is to lose brothers."

"How can we defend Tarrine if we can't even defend ourselves?" Jolan asked, wiping the lone tear from his stubbled chin.

The silence around the room was response enough. Every one of them had thought that same thought, but what does one do with such a thought?

"The Griffin Guard has always protected all the peoples of Tarrine," Melkis' voice broke the quiet. It carried disappointment in the commanders he had led for many years. "Since the inception of Whitestone's fabled Griffin Guard, when Koraal the Wise was king, the Griffin Guard has protected all the people of Tarrine. If a war is coming, it will be fought for all of Tarrine, not Whitestone alone."

Commander Jolan snickered, shaking his head as he intentionally looked to each of the other commanders, save for High Commander Kane. "And what will happen to all of Tarrine should Whitestone fall?"

Melkis reared up, ready to retort, but was halted by Commander Kane's gentle hand.

"Whitestone will stand," Kane said with authority. "It must. If a war is to come, then a war we will prepare for. We will protect Whitestone, and we will protect the other good peoples of Tarrine. I hold that charge to be true from inception to this very day. And if that charge were to be laid aside under my command, then I should be the shame of all High Commanders who have served before me."

The High Commander closed his fist and beat it against the Whitestone crest on his armor.

Pernden and Melkis mimicked the motion, and soon all in the room joined them. Slower than the others, Jolan reciprocated. Whether he was happy about the current state of affairs or not, he was still a guardian, and guardians upheld their duty.

"I will meet with King Garron today at the keep. I will discuss strategy and mission orders for all the Guard. We will be operational again soon. I promise. Until then, prepare. If our enemy prepares, so must we. As our young Captain Pernden reminded us," Commander Kane proudly nodded toward the younger man. "'Bards sing of the glory of battles won, but battles are won by the ones who train the most.' We will train hard, and we will give the bards something to sing about for generations to come."

Unease grew in Whitestone as the people continued about their daily lives. The sight of so many of the Guard around the city, rather than on mission somewhere, was unusual. Buzzing guardians consumed with preparations around the city tied tense knots in people's stomachs. Though admittedly, many of the guardian's spouses were happy to have them home at night.

Pernden walked step-for-step with the older men, his mentors, and, to his estimation, men worthy of the highest honors. He had not seen his cousin since Melkis had brought Garron to visit the Grand Corral.

Commander Kane had requested the young captain accompany him for his meeting. Pernden had served under Commander Kane as the captain of the Guard's Talon Squadron for only a year but had more than proven his mettle in the role. Only the best of the Griffin Guard were assigned to the Talon Squadron, and Pernden was certainly one of the best. All other commanders were in charge of two squadrons a piece, but the High Commander was responsible for the Guard as a whole. The Talon Squadron was considered the High Commander's special operations troop and was often tasked with the most dangerous and important missions.

The three walked swiftly through the castle, no hesitation in their steps.

"How has he been?" Pernden spoke over their echoing footsteps in the long stone hallway.

Melkis wasn't certain how to answer the captain's question. "Something ... disturbs him. He barely eats. I'm not sure he's sleeping. More often than not, he won't even take the time to see me."

"Losing men is a hard thing to swallow," Kane stated. "And then to lose his father so soon after."

The High Commander stroked his neat beard thoughtfully.

"It is ..." Melkis agreed, understanding the truth in the High Commander's thought but unsure the king's difficulties rested solely in those tragic events.

When they arrived at the council room, they found it empty. The large table in the middle of the room was covered with maps and records of troop movements and activity throughout the region. Kane and Pernden looked to Melkis for some explanation, but the old master had no answer for the king's absence.

Melkis slipped from the room and hustled down the hallway to the king's chamber. An adolescent kitchen boy spun around, surprised by the old master's determined approach. Melkis noticed the boy had set a plate of food down outside the door and was returning a plate of day-old food to the kitchen.

The master eyed the boy, irritated. "Has he not eaten?"

"N-no, sir," the kitchen boy stammered, slinking away from the old master's gaze.

Melkis lifted the plate in one hand and banged on the chamber door with the other. The kitchen boy disappeared down the hallway and around a corner.

"Garron! You must open this door! Garron! My King!"

Melkis listened, waiting for a reply. He breathed heavily, his fury overwhelming him. He sucked the air in and raised his fist to beat the door again but was halted by a low response.

"Melkis?"

The weakness in the response broke the old master's heart. His fury melted to sympathy. What was his young king going through? What could render him so weak?

"Yes. It's me, my King," Melkis choked on the words. They sat like a heavy lump in the back of his throat. "You must open the door." His tone had softened.

The large chamber door creaked open, and the young king's face appeared. His eyes were darkened. Heavy bags swelled underneath them. His hair was ragged, and his tunic disheveled.

What a pitiful looking king, Melkis thought to himself.

"Garron," the old master reached out and grabbed the younger man on the shoulder. "We must get you spruced up. High Commander Kane and Pernden are waiting to meet with you in the council chamber."

Garron's faraway eyes returned with the recognition of the guardians' names. "Yes ... Yes!"

He snapped away from Melkis and ran to a table near one of the windows in the king's chamber. The old master followed him, and his heart fell at the disaster of the place. He hadn't been in the room since he personally oversaw its preparation for Garron's move into it after King Farrin's death. Papers littered every surface, even the floor. Letters, historical texts, arcane parchments, and other various documents. Garron frantically grabbed papers and maps on his table.

"I have it right here. It's right here, Melkis."

The distraught king scooped up an armful of materials and shuffled quickly for the door. Melkis stopped him.

"Please, my king. Change your tunic. Throw some water on your face. Run wet hands through your hair. And please," he placed the plate on top of the pile in Garron's arms, then promptly took the load from the young king, nodding to indicate he should keep the plate. "Please, eat something. I will make sure these materials get to the council chamber. Refresh yourself quickly. We will wait for you."

Garron examined himself. He was a mess. His body twitched with a laugh under his breath. He glanced back at Melkis with a sheepish expression. "I guess I am a mess."

Melkis laughed. "Quite."

He waited until he saw his king take a bite out of the bread and turn, set the plate on the bed, and look for a clean tunic. Melkis did not close the door behind him as he left. He wanted to make sure he could get back into the king's chamber if need be. He hugged the mess of papers in his arms as he walked down the hallway toward the council chamber, confused, frustrated, and heartbroken.

"What is all this?" Pernden studied the letters and arcane documents Melkis had brought into the council chamber.

Melkis and High Commander Kane had set to work immediately, trying to fit all the pieces together, laying out parchment after parchment on the massive table, trying to make sense of the mess.

"Many of these speak about a powerful weapon. Magical ..." Kane stroked his trimmed grey beard, puzzling over how they were connected.

"Yes, but many of them make no ties to this weapon at all," Melkis pointed out.

Kane grabbed another parchment. "If we can only find where all of them fit .... Perhaps that will give us more context. I believe the king is working on a plan for us to get some sort of magical weapon that could aid us in the war to come. But where he got such a notion ..."

Pernden watched eagerly as the two older men passed documents back and forth, laying them out and rearranging. Whenever he was with either of these men, he did his best to observe. Melkis had always been like a father to him, as he had been to many. Melkis had overseen his training, and it was the old master who first taught Pernden to believe in himself, to have courage, to overcome challenges, and to treat others with kindness and humility. Melkis was more than a teacher to him.

And then, of course, since Pernden had graduated from training into the regular Guard, he had looked up to High Commander Danner Kane. The man was straight as an arrow. He commanded with authority, and yet, he was approachable—though few knew that fact. All captains spent two active years under another before they become captain of their own squadron, and Pernden had spent two years in the 7th Squadron before Commander Kane tasked him to the Talon Squadron. The timing worked well, for the previous Talon lead, Dahn Barrow, was retiring. More so, Kane recognized Pernden's exceptional ability to rally those around him—no small gift.

As Pernden became the captain of the Talon Squadron, the singular squadron under the direct supervision of the High Commander, Kane took special care to spend more time with the young captain. He mentored him regularly, including Pernden in meetings that didn't require the young captain's presence. He wanted him to learn everything, and Pernden hungrily absorbed all he could.

A sheet slid from the table and swooped past Pernden's leg toward the door. As he stepped to retrieve it, a foot halted the rogue paper in the doorway. King Garron stood there, his foot pinning the paper, his hands carrying a load of other parchments. His face was clean, his hair slicked back, and he looked refreshed. He smiled to his cousin.

"Pernden," he nodded at the paper with a helpless smile and shrug. "Perhaps you can grab this one?"

Pernden returned the smile, surprised at his cousin's sunny welcome. "Of course."

He grabbed the wayward sheet, and the two joined the older men, still working by the massive table.

Melkis looked wearily at the documents the king held in his arms. Garron shook his head in amusement, guessing they had been frustrated in their attempt to piece it all together. "Missing a few pieces to your puzzle, sirs?"

"I suppose you can help us put this all together?" Melkis asked.

"I can."

Garron made efficient work of sorting out all the pieces. He placed specific ones into their rightful spots on the table and threw others, which had not been related in any way, to the floor. Kane breathed quiet chuckles at the discarded documents. That made more sense.

Once he seemed to have everything in order, Garron retreated from the table, marveling at it as if it were some masterpiece of the great painter Jiliana Torver. And then he explained.

"There is a magical item we must secure. An item of great power and importance. It will change all of Tarrine as we know it."

The other three men drew closer to the table, intrigued by their king's statement.

"We need to procure this item to ensure the future of Whitestone."

Too curious to remain silent, Pernden interrupted, "And what is this item with the power to change the world?"

"It is called the Alkhoren Mirror. An old wizard relic that's sat dormant for many years."

"And what does this Alkhoren Mirror do?"

"That I do not have time to explain, for its intricacies are many. But," Garron paused as he grabbed one of the arcane historical parchments and one of the letters and shifted to a large map. "I have learned the location of the mirror. If we hurry, we can acquire it to aid our war efforts."

"If this mirror is as powerful as you suggest, others will know of its existence or even have it in their possession, and they may not lend it willingly," Kane inserted, astutely recognizing it could be a dangerous task to retrieve such an artifact.

"The mirror is forgotten by most. But I have been made aware others do, in fact, know of its existence and will be trying to retrieve it for their own gain."

"So, we get there first," Pernden said eagerly.

"We must." The weight of Garron's words hung in the air while he searched the map. "Here." He pointed.

"The Gant Sea Narrows?" Kane asked, tugging at his beard.

"Yes, an island there. It houses an ancient and decrepit wizard's tower. The waters around it are too treacherous for ships, so sailors never go there. Flying in on griffin-back is the only way to reach the place." He took a marker and set it on one of the rocky islands in the Gant Sea Narrows.

"And how have you come to know about this mirror and this wizard's tower?" Melkis asked, a tone of fatherly concern.

Garron's feet shifted, and his body tensed at the question. He stared intently at the map as his full weight leaned on the table.

A mage ... the whisper planted in his ear.

"A mage," he started. "O-on my journey home. While I was away, after the battle, I met a mage. He was the one who healed me of my wounds before I was able to journey home."

"And why would a mage give us this kind of information?"

Garron shook his head, his eyes never leaving the map of Tarrine. "Because he knows our fate. He knows the fate of all the world."

Before Melkis could question the young man further, loud horns erupted, resonating throughout the city and into the castle. Pernden ran to the western facing window and strained to see what he could in the distance as the horns bellowed again. Commander Kane grabbed a looking glass from a small side table and handed it to the young captain. "What do you see?"

"A troop of wyvern riders in the distance. If we signal for the Guard to mount, the 3rd and 4th Squadrons could get to them quickly enough and take them down."

"Which direction are they heading?"

"North ..." Pernden replied, puzzled.

"North?"

Just then, an aide ran in with the report.

"Sirs, Drelek riders to the west, some distance away, flying north."

Commander Kane swiftly moved to the aide. "Signal for mounting. The Guard needs to catch up to this wyvern troop to figure out where they were and what they were doing. To so boldly fly within view of Whitestone ..." He followed his thought trail for only a second before continuing his orders. "Signal for the 3rd and 4th to ride west and meet them."

Come now, king. Be the king. They don't respect your words.

"Silence!" Garron yelled, halting Commander Kane's instructions to the aide mid-sentence.

"My King, I highly sugg—"

"Silence!" he yelled again, whirling to face the Commander and the aide. He pointed an accusing finger at the aide. "You will not signal anything unless I command it! Leave us!"

The aide hesitated, torn between the tension of listening to his king and the instructions the High Commander had not finished.

"Leave us!" Garron hollered, and the aide quickly removed himself from the room.

Melkis and Kane looked to each other with concern. Their unspoken dialogue communicated the same thing—something about the king's behavior was very wrong.

Garron leaned on the table with both hands again, breathing heavily. "We must get the Alkhoren Mirror. It is our foremost concern. We must secure the future of Whitestone."

He slammed the table and briskly exited the room, leaving the other three stunned. Pernden looked to his mentors. Neither of them spoke; they merely strode to the table and its documents to glean any and all information they could about that magical mirror.

Pernden turned for one last glance at the Drelek riders as they were nearly out of view from his vantage. He set aside the spyglass and joined the other two at the enormous planning table. He did not understand but trusted his elders and followed their lead.

CHAPTER ELEVEN

WHISPERING LAKE

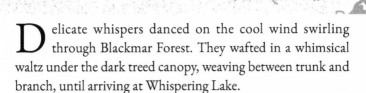

D elicate whispers danced on the cool wind swirling through Blackmar Forest. They wafted in a whimsical waltz under the dark treed canopy, weaving between trunk and branch, until arriving at Whispering Lake.

The *Lady Leila* floated aimlessly in the small lake in the middle of the forest.

The vessel had arrived of its own accord, for none of the companions on board had been conscious to steer. The friends remained motionless in their deeply concussed slumber. The Rolling River had delivered the vessel with haste, and Whispering Lake had hungrily drawn in the boat, like so many before it. The place itched with a strange magic.

After many hours of pointless circling, the *Lady Leila* saw its first sign of life. Coal stirred. The dwarf had been the first to experience the power of the concussive potions hurled by the orc warrior they had encountered, and like many of his kin, he had a hardy constitution. He sat up with much effort, his head reeling. His normally well-braided beard was a ratty mess, and his clothes rumpled in odd places. He tried to focus his eyes to see if his companions were alright, but his head hung heavy and rolled from side to side as he moved.

He found Orin crumpled against the side of the boat. Coal fought to maintain focus. Though he was unable to clearly see the young man, he placed a hand on the guardian's chest and felt his breath. He fumbled over to Ellaria, and relief flooded him as he found her breathing as well. Then to Ezel. His little gnomish friend's body heaved up and down. Even in his delirious state, Coal saw the gnome must have used a significant amount of energy to get the group away from their orc foes. His slight body looked weak—his chest and cheeks more sunken than usual.

Coal hauled himself to the bow of the boat, leaning on the front post so he might be able to pinpoint where they were. He clung to the post, using his sturdy dwarven muscles to hold himself fast. He scanned their surroundings, his head dipping heavily.

"Boehlen's beard ..." he grumbled.

The small lake was enclosed on all sides by trees. No inlet could be seen, nor any outlet. The boat spun evenly, not drifting to one shore or another. He pushed himself away from the front post and trudged each leg forward, feeling as though his boots were filled with lead. Coal slumped into position at the aft control levers and began to sway. The motion did nothing to help his foggy mind.

If only he could get the *Lady Leila* to the shore, they could set up camp, recover, and figure out their next move. But, it was all the dwarf could do to keep himself conscious enough to maneuver the levers. He worked hard at them, throwing all his dense weight into the levers to get the momentum he needed. His looping mind soon became discouraged when he realized that, even though he was moving the boat forward, they were no closer to the shore. No matter what direction he tried, no shore neared.

Whispers on the wind tickled his ears with untranslatable suggestions. His mind rolled backward and then forward. His eyes strained to capture a singular tree on the shore, something to ground him, to steady him. Instead, the shore began to bend in his vision, and the whispering overwhelmed the dwarf, dropping him from the levers into the abyss of unconsciousness.

Sometime later, Ezel jolted awake from an unseen dream. The gnome rubbed at his ribs. He felt as if he'd been hit by an avalanche, a feeling he knew all too well, as he and Coal had been caught in one in their past travels—something he never wanted to experience again.

His head was woozy, and he eased himself to his feet, using the side of the boat as leverage. He looked out over the small lake but saw nothing from that side. After checking on Ellaria, he moved to the other side. Nothing.

The gnome shook his head. *Nothing? How can there be nothing?*

He shook his head vigorously, trying to rattle his confusion. Still nothing. He was unsure whether his mind was playing tricks on him or if their surroundings were an illusion. Surely, they couldn't have entered the lake without an inlet. There must be one somewhere, but he could not see it.

Ezel made his way to the aft and found his stalwart dwarven companion slumped in a heap beside the control levers.

He must have awoken for a time. But what caused him to ...?

The whisper of an ancient and horrible language Ezel did not know breathed into his pointed ears. His greyish skin crawled, and a sudden realization of the danger sobered his mind to a functional clarity.

A runic tattoo on his forehead blazed, giving the gnome the appearance of having three burning blue eyes. His surroundings morphed. The lake was overgrown on the edges, the sunbeams no longer shone through, and bacteria teemed across the water. As the illusion fell away from reality, Ezel identified far off an inlet or outlet—he could not tell which in his hazy state. He quickly turned, searching for another, and spied one nearer to the *Lady Leila*.

Reality continued to unfurl around them. Like drawing back a mystical curtain, the tentacles of a wretched beast came into view. In Ezel's shock, the whispers of the grotesque monster nearly convinced him to go back to sleep. The monster's attempt was half-hearted, for it foolishly thought its little prey wouldn't require much coaxing. Ezel shook his head quickly, snapping back to the beast's grip on their vessel.

Gantendril!

Ezel had not encountered a gantendril before, but during his time on the Gant Sea, he had met others who had. The tales they told were horrifying. Gantendrils found calm, seemingly safe waters where they would wait for unassuming vessels. The gantendril was not a creature that liked to work for its food. Vessels would seek calm waters, only to be confused into unconsciousness by whispering winds. The crew members would eventually starve to death before the gantendril would eat them, boat and all. The obese, tentacled monsters didn't care for their food to fight and wriggle within their bellies. Their illusionary magic was strong enough to trick the eyes and daze the mind. Ezel had to act quickly before the monster realized it needed to enchant him harder.

He was too weakened by his previous battle to fight the monster with magic, especially if he had to hold his vision-clearing spell. He grabbed Orin's sword and cleaved heavily into the tentacle on the starboard side of the boat. A hideous screech resounded as putrid ichor sprayed from the writhing tentacle and coated the boat. Ezel's head lolled as the gantendril attempted to invade his mind once more, pressing in with more force. Ezel hurled himself to the port side, slashing another tentacle as he did. The next pain-filled shriek from the monster broke its mental lock on the gnome.

Ezel shifted his energy to other runes on his hands and pushed with all his might. If he could get them away from the gantendril and heading down the closer of the two waterways, perhaps, with some fortune, they might be able to escape before the gnome passed out again. If the waterway was an inlet though, he feared they would fall right back into the gantendril's trap, and that would be the end of the *Lady Leila* and her crew.

A momentary vision of the destructive power of the young dragon flooded into Ezel's memory.

No!

He couldn't—wouldn't—let them fall prey to such a fate. Their mission was too important.

Arcane energy surged through his tiny frame as he pushed with everything he had. Darkness crept over his mind. His head swayed. The whispers sounded sweet, helpful even, tempting him to sleep. He had so little energy. If he could just rest, maybe he could help his friends later. Just a little rest ...

A hand clamped around the struggling gnome's foot, and a wave of energy washed over him. Ellaria had half-awoken from her own daze and gripped the gnome's foot with all the encouragement she could muster. Swirling green power transferred from her fingertips into the gnome. Though Ezel was confused by the sudden shift in the situation, he also saw the opportunity. He took a breath and focused on tapping into whatever magic Ellaria shared with him. His body tightened as he prepared for one final attempt to blast them free from the gantendril. Without a word, the blue fires roared fiercer, and Ezel let go a blast of energy unlike any he had ever released.

The jarring from the blast and the subsequent release by the gantendril threw the occupants of the *Lady Leila* sprawling onto the fore of the boat, unconscious once more. The boat bounced on the water toward the nearer waterway, which was indeed an outlet. Their vessel caught the swift current of the outlet, and the *Lady Leila* carried her crew down the Rolling River, through Blackmar Forest, toward the coast.

Behind them, the gantendril lurched and writhed in agony and rage. It did not like fighting food. It did not like it one bit. It slumped into the water of the Whispering Lake once again, hungry and angry.

A deer in the wood of Blackmar heard a sweet whisper on the wind flowing through the berry bush it was gnawing. How thirsty it had become all of a sudden. Perhaps it needed to walk to the lake.

CHAPTER TWELVE

THE GOBLIN WAGONER

The mountain road between Cragmok House and Ruk was a tiresome one. The road skirted sheer cliffs regularly, and in places, the wagon Reglese had procured at Cragmok House was barely narrow enough to keep the wheels from slipping into vast crevasses.

The wyvern trainee had been instructed to drop Reglese off near Cragmok House, a large supply depot on the route between Calrok and Ruk, so the goblin entrepreneur could round the bend without anyone suspecting he had received special transport. When Reglese arrived, the hosts at Cragmok, two elderly orcs with an adult son, welcomed him and bade him to have a sit after his "weary journey."

Their usual customers were wagon transporters that brought goods from various places. A fish transporter from Calrok had been there the day before. On the day Reglese appeared, travelers were few. Reglese noticed a single goblin at a corner table. His greyish green skin seemed sickly to Reglese compared to his own vibrantly sunbaked green skin. It had taken him a long time to adjust to living under the sun in Calrok—something he had deemed unnatural for goblins at one point in his life. He wondered if he were the better for it instead.

When Reglese inquired about a wagon to Ruk, the hosts suggested that their boy might see Reglese to the capital. Just before the boy accepted the task, the goblin in the corner offered his services.

"Ima take 'im!"

The hesitation and apologetic ticks on the hosts' faces gave Reglese pause, but the other goblin doubled down on his bid.

"Ima take 'im fer less dan you lot."

Reglese, in a strange place outside his comfort zone, clung to the one thing he understood: saving coin. He was more comfortable with a fellow goblin anyway.

So, at length, he had taken up the goblin's charter. Rocks crunched and skittered away, off the cliffs, under the weight of the old mountain goblin's even older and ricketier wagon. The driver's cloak covered his whole body, and his ample hood protected his pale grey-green skin from the sun.

Navigating the road to Ruk was long, slow work. The goblin, whose name, Reglese learned, was Kig, denounced his years with careful footwork, which increased Reglese's confidence in his choice. Kig knew what he was doing on the treacherous mountain roads, and his strength to pull the wagon had not waned over his years.

As evening drew upon them, Kig deftly maneuvered a side trail to the top of a small plateau where two other traveling wagoners were already setting up camp for the evening. Kig waved a greeting to each, who returned the gesture and continued their business. Kig parked his wagon, very particularly, next to a well-used fire spot where he unloaded a bundle of wood from his wagon. He snatched a handful of kindling from a small wooden box, of which there were many in the back of his rickety wagon, and quickly lit a fire. He grabbed two woolen blankets as well, laying them down with care near the growing fire, and returned to the tiny wooden boxes. He retrieved a pot, a couple pieces of meat, some water, a few vegetables, and some seasoning.

Kig caught Reglese's curious look out of the corner of his eye and flashed him a sly grin, "Just causin' were on the road donnit mean we cannit eat good!" He laughed a raspy laugh and cooked away, humming a mountain melody Reglese didn't recognize.

The two sat in the glow of the fire, the stars ablaze above them. Occasionally, the wind swept away the smell of the fire and stew, and Reglese's capable nose caught the sweet scent of crisp mountain air. Reglese, who was used to the hustle and bustle of his beloved Spinefish Tavern back in Calrok, enjoyed the pleasant stillness. His nights were never quiet but always filled with boisterous orc conversation, music, and raucous laughter. The quiet hum of the old mountain goblin's tune, the warmth of the licking fire, the woolen blanket ... He could get used to those, he thought.

Kig dished the steaming stew into two bowls, passing one to Reglese. "Carful na, itsin hot," Kig warned.

The steam swirled into the cool evening air, enveloping Reglese in its aroma. He blew away the steam several times, dropping it to a temperature at which he might take his first sip. When he did, he looked at Kig with astonishment. It was incredible.

"Where did you learn to cook like this?!"

"Ah," Kig chuckled. "Me fadder was a good cooker. Afore Isa leff 'im tinkin' Isa smerter dan 'im."

He shook his head, laughing to himself and reflecting on the folly of his youthful perspectives. Wisdom had greyed the hairs on his head and deepened his thoughts.

Reglese gazed upon the old wagoner with wonder, blowing and sipping at the stew hungrily. He hadn't been terribly hungry, but the richness and depth of flavor of the stew had stirred his stomach to a ravenous state. The wheels of his proprietor mind began to turn. The old goblin couldn't have too many more years in the mountains. Surely, his strength would fail him as it did everyone who eventually succumbed to age.

Perhaps ...

"Kig," he started, picking his words carefully. "What would you do if you weren't wagoneering?"

"Isa donnit know." Kig set his bowl down to secure the woolen blanket around his shoulders. Once he was comfortable and had his stew back in his hands under his chin, he continued, "Isa supposin ... Ida be dead."

The frankness caught Reglese off guard. He was almost sad for the old goblin. What legacy would he leave behind him? Reglese's mind was made up. "What if I could offer you a new life?" Kig looked at him incredulously, taking another sip of his stew. "If you can cook like this, you could cook for me."

Kig laughed. "Isa just madin some dis stew."

"No really, Kig. This stew is amazing."

Reglese set down his stew and scurried to the back of the wagon, where he had placed the half-sized tankard barrel he had strapped to his back when he arrived at Cragmok House early that morning. He grabbed two mugs the old goblin had stowed in a wooden box and filled them with his proprietary glorb wine.

He handed one to Kig and explained. "This is my famous glorb wine. I make it back 'ome in my tavern in Calrok. I'm going to Ruk to expand—you know—start a tavern there. And then 'oo knows where from there." Reglese's look drifted, lost in his dream.

Kig chuckled again at the younger goblin, so full of excitement. When he took a swig of the glorb wine, he stopped.

Reglese, back from his dream, watched with anticipation, waiting for the old wagoner's verdict on his prized glorb wine. Kig swirled the glorb wine in the mug and sniffed it closely with his long nose. It was good. Maybe, just maybe, the greener goblin had something here. And certainly, Kig was feeling his age with every charter he took. Maybe it was time for a change.

"In Ruk?" he confirmed.

"Yes, in Ruk. I will need a cook for the tavern there. And if your other dishes are 'alf as good as this stew, we'll be the talk of the kingdom together."

Kig looked at the stew in his one hand and the glorb wine in his other as the firelight danced shadows all around. He grinned widely, his smile missing many teeth.

"Isa tinkin Ida likin dat."

The new partners clinked their mugs and drank and ate heartily. Both of their bellies were filled; moreover, their minds were filled with thoughts of potential. Soon enough, they fell asleep next to the fire, on the refuge plateau, under the starry night.

On their flight back to Ghun-Ra, the orcs utilized the cover of darkness. They had stayed in the ruins an extra day, that they might have a full night's cover to travel back to Drelek. While Gar Nargoh, with his pompous attitude, suggested he didn't think it necessary to wait for nightfall, Karnak insisted. Night operations were always safer, and in turn, more successful. Though he didn't doubt the dragon would tear through any enemies that impeded their flight home, wisdom suggested they keep the creature hidden as long as possible.

Karnak thought about the young huntsman. A scowl edged across his face as Smarlo flew nearer. The commander's vision had returned fully, given the extra day to recover, though he had spent most of that day hiding in the shaded spots of the ruins while his eyes were still sensitive. Orc eyes attuned well to the darkness, and Smarlo clearly saw the grim visage on his gar's face.

"I disappointed you, my Gar."

Karnak looked over at his second-in-command, surprised. The statement had brought him out of his own thoughts. He loosened his hold on the reins, not sure how long he'd been gripping them so intensely. "No," he said slowly. "Something is not right."

The concern the gar showed to his most trusted friend caught Smarlo off guard. He knew Karnak to be a thoughtful orc, but in the many years of their companionship, he had rarely seen him in doubt. "What do you mean?"

Karnak stretched his back and cracked his thick neck, adjusting his posture on Ker's back. He tightened the knot of black hair on the back of his head, unsure what he meant, himself. "I told you of Jaernok Tur."

"Yes, King Sahr's new sorcerer. The one from Kelvur."

"That one ... He was strange, Smarlo," Karnak's tone was one of a friend speaking with a friend rather than a gar to a commander. "There was this ... aura about him. Like the very essence of darkness."

"So you've said. What's got you troubled?"

"I'm not sure yet."

The wyverns clicked at one another as they felt the wind off each other's wings, not overly happy with the tight flight pattern. Karnak gathered his thoughts under the watchful stars. His eyes landed on the dragon ahead of them. The beast was a force to be reckoned with, to be sure, but its appearance coincided with the appearance of Jaernok Tur. Karnak didn't like any of the implications.

"Strange to see a gnome with humans," Smarlo thought out loud. "And a dwarf. An odd lot that was."

"Another wrinkle in all this. I've not seen a band like it before."

"Likely won't again," Smarlo chuckled. "I know my aim was true with the blast potion. I saw it land its mark before the orb of blindness hit me. Even if they survived the Rolling River's treacherous waters, they would need a serious amount of luck to survive the dangers of Blackmar Forest. Can't defend yourself unconscious."

Karnak nodded his agreement. Blackmar Forest was infamous, even in tales among their own people.

"Even if they survived the forest, they would wash out to the Tandal Sea, and their vessel would be drowned soon enough. That boat was no seafarer."

Karnak warmed to Smarlo's reasoning, deciding his friend was right. The huntsman would face his own deadly trials in Elderwood Forest, host to its own ancient magics and savage creatures. The group's survival chances were slim, but a solo huntsman lost in Elderwood Forest had little chance at all. Then again, huntsmen made their living in the wilds.

It is not impossible ..., Karnak thought.

The curious makeup of the group nagged at the back of his mind. Even as Smarlo soared a little distance away, to the relief of both wyverns, Karnak stewed on the unusual band. They were clearly not of the Griffin Guard nor of the Loralith Riders. Perhaps they were of the dwarf city of Galium, but there was only one dwarf. If by chance they were some sort of joint task force and managed to survive, the peoples of Tarrine might band together, and King Sahr's war could be over before it really began.

A peculiar bunch, indeed.

Karnak looked up at the stars, wishing he was home with Tanessa. As much as she would argue the opposite, Karnak always thought her counsel wiser than his own. Or, perhaps, her counsel merely comforted him. Surely, she would have thoughts on the matter.

"I can't help but feel there are bigger forces at work here," he said to her, though only the stars and Ker heard him.

Ker clicked warmly, glad to have a little distance from the rest of the group. Karnak patted her smooth, scaly neck in reply. The methodical motion of Ker's deliberate wings comforted the large orc as they flew north through the night.

CHAPTER THIRTEEN

ELDERWOOD FOREST

The tops of the trees swayed in the early morning wind, allowing sunlight to peek through the thickly shaded wood and cast shadows on the refugees inside Elderwood Forest. Sweat rolled and flicked off the ends of his hair as Merrick sat on a stone, rocking his falcon, Rora. He clutched her against his chest.

She laid limply in his hands. He couldn't feel her breathing anymore and tried to remember when he'd last felt her small figure move.

Merrick had run through the night. He did not know how well a wyvern could track through the great canopy of Elderwood Forest, but he felt his best chance to evade their detection was to run and not look back.

Forcing himself to do so, Merrick slowly lifted the bird to look at her. She didn't breathe. She didn't stir.

Rora was gone.

Tears streamed down the huntsman's face, mixing with his sweat and dripping off his chin.

"Rora, I'm sorry," he whispered to her.

Though truly, he knew he could have done nothing to save her. Her loyalty to him was unyielding, and she had sacrificed herself to save him. And save him, she had.

He cut a piece of cloth from his cloak with his dagger and wrapped her broken body with delicate purpose.

He sat, catching his breath, for a long while. He didn't move. So still was he that a deer walked beside him, startling him back to his present predicament, which in turn startled the deer that scampered off through the thick wood.

Merrick realized then he had no idea where he was. He did not know in which direction he had run the night before and did not want to stay in Elderwood Forest longer than he had to. It was a dangerous place, filled with vicious beasts and unknown magics. He reasoned that, if the wyvern riders hadn't found him at that point, they likely had stopped searching. He tried to see the sun through the thick canopy but only got glimpses when the wind moved the treetops just right. He was an experienced huntsman, however, and found his bearing. South would be his best bet; maybe he could make it back out to the plains.

When Merrick stood, he rocked. He hadn't examined his own condition while he was sitting or realized how exhausted he was. He determined to set out anyway and walk as far as he could before the early evening shifted to night. He hoped to find a good place to make a fire and find rest. Maybe he could even set up some hare traps and provide his weary body sustenance.

The huntsman walked all day, twisting and turning through the thick tangled forest. He stopped often, realigning himself with the sun, whenever the encroaching canopy allowed. He continued until he reached a small natural well. The sun shone full on the singular oasis, and Merrick was pleased to find the sparkling water to be crystal clear. To the other side of the waterhole was a small cave that could provide shelter for the night. That spot, of any in the entire forest, seemed the only one with a sense of peace.

It would be a good spot to bury his friend.

After resting for a while and grieving his loss, Merrick found a heavy stone a few feet from the well. He dug a hole large enough for Rora and placed her wrapped body into it with care. He buried her, glad he had found one spot in that crooked wood that would grant her a peaceful rest.

He knelt for a long time, saying goodbye to his companion.

Afterward, Merrick set up a small camp for himself. He gathered wood and placed it near the mouth of the cave. He pulled his extra bowstring from a pouch and set it as a trap on what appeared to be a small game trail. As he made his way back to the cave with kindling, he noticed how thirsty he was. He had been so busy preparing for the night he had forgotten to drink.

Merrick knelt beside the pristine waterhole. The water sparkled in the late evening sun that shot through the biggest window in the canopy he had seen all day. He cupped his hands and scooped water to his mouth, splashing some down the front of his tunic in the process. He took some more and poured it on his hair. The water was crisp, refreshing, and sweet. He drank more.

The water replenished more than the physical; it did wonders for his mental state, too. He felt revitalized. He retrieved the kindling and stood, swaying right and almost falling to the ground. Merrick tried to shake the exhaustion from his head. He needed a good night's rest. He took a few steps and swayed again. All of a sudden, he felt top-heavy, as if his legs could no longer carry his body's weight. He turned a contorted face to the natural well.

What was in that water? he thought.

Recognizing he may soon black out, Merrick lurched toward the cave, praying he might get far enough to cover himself for the night. He sprawled on the ground just inside the mouth of the cave. The world spun, and just then, he noticed a large opening in the back of the cave. He cursed himself for not checking it further before landing himself in his predicament. The dark of the opening grew in his delirious vision until he was swallowed by the void of unconsciousness.

When Merrick awoke, he wasn't quite sure he had. In his groggy state, he opened his eyes and saw only the obsidian of darkness. He raised a hand to his head, which throbbed. He could not even see his hand when he waved it before his face. He groped around, plying his fingers across the stony floor. He blindly navigated his way to a wall of the cave, stepping in a puddle of water—at least he hoped it was water.

He wet the front side of his hand and raised it ahead of him, hoping to pick up a sign of wind or fresh air in the darkness. He held as still as possible for as long as possible until he thought he had caught the slightest of breezes.

That way, he thought to himself.

Gingerly, he felt his way down a corridor. One hand slid along the wall to keep him grounded, and the other he held high in front of his face, hoping to detect any low-hanging stalactite that might threaten a concussive blow. His feet made short, deliberate sweeping motions to test his walking path before every step. Falling into an abyssal crevasse was a legitimate concern.

Despite his care, Merrick banged his feet and hands often, and occasionally, his head, as he continued through the corridor, until his eyes began to work again. He shook his head a few times to make sure he wasn't hallucinating, but sure enough, he saw an eerie blue glow ahead. As he approached, the corridor curved into a wider section filled with a million glowing fungi. The scene was breathtaking. Merrick stopped in awe, taking it all in. The fungi grew from floor to ceiling, dangling from stalactites and clinging to the walls.

Even more beautiful, Merrick felt a light breeze brush past him, a sign that he was, in fact, going the right way. The cave floor was devoid of fungi, revealing to the huntsman it was a well-traveled path. Taking a moment to inspect himself and his situation, he noticed his cloak was mangled and torn and reasoned he must have been dragged into the cave by some unknown monster. The thought did nothing to relax him, and a sudden noise stiffened him.

Clacking echoed through the corridors, bouncing off the walls. Merrick instinctively sought somewhere to hide. He was in no shape for a fight with an unknown assailant. He saw a particularly thick grove of fungi nearby and dove into it. Glowing blue spores transferred to his clothing like they were magnetically drawn. Realizing he might be a dark spot among the fungi, he rolled a few times, covering himself head to toe with the glowing spores.

The noises continued to *click-clack,* and the resonating sounds indicated the creature was nearing. A loud, pitiful screech rang out. There was a flurry of clacking, like some sort of scuffle, followed by a loud *crack!* And the struggle was over. Merrick laid there, silently controlling his breathing. He waited for a long time before the clacking began again, and the creature skittered into the fungal corridor.

Merrick couldn't get a glimpse of it. He laid perfectly still, hoping he'd blend in with the fungi. As the mystery beast approached, Merrick smelled and heard its rancid, belabored breath. Finally, it came into view. It was a rinont!

Rinonts were hideous, heavily armored insectoid monsters. They had six legs that ran down their bodies like razor sharp swords. Their massive heads were long-snouted and covered with horns. Thick, naturally developed armor plates ran along their hides. Merrick had never encountered one before. He had only heard tales of rinonts in the caves of the dwarves.

The massive rinont dragged its latest victim, clamped in its horned maw. Like Merrick, the deer must not have suspected the dangers of the waterhole and taken a drink.

Quite the efficient system for the rinont, though, Merrick thought.

The creature halted near Merrick. It wheezed as it sniffed the air, confused by the scent. Merrick gripped his dagger, relieved at the small victory that it was, indeed, still attached to his belt.

The rinont slowly turned in Merrick's direction. For a split second, the two stared hard at each other, neither making a move.

He was caught.

The rinont rushed straight at Merrick and slammed into the wall next to him with a *bang* that echoed through the fungal corridor. Spores flew in every direction, coating the rinont and everything else in its glowing powder. The creature flailed its legs wildly, attempting to stick Merrick with one of them.

The huntsman drove his dagger into the underbelly of the rinont, its weakest point. The monster screeched with horrific rage as it stumbled backward, its horrifying legs clacking feverishly. It charged again at Merrick, trying to catch him in its terrible, toothy maw, but it had forgotten the deer stuck in its mouth. The beast shook savagely, trying to free itself from its victim so it could finish the huntsman as well. Merrick, however, saw his opportunity.

He bolted down the corridor, following the weaving of the caves until he had run so far he no longer had light from the fungi. He threw out his hand to ground himself on the wall and ran on. He stumbled and banged along until he tripped on a low stalagmite that sent him sprawling to the cool stone floor, shaking much of the glowing spores from his clothes.

The clacking behind him closed in.

Merrick jumped to his feet and continued running. Finally, a glimmer of faint light up ahead—the shine of the moon in the singular clearing he had found?

Yes!

He burst from the front of the cave, not stopping to look around. He raced to the other side of the clearing and hid behind an ancient tree where he could catch his breath and watch the cave and his pursuer.

The rinont stormed out of the cave, a piece of the deer hanging from the side of its jaws. It screeched furiously as it looked this way and that, trying to pinpoint its escaped prey in the moonlight that bathed the clearing. It grunted and shook its massive head a few times, disappointed at losing such a special meal. It did not often have humans in its diet. Eventually, it clacked back into its cave, defeated.

Merrick exhaled heavily. How on earth did he manage to survive that? The rock next to the water glimmered and caught his eye.

Perhaps one last gift from an old friend, he thought, nodding to Rora in her final resting place.

He sat there for a long time, not so foolish as to go back into the clearing, but also not eager to go farther into Elderwood Forest at night. Not in his state, anyway. He needed to rest. He looked at all the trees around the clearing for one he could climb and perch among the branches to get some rest.

Crack!

The sound of a broken stick behind him caused Merrick's head to droop in defeat. He was exhausted.

What now? he thought.

He turned and came face-to-face with an enormous bear looming over him.

"Oh, come on!" Merrick yelled.

The bear's humongous paw came down on him like a hammer.

Chapter Fourteen

Storms Over The Narrows

The seaside city of Dahrenport buzzed with life, even as the sun set. The port city rested easily in a bay on the eastern coast of Tarrine. Pernden breathed in the smells of salt and the catch of the day as they swirled in an ebb and flow with the sea breeze. The harbor bells rang as the remaining fisher boats entered port. Dockworkers hurried about, running from one ship to another, unloading the final boats.

Pernden found his surroundings fascinating. One of his favorite things about being a Griffin Guardian was the travel. As he experienced the buzzing port city, he realized most of his travels had been entirely predicated on the whereabouts of a goblin or orc threat.

He reflected on the argument around the war room table at the Grand Corral. Had the Guard become calloused to the people of Tarrine? They had been fighting for so long on the front lines, isolated from the rest of the peoples, perhaps they had forgotten what they were fighting for. When their mission was over, Pernden would suggest squadrons do rotations in cities and towns across Tarrine to remind themselves of the people for whom they fought.

His eyes landed on a familiar face. Nera's bright smile stood in contrast to her ebony skin as she shone radiantly in the evening colors. Pernden's heart skipped a beat. He was surprised at her fairness, not because she lacked beauty but because it was often overlooked beside her skill as one of the Griffin Guard's elite Talon Squadron warriors. Her dark brown eyes, which had been lost in the wonder of Dahrenport, met his, and she crinkled her nose at him.

"What?"

"Nothing," Pernden said quickly, shaking away his daze. "I was just ... thinking."

"Isn't it beautiful," Nera said, getting lost in the view of the sea again. "You forget sometimes there is more life than just that found in Whitestone."

Pernden smiled at her words. He was glad to know he wasn't the only one with such thoughts, and he couldn't have hoped for anyone better to have said it. In addition to being an extremely capable guardian, Nera was also sound of mind and full of wisdom. Pernden trusted her judgment above anyone else's in his squadron.

"I've procured us an audience with the master of the fishermen's guild here in Dahrenport," she stated, leaving her eyes on the rarely experienced view. "He's waiting for us at the tavern by the northside docks."

"Let's not keep him waiting, then."

Pernden wheeled on his heel but stopped when Nera's hand grabbed his. Her gentle grasp held him captive in the sunset. She gazed across the bay, soaking in the view as long as she could.

She finally released his hand, whirled into a determined pace, and said, "Alright, then. Let's see to this guild master."

They fell into step together naturally, a result of marching drills during their trainee period at the Corral. Some of the young dockworkers—never having seen members of the Griffin Guard—gawked as they passed. Two boys grabbed poles and started sword fighting, only to get scolded by their father a moment later. Nera laughed at the poor boys, who quickly returned to work.

The tavern at the northside docks was well lit from the inside and easy to spot in the evening dim, even without a sign or designation on the old building itself. The noise coming from inside, in contrast with the well-quieted docks, indicated clearly to the two guardians they'd arrived at the right place. They stood out as they entered, since the tavern was filled wall-to-wall with fishermen, who erupted with excited conversation at the sight of them.

"I guess our guild master was eager to share this glorious opportunity of his," Nera muttered, her voice dripping with sarcasm.

Word had gotten out, and every fisherman in the northside docks had rushed to the tavern for a good look at the visiting guardians—a rare treat, indeed.

A rather hairy-armed man with a bushy mustache waved them to his corner table. Nera nodded his way and fell in line behind Pernden as they waded through the crowd. Fishermen eyeballed them from all sides. Some shook their hands, thanking the guardians for what they do. Pernden merely shook the hands and nodded, uncertain how to respond to such greetings.

When they got to the table, the big man's mustache bobbed with his giant grin. Another man, who Pernden had not seen earlier, sat next to the mustached man. With his light armor and less sunbaked skin, the second man didn't look much like a fisherman. Pernden and Nera took seats, and before the guild master could get a word out, a couple of barmaids unloaded handfuls of drinks for them. Apparently, everyone wanted to show their appreciation for the guardians. The mustached man shooed them away, looked down at the table full of drinks, and shook his head.

"The fishermen of Dahrenport thank ya fer yer service!" he yelled from behind his bushy mustache. A raucous cheer resounded through the whole place, and Pernden nodded his head and waved his hand in thanks to the good people, who settled into their own conversations around the room.

Pernden turned to the two men. "Thank you for the hospitality. I've never ..."

He trailed off as a distraught barmaid eyed the full table, wondering where she might set the next batch of drinks she held precariously.

"I think we have plenty, thank you. Perhaps the fine gentlemen at this next table?" Pernden motioned to a nearby table where the barmaid quickly passed the drinks to some ever thirsty fishermen. She shot a thankful glance back at the guardian, relieved to be done with the balancing act.

"It is our pleasure, Sir Guardian," the light-armored man said with a nod.

"Ah yes! I met the beautiful Miss Nera," the mustached man remembered. "But I haven't met yerself, Captain. I'm Trent Goffer, master of the Dahrenport fishermen's guild." His proud words wobbled his mustache. "Oh, and this be Marlon Kirt, dock guard."

"Mr. Goffer. Mr. Kirt—"

"Oh, Trent be fine!" he cut in. He motioned to Nera to see if she would be offended if he helped himself to one of the many drinks covering their table. She nodded her approval with a scrunched nose and a grin.

"Marlon, for me," the guard added, also helping himself to a beverage following Nera's approval.

"Sure, Trent and Marlon. Thank you, truly. I take it Nera has briefed you on the necessary details of our mission here?"

"Yes, yes," the big guild master leaned in. "Very dangerous task, that is. Goin' to the Gant Sea Narrows at night. Dahrenport fishermen don't go there at night. It's too dangerous fer ships to be out there. Too dark. Treacherous rocks. And death wings!" His whole body shook, and his mustache bristled at the thought.

"Yes. Death wings ..." Marlon nodded, taking a swig from his tankard.

"Death wings?" Nera asked, never having heard of such a thing.

"Giant bats," Marlon answered. "They are ravenous monsters. They are active at night, flying around the Narrows searching for fish or birds that might have landed for a poorly laid bed. As big as dolphins, they are!"

"Has anyone been out in the Narrows recently?" Pernden asked, grabbing a tankard for himself.

"No," Trent replied, replacing his quickly emptied glass with a full one. "Like I said, treacherous rocks. Most fishermen don't get too close to the Narrows. We been fishing here fer generations. Lessons learned."

"Well, we'll be looking for a specific island that has a tower on it, or perhaps only ruins of a tower. Our understanding is it was once a wisdom tower for wizards. Our information comes from a mage who met our king. Has anyone seen anything like that?" Pernden asked, hoping for useful information for his squadron.

Marlon and Trent looked at each other. "Well ...," Marlon started.

"No, no, no," Trent grumbled. "Not ole Barnett—"

Marlon shushed the guild master, waving him away with one hand and grabbing another glass with the other. "Well, there's an old man here, named Barnett. I speak with him regularly."

"Ya mean he talks at ya because yer walking 'round the docks all day, and the old man has nothing to da but tell crazy steries!"

"He's the only one who's ever said anything about weird goings-on in the Narrows!" Marlon snapped back, losing some of his well-trained composure.

"Ah, fine then! Let's invite him aver ta the table, then!" Trent's stocky body clambered onto his chair, and he shouted over the tavern's noise. "Oy! Barnett! Barnett! Get aver here! The guardians want ta talk ta ya!"

The tavern hushed into gossipy whispers as the old man maneuvered through the crowd with a soft clicking. He worked his way to their table and reached out a hand as he neared.

"Aver here, Barnett," Trent's voice guided him.

The old man stopped next to the table and angled in Trent's direction. Pernden noticed the old man's grey eyes and realized he was blind. Nera's puzzled face mirrored her captain's, as their hopes for real or useful information slipped away.

Marlon seemed to have much more compassion for the old man. "Barnett, it's Marlon here."

"I knows ya. I'm blind, but my ears werk perty gud."

The old man shook when he talked, gripping his walking stick with white knuckles, trying to keep his balance. Pernden thought the man a pitiful sight and offered him his chair.

"Please, take my seat," he said.

The old man looked surprised at the guardian's kindness, his wrinkled face showing every ounce of gratitude. He gratefully accepted.

"Hello, Captain," he said.

"Hello, Mr. Barnett," Pernden replied, unsure how the man knew he was the captain. "How did you ..."

"Officer and gentleman," the old man quipped, answering Pernden's question before he had finished asking. "I s'pose if yer talkin' ta me, yer wantin' ta knows 'bout the Narrows."

"Yes, sir. Anything you can tell us would aid our mission greatly."

The old man beamed at being addressed as "sir."

"I was thinking you should tell them about the lights," Marlon suggested.

"Aye." Barnett agreed, a far-off look in his blind eyes. "See, I wasn' always blind. Was a time I wasn'. But long ago, when I was a young'n, I tooked my daddy's boat to the Narrows—fer a girl, of course. Mind ya, not as perty as the one sittin' next ta ya. If she was, I mighta got myself inta even more trouble," he mumbled.

Pernden turned to Nera, completely baffled by the old man. Nera only smiled back, not sure herself.

"Anyhow," Barnett continued. "I heared tale of an old wizard's tower that was filled with treasures, see. I wanted ta get her somethin' special. Some kind a' treasure. I loved her! Oh, I did ..." He mumbled under his breath, again. "Anyhow, I found it, I did—the tower. But, the Narrows are danger'us at night. I couldn' control my daddy's boat. And anyhow, I'da died if I tried ta get inta the tower. Lightnin' flashed! And fire! Red and blue, green and orange. All colors a' light flashin'! I seen the tower blowed up, and one a' the red lightnin's came right at me! Knocked me undone. When I waked, by some miracle, I was floatin' just outside the bay. But I was blind. A friend a' mine was in his boat with his daddy, and they camed and helped me get back inta port."

"Mr. Barnett, I think this tower is the one we are looking for. Is there some way you could help us find its location?" Pernden was excited to finally have some information for their mission.

"I'm not so gud at maps no more." The old man let out a raspy laugh at the younger man's excitement. Nera couldn't help but snicker. Barnett easily grabbed a full tankard from the table, took a big swig, and continued. "I can tell ya the route I taked, and hopefully, it helps ya."

"That would be much appreciated," Pernden conceded.

The old man told them how he had followed the Narrows, starting from the north coastline of the bay. He had traveled for hours circling, winding, and navigating as close to each island as he possibly could without wrecking his boat.

Apparently, he had nearly wrecked himself on multiple occasions. But love is love, after all, and he was already wrecked.

He couldn't say exactly where he found the small island with the wisdom tower, but he knew if they followed the Narrows going east, certainly a squadron of the famous Griffin Guard would find it. That is, assuming there was anything left of the tower.

While the information they gathered from the people of Dahrenport wasn't entirely concrete, the renewed sense of purpose for the young guardians was already worth the trip's price. They were thrilled to see those people living their lives in freedom. Their liberty was what the guardians were fighting for and why they sacrificed so much.

A massive storm rolled heavily off the sea from the south and barraged the Talon Squadron as it flew under the cover of night. Lightning streaked across the sky at unpredictable variables, and the raging winds pressed hard against the determined troop.

The griffin formation bobbed and weaved as gusts forced them off their direct course.

Griffins produce natural oils for their feathers that whisk the rain free with every flap of their wings. That brought little comfort to the guardians, however, whose armors were drenched and reins slick. They were the toughest of the tough, though, the hardiest of all their stock. Though cracks of thunder might downcast the hearts of other men, Talon Squadron remained stoic; their vision unwavering.

A bolt of lightning streaked closer than one of the guardians liked, and he tightened himself to the formation. They had been flying over the Gant Sea Narrows, headed east, as old blind Barnett had instructed, for some time. They still hadn't found the lone island with the tower. Pernden doubted there would be a tower to find. Perhaps they would find some ruins, but in the deluge, it was hard to make out any details on the islands below.

Nera flew nearby. "Captain, we need to fly lower. It's impossible to see from here, and the storm is going to get worse before it gets better!"

Pernden knew she was right. Their elevated altitude gave them a stealthier approach to obscure them from anyone who might be waiting. But it was a difficult task to see the islands below. Though battle-hardened and tough as they come, the griffins could not hold up forever under such conditions either. He patted the neck of his griffin thoughtfully. He and Rocktail had flown through storms before, but this one raged with the heart of the sea.

"Alright!" Pernden yelled out right after another bang of thunder. He signaled to the Talon Squadron to lower their formation.

The maneuver would have been a sight to behold, had it not been for the raging storm, as the skilled squadron smoothly dove into a pattern they had performed countless times. They leveled out at a lower altitude, able to see more clearly, even as the storm continued, unrelenting. Their formation spread again as each looked for remnants that might have been a tower.

Rocktail roiled uncomfortably, sensing something Pernden did not. A streak of grey-black flesh blasted in from out of nowhere, nearly knocking Pernden out of his saddle. Rocktail screeched a violent warning. As Pernden regained his seat and looked out over his squadron, he realized they had made a mistake.

"Death wings!" Nera yelled.

What seemed like a hundred large bat creatures flapped in mass chaos, enveloping the guardian squadron. Griffins outstretched razor-sharp talons and ripped at the monstrous bats' flesh, tearing at whatever they could sink their claws into. Guardians swung swords, lopping off grey-skinned wings, forcing some of the bats into twisting tailspins toward the rocks below. Others jabbed at the monsters with spears. In the flurry, Talon Squadron had broken formation to take on individual assailants as best they could. Between the chaos of the battle and the storm, it was hard to see even the nearest of their fellow guardians.

Ba-boom!

A massive lightning bolt struck one of the nearby islands, blasting with an intense light and crack of thunder. It seemed to stunt the death wings' onslaught as they skittered wildly in response. The momentary reprieve gave Pernden an idea and spurred him into action, once more commanding his guardians.

"Fly into the storm!" he yelled. "Fly into the storm!"

Instantly, the guardians of Talon Squadron rocketed through the air flying high into the storm. The giant bats raced after them, hungry for the unusual meat.

Kra-kow!

Another strike sent the monsters into a frenzy. They seemed to hover in place for a while, deciding whether the meat of that crazy prey was worth facing their archnemesis, the storm. Another flash of lightning made the choice for them.

The angry horde flew chaotically back down toward the Narrows. Some nipped at others. Some made swift dives for the ocean, hoping for fish. And still others crashed upon their wounded brethren to feast on the no longer viable members of the pack.

Once sure the monsters had relinquished their chase, Pernden looked around to his fellow guardians. No one had been lost in the vicious attack, but some nursed bloody slices. Meanwhile, some of the griffins nuzzled at savage scratches and bites the monsters had gotten in.

This could have been a lot worse, Pernden thought to himself.

He stroked the neck feathers on Rocktail, who did not seem pleased about the ambush.

Pernden flew alongside Nera, who was leaning forward, looking ahead. She turned to him, a relieved smile etching her face.

"Well, I think we found our tower," she said.

Pernden turned his surprised gaze to where she pointed, some distance below and farther to the east than the horde of death wings. Sure enough, there it was—not a whole tower, but a tower nonetheless.

"Thank you," Pernden said under his breath.

With a quick signal to the others, he led them onward through the storm.

Talon Squadron landed silently under the cover of the pouring rain. Only Pernden, Nera, and Tozer landed on the small island with the tower. The others put down softly on nearby islands, alert and ready to fly at a moment's notice should anything go awry.

Tozer took point and led the younger guardians toward the old wisdom tower. He was the eldest member of Talon Squadron. In fact, few had ever made it to his age and still been part of the elite group. Pernden appreciated the man's wealth of knowledge and experience and often looked to him for counsel on missions. Tozer skillfully navigated them around pieces of rubble and half-fallen walls, while the other two kept their heads on swivels, looking for any trouble.

What was left of the tower stood at an awkward angle and looked as though it were at home in the terrible storm. Many of the massive stone pieces the guardians weaved around were charred, lining up with the story Barnett had told them. To Pernden's estimation, that place had seen an epic battle indeed. He wondered at what kind of magic the place had witnessed as he looked up at the looming, decrepit tower before them. Who knew what kind of wizard power had been used there?

A sound halted them. Tozer's commanding fist signaled for them to hold fast. The rain continued to fall in sheets, and the waves crashed against the many islands, while the three listened intently.

"Perhaps a loose stone from the aging tower finally gave way," Tozer whispered back to the others after a long pause.

Satisfied with the answer and trusting Tozer's experience while also acutely on guard, the three pressed forward toward the tower. Tozer reached the tower door and began the work of unlocking it, as Pernden and Nera swept to either side, clearing the area. Pernden rounded the corner of the tower, looking it up and down. Higher up, the tower had been totally blown open by the force of some massive energy he could hardly imagine. The tower had clearly been built sturdy, as the bottom half remained intact. He turned and rejoined Tozer at the same time as Nera, their movements fluid and well rehearsed.

There was a heavy clunk in the door, and Tozer nodded to them that he had gotten it unlocked. Without saying a word, the three formulated their plan. Tozer would swing open the enormous doors. Pernden would slide in first rounding to the right with his sword at the ready, clearing his area. Nera would round to the left to fend off any attackers with her spear. And Tozer would come flying in behind them with his trident to round up the rest.

The three-man squad executed the maneuver to perfection. To their relief, they found the foyer of the great tower empty. A great streak of lightning illuminated the foyer briefly, and Nera noticed a candelabra with a flint spark lighter next to it. Tozer grabbed a torch from the wall, and the two ignited them to light the interior.

Pernden was drawn immediately to a large table in the middle of the room which had scrolls and parchments thrown all about. He looked up from the center of the room to the zig-zagging stairways leading to the upper levels of the tower. Rooms and nooks were nestled all around the exterior walls, and from his vantage point, it was hard to guess how many there might be. As the glow of the candles and multiple torches began to illuminate the tower, Pernden was struck by the disheveled tomes, scrolls, and parchments that were strewn about.

The place had been ransacked, to say the least. Judging by the vast number of shelves around them, it was clear the place had been a wisdom tower. Pernden had heard tales of such places, where mages came and brought together their collective wisdom of the magical arts. He had even heard wizards were the ones who originally established these places long ago. He knew of the locations of only a few active wisdom towers—actively inhabited by mages, anyway. He had never actually seen one in person.

Tozer snapped his young captain back to the present as he handed him a blazing torch.

"Right," Pernden nodded. "We're looking for a mirror. The writings that King Garron procured called it the Alkhoren Mirror. To this point, we don't know its magics, so be careful. The king believes it's vital to our efforts against the rising threat of Drelek. We must find it."

Tozer studied the ancient stairways while his captain spoke. "I should start on the third level," he offered.

"Good," Pernden permitted. "Nera, you take this level, and I'll take the second level. If we can't manage to find it, we'll climb higher. I'd prefer we didn't have to, though. The tower has far more damage higher up."

Without another word, the three split up to search the tower. The stairs creaked under the weight of their footsteps. Tozer continued to climb as Pernden began his search of the second level. He followed the shelf-lined walls to the first alcove, only to find a mess of parchments that whoever had ransacked the place hadn't cared about. He moved on to the first of many rooms with its door splayed open.

Nothing here, either, he thought.

The process continued, as he found rooms for all sorts of magecraft. There were rooms for quiet study. Rooms for what seemed like the practice of magical arts. Rooms for potion making. And of course, he found rooms for sleeping. The old wisdom tower must have been quite the sight in its prime. Pernden could only imagine. He leaned over the railing in the center, not surprised to see Tozer pop his head over the third level railing to his left.

"Anything?"

"Nothing, Captain. The King was sure the mirror is here? This place looks like it was picked clean, at least of anything of value."

"Seems that way to me, too," Pernden nodded.

Nera slid into view below them.

"I've found a locked door down here. I almost missed it in the dark. It's in a back corner behind the hearth."

Pernden and Tozer glanced at each other before making their way to the stairs. If they were lucky, the mages may have stowed away some of their most prized possessions in a hidden vault in light of the attack. Maybe the mirror would be among them.

Tozer set to work on the hidden door.

"I only just noticed it. I was illuminating this ornate banner and happened to notice the hidden door on the edge here."

"Hidden back here, the attackers may have thought the banner worth nothing and never noticed the door behind. We may be in luck." Pernden said.

After a click and a long groan of the hinges, Tozer looked back, a glint of excitement in his eyes. The three stepped into the room, and in the light of their torches, they saw a singular item, standing as tall as any man and wrapped in a heavy cloth. Pernden followed the binding with his hands and untied the knot that held the heavy cloth together. He pulled the cloth away to reveal the Alkhoren Mirror.

The mirror was an ornate piece, its frame beautifully crafted. Magical runes etched the frame on all sides. The blazing torches reflected brightly off the pristine mirror.

"I think we've found it," Pernden stated and smiled his relief at their luck to the others.

They quickly rewrapped it in its protective cloth. Pernden and Tozer each pulled out an extra cloth and rope they had brought. They had no way of knowing what condition they might find the mirror in and wanted to be able to wrap it well for the return journey to Whitestone. After wrapping the Alkhoren Mirror, they worked together to lift and carry the massive piece.

Nera, who had been holding her torch high so the other two had good visibility, noticed a long shining item in the corner of the small room. They hadn't noticed it before, but it was the only thing left in the room. As she neared the shiny object, she realized it was a spear covered in ornate scribblings and runes. It had a small parchment attached to it that she untied and read to herself.

Santoralier – Lightning Rider.

The mages had marked the artifact and clearly thought it the only other piece worthy of being hidden with the mirror in their haste. She looked the spear up and down once more. It was a fine weapon, and as it did not appear to have a master at present, it seemed quite the waste for it to remain in such a dank room. She slid her fingers along the ornate scribblings and a small yellow stone centered on the spear. She could feel a light energy flowing through the whole thing—a fine weapon, indeed.

She grabbed the spear, Santoralier, and sauntered out to join her friends. Though they had found the mirror, the raging storm was a stark reminder their mission was not over. They would head back to Dahrenport for some rest and embark the next day on the long journey back to Whitestone.

CHAPTER FIFTEEN

A DEADLY GAME

Waves lapped harmlessly against the *Lady Leila*, securely beached in the morning fog. Orin groaned. Everything hurt. His ribs ached as he rolled over on the hard planks of the wooden boat and pulled himself upright. With a groan, he remembered he had not fully healed before embarking on the journey home. Not only was he not in Whitestone, but he had important information to bring to his commanding officers in the Griffin Guard. At that point, though, he had no idea where he was.

The fog rolled off the sea in thick blots, but not so thick he couldn't see his friends' silhouettes where they conversed on the beach nearby.

"Orin!" Ellaria started. She dashed to him. She helped him stand and get out of the boat. "Hey you, how's your head?"

"My head's a little fuzzy ... but my whole body hurts."

"Can't imagine why," Ellaria said, dripping with sarcasm.

Her face was covered in drying tear streaks. They had discussed Merrick and how he'd helped them escape the orcs at Macintroh's farm. For all she knew, he was dead, having sacrificed himself for them. Though she knew she must bury her feelings and get on task. Their new mission was vital and required her to focus. She would have time to grieve later. And if she was honest with herself, Ellaria still held hope that Merrick had also escaped.

"Come here. We're trying to figure out where we've landed."

They joined Coal and Ezel a few paces away. The mighty black-bearded dwarf and the scrawny hairless gnome were signing feverishly in their usual manner. Orin could only watch helplessly until Coal said, "Bah!" waving a dismissive hand at the little gnome.

"He says we ran into a gantendril in Blackmar Forest at the Whispering Lake. Which ... come to think of it, makes a lot of sense ..." Coal tugged at the braid in his long beard as he trailed off. "But now he thinks we're on an island somewhere in the Tandal Sea, which, of course, is a long way from the Whispering Lake. I'm not saying he's wrong. I'm just wondering how he's supposed to be knowing this with all the fog."

Ezel placed a hand in the sand and raised one high above his head. Blue fire burned in his eyes, and several of his rune tattoos glowed. Coal rolled his eyes, and his whole body shrugged. "Yes, yes. But we won't know where we are until the morning fog rolls out and we can check the island."

Ezel's magic diffused, and the two fell back into a signing argument.

"They've been at this since I woke," Ellaria muttered to Orin. "How long?"

"A couple hours mayb ..." Ellaria stopped, realizing they had been arguing about the fog for much longer than they should have. "Hey, you two! How long should the morning fog last in these parts?"

Coal half-turned to her, not wanting to concede the argument he and Ezel were engaged in. "Maybe an hour or s ..."

The dwarf comprehended her point, and Ezel's face shifted as he recognized the same. The dwarf signaled to the gnome, who readied his stance. Then, Coal signaled to Ellaria and Orin to fall in with them, taking his mighty battle hammer into his tense hands.

They slowly moved through the sand of the beach, up and away from the water. As if they walked through some magical barrier, the fog peeled back behind them as the interior of the island came into view. The island was covered by a beautiful jungle. Butterflies flitted to and fro, and in the distance, they saw what looked like an ancient palace, gleaming in the sunlight. A butterfly floated near Ellaria, stopping for a short rest on her necklace, only to pop up and fly away again a moment later.

"What is this place?" she asked.

"I do not know ..." Coal answered slowly.

Ezel's hands flowed, signing a thought to the suspicious dwarf. Orin wasn't sure what he'd signed, but the gnome's face was a mix of fear and intrigue.

Coal only replied with a low, "Maybe ...," his hammer firmly at the ready.

"What kind of dream is this?" Orin asked.

"There is some sort of magic about this place. Powerful magic, if Ezel didn't see it. My guess is it's some sort of illusion spell to protect this place from fishermen or other vessels."

The dwarf did not look pleased about what that might mean about the place. A dozen more butterflies floated about, a few of them flitting around Ellaria, who looked at them with awe. Their colors were unlike any she had seen in Tamaria at Lady Bird Hill. They were quite the spectacle.

Ezel prodded a hand through the fog barrier, trying to feel the magic and get the sense of it. Suddenly, a thought struck the tattooed gnome, and he bolted back into the fog.

The other three followed him through the barrier, the dwarf never looking away from the interior, in case something followed them. The others had suddenly stopped, and Coal's backpedaling had to halt. He turned to see what his companions gawked at, and his hammer slipped into one hand, the head falling heavily, landing a crater in the soft sand.

"Boehlen's beard ..."

The *Lady Leila* was gone.

Coal's dwarven feet stomped through the sand of the beach as the crew followed the edge of the island, hoping to find any sign of their boat. The heated dwarf was furious at the predicament. Ezel had used his magic in an attempt to spot the *Lady Leila* adrift somewhere in the fog but was unable to see the small vessel.

The two were experienced with their boat and had left it secured. It seemed unlikely it had been taken away by the waves in the brief moments the crew had gone through the veil of fog to the interior of the island.

Ellaria and Orin trudged through the sand helplessly, several paces behind the brisk dwarf. A blue butterfly floated near Ellaria as they walked.

"What'll we do if we can't find the boat?" Ellaria asked.

"Oh, we'll find her!" came a yell from Coal, who never looked back.

"We have to trust that Coal and Ezel will find a way. We have to. I'm no seafarer, but I must get back to Whitestone to report to High Commander Kane. Drelek has a dragon ..." Orin said the words, hardly believing them himself.

"Aye," Ellaria nodded. "I'll admit, I wasn't expecting that. Do you think they might have more? Where did it come from? I thought dragons went extinct during the Second Great Black War."

"As far as I have known, that was the case. A dragon hasn't been seen in Tarrine since then."

Orin bit at the inside of his lip, pondering the new development. Finlestia was bigger than just Tarrine, he knew, but little was known about the other places beyond the seas. It was not impossible that the dragon had come from elsewhere. He'd never seen a dragon in real life, only in the annals of the Grand Corral. How would Drelek have gotten hold of such a creature? Ellaria's question about them possibly having more of the beasts fueled his desire to get back to Whitestone. The surprising boldness of the wyvern squadrons of recent months made more sense. As far as Orin knew, he was the only guardian who knew about the dragon they had run into at the Palori Ruins.

As the guardian walked beside the young woman, her red hair waving in the sea breeze, another question sparked in his mind. "Ellaria, how long have you been able to wield magic?"

"I hadn't!" she confessed. "It was a surprise to me as well. I don't understand everything Ezel was trying to say to me on the beach, but we were trying to figure out why ..."

"Ah, no, no, no, no, no!" Coal pumped his short dwarven legs and sprinted ahead in the fog. His battle hammer waved wildly as he high-stepped through the sand.

Ezel's magic lights dimmed, the seeing rune on his forehead returning to its normal tattoo state as he ran to catch up to the dwarf. Orin and Ellaria ran up behind them, only to find them standing at an edge of the island that appeared to be an outlet for some kind of river.

"It's two islands," Coal grumbled.

"Two?" Ellaria asked, the blue butterfly landing on her shoulder for a momentary respite.

"Aye, two. The island is split. See there?" He pointed a little way ahead of them, and through the thick fog, the crew could just make out more beach on the other side of the waterway. "It's not a river like we know it. Not like the Rolling River or the Palori. This is a seaway. It seems like a river, but it's really just the sea running between two close islands."

"What does that mean?" Orin asked, hoping there was something he could do to help.

"It means ..." The dwarf flicked his hands in a quick sign to Ezel. "Someone's stolen our vessel!"

Ezel whirled around, eyes ablaze, runes on his hands lighting in a burst of magic. He lifted the blue butterfly and held it in the air between the companions. Following Coal's lead, Orin drew his sword and held it at the ready. A low squealing noise came from the writhing butterfly as it mutated and transformed. The squeaking twisted to a reverberating howl, as the creature gave into its new form before their eyes.

A faery!

"T-that j-just hurts!" the faery cried out. His voice vibrated when he spoke. "N-not fair. N-not fair at all!"

"Where's my boat?" Coal growled, gripping his war hammer tighter, shoving his face closer to the little creature.

"N-not fair. Y-you cheated!" the faery cried with a chime in his voice.

"I cheated?"

Coal grabbed the faery by the leg and gave him a good shake. Hanging upside down, the faery had been released from Ezel's telekinetic hold but found himself in a less fortunate situation in the angry dwarf's grasp. His little brain rattled as he blinked crazily, trying to regain his faculties.

"Let's try this a little slower. Where-is-my-boat?" Coal asked, again.

"Glintz doesn't c-cheat. N-no, no!"

"What? This isn't a game, you little pixie!" Coal growled, shaking the faery more for good measure.

His wings fluttered wildly, and he grabbed at the dwarf's linen hand wrappings, trying to gain some stability.

Glintz's eyes lolled in his head.

"L-life is a g-game," he said defiantly.

"Listen!" Orin cut in. "Many lives are at stake! We're on an important mission for the Griffin Guard of Whitestone. There's a war coming!"

"W-war is a g-good game," the little faery grinned evilly.

"His people would know nothing of that here," Coal said to Orin. He understood the man's thought but also knew the futility of the attempt.

"B-but we play h-hide and s-seek."

"Ah!" Coal shook the faery by the leg again.

"Wait, wait," Ellaria stopped him. "Glintz, was it?"

Suddenly, as Ellaria leaned in, the little faery's focus sharpened.

"Y-yes," he replied, nodding his head. He stared, transfixed, at the green stone that hung from her neck.

Ellaria grabbed the necklace and waved it back and forth ever so slightly, watching the faery's gaze follow its movement.

"Do you like me necklace?"

"Y-yes. Y-yes!" his voice vibrated excitedly, his wings fluttering like crazy.

She covered up the stone with her hand, jolting the faery's attention, bringing a sad look to his tiny facial features.

"I like to play games, too. Used to play them with me brothers when we were young," she continued. "But you see, these guys don't know the rules. They don't want to cheat; they just don't know how to play."

Glintz's mouth gaped as he looked around at the others, as if suddenly he understood why they were cheating. Certainly, it was by accident.

"Y-yes. C-cheating is for l-losers."

"Right," she said. "And no one wants to lose. Winning is much more fun."

"Y-yes!"

"But it's not a fair game if me friends don't know the rules. Maybe a clue would be helpful."

Glintz opened his mouth wide, ready to teach these silly folks how to play. But he stopped suddenly, thinking perhaps maybe he shouldn't. Ellaria revealed the stone on the end of her leather necklace, again drawing a mystified gaze from the faery. His face contorted as he tried to decide what to do.

"You know, if you don't give them a clue, then really, you're not playing fair," she pushed him harder. "That sounds like cheating to me. And I don't think Glintz is a loser, is he?"

"N-no, no!" He straightened his upside-down posture and crossed his arms proudly. "Glintz wins a-all the t-time."

"So, a clue then?"

Glintz hesitated, not having a great argument to defeat Ellaria's logic. He was no cheater. Well, at least he wasn't when he didn't think he could get away with it. As an idea revealed itself in his mind, a wicked grin scrawled across his tiny face.

"A c-clue!"

He reached for a pouch on his belt with both his hands, and as swift as his rapid wings, he pulled out a tiny dagger, jabbing it into the dwarf's massive thumb. In the split second of confusion, the faery smashed the tiny pouch on his own chest, which exploded into a small cloud of dust. Ezel's tattoos blazed as everyone glanced around, feverishly searching for the tiny faery. From a distance, they heard his vibrating voice.

"Oh, there's s-so many b-boats. Our g-great king loves how they f-float. But w-where does he k-keep his m-moat? The d-dwarf and his t-team should follow the s-stream, but n-nothing is as it s-seems!"

Glintz's vibrating voice sang out hauntingly as he flew away in the fog.

Coal grumbled as he sucked on the side of his thumb where the faery had stabbed him. He did not like it, not one bit. It had taken him time to get used to Ezel's magic, and he did not care for the magics of such deceitful little creatures as the faery.

The blood on his thumb was a stark reminder of the danger they faced, and Coal did not take lightly the mission with which Merrick had charged him. Orin and Ellaria depended on him to get them to Whitestone safely. More than that, all of Tarrine was in danger, with Drelek in possession of a dragon. His and all the other people's lives as they knew them could soon be over if they failed.

He looked up to the two man-kin in his care and then over to Ezel, who nodded, suggesting he also recognized the weight of their mission.

Onward then.

Coal's heavy boots trudged through the sand as the crew fell in behind him. They headed upstream through the fog, toward the interior of the island. Toward what, exactly, they could not guess.

Along the way, the illusion fog had dissolved to reveal the reality within. The vibrant colors of the jungle-covered islands mixed with the array of brilliant butterflies was almost too much for their senses to take in. This time, they were not fooled by its beauty. Ellaria did not marvel at the variety of butterflies. Instead, she felt the weight of thousands of eyes watching her every movement. As some floated near, she waved them away.

Ezel's head turned right and left, eyes darting around, trying to be prepared for anything. The hairless gnome had taken personally his inability to recognize the magic that had landed them in their situation. He desired to protect his friends at all costs and felt he had failed them. He looked ahead to the dwarf, stomping onward, following the waterway, face set like flint. He and Coal had traveled together for a long time, and the gnome had seen this side of the dwarf before. Coal's singular focus on getting the *Lady Leila* back was a strength that could certainly help the team find the boat, but such bullheadedness also posed the risk he might miss a trap or an ambush. Ezel tried to keep a cool head, knowing his constant vigilance coupled with the dwarf's heat may lead them right.

Orin took note of the sky while they were inside the fictitious barrier. The sun was already on its descent, and he realized they had lost nearly a full day to the faery island already. Anger rose within him as he saw dozens more butterflies floating on pace with them across the waterway, observing their progress. But their progress was suddenly halted by a curve of the waterway and an outstretched signal from Coal.

The dwarf slid his grip to the end of the long handle on his hammer and poked the weapon out ahead of him. He sniffed the air, trying to smell something the others could not identify. His hands flicked a quick comment to Ezel, and a couple of the grey gnome's tattoos roared to blue flame.

As if it were coming alive, the waterway snaked itself into a new position that ran in the opposite direction. Apparently, the crew had lost the waterway a while back and had been walking far from it since. A resounding chorus of vibrating snickers rolled through the jungle around them.

"I'm tired of these games!" Coal growled, his eyes seeming to blaze like those of his gnome companion, but the dwarf's smoldered with the fires of rage instead of magic. "The waterway is over there. Ezel, have you figured out how to keep these tricks at bay?"

Ezel signed to his friend that he was working on it. That time, when he revealed the truth of their surroundings, he had used a combination of his rune tattoos he had not attempted to use before. Faery magic was quite different from his own. The bald gnome was still experimenting to figure it out.

"I don't much care for these faery tricks myself," Coal grumbled aloud.

He led them back to the waterway. Ezel revealed what he could, so they were able to pick through the jungle and get back on course. They managed to follow it only a short way before Ezel stopped the crew in their tracks. Coal poked around with his hammer again, while Orin peered through the trees and brush, trying to see anything that might pose them a threat.

Ezel's hands flashed to Coal that he wasn't sure what the danger was, but he could sense it. He felt the tingling in his small frame but couldn't figure out how to reveal it.

"Ahhh! Enough with the games!" Coal yelled through the jungle. He lifted his hammer into a ready position with both hands clenched tightly around the handle. "Come out and show yourselves! I've got a game for you!"

Several butterflies had begun to hover a little too closely for Ellaria's liking. She wafted her hands to shoo them away, but the swarm only grew.

An idea struck the little gnome as he remembered Whispering Lake. With Orin swatting at the butterflies too, Ezel ran up to Ellaria, reached up high to grab her hand, and shot the other hand out wide. A combination of runes sparked to life. Realizing what the gnome was doing, Ellaria closed her eyes and set her will with his.

Emerald whisps of magic rolled off the woman, her red hair flowing with the winding force. Her magic twisted and turned, seeming to intertwine with and energize the gnome's magic. Orin and Coal could only watch the spectacle, neither understanding what was happening.

Around them, the veil faded. Trees and bushes dissolved into nothing. Butterflies twisted and contorted as they mutated into their faery forms. A massive pit trap covered in gnarly spikes at odd angles opened a few steps ahead of where they had been walking. Small stone huts emerged, covering the hill leading up to the ancient palace, which was visible. The palace's luster lessened as the hallucination gave way to authenticity.

To Coal's great relief, the *Lady Leila* appeared, in fine condition. The boat looked to the dwarf as beautiful as the woman she was named after, safely nestled in a tiny offshoot of the seaway that split the islands. She was flanked by several larger vessels, and for a brief second, Coal wondered what had happened to those crews. He turned to face the ambushers. His eyes no longer raged with embers of anger but rather had a giddy sparkle at the newly even playing field.

"Coal ..." Orin started cautiously, recognizing the shift in the dwarf's stance and settling into his own ready posture.

As the magic simmered, the world appeared as it truly was. A pair of faeries caught in the dwarf's wild gaze glanced nervously to one another. A menacing grin rolled in behind the dwarf's great black beard.

"Game on," he said, laughing as his mighty hammer swung right through the pair of nervous faeries, connecting hard and blasting them into dust.

The battle broke out in a frenzy. Some faeries dashed about, wings flitting. Others exploded magic dust on themselves to disappear and reappear out of harm's way. Faeries dipped and darted, jabbing with their tiny knives.

"W-war! W-war! They want to p-play war!" reverberated from all around as the tiny monsters swarmed.

Orin's training superseded his body's aches and the faeries' speed. He sliced and hacked, his sword ringing with a *ting* here and a *thuk* there, as it landed its marks. The nuanced display would have been dazzling to see, were his companions not occupied with their own attackers.

Coal laughed crazily as he swung his war hammer out, obliterating the tiny creatures. He took no notice of their stings when some got through to poke at him. The mighty head of his hammer met the minuscule monsters as though they were bugs, swatting them easily.

Ezel produced a large, glowing blue orb above himself, capturing many of the faeries. They furiously stabbed at it, trying to break free. Others came to help but found themselves sucked into the orb.

Ellaria pulled back the drawstring on her bow. Her sleek muscles, as taut as the string, didn't waver as she focused her energy into the release. Green magic swirled around the arrow as it took flight and burned through the air, catching up more faeries in its whirlwind before colliding with the blue orb and exploding.

The shock stopped Orin and Coal mid-attack and sent the rest of the faeries skittering in all directions. None of them had seen such power before, and they weren't quite sure they could win the game without cheating.

Ezel saw the opportunity and didn't hesitate to lead the charge to the *Lady Leila*. They ran to the left through the brush, palm leaves whipping against their fresh nicks and cuts. They were nearly there when a sudden chorus of vibrating laughter rippled through the surrounding trees. The companions formed ranks, back-to-back, preparing for another swarm. Instead, little cheers popped up in waves from the direction of the palace. And then Ellaria saw him.

The faery king had come.

"Guys ..." Ellaria said nervously over her shoulder.

The others joined her gaze to take in the sight. The faery king was much larger than the others. He was taller than Coal but shorter than Orin. He was slender, and his wings held him in a regal pose above the ground. He was decked out in flamboyant colors, and the fabrics changed hue as the sunbeams bounced off him through the swaying trees. His hand gripped down on a pouch tied to his belt, and an arrogant, almost knowing, pride etched his face.

"Time to go," Coal said to the others, spinning on his heel and bolting for the *Lady Leila*.

The others wasted no time. Orin and Ellaria's longer legs carried them past the dwarf at a full sprint. Curdling squeals welled behind them as the faeries gave chase. The crew jumped into their boat at full speed, Ezel pausing to throw up a small magical barrier to block an incoming pouch that exploded into glittering dust.

Orin grabbed another bow from inside the boat, joining Ellaria's barrage of arrows hurtling at their pursuers and slowing them down. Coal's dwarven banded muscles tensed and contracted furiously at the controls of the vessel. Ezel swirled his arms around, building up magic for a massive discharge.

"Any time now! Any time now!" Coal yelled through gritted teeth.

As though time had stopped, everything went silent, like the calm before a storm. Ezel's little gnome body trembled with built-up energy, then he shot both hands out in front of him, aiming out the back of the boat. The magic exploded through the water, launching the *Lady Leila* forward, slicing down the seaway. Ezel quickly shifted what energy he had left to help Coal maneuver the levers, building on their momentum. Ellaria and Orin held their bows ready for pursuing faeries but saw only a few glittering creatures through the trees on either side.

They picked up even more speed as their boat caught the current where the waterway met the sea once again. They didn't change course as they slipped into the open sea and back into the fog surrounding the island. The farther they got from the island, the more the fog dissipated. Before they were clear, they heard a familiar vibrating voice call in the distance.

"C-cheaters!"

Ellaria shook her head to the others, not quite believing what they had experienced. As the fog dissolved with distance and the clarity of the cool evening fell upon them, Orin took a turn at the levers so Coal could rest and prepare to navigate them through the night. They still had no idea where they were.

CHAPTER SIXTEEN

GATHERING AT GHUN-RA

Ghun-Ra sloped and merged with several other mountains, connecting with them in wide ridges. It didn't stand solo like some of the other mountain castles of Drelek, but rather the town was built throughout the slopes, spreading out from the fortress that was dug into the side of the Ghun-Ra peak. The several attached peaks had tunnels and steads dug within, making it an interweaving network city.

The town, one of the southernmost in all Drelek, served as a frequent operations base for orc troop movement. Raiding parties were often launched from the base and sent over the southern ridges.

Ghun-Ra also had a long and cherished history among their peoples. During the Second Great Black War, the commanders and generals operating out of Ghun-Ra were the ones that landed the final blow to the mighty elvish city of Palori. When the war was coming to an end, it was at Ghun-Ra that the enemy forces were halted and kept from riding farther north into Drelek. The town had much pride.

Gar Nargoh's dragon swooped over the valley, casting a strange shadow in the moonlight as they came in for a landing. The morning was not far off, and it had been a long night. They would need to get some rest before meeting with Gar Jergahn in a few hours.

Karnak and Smarlo floated to a wyvern landing zone perch Nargoh had pointed them toward. He and the adolescent dragon flew to a larger zone nearby. A couple of goblin guards directed the orcs from Calrok to open stalls where their wyverns could rest.

Karnak recognized many of their Scar Squadron wyverns. Having been to Ghun-Ra once before, he knew many of the other areas would also be filled with wyverns from other squadrons around Drelek.

The orcs settled their wyverns in. Karnak grabbed an extra hare from a barrel nearby and flipped it to Ker before bidding her goodnight. She had earned it. She caught the rabbit in her maw, chomping it with her many teeth and working it down her long neck and into her belly. Ker clicked happily as she made herself comfortable in the stall.

Smarlo motioned the lead to his gar as they followed a dark hallway. The tunnels were barely illuminated by a torch far inside. Orc eyes, like goblins', could see even in the blackest pitch of tunnels at night. Doors led to chambers lining the length of the corridor. Smarlo found his door and nodded his regards to his gar before slipping into the small room for the night.

Karnak found the gar chamber at the end of the hall. Gar chambers were always deeper in the tunnels that they might be protected from an ambush or attack. In open battle, Karnak did not know a single gar who would not take the lead in a charge.

As Karnak crashed onto his bed for the night, discomfort swept over him. He couldn't tell if it was the millions of tons of rock that hung above him or if it was the weight of everything he'd become privy to in recent days. One thing was sure: if he had any kind of role to play, he would need rest to be at his best.

He closed his eyes, seeing his wife Tanessa and his little monster, Gernot. He breathed in deep, a smile scrawled across his tired face, and he followed the two into his dreams.

The sun poked over the ridges of the narrow valley of Ghun-Ra, finding its way into the plethora of window holes that had been carved throughout the city. Light poured through some, wider than others. In other places, goblin engineers had fashioned intricate mirror systems to illuminate deeper chambers.

Smarlo had gotten up early enough to fill Belguv in on what he and Karnak had experienced on their mission with Gar Nargoh. Belguv was stunned to hear of the dragon and baffled that none of Nargoh's orcs had mentioned anything about it. It was not uncommon for orc squadrons to boast about their prowess when brought together. He thought, surely, they would have considered a dragon worth boasting about. Clearly, they were all bound to secrecy on the matter.

Belguv didn't have much to report to his commander. The Scar Squadron had not had any issues. Their youngest rider, Tark, had gotten a little rowdy one night in the excitement of his first mission. Smarlo laughed. He remembered being that young. Other than that, Belguv reported there were at least four squadrons from different places around Drelek stationed there at the moment. As he'd asked around, none of them knew exactly why they had been summoned. He assumed they would all find out during that day's meeting with Gar Jergahn.

When Karnak joined his two orcs, they filled him in as they navigated through the winding tunnels, headed for the meeting chamber. They ran into the gar from Dak-Tahn and his commander as they passed the barracks tunnel where that squadron had stayed. Gar Dahno seemed to know his way, and they continued along the same path, weaving through the maze.

Gar Dahno cringed and raised a hand to protect his face as sunlight poured through a window in a long straight hallway. Dak-Tahn was a mountain fortress in the far north of the Drelek Mountains. They had almost no windows, and their wyvern riders operated almost exclusively at night. While Karnak and the orcs from Calrok lived mostly in the sun, Gar Dahno and the orcs from Dak-Tahn lived almost entirely in darkness.

As the tunnel widened, they came upon a set of large double doors guarded by two goblins. They stood rather straight for goblins, seemingly very proud of their positions, and rightfully so. The rich military history of Ghun-Ra was not only for orcs, but for all the members of Drelek. Goblins and trolls had integral roles in the Second Great Black War, and there didn't seem to be any division among the races. They were all on a mission, all the time.

"Good morning, Gars," one of the goblins said, placing a finger to his brow and giving a slight bow. The other swiftly opened one of the large doors and ushered them into the meeting cavern.

The chamber had been a natural cavern originally. The floor had been ground down to a flat surface, but the ceiling was covered in patches of stalactites. Light filled the chamber from several different holes in the ceiling, obviously paired with mirror contraptions to bring the sunbeams into the deep room.

Gar Nargoh chatted with Gar Jergahn near a table in the chamber's center, as Karnak and the others entered the cavern. They crossed to the table, and before they had reached it, the last gar, a rather fat orc named Klentja of Borok, and his commander arrived.

The whole group was present and waited patiently for Jergahn and Nargoh to finish their side conversation.

"Welcome, Gars. Commanders," Jergahn started, turning to the table before them. "I trust your travels were swift?"

The grunts and nods around the table were all the reply necessary.

"And the barracks and food have been to your liking?"

"There wasn't much left after Klentja got to it." Gar Dahno roared. Laughter resounded at the ribbing, except for Klentja's commander, of course. Klentja, himself chuckling, held a hand out to stay his offended young commander, Genjak. Dahno and Klentja had been friends for many years.

"The early orc gets the glorb! We weren't hiding from the morning like you vampires." Klentja shot back in his rough orc voice, to the delight of all present.

"And at least we know how to navigate tunnels to make it to a meeting on time," Genjak added with a pop of his eyebrows. The others rolled with laughter at the young commander's bold jab.

"I only wanted to make sure the Calrok sun-lovers would be able to find it in the dark tunnels," Dahno chimed.

"Yes, how we love the sun's scary light and horrible warmth. Is that why you hide away in that frostbitten hole up north near the Frozen Lake?" Karnak threw in. Several of the orcs held their aching ribs as they tried to control their mirth.

"Good, good," Jergahn continued, as the laughter died down. "I know some of you might be wondering why King Sahr has ordered us to gather here."

Again, the grunts and nods around the table answered his question.

"Drelek is about to come into its glory of former days. For too long, the people of the south have spat in the face of our traditions and honor." A couple orcs spit in response. "No longer. King Sahr's new ally has procured for us the means by which we will assert our power and might over all Tarrine!"

While the others leaned in to hear of the mighty weapon, Karnak tightened his knot of black hair, crossed his arms in front of him, and leaned back, thoughtful. Smarlo shot him a glance, trying to read his gar but also displaying his own concern about what they had seen the other night.

"A dragon," Gar Nargoh proudly answered their inquisitive looks.

"What?" Gar Dahno's commander reacted.

"A dragon?" Gar Klentja repeated, processing the answer.

"Yes. A dragon," Gar Jergahn continued, while Nargoh brimmed with pride and satisfaction at their reactions. "Gar Karnak arrived before the rest of you, and he and his commander witnessed the creature's mighty power."

The others looked to Karnak for his input. The young gar was slow to speak, not initially wanting to comment on the matter until he was more aware of the intricacies of what was going on. All the leaders from the far reaches of Drelek stared at him, awaiting his thoughts. The silence was deafening as his muscles twitched and rolled under his deep green skin. Karnak adjusted uncomfortably in his seat.

"I've seen the beast," Karnak finally gave them.

The answer did not satisfy the onlookers.

"And? What of the beast, young Gar?" Gar Dahno prodded, not liking the unresolved reply.

"It is young and still has wild horns," Karnak continued, thinking aloud. "It would not be wise to rush into open war while the creature is still so untrained. It's mighty, to be sure. But should its unbridled power remain untamed in the midst of battle, it could mean disaster."

Disappointed huffs rolled around the table. A growl emanated from deep within Gar Nargoh.

"So, the monster must be trained," Gar Klentja cut the tension.

"The beast is trained!" Nargoh shot back, unable to stay his mounting rage.

"Unless it wants a snack," Smarlo rebutted.

Nargoh shot up, his chair flying backward and his hands gripping the table's edge. Gar Jergahn placed a big hand on Nargoh's tensed arm, his steely eyes regaining control of the meeting.

"Gar Nargoh has been training with the dragon for many weeks now, and the incidents of the other night have been reported. I still believe it to be a capable weapon against our enemies," Jergahn reassured them.

"If the beast isn't ready and we start a war against the man-kin, we could lose before we start. And Borok doesn't intend to fight a war that's already lost," Klentja stated the obvious concern in the back of all their minds.

"The creature is ready," Nargoh growled, again receiving a staying hand from Gar Jergahn.

"This is why we won't test its battle prowess on man-kin yet," Jergahn said.

"The dwarves? Elves? Who?" Klentja questioned, an incredulous look on his aging face.

"The rebellion."

Silence filled the room. Gar Klentja leaned back in his seat, his chin raised at Jergahn's answer. The others waited for more.

"As you know, Gar Nargoh and Gar Karnak are here with us now because the traitors abandoned their seats. They lost faith in our king. They lost faith in their brothers—in us!"

While others around the table nodded in agreement, Karnak noticed Klentja's demeanor shift. His pensive look eased Karnak's concerns about his own misgivings. He would have to speak with the older gar more about the whole situation later.

"This is why we are meeting this morning: for all of you to witness the might of the dragon and to spark the flame of courage in our bellies for the war to come. For the glory to come! For the honor to come!"

Approving grunts at Jergahn's words rolled around the table from many of the younger commanders.

"Gar Nargoh will lead his squadron in a battle against the rebels at Renjak. The Scar Squadron is the most rested and will provide backup should Gar Nargoh need it," Jergahn nodded the order to Karnak, who listened intently. "Though I don't foresee any problems arising. Gars and commanders will stay airborne with the Scar Squadron to witness the events. Should all go accordingly, we'll reconvene here for the next phase of the plan."

The chamber was quiet, almost somber. Belguv and Smarlo looked to their gar. Karnak dipped his chin to avert their looks. They would discuss the matter privately. Karnak was caught in the stare of Gar Klentja, and Karnak worried the older gar might be able to read his expression, and by extension, his thoughts. The gar nodded slightly toward him, almost as an invitation for the younger gar to seek him out later.

"Start preparing yourselves," Jergahn said resolutely. "We will fly for Renjak and put an end to this rebellion."

Karnak walked through the tunnels alone. Shortly after Gar Klentja left the dining hall reserved for special guests, Karnak also excused himself from lunch. The commanders and the other gars paid no attention and continued their own conversations. Karnak hoped he would be able to catch the gar from Borok and speak with him alone. Did Klentja know something he didn't know about the rebellion? What could he tell Karnak that might put the younger gar's heart at ease within him?

When he first entered the hallways, he had expected to see Klentja right away. Instead, he found an empty stone walkway. Karnak weaved and poked in and out of side passages that crisscrossed his path, hoping to catch a glimpse of the older gar. When he had found no trace of him, Karnak decided to search for him in the Borok squadron's barracks tunnel.

He found the barracks empty as well. Karnak noted with appreciation that those rooms were also unkempt, relieving his concerns about the messy young orcs in his squadron. Realizing he may not get a moment alone with Gar Klentja if he was with his squadron, Karnak decided to visit Ker in her stall and try to catch the older gar later.

He walked through the maze of tunnels, knowing that route well. His big paw of an orc-hand slid across a natural, rippled pillar of stone as he rounded the corner to a long hallway. The passage was unique. One side of the hallway was completely exposed to the air. The backside had a few side passages. In the afternoon sun, the shadows of those tunnels were a hard contrast to the open-air hallway.

Karnak leaned on the low wall that overlooked the slope below. He took a deep breath; feeling the sun on his face infused vitality to his bones. He smelled the fresh mountain air, a relief from the damp tunnels. He gazed across the narrow valley, seeing orcs scattered around. He spotted some catching fish in the river and noted how deep green they were, much like him and the other orcs of Calrok. As one pulled in a fish, Karnak was struck with a sort of homesickness. How different Calrok was to many other orc strongholds. But then again, how very similar were those orcs wading in the river, filling baskets of fish.

"I knew you cared."

The gruff voice behind him snapped Karnak from his thoughts as he whirled around to confront it.

Gar Klentja emerged from the dark shadow of one of the side passages. His gaze locked onto the younger orc. He inspected Karnak and slapped his hand on the large orc's shoulder, gripping down to feel the muscle. Karnak stood, accepting the inspection from his elder. When Klentja appeared to have seen what he needed to in the younger gar, he leaned against the wall next to him, squinting his eyes in the bright sun.

"I was hoping you cared," the older orc said, hairs from his greying head catching some of the mountain breeze. "There can be no doubt you are a son of Calrok. Born to the sun, those ones."

The wrinkled smile on Klentja's face put Karnak at ease. Again, he leaned on the wall next to the older orc to enjoy the view.

"Your father was sensitive, too," Klentja continued. "Plak cared deeply about those around him. He was a good friend. I was very sad when he died."

Klentja rubbed the back of his thick neck, turning away from the younger orc to hide the sadness that welled within him.

"You knew my father well. I remember his stories of you."

"Ha!" Klentja laughed and slapped his big belly. "I wasn't always this old and fat! Back in the day, Plak, Zotar, and I were unstoppable. Your father was a mountain of an orc. Just like you, I suppose ..." He paused, recognizing his old friend in the young orc. "We were a force to be reckoned with."

As he turned, the older orc's gaze was no longer on the narrow valley, but rather years away in a distant past.

"Best orc I ever knew," Karnak said honestly.

"Yes ..." Klentja agreed. "He was wise. Always thinking, Plak was. He had great instincts. Always knew what was right and wrong ... I miss him ... I miss my friend."

"As do I."

The two leaned on the wall, feeling the mountain breeze, enjoying the moment in the sun and the quiet memories each of them held dear.

"I saw my old friend again this morning," Klentja broke the silence. "When I saw you, it was like seeing Plak again. It stirred something in me I can't quite explain. I could see his same thoughtfulness. You chose your words deliberately and spoke what you thought right, whether Gars Jergahn and Nargoh wanted you to or not. You get that honestly."

Klentja's shoulders and belly rolled as a chuckle worked its way through his body. Karnak decided he could ask some questions, the older gar having opened the door.

"Zotar is one of the rebel gars?"

The question stung Klentja, and he winced.

"Zotar and Maktom, yes."

"But why? What happened? What would make them rebel against King Sahr and the rest of Drelek?"

Gar Klentja inhaled a long draw of mountain air, his lungs emitting a low wheeze under the strain.

"I cannot say for sure. Before Zotar left, he told me of King Sahr's new sorcerer adviser, an orc by the name of Jaernok Tur."

Karnak's heart stopped, a million thoughts flooding his mind. He had met Jaernok Tur as well and worried more about the sorcerer from Kelvur than any potential enemy they might face. Karnak wasn't sure Jaernok Tur had the best interests of Drelek in mind. Further, he feared the sorcerer was leading their king down a path of destruction. Where the head goes, the body follows. He did not want to see Drelek led into destruction, especially not Calrok.

The older gar stared at Karnak, studying his face. Karnak straightened, and worry flooded his thoughts.

Does he see my reservations?

Would Klentja recognize the young gar's worries? Would he share them? Or would he see them as traitorous thoughts about Drelek? Too many things were at stake.

"You've met this Jaernok Tur?" Klentja asked in recognition.

"I've met the sorcerer," Karnak replied, choosing his words carefully.

"And what are your thoughts, son of Plak?" the older orc pressed. His eyes narrowed as he tried to read the younger gar.

"I ..."

Smarlo and Belguv rounded the corner, laughing about something they had been discussing. Klentja straightened and turned to face the two Scar Squadron leaders coming down the hall.

"You've found the best sun in this fortress, my Gar!" Belguv roared excitedly.

"Gar Klentja," Smarlo acknowledged him with respect, placing a long finger to his brow and dipping slightly.

"Commander," Klentja returned the greeting. "I'll be taking my leave now. It was a pleasure to reminisce with you, Gar Karnak. I look forward to more times like this."

Klentja's even stare told Karnak nothing of what the older orc was thinking as he left them. Karnak knew in his bones something wasn't right with the whole situation. But Karnak was no traitor to his people. How could Zotar, one of his father's best friends, have betrayed Drelek? Karnak had heard many stories about their exploits while he was young. It was hard to imagine how their situations had all gotten so messy.

An image of a raven pecked at the edge of his mind. It crept in like some mutating monster and took the shape of the sorcerer, Jaernok Tur. Karnak shuddered at the image, shaking it from his thoughts.

"Belguv."

"Yes, Gar?" he responded promptly, pulled out of his side conversation with Smarlo.

"I need you to fly to Ruk."

"Yes, Gar. What shall I do once there?"

"I need you to find out everything you can about the rebellion. Something doesn't feel right about all this. We need to know why."

"Yes, Gar."

The wind blew through the open wall and whistled along one of the side passages, reminding Karnak that anyone could walk up on their conversation from many routes. He pressed closer to the other two, intentionally placing the low wall at his back so he could keep a wary eye on the side passages.

"Our squadron could use a refreshed supply of glorb wine," Karnak continued, using his eyes to express the ruse. "The best glorb wine maker we know is in Ruk, and I think we should procure some."

Belguv nodded, recognizing the shift in his gar's countenance.

"And since our supplier is so good to us, perhaps you make it known to everyone you run into while you are there why it is that we would send you on such a trek to get us that glorb wine—the best in all Drelek, after all."

Belguv nodded again and then added, "Maybe I should stay a day to ensure the supply will continue to flow. We'll need as much as possible."

"Yes," Smarlo joined in. "Once it flows out, it's out. Leaders at Ruk will certainly enjoy the glorb wine and gather for it."

"But new friends don't know that glorb wine loosens lips," Karnak finished, his gaze turning back to the narrow valley that sprawled below them. "I hope our supplier is able to get us what we need."

His genuine concern hung on the wind with his words.

Reglese and Kig had gotten to work straightaway once they arrived in Ruk. The capital stronghold was large and bustling with life but had a tendency to chew up and spit out those that weren't as skilled at their craft as they had believed themselves to be. That created a transient culture around the place, especially in the market areas. Orcs and goblins, and even the occasional extra-spirited troll, would come in, set up shop, and move on to another place if it didn't work out.

Finding a location for their tavern was easy. The spot had been used as a tavern in the past by previous entrepreneurs. None of those failures had Reglese's proprietary glorb wine. He knew he could succeed. After all, his Spinefish Tavern, back in Calrok, had done quite well. He knew what he was doing.

Once they garnered the location, the goblins began preparations. Reglese immediately started making more glorb wine, while Kig fixed up the kitchen for the mass amounts of cooking the old goblin dared to dream would take place. He had sold his wagon when they had arrived. He was all in. Between his money from the wagon and the gold Reglese had brought with him from Calrok, they easily acquired all the things they needed.

They furnished the tavern to Reglese's specifications, him having the experience of producing an attractive environment for patrons. The kitchen was entirely Kig's project, Reglese deferring to the old goblin's judgment and preferences. Of course, Reglese marked off a large area for the glorb wine he would need to continue making. He already had six new barrels going.

They even managed to find a young orc woman named Getta to serve the patrons and offer great hospitality. It was all coming together, quite to Reglese's liking.

He stepped outside the tavern doors to look at where his new enterprise would make its fortune. The tavern was on the edge of a main tunnel leading into a massive cavern that housed many shops. The high ceilings made the place feel spacious, and the numerous beams of light that spilled in from windows gouged into the rock illuminated it well. A singular stalagmite was left in the center of the cavern, rightly so, as it was enormous, standing a few hundred feet in height.

A heavy clanging of a hammer grabbed Reglese's attention from the awe-inspiring cavern. He looked across to the other corner space, an open-faced shop. A large troll, a blacksmith by trade, methodically hammered molten metal. He stopped when he noticed Reglese observing him and returned the stare, a dumbfounded look on his large troll face. Reglese flashed a toothy grin to his new neighbor and gave a short wave.

The troll didn't immediately return the gesture, confused at the random goblin making faces at him. When he decided that, perhaps, the goblin was just trying to be nice, he returned a hideous smile, his face scrunching up in odd places, and waved his hammer. Reglese was taken aback by the troll's inability to smile but nodded kindly to him, nonetheless.

As Reglese turned and marched off, intending to make his face known to all the other shops that meandered around the center monument in the large cavern, he heard the blacksmith's methodical clanging start again. There was a lot of activity here, a rather busy market cavern in Ruk; and as Reglese strolled along, greeting others as he went, he felt good about his position. His glorb wine was going to do well here. He couldn't help but think about all the coin he would make.

CHAPTER SEVENTEEN

THE END OF A WALK

Leaves rustled throughout the forest as the wind stirred them to life. The breeze blew locks of Merrick's brown hair over his face, some of it sticking in the scruff on his chin. The tickling hair woke him. He did not open his eyes at first. Rather, he listened to some woman he did not yet know, humming over the crackling of a fire in the early morning cold. He smelled the smoke but something else as well.

Meat?

Though he had cooked many types of game on a fire in the wild, he couldn't quite place the scent of the one currently cooking.

He listened more carefully, seeing if he could pick up any of the words in the woman's song. The lyrics seemed jumbled and made no sense, like another language. He wondered how hard he had been hit by the bear, that he could no longer understand words.

And then it dawned on him, the bear! How was he still alive?

What happened?

Without a flinch, he took a quick mental inventory of his body. He was bruised in many places. His legs were filled with the fire of fatigue. His head had taken some lumps, and the dull ache that still rang around inside his brain wouldn't let him forget it.

Hot breath rolled over his face as the bear grunted. Merrick's entire body tensed as he realized the danger might not be over. The bear was still here, but for whatever reason, the beast had not finished him.

"Did you think to get the jump on me if I thought you to still be asleep? You are not much of a trickster, man-kin," the woman's voice said matter-of-factly. "Lucky, yes. Brave or stupid? Still to be determined."

Merrick relented and opened his eyes. The bear's nose was inches from his own, but the creature merely stared curiously at him. He tried to glance at the female voice without moving his head but couldn't get a visual.

"Perhaps a bit of both," he admitted, still lying prone and as still as possible, under the watchful lavender eyes of the bear.

"Ha!" the woman laughed. "Maybe honest as well."

Merrick exhaled a short burst of amusement himself, startling the bear, whose confusion was evident in its contorted face. The purple in its eyes flickered.

"Is this, uh ... your bear?" Merrick asked, utilizing their shared moment as a building block to get himself out of whatever situation he had woke to.

"She is no one's bear. She is her own, though she has been very helpful."

The bear took a few heavy steps backward, giving Merrick breathing room, but never taking her lavender-laced glare off the man. Merrick lifted himself to a sitting position with great struggle. He was sorer than he had realized. His body had taken a beating the last few days. He noted the distance the bear had granted him and that the beast was still within striking distance if Merrick's stupidity decided to rear its ugly head. Sadness washed over him as he examined the strange bear. As if the woman sensed his emotions, she reacted, "Hmm."

And then he noticed her.

Her slender elvish form gracefully maneuvered about the small fire. Her pale skin glowed like the moon. Her thin silver hair floated in the breeze. She tried to wrangle it with one hand, tucking it back behind one of her pointed ears, and revealed a rosy blush on her cheek. She was quite stunning as she tended to whatever she was making, seemingly paying no mind to the huntsman, who stared with his mouth agape.

"I am making breakfast for us. You don't have to catch flies," she teased him, not even looking in his direction.

Merrick sheepishly snapped his mouth closed, not realizing it had slipped open. "How …" he stopped, rethinking his question. "Who are you?"

She paused, silvery strands of hair jumping free from behind her pointed ear to fly in the breeze once more. Her mouth twitched thoughtfully while she decided whether to tell him or not. Finally, having convinced herself it mattered not whether the huntsman knew her name, she said, "Ralowyn."

"Ralowyn," Merrick repeated, committing it to his memory, though he didn't think he would forget her any time soon. "I'm Merrick," he offered.

"Merrick," she nodded quietly, still not taking her eyes away from the task at hand.

The silence between them let the crackle of the fire speak out. Merrick glanced back at the bear, whose lavender gaze had not left him.

What a strange bear, Merrick thought to himself. He had a lot of questions, but before he could ask any, Ralowyn paused again.

"Do you mean me any harm, man-kin?"

Merrick was surprised by the question, not totally sure where it had come from. By all accounts, she had him at her whim.

The bear had dealt him a heavy blow to the head. He wasn't quite sure how long he'd been unconscious, but judging by the fact it was morning, at least a whole night. Certainly, she could have done many things to harm him in that span. It was at that moment he realized he didn't have his bow, quiver, or knife.

Panic swept over him but faded quickly as he watched the young elf woman, totally still, save for the floating silvery strands. He did not mean her any harm, and at that point, it seemed she did not mean any toward him, either.

"No. No, I do not."

A thankful smile spread across her face. She grabbed a piece of meat next to the fire. The piece was too large for the breakfast she was preparing. She moved slowly toward the bear, still not looking Merrick's way, and greeted the large creature with the chunk of meat. She stroked the bear's head, scratched behind its ear, and whispered, "Thank you, my friend."

She stepped back, and the purple glint in the bear's eyes flashed and disappeared. It blinked in confusion, looking to Merrick and then to Ralowyn. The elf nodded approval to the furry creature, who decided to take that as its sign to leave.

Merrick watched the scene in awe. The bear happily took its tasty treat and rambled off through the wood. Ralowyn watched the bear disappear into the overgrowth of Elderwood Forest, clearly satisfied with the outcome of their encounter.

"Are you hungry?" she asked, finally, grinning from ear to pointed ear.

For the first time, she looked at Merrick. He was struck by the young elf woman's beautiful lavender eyes.

They had eaten breakfast in relative silence. Merrick had graciously accepted the cooked meat, still not sure what animal it had come from. Ralowyn had seasoned and cooked it well, and he had no complaints.

By the time they were finishing, he had gotten a good long time to inspect his ... captor? Savior? She was a slight elf woman. She ate her breakfast with a certain grace, deliberately pulling the meat apart into smaller bites. Her silver hair was so fine it didn't stay in place behind her pointed ears. She often let it fall in front of her face and hide her fair features.

He noticed a staff standing upright nearby. The staff was made of some sort of silvery metal Merrick was not skilled to identify. Scrollwork ran in intricate weaving patterns the length of the tall staff all the way to the ornate head, which branched apart delicately and then back inward to a swirling point. A purple glow seeped out between the finely crafted branches of the pinnacle. He did not know how it managed to stand in place by itself, but Merrick assumed it was some magic of the elves that he could not comprehend.

Finally, he asked, "Ralowyn, what happened?"

The question was funny to her. She replied, "It seemed to me you had an encounter with a rinont."

"Yes," he remembered that part quite well. He rubbed at the bruises on his lower back and hip. "The creature has found itself quite the spot for trapping prey. I'm ashamed to say I didn't see the signs in my exhaustion."

Ralowyn smirked. "You weren't quiet, running through the wood. I heard you from far off."

It hadn't occurred to Merrick that Ralowyn could have been keeping tabs on him even before his run-in with the rinont at the sparkling well. He certainly hadn't been quiet as he ran through Elderwood Forest, attempting to lose any wyvern riders floating overhead, searching for him. Even after he had run for a long time—once he was certain no one was looking for him—he had continued to run, purely out of grief. For while he was running, he wasn't sure what he was going to do with the lifeless Rora cradled in his arms.

The thought of the loss wrenched his heart again. As much as he didn't intend to show his pain, Ralowyn noticed instantly. "The bird was a companion of yours?"

"A friend," Merrick agreed. "I caught her when she was very young." He realized Ralowyn had heard him running through Elderwood Forest and had seen him bury Rora. It was the only way the elf would know Rora was a bird. "Why didn't you tell me of the rinont's trap?"

Another smirk revealed Ralowyn's amusement at the question. "I did not know. I had not found the well before." She shrugged, clearly telling the truth.

"Why are you out here?"

Ralowyn did not smirk at that question. Rather, she hesitated, looking at the tall staff, teeming with magical energy. "I am walking."

Merrick shook his head, not understanding.

"I was sent into the wood to walk—to learn who I am."

"I'm not sure I understand."

Ralowyn stood and turned in a single motion with a dance-like grace, stretching her arm out wide, beckoning the staff. In a flash, the shining silvery staff responded to the call, smoothly landing in her outstretched hand. A surge of energy rippled into lavender ribbons of light that swirled around her—a spectacular display to Merrick but hardly a test of the elf's abilities.

"When it was discovered I had an aptitude for the arcane arts, the elders of the wisdom tower at Loralith brought me in. I was only a girl then." The memory took her lavender eyes to a distant time. "Strangely, many of the artifacts in the tower repelled me or didn't respond to me at all. Until the Staff of Anvelorian."

She effortlessly twisted the luminous staff in her hands, her eyes glowing with similar intensity. The staff hummed slightly with each twist and flick.

"None had been able to activate the power in the staff since Anvelorian himself," Ralowyn continued, not reserved about sharing with the huntsman. "The staff had hung over a mantle as a relic for many years while I studied at the tower, learning everything I could. When I took hold of the artifact and it burst to life, the elders didn't know what it meant and were fearful of the power. Moreover, they were afraid of the power in the hands of someone who had not yet been tested. I was coming into the age of testing anyway, and it was time for me to take up an artifact and go on my walk to learn who I am."

"So, you came out into Elderwood Forest to train?" Merrick asked, not well versed in the cultural norms of the elves of Loralith.

"To train," she dipped her head to the side, not convinced the phrase accurately reflected what the walk meant. "But also, to find out what I would become. Who would I be, should I master the magic of the Staff of Anvelorian?" She paused and eyed the intricate lines running the length of the unique artifact. "Or would the thing master me?"

"How long have you been out here?"

The question made her ponder. It had been a long time, but not so long for an elf. "Forty years," she replied.

Her answer shocked Merrick. The elf looked to be no older than himself. He had met elves who were several hundred years old back in Tamaria who looked no older than his father. More surprising was the fact that she had been alone in Elderwood Forest for so long. As a huntsman, Merrick knew well the solitude of the wild, but he had always returned to his family after short stints.

"Do you have no family?"

"No," the purple of her eyes glinted as she answered. "Though Master Tenlien at the wisdom tower in Loralith has always treated me with great kindness."

"But you haven't seen him in forty years?" Merrick pressed.

"I have not."

Merrick didn't know how to respond as Ralowyn swished the staff in an arc over the campfire. Again, lavender light rippled in choreographed swirls, putting out the campfire and rustling the remains, erasing all signs it was ever there. She clanged the bottom of the staff against the ground and faced the huntsman directly.

"The real question is," the smirk returned. "What are you doing in Elderwood Forest, man-kin?"

They hurtled through Elderwood Forest at a blistering pace, the huntsman keeping up well with his new elf companion, though he was sure she was holding back so she wouldn't lose him in the thick overgrowth. He marveled that her footfalls made no noise and that she somehow avoided every swiping branch, bush, and limb. Merrick was a skilled huntsman, but the ease with which she maneuvered the congested forest was a sight to see.

She veered off their direct course to stop in a tiny open field. The huntsman thought it hardly an opening at all, as the canopy of trees still shaded the whole area. Ralowyn knelt at a small natural well and filled an ornate drinking pouch she carried about her waist. Merrick hesitated, remembering the last time he drank from a natural well—or rather, an unnatural one—in the mysterious forest.

"It is fresh. I have used this well before," Ralowyn comforted him.

Thankful for the brief rest, Merrick retrieved his own water skin from behind his quiver and filled it. He tried to take slow sips in between heavy breaths.

He had told Ralowyn everything. How a battle between the Griffin Guard and wyvern riders from Drelek had been fought too near to home. How his sister had found one of the guardians still breathing and nursed him back to health. How they had joined forces with Coal and Ezel to investigate the strange happenings at Palori Ruins en route to Whitestone. How they had engaged orcs and goblins there. How he had stayed so his companions could get away. And how he had escaped through Elderwood Forest, running until his body gave out.

And of course, he told her of the dragon.

When he had finished his tale, Ralowyn, who listened intently, looked up from her thoughts and said only, "It appears my walk has ended."

The two had quickly gathered their belongings, and Ralowyn returned Merrick's weapons. Once they had cleared the camp, she turned to him and spoke intentionally. "We must make for Loralith. The elders of the city must know all this."

They had been running through the Elderwood Forest since.

While Merrick refilled his water skin a second time, finding the water from that well to be clean and refreshing, Ralowyn asked him what she had been wondering while they ran. "There was a rider on the dragon?"

"Yes," Merrick said after another gulp. "An orc, I think. But I'll admit, I was a little more focused on the dragon. I thought them to be extinct."

"As did I," Ralowyn confessed. "Did the orc appear to have control over the creature?"

"I wouldn't say that," Merrick said. "The monster broke through pillars and walls chasing after Rora ..." He winced at the reminder of his fallen falcon.

Ralowyn placed a sympathetic hand on the huntsman's shoulder. "As you have told me the story, the bird sacrificed herself for you. A brave and honorable act."

Merrick nodded solemnly. She was right, of course, but it didn't ease the heartbreak he still felt.

"So, the orc did not have control of the dragon?" Ralowyn pressed.

"I wouldn't say that." Merrick searched for an explanation. "It was like a pup, training to be a good hunting hound. When it's not fully trained, it can get distracted by something it doesn't recognize and chase after it. My uncle had a young hound that chased after a skunk. The poor thing scratched at its nose for weeks trying to get rid of the stench."

"So, the dragon is young?"

"Perhaps. But again, I don't know how a young dragon should look."

Ralowyn topped off her water skin, deep in thought, clearly still shaken by the news of the dragon's existence.

"How did you control the bear?" Merrick asked.

His sudden question surprised her. In truth, she didn't know the answer, but she tried to explain.

"It is not really control. It is more like focusing the creature's thoughts. I have found that I can focus the thoughts of some creatures to help me if they are willing—but only if the creature is willing. I once asked a badger to help gather a branch for a fire. The thing looked at me and walked away. The bear, however, was startled by your presence as well and was willing to help." She dipped her head to the side in a shrug that said she did not understand the power fully, but that was the best explanation she could muster.

Merrick took it, content she was willing to share with him, even if he didn't totally comprehend.

"Are you ready to run again?" she asked, an empathetic smile on her face.

Merrick shook his legs out. They were in a state somewhere between fire and jelly. He took a deep, resigned breath and said, "Lead the way."

The two bolted out of the tiny clearing, back into the twisting paths of Eldwerwood Forest. They still had some distance to cover. They needed to reach Loralith as quickly as possible and would face more dangers of the forest should night fall upon them again.

CHAPTER EIGHTEEN

THE ALKHOREN MIRROR

K ing Garron had scarcely left his chambers. Few dared enter, for fear of rebuke. His callousness toward any intruder, though they came in the spirit of service, was venomous. Rumors circulated among the castle staff that the young king was turning more creature than man, wallowing away in the darkened room, hunched over various scrolls and parchments.

The only welcomed visitors were those who brought him more scrolls from Whitestone's library. The records he requested didn't seem to be connected in any way the couriers could make out. Plus, the young king asked for a new courier each day, making it impossible to follow his thoughts.

When Melkis arrived at the chamber doors, two plates of food slowly decayed on the floor, having been set in the hall early that morning. Melkis banged on the door with his bony hand. Two aides, concern etching their faces, shifted carefully to adjust the considerable weight of the wrapped mirror they had hauled from the Grand Corral. Melkis rapped on the door again. After no response, the old man tried to open the chamber doors, which, of course, were locked.

Melkis sighed. He smoothly removed Wintertide, his curved sword, from its scabbard. The metal rang with a twinge of energy as it came loose. The old guardian motioned for the aides to step back while he worked on the door. He whispered something to the beautiful silver sword and thrust the tip of the long blade into the keyhole on the door. Ice crystallized around the mechanism, weakening the door's internal integrity. Melkis leaned into the action, spurring the sword onward. Eventually, a *click-clunk* sounded inside the door, and it swung open.

The two aides hoisted the massive mirror they had set down, not expecting the old guardian to have managed the door so quickly. Melkis relished proving them wrong. He may be old, but he wasn't dead. He could still surprise some people. Sometimes, even himself.

He led the way into the chamber, kicking parchments on the floor as he went. The place was a disaster. The stench was pungent. Wax candles burned all over the chamber. Many more had finished their wicks and been hastily pushed aside to make space for new ones, the wax spilling in wild angles and hardening to form eerie statuettes.

Melkis kicked more scrolls aside as he waded to the window and cast open the curtains, allowing light to pour into the room. King Garron recoiled as though the light burned him but continued reading the scroll in front of him.

"Start cleaning this place up," Melkis said to the aides, who promptly began to collect random items from the floor.

"No!" Garron yelled hoarsely. He jumped to his feet to halt them but tripped over the rather large pile of articles surrounding his seat.

Melkis stepped forward to help his king up, signaling the aides to keep cleaning. "My King, please. What has you so distressed? You've been in here for days."

The disheveled king breathed heavily and said, "My house is fallen, Melkis," Garron cried, finding his way to a kneeling position.

Melkis also knelt, leveling his wise eyes with those of the king. The old man saw that tears had streaked the king's face, driving hard lines. "Perhaps it has tripped, but it has not fallen. You've been lost in the wildlands ..." Melkis glanced around at the mess. "When you trip, you get back up. Stand with me, as I stand with you."

Garron weakly took the outstretched arm, and by no strength of his own, returned to his feet. Melkis guided him to another set of curtains that he threw aside, revealing a balcony beyond. They stopped at the railing; the breeze breathed new life into Garron as he took in the fresh air.

"I'll be right back," the old master assured.

Melkis slipped back through the portal into the chamber. One of the aides was gathering scrolls into one place, so he might organize them. The other had gathered some of the strange wax forms and was attempting to remove hardened wax from one of the furs that had fallen on the floor. Melkis paid them no mind, on his way to the door.

The lock mechanism inside the door had completely cracked by the expansion of the ice, which was melting and dripping into a small puddle on the chamber floor. The old man crouched and prodded at the food on the plates, determining which was fresher. He picked one of them up, sniffed it, squeezed the bread, and decided it was still edible.

As he stood, High Commander Danner Kane and Commander Jolan rounded the corner and stopped, each glancing between Melkis and the disheveled chamber beyond him. Melkis answered their unasked questions with a heavy sigh, a raised brow, and an unknowing shrug before he whirled back into the chamber and toward the waiting king.

The two commanders paused, baffled. Commander Jolan didn't hesitate long. The mountain of a man walked to the table and hunched over it to see what he could glean from the parchments. Danner Kane chose the pile on the king's bed.

"Eat," Melkis said, forcing the bread into Garron's hand.

Garron took it slowly. When its scent caught his nose, he realized how famished he was. He took a bigger bite than intended and chewed awkwardly, while the breeze cooled his streaked face.

"You look unwell."

He mocks you ... the whisper on the wind said.

"What do you know of it?" Garron growled in the old man's face, bits of bread spraying from his mouth.

Melkis was shocked by the sudden shift in the young king's demeanor. In his rage, the king looked more rabid than pitiful. And it was in that moment Melkis realized his hand had instinctively latched onto the hilt of Wintertide. He did not want to use the sword on his king, of course, but his instincts had rarely been wrong all these years—one of the reasons he had lived so long.

"Beware an old man in a profession where men die young," he'd say to the young guardians who sparred with him. Instinct and training are a deadly combination.

"Garron," his voice was gentle. "What do I not know?"

"My house is fallen!" Garron threw the remainder of the bread off the balcony, and tears streamed down his face once again.

"But it hasn't," Melkis assured him. "You still stand. I know the loss of your brothers was hard. And your father and mother. But Garron, you are not alone. I have always thought of you and your brothers and your cousins as the sons I never had."

Lies ... You have seen the fall for yourself. I have shown you.

"No ... No! I am the only one left. I must save my house and Whitestone. Nothing else matters!"

Melkis didn't know what to say as he watched the king mumble to himself, caught in some sort of unseen calculations. The sight reverted to pitiful, and Melkis's heart had a hard time bearing the king's pain.

Movement in the room behind them reminded Melkis of the reason they had come to the king's chamber in the first place: the mirror. Garron had been adamant about retrieving the mirror for its magical powers, which supposedly would be a positive agent for the coming war.

"Whitestone has not fallen yet. And to my last breath, I will defend it. If you believe the mirror to be the key to our future—"

The mirror is here ...

"The mirror! Where is it?" Garron's eyes widened hungrily.

"Pernden and the Talon Squadron retrieved it from the Gant Sea Narrows. We have brought it here to your—"

Garron didn't wait for Melkis to finish. He spun on one foot and darted through the opening, into the chamber. It was the hunger in the young king's eyes that gave Melkis pause. He had always known Garron to be determined and strong, but he also understood how much the young king had lost and how loss can change a man. He wondered, however, who was the mage who had given him the location of the mirror? How long had the king been exposed to the mage? And with what, exactly, had he filled the young king's mind?

Clawstone was a well-kept secret of the Talon Squadron, a place of the elite group's own from which to run covert missions that required utmost secrecy. The place was aptly named for the four jutting white stones that broke the tree canopy in a strange formation rather like talons. It had been used as a secret training space and occasional base of operations for the elite members of the Talon Squadron since its inception.

Its location was kept sacred by the indomitable loyalty the elite guardians had to their brotherhood. Generations of Talon members held it close to their hearts. It had become a place of tradition, honor, celebration, and remembrance. To some, it even felt more like home than Whitestone.

Griffins perched in ancient pines surrounding the area. Whitestone Forest had grown at odd angles around the area, as the massive jagged stones broke earth and sky. No one ever came near. The northern road between Loralith and Whitestone swung around the edge of the peppered forest. The southern route veered farther east of the location, having been trampled on an easier path long ago. Clawstone was quite isolated, and to many of Talon Squadron, it was one of the few places they found solace.

Nera swept her loose hairs back into the singular braid that sloped off the back of her head, rather like the mane of a beautiful mare. With a flick of her foot, she launched the leaning spear into the air, spun, and caught it so smoothly, it appeared as though she had done it thousands of times; which, in fact, she had. Not with that spear, of course, but with many others before.

Santoralier, Lightning Rider as the sorcerers had labeled it, was a spear set apart. As she twirled it in a well-rehearsed routine, Nera marveled at how it appeared lighter and lighter in her hands. With each swing, the weapon hummed in delight as though it had been waiting for such a skilled warrior to use it again. The golden metal was hardened by magic that imbued the spear with powers yet unknown to the guardian.

Nera's movements were swift and calculated, every action setting up the next. She swirled and twirled, appearing to others in some sort of war dance. The spear bristled with energy, and she felt its tingling within her body. Arcs of electrical power jumped in random chorus, joining her movements. And finally, out of pure instinct, she feigned a parry left, a parry right, a spin jump to the rear, and let the spear loose toward a target sitting near one of the massive white stones.

It was as though the spear became pure electric energy and flew as a lightning bolt directly from her hand, exploding into the target. The force of the bolt sent arcs of energy splattering around where the target had been, leaving jagged scorch marks all over the ground nearby, even lighting a patch of grass on fire. Not only had the spear blasted its intended target, but it had ridden the lightning back into Nera's hand, as though she had never thrown it.

"Wow," Pernden said, putting his hands together for a few astonished claps. "'Santoralier,' you called it?"

"Yes. Or at least the keepers of the wisdom tower at the Gant Sea Narrows had marked it so. 'Lightning Rider.'"

"A weapon of similar stature to Master Melkis's Wintertide, I'd say." He laughed to himself. "Though many of us have tasted the playful sting of Wintertide—and many orcs, the more deadly sting—I don't know that I would want to taste any sting from this spear. Playful or otherwise."

Nera agreed. She traced her fingers along the mysterious scrollwork spanning the spear's length and halted in the middle. The yellow stone brimmed with energy. She did not understand why the destructive force of Santoralier did not bite her, but she knew this was a special weapon, indeed.

"Nera ... Whoa!" Pernden recoiled his hand.

When Nera had gotten lost in thought, he had touched her to get her attention and received a painful shock.

Nera gazed at the small arcs of golden electricity jumping in bold contrast between her dark fingers. She looked up at Pernden with a huge grin. He feigned hurt, but his countenance shifted to surprise.

"Your eyes are gold ..." he said, staring.

She looked back to Santoralier, still humming slightly in her hand.

A special weapon, indeed.

Garron kicked at scrolls and parchments that impeded his progress toward the table. He grabbed a dagger and waved it wildly as he stomped over to the mirror. Melkis reentered the chamber from the balcony as the king hesitated.

Do it. It's time! With this power, you'll be able to save your legacy!

Suddenly, Garron raised the dagger high and slashed down at the coverings. Fabric ripped under the heavy-handed blade as everyone in the room watched with anticipation. Even the aides stopped what they were doing to watch curiously. As the shreds of fabric fell or were ripped free by the king, the Alkhoren Mirror shone in the early evening sun.

Garron stumbled back in awe, the large mirror framing him from Commander Jolan's perspective.

"What is this mirror?" Jolan's words sounded far away.

The mirror emitted a low hum as ribbons of light bounced off the runes marking its edges. The magical energy swirled, forming a singular stream that ran around the frame. Melkis moved past the mountain of a guardian—for Jolan was stunned—and grabbed Garron by the shoulder, trying to move him back.

Don't let him interfere!

"No!" Garron barked at Melkis, sloughing off the old man's protective hand.

"Garron please! You must back away! Do you even know what this mirror can do?"

The hum of the mirror reverberated around the chamber, and the corners of the room bent in weird directions.

Danner Kane grabbed the two aides and shoved them toward the door and safety. "Go!" He shouted to them over the thrumming.

He ran to join Jolan and squared up defensively, not knowing what to expect but ready to fight the only way he knew how. Jolan watched, mesmerized.

"Garron, please!" Melkis yelled again. "You don't know what magics this mirror might contain!"

A flash of sinister smoke rose inside the mirror, and darkness gathered within. Melkis stopped grabbing at the young king, enraptured by what the mirror was revealing. A face in the smoke flashed and flashed again, as if someone were on the other side of the glass. And then, briefly, the picture flickered clear—the grin of a shrouded orc.

Melkis unsheathed Wintertide, leveling it straight at the mirror as he stepped between his king and the unknown threat.

Don't let him interfere! The old man would steal your future! He would steal your very life!

Garron cried out and lunged at Melkis with the dagger in his hand, bringing it down hard into the old man's back.

Melkis hollered in pain, lowering his sword to his side out of shock.

Garron pulled the knife back savagely and stabbed again as the old man turned to the young king with a confused look on his face. This jab was true and landed deep into his old mentor's chest.

For the two commanders, time stopped as they witnessed the king's violent outburst toward the beloved master.

Suddenly, a burst of magical force erupted from the mirror, sending all in the room flying in its blast. Parchments and scrolls fluttered through the air, and all became silent. The mystical energy continued to move around the frame, but the mirror was no longer a reflection. Rather, a wall of smoke existed within the borders of the runes.

Sobs rolled from the king, as he beat at Melkis's chest where they lay on the ground.

"I told you! My house is fallen! This is the only way! The only way ... The only way to save Whitestone. The war is already lost! Don't you see that?"

Garron slammed heavy fists onto the old man's chest, but his tears dropped heavier.

Melkis's glassy eyes looked to the young man he had helped raise. He was confused by the attack, but he had been a faithful man and knew death would come eventually. Tears of his own flowed out the crease of his eyes, running down the side of his face into his ears.

"Garron ..." He coughed. "I do not know what voice has twisted you against me ..." He took in a struggled breath. Knowing it might be his last, he told the king the only thing he thought worth saying in his final moment. "I have loved you ... like a son ..."

The words stunned Garron, and he stared at the old man.

Melkis's spirit departed.

Sudden realization rolled over the young king. "No! No, no, no ..." He cried to himself. "You don't understand. It's the only way ... it's the only way! Why didn't you listen to me?"

He shook the limp form of his former master and whimpered.

In the blast, Commander Jolan had been thrown to one side of the room, and Danner Kane was sprawled out near the balcony. Jolan had already risen, hand on the pommel of his still-sheathed sword. He watched his king, a wretched sight, and knew how the king felt. Jolan had lost his world as well—his own son—in this war that hadn't really even begun. His empathy stayed his hand.

Danner Kane kicked something hard as he came to a seated position. Wintertide glinted in the evening sunlight near his foot. He grabbed the old master's sword and sheathed his own as he stood.

He glanced at the king, hunched over the old master. When he locked eyes with Jolan, they sensed a turning point. Both made an instinctual decision, not based on reason, but rather on years of experience in battle, loss and regret, and pure unbridled emotion. In that moment, they realized they stood on opposite sides of the decision.

"No!" Jolan roared.

The massive man bolted to intercept a sprinting Danner Kane with Wintertide poised to strike down the unwary king. Before they collided, a black orb, rather like the darkest of nights, blasted into the High Commander, sending him reeling back past the king's bed, toward the balcony.

It was then that they saw him. A tall orc sorcerer stepped through the smoke in the Alkhoren Mirror, his movements serpent-like. The shroud of a dark aura surrounded him, and smoke slithered behind him. He held out a tall staff that shone in a strange hue. The small tusks of the orc parted his lips, which upturned into a wicked smile.

The orc turned to Jolan, who stood nearby. "A new age has dawned man-kin. Your king has saved you," whispered echoes chased his words.

A singular tear rolled down the commander's cheek, weaving its way through his stubble to the bottom of his chin. He stood perfectly still, a vision of stoicism.

While the orc looked the commander up and down, Danner Kane pulled a small whistle from a pocket under one of the many plates in his layered armor. He blew it, and no sound came out—at least no sound audible to men.

Orcs, however, hear that pitch perfectly well, and the whistle alerted the sorcerer to the guardian crouched behind the king's bed. "Come out man-kin. I will give you a choice."

Danner Kane cursed the whistle's betrayal. He stood and faced the orc, Wintertide in his hand. After a good look at the intruder, Kane realized this was no ordinary orc. One of the sorcerer's arms appeared to be made of stone, and smoky tendrils wisped from the bottom of his long cloak.

When their eyes met, both knew Kane would not choose what the sorcerer offered. An annoyed look replaced the orc's wicked grin. He lobbed another pitch-black orb toward the man.

Danner Kane dove and rolled to the side, closer to the balcony. He popped up quickly, muttered a prayer under his breath, and launched himself off the high castle balcony into the evening sky. Wind rushed past his face as he fell. The ground came fast, but not as fast as the High Commander's griffin. The creature swooped in, catching the commander with its talons and carrying him off into the distance.

The sorcerer stood on the balcony, observing Kane's escape. He did not show displeasure, though he certainly felt it. He merely turned to Commander Jolan, who also watched. The orc's eyes blazed with an obsidian fire. Jolan visibly winced under the sorcerer's direct gaze. The guardian couldn't move. He stole a quick glance at the king who knelt absently next to Master Melkis's body.

Jolan felt pressure on his heart and his mind, as though they were being squeezed inside of him. It took every ounce of willpower he had left to meet the sorcerer's eyes again. When he did, dread crackled through the air around him.

The sorcerer's wicked smile returned, and he said, "Find him. And prepare for war."

CHAPTER NINETEEN

THE SEA & THE STRANGER

The *Lady Leila* bobbed wildly in the chunky waves. Though the vessel had not been built for the open sea, the dwarf and gnome worked it like they were born seafarers. For the last few days, they had been skirting the Stranded Coast on the western edge of Tarrine. They were headed north toward the dwarven port of Crossdin, a spot populated by peoples from throughout Tarrine where work could always be found, especially among fishing ships. The colder water of the Tandal Sea made it a happy home to many fish species. Crossdin's location made it the main supplier of fish to both the dwarven city of Galium and the elven city of Loralith.

Coal had used the stars to determine their location, and he had immediately gone to work getting them to the coast. The *Lady Leila* would not survive a storm in the open sea, so they needed to be close enough to quickly put in to shore should the need arise.

Once the pair of experienced sailors found the coast, they discussed their options and settled on heading north toward Crossdin, where they would find port and hopefully procure some steeds.

They planned to press on to Whitestone by way of the northern road from Galium.

That route gave them the added benefit of spreading the news of the dragon to the dwarven city, which they hoped would join the war efforts against the rising threat. It wasn't a perfect plan, but it was as good a plan as they could come up with in the situation they had found themselves.

They had no food left and were unsure when they had lost most of it. Whether it was when the orc had blasted them with a concussive potion or if it had been the faeries indulging themselves with whatever goods had still been in the boat, they couldn't say. Either way, it had been scarce rationing for the last few days, and the whole crew was tired and hungry.

The first couple of days on the sea, there had been a lot of talk as they planned for what was ahead and discussed what they'd already seen. By that point, their bodies had no energy to waste on talking. None of the companions held it against the others. Instead, they let the sea serenade them with its rolling waves and rotated like a machine, each taking turns on the levers. Coal took the more difficult waters with his constitutionally sturdy frame.

Orin looked on at the weary crew. Coal had taken over maneuvering the levers in the choppy waters. The muscles in the dwarf's arms twitched with whatever energy they had left. Ellaria sat near the post at the front, looking ahead for any rocks on the coast that might surprise them. Ezel looked pitiful, indeed. The little gnome appeared more grey and scrawny than ever. He had taken off his shirt earlier in the heat of the day, revealing more blue-black, runic tattoos. Orin could see the poor gnome's ribs, as well.

Unable to stand with the intense rocking, Orin crawled to the gnome and placed his hand on Ezel's tiny shoulder. Ezel opened his eyes and looked up at the human.

"Are you okay, Ezel?"

The gnome responded with a tired smile and signed that he was fine.

"He says he's fine," Coal said from the levers.

Orin nodded, patting the small gnome softly and letting him return to his concentrated meditation. Orin guessed the little gnome had learned ways to use magic to heighten concentration and wondered if Ezel was able to shut out his hunger altogether.

"We're going to have to put into shore soon and hunt or gather some food. How many more days to Crossdin?" Orin asked.

Coal tugged at the bottom of the braid on his beard, calculating his best guess. "Two days. Maybe three in this boat."

"Maybe three?"

"Maybe. Can't say for sure. Most of my sailing was on the Gant Sea. All of what I know of this wretched sea comes from maps ... and only maps in my memory."

Helplessness overwhelmed Orin, as he realized there wasn't much they could do in their current predicament. He shifted his worries off his stomach and onto the dragon of Drelek.

"I don't doubt whatever Drelek has planned with the dragon will be moved up now. How could they not after we saw the thing? They know they didn't kill us. Surely, they'll want to surprise the Griffin Guard before they know of its existence."

"Maybe they thought we wouldn't make it out of Blackmar Forest. And even if we did, the sea should have swallowed our little vessel. We've been quite fortunate," Coal reasoned.

"Fortunate?" Orin blurted, more angrily than he'd meant. "We barely survived a run-in with a gantendril—which I only heard about after the fact. Then our boat was stolen on a faery island where we nearly died. And now we've been stuck at sea on a boat that is hardly seaworthy with no food to speak of. At the end of it all, none of this matters if we don't get to Whitestone!"

"All of this matters," the dwarf said sternly. "Every bit of it. Think of what we've come through already. Let that spark your hope! Our part in this tale is not done, Guardian. That I believe."

Orin was taken aback by the dwarf's positive resolve on the matter, and he felt as though his weariness had gotten the better of him in the moment. "I ... I'm sorry."

"It's okay, lad. It's the tired shaking you," Coal's face revealed a genuine forgiveness and understanding of the ache inside him. "The stars will be out soon. Get some rest. I'll wake you when the moon is high to take another turn."

Orin nodded his head in thanks, tried to make himself comfortable against a pack that was still on the boat, and closed his eyes. The waves sang him a lullaby, and the boat rocked him into a deep slumber. Apparently, he was more exhausted than he even realized.

The storm crept in through the night like a silent thief slips through a raised window. Though Coal did not know the Stranded Coast well nor did he know the Tandal Sea, he understood the dangers of being caught in a storm too near the coastal cliffs in such a small vessel.

He'd whistled to Ezel, who had been at the front, eyes a blue blaze in search of well-shrouded rocks in the coastal waters that held the potential to wreck them. Ezel had felt the shift in the waves and the pressure in the air as well. Hidden rocks were no longer their primary concern. At this juncture on the cliff-adorned coast, there was no place to put into shore. They worked the levers together in a hurry, trying desperately to get farther out to sea to avoid being caught in the collision of storm, sea, and cliff—a lethal combination for their small boat and crew.

As the waves increased, the *Lady Leila* whipped upward onto watery peaks and dropped heavily into rolling valleys, waking the two humans. The storm rushed upon them in a fury of wind and water. The rain drenched them from crazy angles.

"Coal, what can we do?" Ellaria yelled over the noise of the raging deluge.

"Hold on!"

Coal and Ezel continued to work the levers together, but the boat seemed more like a fishing bob with a life of its own in the great swells. The boat rocked awkwardly, sending all of them to their knees in one fell motion. Ezel flicked a sign to Coal with a quick flurry of his hand, and the dwarf agreed.

"Lash us down!" He yelled to the other two, pointing to a wooden box built into the side of the boat where the ropes were kept.

Orin and Ellaria went to work tying themselves in first and then each crawling over to tie on the others. Orin slid on his knees with another great rock while he tried to fasten the rope around the dwarf's waist. The guardian regrouped quickly and cinched the rope securely, evoking a gasp of discomfort from the dwarf. A little tight maybe, but at least he wouldn't be launched from the boat. Coal slid as well but never lost grip on the levers.

"I can't see the coast!" Ellaria yelled, gripping the bow of the vessel, peering out with eyes narrowed by the storm's fury.

The seasoned seamen exchanged a glance. They both knew the waves were pushing them ever nearer to the boat grinder of rocks and waves. Suddenly, Ezel stopped fighting the levers, and his face contorted. The gnome narrowed his eyes to gaze through the deluge, and after only a moment, he spotted what he had already felt.

A bright light shone through the storm in front of their bow. It was distant, and it disappeared behind rolling waves for brief seconds at a time.

"What is that?" Ellaria asked.

"Maybe a lighthouse!" The dwarf answered the woman, though it came out as more of a question because he was confused as well. "Stroke!"

Orin jumped to it, grabbing one of the levers and finagling it with all his might in rhythm with the dwarf's cadence. Ezel used his magic to aid them. They maneuvered the levers at an exhausting rate, but even when their muscles were spent, they dug deep, finding reserves from somewhere within. They couldn't stop. To do so meant certain death, and their mission was too important.

They cut through the waves with slow methodical work, finally reaching the edge of the light beam that beckoned them to safety. Ellaria was the first to see the strange magic at hand. It was as though they entered an invisible tunnel where the water calmed. The storm rain splattered on some unseen shield above them, and the mountainous swells splashed overhead, leaving the *Lady Leila* untouched. The only drops of water that landed on the boat were those that fell from the soaked crew.

The boat glided along the strange path of calm water from the momentum they had created working the levers. The sound of the raging storm was muffled.

What magic is this? Ellaria thought, though the question had struck every one of them. And then, in the distance closer to the point of the light beam, she saw a silhouette.

"I see ... I see ... a man?"

The silhouetted figure seemed to be walking away from them. Coal pulled at the levers, jolting Orin back into rhythm with him. Though, they now moved easily through the calm water tunnel. The farther they rowed, the farther the figure moved, and the calmer the waters outside the protective barriers became. After a long while, it appeared they had maneuvered outside the storm's range, and the beam of light vanished.

They frantically looked about, searching for the light or its source, but none could spot it. The Tandal Sea had calmed, and the stars made unstable appearances behind dispersing clouds.

"We need to get back to the coast," Coal broke the silence.

"But what about that man?" Ellaria asked.

"I don't think that was a man," the dwarf tugged at the braid in his beard.

When they turned to the coast, in the distance, they saw a campfire—yet another beacon of light to guide them. Without any discussion, for all of them were spent and none would argue they didn't need to rest, they pressed on toward the light on the shore. Orin and Ellaria untied everyone's straps. Coal continued to work the levers, easier as they flowed with the waves, and Ezel watched for hidden rocks in the dark waters.

They came ashore, finding a quiet sandy beach and what appeared to be an old man waving to them from near the fire.

"Come, my friends!" He called to them. "Come and eat."

As expected, the spent crew of the *Lady Leila* ate ravenously. For some reason—and they couldn't figure out if it was their pure exhaustion, their unbridled hunger, or that the old man was a fantastic cook—the fish was the best any of them had ever eaten.

The man ate only a little himself and let the weary crew eat to their filling points. He grabbed a large staff that twisted beautifully at the top. He leaned into the long staff, and the curled top swung around. His kindly eyes watched them with joy as they gobbled the food.

At the sight of the staff, Coal recognized this was no man. The dwarf narrowed his eyes to get a better look at him in the flicker of the firelight. The man had a long grey beard that hung to his stomach. His flowing cloak was muted burgundy with golden accents. Knowing Coal was trying to see his ancient face, he pulled his hood back, not looking directly at the dwarf. His face was creased with smile lines that had grown over an era. When he finally turned toward the dwarf, a half-smile grew across his visage.

When recognition struck him, Coal flopped a limp hand against the little gnome's shoulder to get his attention. Ezel, mid-bite on another piece of fish, leered at his companion. When he saw the dwarf's mouth agape, he followed his gaze to the de-hooded man. Ezel's own mouth fell slack. They had met before.

Though he had shown no sign of magic in their first meeting, he clearly was no man. He was a wizard.

A massive grin spread across Coal's face as he stuffed another bite into his mouth, crumbs falling into his thick black beard. Ezel could only smile back in defeat. The dwarf had been right all this time. The wizard glanced at the little gnome and gave him a sideways wink.

Finally, Ellaria could eat no more and felt it was time to ask her question. "Was that you out in the storm?"

"It was," the wizard replied.

"Who are you?"

"I am Enkeli."

"How did you—"

"He's a wizard!" Coal butted in, happy to gloat.

"I am."

"Why did you help us?" Orin asked, not understanding.

The wizard smiled at the question. "It appeared to me that you were being tossed by the wind and waves and that perhaps you needed some direction."

"More than that! We were going to be drowned," Ellaria piped.

"Ah, but see," the wizard took a few steps away from his staff, which stood on its own like a flagpole. "Your part in this tale is not finished."

"What do you mean?" she pressed.

"You have been given a very special gift. Each of you has." He waved his arm over the whole group but continued to address her.

Ellaria grabbed at the green stone hanging around her neck, thinking he meant the powers within it. The necklace had proven to be quite the surprise on this journey. She had never noticed anything strange about it before, but since it had roared to life at the Palori Ruins, she had been able to sense its magics and tune into them. Enkeli knelt before her and placed a warm hand over hers, shaking his head.

"Each gift is different, and all are necessary. In the end, it isn't what your gift is but rather how you use it that matters. Will you give of yourself and serve others with it? Or will it lead you to your own downfall?"

A surprise tear rolled down her cheek. The thought of Merrick's sacrifice stirred up heartbreak within her again. When Coal had first told her Merrick had stayed behind, she had assumed he'd been lost in the battle. Though she knew her brother to be a capable huntsman, and man in general, he was no guardian of Whitestone. What chance did he stand against orc warriors of Drelek? She had cried heartily on the foggy beach of the faery island before Orin had awoken and their haste had ramped up.

The old wizard's kindly face crinkled in sympathy, as though he knew what Ellaria was thinking. "Do not give up hope so easily. When things are hardest, it is hope that pushes us onward."

Tears flowed abundantly from her eyes, for suddenly, she no longer believed her brother to be dead but merely lost. She lifted a hand to her mouth. In her being, though, she knew to trust the wizard's words and the twinkle in his eye. He wiped the wetness from the side of her face, pushing strands of blazing red hair behind her ear with his warm hand.

He stood and shuffled toward Orin. "Walk with me?" Orin hesitated, seeing Ellaria's tears, but she nodded her approval and put the guardian into motion.

The two walked in relative silence until they were out of earshot of the group. They curved up a thin trail that led to a higher point above the fire. The sun had still not crested in the east, but the color of the sky looking over the Tandal Sea to the west was already shifting, preparing the stars for hiding. The sound of the waves crashing against the cliffs farther down the coast beat like the heart of the world.

"I have always found the sea to be beautiful," Orin finally said, unable to remain silent.

"Ah, but you have always seen it from high above, floating through the clouds."

Orin shrugged. Admittedly, the view from the back of a griffin does give one a particular perspective. And his experience down upon the waves of the sea had been less than serene.

"There is a war coming," Enkeli said. Orin noticed the gloss that rimmed the old wizard's eyes. "You will have to be willing to let go of everything you feel you know."

"What do you mean?"

"You will be where you are needed soon."

The cryptic answer didn't satiate Orin's frustration. "What does that mean?"

Enkeli, holding his beautiful, curved staff in one hand, reached out the other and landed it around Orin's shoulders comfortingly. "You have lived your life with a singular purpose. You have been focused. You serve without hesitation. While your purpose does not change, the way you play your part will."

"You speak in riddles, wizard."

The right corner of Enkeli's lips shot up, humor creasing his old countenance.

"To speak plainly of the future puts that very future into harm's way, for time is a delicate thing. Perhaps you would run into the future, hoping to get ahead of it, but merely rewrite it in your own fashion, with every flaw in tow. Or perhaps you would run from it, sending it crashing into oblivion."

The old wizard turned away from him and gazed over the sea. "No," he continued. "No, yours is to be present. If you are, when the time comes, you will know the right thing to do."

"What I know is that the Griffin Guard needs to hear of the dragon. It could reshape the world. You speak of oblivion. The dragon could be the herald!"

"Your journey is far from over, young guardian."

"Er ... excuse me, Master Enkeli." The dwarf's normally gruff voice came in an uncomfortable timbre. "I believe I was called."

Orin blinked in confusion. He hadn't heard the wizard call out for him; nonetheless Enkeli replied, "Yes. You answered my call Colahr, son of Onik of clan Carraignyk."

Having heard the dwarf's full name uttered by the wizard on the cliffside, Orin studied Coal. He felt a vague familiarity with it, though he could not put his thumb on it.

Coal bowed slightly and responded, "I am at your service."

"Come close, my friend. Orin returns to the fire presently."

Enkeli gave him a sideways wink, and Orin assumed the old wizard thought himself rather clever with his wordplay. Though Orin was conflicted inside, he did not linger to ruin his companion's time with the wizard. Coal gripped the guardian's hand quickly as he passed. The two exchanged determined glances, and Orin went his way.

When Orin sat down near the fire between the woman and the gnome, Ellaria's tears had ceased, and both regarded the sea beyond the flickering flames. Ellaria took Orin's closest hand, squeezing it softly. His eyes slipped from their clasped hands to the woman and then to the gnome on his other side. He reached out and enveloped Ezel's small hand in his large one.

The three sat for a long time, watching the changing colors of the sky as their world began to rise, and were content in their circumstances. For his part, Orin was mindful of being present.

On the trail above them, Enkeli the wizard addressed their dwarven companion. "You have a much bigger role in this tale than you realize, Clan Prince."

Chapter Twenty

Renjak

T he tavern bustled with excitement. Reglese happily poured more glorb wine into new mugs and loaded a carrying tray for Getta. The barmaid was a lovely orc, but it was unwise to credit her for her looks alone. She had more than proven she could handle her own when orcs got too rowdy.

Already, she had socked an overly zealous orc right in the nose, sending him sprawling to the floor, and kicked his rear all the way to the door as he scampered out of the place. She intended to keep the tavern a respectable establishment. There was room for fun, as long as they remained respectable.

Reglese loved her. He had never been in love, but he thought for sure how he felt about the brash orc woman must be it. He loved, too, that the tavern was making waves in Ruk.

Kig's dishes got better every time he made something new, and the younger goblin had thought himself very clever indeed for extending the partnership offer. Reglese had loads of barrels of glorb wine going, and the patronage had grown each day to the point where the place had been full for several days running. They were a hit.

Patrons left filled, quenched, and happy, and they would tell others and return the next day with more friends. Even some of the higher tunnel leaders were coming to the tavern to experience Reglese's glorb wine. The goblin brimmed with pride as he overlooked the lively room.

His mood shifted, however, when he noted a cantankerous-looking orc sidle through the doorway, his deep green skin giving him away. Belguv snarled at a rather loud group of goblins at a table near the entrance.

In all his excitement about the new enterprise, Reglese had remembered little of the purpose of his presence in Ruk. Truly, he had not had much opportunity for spying, as launching a new tavern was a time-consuming endeavor. Plus, the upper tunnel leaders had only just discovered his place in the last two days. He had very little to report and didn't like the idea of making Belguv, already sporting a gruff exterior, more irritable.

Reglese shuffled to the opposite end of the bar where it met the cold stone wall, slipped a fresh mug into the hand of the shaky goblin sitting there, and said, "This one is on the house. You will find yourself a new seat."

The goblin marveled at the full mug with wide eyes. He thought for a split second, hopped out of the seat, and ran off to find a new spot, content with the arrangement.

Belguv maneuvered through the crowd to take his seat at the end of the bar. "I hear you have the best glorb wine in all of Drelek."

"Yes. 'Ere we 'ave the best glorb wine in the 'ole kingdom. And if you're 'ungry, we can 'elp with that, too."

"I could eat."

Reglese whirled around and slipped into the kitchen, receiving a rather bewildered look from Kig as the younger goblin dished out a bowl of the thick hare and rice concoction. Reglese shook his head before Kig could ask and left him there to fill more bowls for the packed house.

The nervous goblin reappeared behind the bar and slid the steaming bowl to the cranky orc. The rushing motion wafted more of the fine scent into the room, causing more orcs to raise a hungry hand toward Getta to place their orders. Reglese quickly spun away to fill a tankard for Belguv, as well. His delay was obvious enough to the seasoned orc warrior, who was surprised by his first bite.

"This is good."

Reglese paused. "I found myself a master cook."

"Yes. I see business is good."

"It 'as been a flurry," he sighed, hoping Belguv would understand his predicament. "I 'aven't 'ad time for much of anything other than business."

Belguv chewed a nice piece of rabbit in his mouth, while steadily staring at the goblin proprietor who had begun to feel faint. Reglese had never been a warrior and did not know how it felt to be stabbed by a spear. He decided it must feel exactly like the formidable orc's stare.

He shifted uncomfortably and realized he still had the full tankard in his hand. "Ah, a drink for you."

Belguv downed the drink and handed the dripping tankard back to the goblin for replenishing. Reglese took it promptly. As Belguv was about to start grilling the goblin for answers, a hush fell over the entire room, drawing their attention to the entrance. There, lo and behold, was King Sahr, with his pipsqueak of an assistant standing in his wake.

"It has landed on my ear that there is a new glorb wine here that will be the rave of all Drelek!" The king hacked a disgusting cough. "Where is the owner?"

In unison, the entire room shifted in their seats and looked to Reglese on the raised level behind the bar. Though he was not short for a goblin by any means, he seemed to shrink in that moment.

"Right 'ere, my King!" his voice wavered.

"Well, is your glorb wine the best in all Drelek, as it's been said?" King Sahr yelled back to him across the room.

Reglese's mind raced. If he answered in the affirmative and then the king didn't like it, he'd be a dead goblin. And even worse, his business would be ruined. But if he answered no, he could be called a liar, for he had boasted to all who had entered the place. He was stuck.

Belguv grabbed the tankard out of Reglese's quivering hands, and making a big show of it, stood, drank it dry in one go, and slammed the tankard back onto the bar. Everyone stared at the deep, green-skinned orc in shock.

"It's the best!" Belguv roared. "All hail the king. This round's on me!"

A cacophony of cheers rang out and bounced off the stone of the tavern's walls and ceiling as patrons around the room signaled to Getta for their free drinks. Belguv stepped to a nearby table, growled at the goblins sitting there—who promptly made their exit—and invited King Sahr to join him at the empty spot.

King Sahr's drooling grin did not fade as he waddled over to join the Calrokian orc. His one good eye darted here and there, greeting the overjoyed customers and subjects. It was good to be the king, he thought. He stood near the table, while his attendant slithered around his heft to pull out the chair before he sat. "Join us, Calrokian," he croaked to Belguv.

"An honor, my King."

The king swayed in his seat, looking to Belguv as though the monarch was already in the buzz of a stupor. The opportunity was too good to pass up. Belguv waved Reglese over, who had already started preparing a tray filled with glorb wine for the king. He ambled over with the tray, four tankards full. He slid one to King Sahr, one to Belguv, one to the attendant, and when the king indicated the goblin join them, he kept the other in front of himself.

King Sahr took a long draw on the mug and moved his mouth awkwardly, attempting to taste all its flavor profile. Everyone at the table watched and waited. The king lingered on it, enjoying all the attention being on him, and finally said, "It just may be."

Reglese relinquished a heavy sigh of relief. They all relaxed. Before the aide could lift his mug, the king swiped it out from in front of him, sliding his empty one in its place before the sniveling goblin. Getta craftily swung by with a couple of extra mugs that she placed in the center of the small table and whirled about, bringing more drinks to the clambering customers. Reglese was glad for her indeed.

"Calrokian I'd wager!" King Sahr started. "I saw another orc from Calrok a while back. Gar Karnak ..."

"Yes. My gar," Belguv confirmed, even though the king had called him Calrokian earlier. The king was obviously not at his best.

"Brute like you, I'd have thought you to be a warrior. But the Scar Cliff Squadron is out in Ghun-Ra ...?" He shot a questioning glance at the aide, who affirmed him.

"We are. At the service of the king," Belguv responded. "Reglese here has quite the eye for business. His first tavern is in our home of Calrok. Our orcs know his glorb wine well, and I am on errand to retrieve some for our forces there in Ghun-Ra."

"Splendid idea!" King Sahr spurted some out of the side of his mouth as he spoke. "They will certainly need it!"

The king grabbed another tankard without a second thought. His stupor continued to grow, and Belguv was happy to let the king have first take of the filled mugs. Occasionally, Reglese would excuse himself and beg the king's pardon, but he always brought back more glorb wine to Sahr's great delight. Even the attendant was able to get a tankard with the king's cognizance lowered.

They went around and around on the same topics for a long while, but when the conversation came back to Ghun-Ra, Belguv took the opportunity to press for the information he'd patiently aimed to receive.

"The dragon should easily destroy the rebels," Belguv commented casually.

"Rebels. Rebels!" King Sahr's one good eye rolled erratically. "They don't understand what one has to do as a king! They hold on to some archaic—*hic*—notion of 'orc honor' that makes them cling to old ways! There's no progress in that. What legacy do they leave their children? Nothing! *Hic!* They will be smashed and burned ... their children included. We will end their bloodlines!"

Belguv and Reglese had an unspoken moment, taken aback by how readily the king spat such venom at his own people.

"And they're just the start," King Sahr wobbled in his chair, his head heavy with drink. "They are just a test! Then, the battle for Tarrine really begins!"

"Good," Belguv feigned agreement, though the very idea of wiping out orc bloodlines sat like a spike in his gut. "Where to, after the rebel dogs are burned out?"

"Haha!" the king cackled. "Then it's off to Galium! We'll smash the dwarf pests that have, for so long, lived on the edge of our mountain range! Our mountains!"

King Sahr waved a sloshing mug high, and Belguv clinked his own against it. He would do what he was sent to do. He would gather as much information as he could by whatever means necessary. He would leave first thing in the morning and return to his gar's side.

The early morning air had a crisp bite to it. Clouds rested lazily upon the peaks of the Drelek Mountains. Perfect conditions for a stealthy flight. They'd been flying toward Renjak since well before dawn, Gar Nargoh's dragon setting a brisk pace for the wyverns to follow. His squadron followed closely, the accompanying gars behind them, and finally the Scar Squadron fell in at the rear.

Ker's long neck shook at a splash of early morning sun that peeked through the clouds and landed its beam of warmth on her. As the sun came up, the clouds would dissipate, and the cutting wind would be less bitter. There was strategic advantage to traveling at such a time when enemies could not see them coming, of course. Karnak, however, would welcome the sun.

The big orc's uneasiness about their mission chilled him. Their plan was sound, of course, and he could not deny the logic of it. Giving the dragon every opportunity to train was important if it was to become a viable weapon for the kingdom.

Revealing the dragon too early to Drelek's foes would certainly spur action against them, for which the creature would be utterly unprepared, and could cost them everything before a campaign really got started. To test its mettle in real battle against a rebel orc faction made perfect strategic sense. Killing two griffins with one spear, as it were.

The Scar Squadron was in tow for the sheer purpose of support, should anything go awry. They were to hold back, high above, awaiting a signal from Gar Karnak should Gar

Nargoh's squadron run into trouble. The four gars, Karnak, Klentja, Dahno, and Jergahn, would fly lower where they could observe the action and witness the power of the mighty beast as it worked alongside Nargoh's group.

Karnak thought the show had already started as Ker grunted with effort. Nargoh rode the dragon at a clipping pace to display its superiority. Karnak imagined the dragon-riding gar was enjoying proving him wrong. The younger gar didn't see the wisdom in tiring all the wyverns before a battle. But then again, there can be no wisdom found in pride. So, the mass of riders flew onward.

Ker's membranous wings glided easily for a moment as they tilted. The whole stream of warriors banked to the north, course correcting to follow Nargoh.

Karnak raised clenched fists above his shoulders, flexing his massive green muscles, breathing in a deep stretch in his chest and back. He shook it out as he settled back into the ride. They still had a good distance to go. He adjusted the way his axe, Dalkeri, sat in the saddle. There wasn't much to see when flying through the morning mountain clouds. And while flying in such a caravan, there wasn't much to do, save for pondering, which suited him just fine.

His previous encounter with Gar Klentja back in Ghun-Ra sat uneasily with him as well. The older gar seemed to engage him with kindness and a sort of respect Karnak wasn't sure he had earned. He imagined much of it came from Klentja's relationship with Karnak's father, Plak. Much had been left unsaid between the two of them in that open-faced hallway.

Had he seen my hesitations? Karnak wondered.

He reached up and tightened the knot of hair on his head, frustrated he felt so in the dark about all the things that were happening. He wondered how Belguv's side mission was going. What information would he bring back?

How was Reglese doing in Ruk? The goblin had been one of the very few of his kind Karnak had enjoyed meeting. He worried about Reglese being found out and captured.

Would Karnak be marred as a traitor?

He hated all the doubt that flooded him. He closed his eyes, trusting Ker completely and letting her wings' steady flapping soothe his mind.

Tanessa, I miss you, he thought. And truly, he did. He would rather be near her. With her, he knew he was right where he was supposed to be.

He missed his son, Gernot. Karnak's features brightened with a silent smile as he imagined wrestling with the little tyke. He thought of Calrok and home.

They flew on for most of the day, stopping only once for a rest and to water the wyverns at an elevated alpine lake. The lake was so remote there was no foot traffic, but it was large enough to supply all the riders of their company.

Gar Nargoh made sure to check on the other gars, obviously not caring about their well-being or that of their wyverns. Rather, he remarked his ulterior apologies about how the dragon was so powerful a flyer it took a very firm hand to keep the beast held back so—for their sakes, of course.

Once all the wyverns were watered, the orcs gathered to rehash the plan, making sure they understood their responsibilities. Wyverns perched all over the mountain bowl surrounding the lake while they rested. Once the meeting was over, the orcs dispersed to find a place to rest for the next few hours. Night quickly approached, and what a night it would be.

They would fly to Renjak, and once the moon was high, the battle would begin.

Though it was the middle of the night, the moon illuminated the quiet stead of Renjak, bathing the mountain town in a silvery glow. The stone structures dotted the sluggish slope. Renjak was one of the more remote forts of Drelek, skirting the far western reaches of the mountain range. Usually, it was quiet, and tonight was no different.

The attacking company swooped in like a wraith of the night. Their dark blurs blinked out stars in a way only trained eyes could see. They swung north and approached the fort from that direction to avoid being silhouetted by the shine of the massive moon.

Just like they had discussed, the Scar Squadron waited some distance away to provide backup if they were signaled. Gar Karnak would lift his axe, Dalkeri, and let its magic blaze brightly through the night sky. It would be seen if the time came, but for the sake of stealth, he had covered the weapon with a thick cloth.

Karnak and the other gars flew in close with Nargoh's forces, only separating from them when the final descent began. They would watch from a safe distance. Nargoh would prove his claims and his pride, or he would not. Karnak wasn't sure which he preferred.

The monstrous dragon fell upon the sleepy fort, which, unfortunately for the orcs of Renjak, was built more on top of the long, wide mountain than inside. The beast swooped in with a fury unseen in generations. It opened its giant maw, burning light blazing from within, and unleashed a fire blast that exploded a guard tower at one end of the fort and set several nearby buildings ablaze.

Screams erupted from the nearby buildings, and panicked shouts reverberated throughout the fort. Guards from other towers sounded alarms, sending orc warriors pouring out of their homes like ants on a hill. Wyverns from nearby perches were spurred into action, many swooping in to find their riders; others being cut off by Nargoh's prepared squadron. Those that did manage to connect with their riders turned quickly to face their attackers head-on.

The dragon looped back, Nargoh setting its course to run straight over the fort. It barreled in like a gargantuan winged javelin through the sky, spewing flame over everything in its path. One unlucky wyvern went into a plummeting spiral into the valley below, its momentum only fueling the fire that engulfed its wing. The dragon crunched down hard on another riderless wyvern, crushing the life out of it.

This wasn't a battle. This was a massacre.

Ker roiled anxiously, recognizing Karnak's shift. He hadn't realized his massive body had tensed and his legs squeezed hard against her ribs. He adjusted uncomfortably in the saddle and shot Gar Klentja a concerned glare. The rotund orc, gliding nearby, caught the look and continued to watch with grave visage.

Karnak saw on one edge of the fort a fierce orc riding an older wyvern, barking directions at a rallying group of defenders. That, Karnak figured, was Maktom, the rebel general. Even in the face of such overwhelming odds, Maktom fought and led his rebels with a ferocity and zeal few orcs would be able to muster.

Several of his riders swerved into the sky, headed for Gar Nargoh and the dragon, who was making a wide sweep to pass back over the fort. They flew in with fury, hurtling spears, axes, or whatever they had at the giant beast, quickly grabbing its attention. But that fight turned swiftly, and the dragon gave chase to the scattering wyvern riders.

Meanwhile, Maktom had set another contingent into motion to help orc families escape the burning buildings. That didn't leave many riders to fight off Nargoh's squadron, and they were losing that battle in haste. Maktom was forced to recall his troops not already engaged with the dragon.

It all seemed chaotic as Karnak watched from above. Half the fort blazed in bright orange flame, the silvery glow no longer radiating the greater light. Orc families frantically sought shelter in more fortunate neighbors' homes. Scattered among the inferno of ruins, he heard wails and frenzied cries.

Nargoh's wyvern riders cut through the rebels easily, in some cases coming up against them four to one. Maktom barked something to his few remaining riders, and they scattered amongst the carnage, all of them swooping into crevasses and loading a passenger or two onto their wyverns. Nargoh's riders were relentless, though, and didn't allow the rebel riders to leave the ground again. They dove on the rebels, tearing at them like wild beasts.

The rebels of Renjak didn't stand a chance.

Nargoh and the dragon swept back over the fort, having killed the pesky rebels that attempted to distract the monster. The dragon unleashed a wave of flame, igniting more of the fort. Some of Nargoh's own squadron skittered away, nearly caught in the dragon's frenzy.

It was as though everything slowed down at that moment for Karnak. His eyes fell upon a young orc child framed in a small market square, surrounded by debris, crumbling stones, and burning buildings. The child was no older than his son, Gernot, and he stood in the middle of the square, covered in ash, tears streaking his tiny face.

Karnak gripped his axe. Dalkeri hummed silently in his hand, joining the welling rage flowing from the orc into the axe and back—the two melding together like hot pieces of iron.

Is this the legacy of the dragon? He thought to himself. *Is this the future of Drelek?*

Karnak started to rip at the cloth covering the razor-sharp, double-bladed head of his axe but was stopped by a lance that landed heavily on top of it. Gar Klentja had extended the lance to stop him. Karnak blinked in rage at the old orc.

"How can you stand by and watch this happen to our own people!" He hissed through clenched teeth.

"You can do nothing here!" Klentja spat back, trying to keep his voice down as not to draw the attention of the other gars, who were enraptured by the dragon's destructive show. "The outcome of this battle is already written."

"This isn't a battle! It's a slaughter! There are children down there!"

"And you can do nothing for them—or the ones that may need your help in the future—if you throw your life away tonight!"

The words of his father's old friend stung, shooting waves of sickness into his stomach. He knew the old gar spoke truth, even if he hated it was so. Ker clicked and clacked at Klentja's wyvern, not loving the close encounter, especially with all the tension she already felt. Karnak shot a glare at the old gar, hating him in that moment, and shifted himself in the saddle to try to spot the little orc boy.

His eyes fell upon him just as Gar Maktom swooped in and grabbed the child in a particularly acrobatic move for the old orc. The two raced wildly, weaving through fiery pillars, trying to escape the attackers giving chase. But their flight was of no use. Before they could even get into open sky, Nargoh's dragon fell upon them like a cat on a mouse, blasting them with his raging flame and then clamping down on them with his devastating jaws.

Karnak winced and looked away. Klentja had released him to watch the encounter as well but turned to the younger gar.

The screams continued from various collapsing holes in the fort below, drowned by the sound of the dragon's breath raining down more destruction.

Karnak stared into the night sky. A single tear rolled down the mighty orc gar's face, sliding around his tusk, dripping off his chin, and plummeting like a lifeless raindrop into the darkness.

CHAPTER TWENTY-ONE

A MAN AMONG ELVES

M uch to their relief, Merrick and Ralowyn survived another night in Elderwood Forest without any monstrous encounters. Merrick had slowed significantly as they ran, his legs depleted and body aching from his previous days in the challenging forest.

Ralowyn appreciated the man's determination. He would have run, even at his slow grinding pace, all the way to Loralith. The elf recognized Merrick's exhaustion, though, and forced the stop for the night.

It hadn't taken Merrick long to drift off. When he woke the next morning, he felt immensely better. He wondered if Ralowyn had used some sort of healing magic on him while he slept, but he did not ask. He was glad for whatever she might have done.

Onward they ran, until Ralowyn halted them again.

"What is it?" Merrick huffed.

"We are here."

She stood straight, both hands poised on her staff, her eyes closed as if she were in a trance. Merrick looked around, peering through the trees and overgrowth in all directions. He saw nothing, save more forest. For the first time, he doubted the elf woman. She had been out in the forest a very long time, and he didn't really know who she was.

He watched as her silvery hair blew in the light breeze. Her slender form was unmoving.

"I don't see anything."

Her smirk returned. "I should say ... they are here."

Merrick retrieved his bow, nocked an arrow, and readied himself out of pure instinct. For what? He didn't know, but the mere action seemed to trigger everything into motion.

Four elves silently appeared, slipping around trees from where they had been hidden so perfectly the huntsman had been unable to sense them. Ralowyn did not move. The elves circled the pair menacingly, and when they were all in position, a fifth elf revealed himself. He wore an ornate cloak of blues and greens, different entirely from the others. He carried a strangely carved stick in his hand that Merrick guessed to be some sort of magic wand.

"The Staff of Anvelorian," the lanky elf acted impressed. "I know of only one who has been able to spark it to life since old Master Anvelorian himself."

Merrick did not understand the elvish tongue. He watched the elf carefully move toward Ralowyn until he closed the distance between him and the slender she-elf. Merrick's fingers twitched around the string and arrow nervously; the surrounding elves' eyes were locked on him.

The cloaked elf circled Ralowyn, inspecting her as one would a priceless statue. She stood as stone, giving him nothing. He stopped in front of her once more. "You have grown quite fair, Ralowyn."

Merrick's features scrunched; he recognized Ralowyn's name as the lanky elf spoke.

"You remain the same as my memory, Lanryn."

"You wound me," he mocked, placing a hand to his heart.

"And your jealousy is thinly veiled. As thinly veiled as this illusion."

Ralowyn leaned the staff in front of her, pursed her lips, and blew through the pinnacle. The magic, made entirely of light, swirled like specks of dust. Purple embers floated and fell upon the cloaked elf, enveloping him and seemingly devouring his form. In an instant, he was gone.

A hearty laugh rolled from behind Merrick. He turned to see Lanryn, the real one, slip out from behind another tree. He called from there, not daring to come closer quite yet. "And why, pray tell, would Master Tenlien's favorite pupil be jealous of the second?"

"I did not say I was jealous of you."

Lanryn laughed again and edged closer to the statuesque Ralowyn, inspecting her with his own eyes. He twiddled the wand in his hand, flipping it in his fingers with well-practiced ease.

"My wand has served me quite well. It has vanquished many foes." He held it close between his face and hers.

Merrick tensed. He didn't need to understand the words to know the stance of the elf did not look friendly.

Lanryn stared at Ralowyn. She remained stoic with her eyes closed. Merrick noticed then she hadn't even opened them to detect the initial illusion. After a long pause, Lanryn dropped his wand hand down to his side and smiled.

"How was your walk?"

As the group walked, Ralowyn promised the tired huntsman Loralith was nearby. After Ralowyn insisted on switching to the common tongue, as to not exclude Merrick, she and Lanryn spoke like old friends—though he spoke enough for the both of them.

Merrick learned they had known each other since childhood. Lanryn had been brought to the school of magic as a child a year or so after Ralowyn. Orphans that proved adept at arcane arts were usually identified earlier than those living with parents. The orphanage did not have the capacity to foster such elves, so they would send them to the school of magic as soon as possible.

Both elves had studied under Master Tenlien for years before Ralowyn left on her walk into Elderwood Forest.

Lanryn updated his friend on the subtle shifts in the hierarchy of the highborn families of Loralith. He described some of the promising young students studying under Master Tenlien at the wisdom tower.

He also explained why he, a mage of such quality, was on patrol with a small band of warriors.

"Seer Zelor has been speaking to the high council about a darkness edging across Tarrine. Something from a distant land that is unknown to us. The king has put all of Loralith on guard."

"I believe we may know something of this shadow," Ralowyn replied, lifting a hand toward Merrick.

For the first time, Lanryn regarded the human walking with them. He had been so wrapped up in speaking with his oldest friend, he'd completely forgotten about the huntsman's presence.

"Indeed," he said, shifting back to Ralowyn. "Did he disturb your walk?"

"No. I believe I found what I needed to find."

The Staff of Anvelorian hummed each time it hit the ground as Ralowyn swung it forward like a walking stick. It sparked and glowed in purple spurts.

"I see you have more control over the staff."

"Forty years of practice helps."

"Ha! I suppose it does."

Merrick watched and listened as they followed some unseen trail. Shortly, they rounded a small treed knoll, and the elven city of Loralith sprawled before them.

Towers and buildings cut upward, covered in vines blooming with a stunning array of flowers. Every building appeared to be growing, though it was an illusion. Small trees grew on top of some buildings. Others had tendrils of vines sprouting out and hanging from the roofs. Even the main castle keep was covered in flora, making it appear as one giant growth.

Merrick saw, to one side of the city, a road that cut through the forest. His experience in Elderwood Forest had been challenging, and he was one who willingly embraced the wilds of the land. He wondered how difficult the forest would be to traverse for merchants and traders hauling their wares.

As they passed the outer walls and pressed through toward the castle, Merrick looked down street paths between buildings, noticing elf children at play and adults going about their business. The city teemed with life.

They navigated the area with ease, though it was a maze to Merrick's mind, and soon arrived at the main keep. Lanryn and Ralowyn spoke to the guard, who looked past them to inspect the human and, after a pause, nodded them through. The inside of the castle was the opposite of its exterior. The place was built with stone as smooth as pearls worked into ornate curves, uncluttered by flora. They stood in a great foyer with high ceilings. Two sets of stairs curved beautifully in front of them.

"A man has not set foot in this keep for many of your generations, man-kin," a voice came from a landing where the stairs met before splitting again.

For the first time since they had rallied with Lanryn's crew, an elf addressed Merrick directly. The voice belonged to an elf who wore a golden robe covered in green scribblings. Her eyes, though, were covered by a single cloth wrapped around and tied at the back of her head. The covering did not seem to be of any special design, simply an old cloth.

Merrick stepped forward between his two elven escorts. "I am Merrick, son of Grell, huntsman of Tamaria. I come with news for the lords of Loralith."

"You involve other peoples in your own mess."

He shook his head. "No. I bring news of warning for the safety of all our futures."

"The wheels of death have already been set into motion. You are merely a messenger, a catalyst to spark the flame of war."

"You talk about flame, but you don't even know of the fires coming to this world!"

"I see far more than you know, man-kin!" She reared up, her voice becoming harsh. "I have seen a dark tide wash over the land, covering the world and drowning it all."

"That's bleak," Lanryn murmured.

"Then you know that I must warn the lords of Loralith," Merrick continued.

"You rain death upon us all," she spat.

"Always the optimist, this one," Lanryn mumbled to Merrick as he stepped past the huntsman again. "Seer, we must speak to the council—"

"You don't know what you've wrought!" she cried.

Before anyone could speak another word, an elaborately crafted door at the top of the stairs to the right swung open with a sucking force. All the tension in the foyer dropped as the elves surrounding Merrick bowed gracefully. At the railing stood a beautiful elven woman. She was dressed in a decadent gown adorned with lace and ornamentation. Her hair was braided like an intricate net and strewn with flowers of different colors.

"Merrick, Son of Grell," the sweetness of her voice lulled him. "You are most welcomed."

"T-thank you, my lady," he stammered.

A kind smile spread across her visage. "I am Queen Velari. The council will see you now."

Sun flooded through open windows into the council chamber. The room smelled of sweet spices and incense. While the place was comfortable, the company was not.

Merrick stood before the table, where twelve elves were seated, listening stoically. The only one who showed any emotion was Queen Velari, smiling at him more out of compassion than at the content of his message. For his message was bleak, indeed.

He told them of all that had happened with Orin, Coal, Ezel, and his sister, Ellaria. He told them of Rora, though it pained him to do so. He spoke deliberately about the encounter with the orcs and the dragon, trying not to miss any details. He got a raised eyebrow from the elf sitting to the king's right-hand side when he described the blazing magical axe one of the orcs wielded.

While he spoke, Merrick looked to Ralowyn for confirmation or help. She only nodded affirmation for him to continue his story. He described to them his days with Ralowyn. He told of her kindness and aid and didn't leave out any details on their time together, not about the rinont encounter and his stupidity or even the bear that had worked with Ralowyn. That brought an approving nod from the elf to the right of the king.

When he finished recalling all he could, Merrick stood before them, waiting for any kind of reaction. He glanced to Ralowyn again, wondering what was happening, but she gave him no indication she knew any more than he did. He fidgeted, awkwardly adjusting his weight to the other leg in the tension of the silence. The queen's kindness saved him again.

"Thank you, Merrick," she said. "You have given us a thorough account of—"

"Thank you?" Seer Zelor spat. "He brings tidings of death, and you thank—"

"You will remember your place, Seer!" The king slammed a fist onto the table. "Interrupt my queen again, and you will be removed from this council session."

The seer scowled but shut her mouth.

"Do you know what became of the dragon after your encounter?" The queen started again.

"I do not. As I said, I did everything I could to give my companions a chance. I do not even know if they were able to escape. Another orc chased them ..." Merrick trailed off.

He had thought much of his friends' well-being while he ran through the forest with Ralowyn. He did not know if they had made it or not. If they hadn't, the burden of delivering the message rested with him. "I must bring this news to Whitestone, as well. If my friends didn't make it, then the Griffin Guard will be caught unaware."

"I am sure we can aid you in that," the queen offered.

"What?" Seer Zelor reacted with vitriol but quickly softened her tone at the glare of the king. "We cannot help him. It will only bring tragedy."

"Then I will help him," Ralowyn piped up, drawing offended looks from several around the table.

"And you should remember your place, young mage," the elf to the right of the king corrected her as softly as correction can be dealt.

Ralowyn bowed her apology to the elf.

"If Drelek has somehow acquired a living dragon, it is imperative we act decisively," he continued to the king.

"Do you intend to bring the wrath upon our own people, Tenlien?" Zelor griped with familiarity.

"As I see it, all of Tarrine would be in peril should Drelek have plans to attack with an army of dragons. Perhaps even all of Finlestia! Are we not citizens of this world?"

"Please, listen," the seer pleaded. "This is only the beginning. This is—"

The king halted her words with a raised hand. "You only saw the one dragon?" he asked Merrick.

"Yes, my Lord."

"Then we do not know how many they have." He turned to Tenlien. "I thought them to be wiped out during the Second Great Black War."

Tenlien shrugged. "As far as we were aware, that was the case. But if they have one, who is to say they don't have more? Where did they come by a dragon? Certainly, one hasn't been reported in Tarrine for generations. Large wyverns, but no dragons."

"A dark shadow rises." Seer Zelor stood upright, sending her chair skittering behind her. "A wave of destruction comes to thieve. Stealing life. Stealing joy. Stealing peac—"

"Enough!" The king slammed his fist on the table again, shocking the foreteller back to the present. "I have heard enough of your laments. What do we have if we have no hope? I will not sit idly by while a very present threat rises.

"If there is only one dragon, then praise the Maker for our fortune. If there are more, praise him even more that he might go before us and make a way for our victory!"

The seer began to shrink back and grab her seat.

"No!" the king continued. "You are dismissed, Seer."

Her jaw trembled below the ragged cloth that covered her eyes. A tear rolled from behind it. She wiped the repulsive droplet from her chin and stormed out of the chamber. The room remained silent for a long time, her words of despair hanging heavily upon them all.

"Merrick will need to fly with haste," Queen Velari finally broke the silence.

"Yes, my love ... Yes. You are quite right." The king turned his gaze to Merrick, still standing at the end of the table. "If Tarrine is in danger of Drelek's threat, Loralith will answer the call to arms. We will remember our oath with Koraal the Wise, King of Whitestone. We will stand in defense of all Tarrine."

"By order of King Solorin, let it be decreed," Master Tenlien offered.

"So it is," the king proffered the customary response.

All the council members faced Merrick. Though he was flanked by both Ralowyn and Lanryn, he felt utterly alone under their full attention once more.

Master Tenlien spoke to him directly. "Master Merrick, come." He motioned toward the empty seat next to himself. "We must draft the course of our future. Together."

They spent several hours devising a strategy to meet the new threat. The council members offered plenty of advice from their long, experienced lives. Merrick felt out of place when they asked him of his opinions on different parts of the planning. Master Tenlien was kind, though, and reminded Merrick it was wise for them to hear the thoughts of a man. Many of the peoples of Tarrine they sought to protect were man-kin and saw life differently than the long-lived elves.

Master Tenlien also invited the thoughts of the younger mages in the room. Lanryn was more than happy to share his opinions on all the matters where he was given voice. Ralowyn was pensive and chose her words with methodical care.

They worked over the plans long into the evening. The royal staff brought platters of food and grails of drink into the chamber. The smell of the herb seasoned meat caused a renewed fervor from the weary huntsman. He dug into the platter set before him. Everything hit his tongue with vibrancy: the vegetables, the meat ... even the elvish bread. *Etchlin* was a sweet bread, made with honey, which added a tasty treat after the hearty meal.

When all was said and done, they had devised a plan that satisfied King Solorin. Several of the elven commanders would take their pegasi squadrons to strategic places around Tarrine and prepare those places for defense. They appointed Commander Fario to gather his squadron and lead Merrick onward to Whitestone.

Master Tenlien offered to act as the huntsman's sentinel, ensuring his safety. However, the council thought it unwise for the master to leave his post in such dire circumstances and with so much uncertainty of the future. He offered Ralowyn as an alternative, should she accept the honor. She nodded her acceptance, and all agreed her to be a good fit. Though Merrick believed the master to be quite capable, he was relieved Ralowyn would accompany him. He trusted her and had been glad for her companionship.

When the meeting was over and all had departed for the evening, Master Tenlien led Merrick and Ralowyn out of the castle toward the stables. The city of Loralith glimmered in the night. Magical lights glinted with faery fire in a myriad of colors, mirroring the flowers of the daytime. It was a sight, Merrick thought, that could not be seen anywhere else in the world. He had certainly never seen the like.

They met Commander Fario at the stables. The elven commander's stern face surprised Merrick, as most of the elves he'd met had much softer features. This elf was a warrior. Who could say whether it was birth or war that had hardened his countenance so?

Tenlien greeted the commander, and the two hurried into a conversation in elvish that Merrick did not understand. Ralowyn grabbed him by the arm and led him to an open corral.

A sleek light grey pegasus with dark grey spots neighed at the intruders. Ralowyn raised her hand and hushed the spirited creature. Its massive wings furrowed as it calmed. Merrick stood back and watched as Ralowyn drew near to the animal. They met easily, and she prompted Merrick to join them. He reached out to pet the great creature, stroking its beautifully spotted fur. He had never seen such a majestic beast.

"Have you ever ridden?" Ralowyn asked.

"A horse, yes. I've only seen pegasi in paintings." He shook his head in disbelief.

"They are much faster than a horse."

"I could guess."

The pegasus nuzzled Merrick's stubbly chin.

"I think he likes you."

Merrick laughed and brushed his hand along the animal's neck. "I like you, too," he said. His hand followed the creature's creased muscles until he paused before the wings. "May I?"

"Of course."

He stroked the large wing, feeling the enormous feathers against his fingers.

What a magnificent creature, he thought.

He stopped suddenly as he remembered petting Rora's feathers, which made him think of his sister. Ralowyn did not miss his shift into worry.

"You are worried for your sister?"

"I am."

"She was with the guardian?"

"She was, but Orin was not at full strength. I know Coal would do everything in his power to protect her."

"The dwarf ferryman?"

"Yes. And Ezel wields magic from his body. How that kind of power comes from such a small form, I do not know." He shook his head at the thought. He was suddenly feeling better about their chances. They may yet have survived.

Ralowyn sensed his change and smiled at him.

"Commander Fario will have his troops prepared for tomorrow," Master Tenlien called to them as he rounded a stable building. "We must get to the wisdom tower. I have something for you there."

They walked through the city beneath the buildings' dancing glow of vibrant colors. The old master spoke with the fervor of a younger elf, as he asked Ralowyn questions in elvish about her walk in the wood. He asked what she had learned about the Staff of Anvelorian and what abilities she'd found within herself. He told her how excited he was that she had come out the other side of the trial without losing her compassion.

Tenlien was like a proud father, doting on his prized daughter, though they shared no blood connection. Ralowyn, for her part, was amused by his excitement and gladly offered answers to every one of his questions.

When they arrived at the wisdom tower, Tenlien led them through the place, winding up the stairs to the highest level. There were two rooms on that level. One was a training room, long and wide enough to be used for some of the more dangerous spells that younger acolytes weren't ready to learn. Tenlien led them to the other room, the master's chamber.

Though outsiders were in his room, he did not hesitate to open a secret door on the side wall. He swirled his arms, twisted his fingers, and whispered an incantation. The wall shifted and settled into a heavy swing.

"Is this where you hid the staff before I was old enough?" Ralowyn asked, less than amused by the old master's facetious smile.

"Perhaps," he replied with a raised eyebrow. "One moment."

He slipped into the hidden closet, and Merrick and Ralowyn heard him jostling items.

"Ah, there you are," they heard him say. "Oh yes. Yes!" he said, seeming surprised he hadn't thought of something before.

The old master shuffled out of the secret room, knocking something over along the way, and used his foot to slide some brass artifact back into the closet. He whispered a command to the door, which seamlessly closed back as part of the wall, and turned bashfully toward them. He held in one hand a magnificently crafted elven bow and in the other a small pouch.

"Here, here, here," he shuffled over, handing Merrick the small pouch. "Open it. Open it."

Merrick could feel some hard object within the velvet pouch. He could not determine its shape, so he untied it quickly, slipping the item from its concealment into his other hand. A crystalline-stone bird, made of some material he did not know, landed in his hand. The stone was of blue and orange tint and had ribbons of black pepper and white crystal throughout. Its smooth surface was cool to the touch.

The huntsman recognized it to be a falcon.

"Valurwind," the old master whispered, his features full of glee.

"Valurw—"

"Shh. Shh! Not yet!" Tenlien stopped him. "I will teach you how to call upon the great falcon."

"A calling crystal for an astral creature?" Ralowyn asked, leaning in to see it better.

"Yes. Very good!" he replied. "This one summons the great falcon to whomever calls upon its name."

"Valurw—"

"Shh! Not yet!" the master scolded Merrick again.

Discouraged by the scolding, Merrick moved to the next item and asked, "What power does the bow hold?"

Master Tenlien chuckled and looked down at the bow. "It is not imbued with any magic other than love."

Ralowyn and Merrick exchanged glances, neither of them understanding his meaning.

"This bow is of the finest quality you will ever see in Tarrine," he continued. "It has no magic. But it was crafted for me by the greatest weapon-smith Loralith has ever known. My father."

"I could not take it." Merrick waved it away. "I have a bow of my own. I made it myself. I could not take such a prize from you."

"I would not give it to just anyone," the master said and looked at Ralowyn's violet eyes. "I give it to you, huntsman. For I would have you protect her as much as she is charged with protecting you."

Ralowyn pulled at Merrick's bow, which he let her remove from his sling. The man accepted the elven gift with as much gratitude as he could offer.

"Very good. Very good," Tenlien stated, happy with the man's new gear. "Off to the training room," he barked. "I hope you aren't tired, huntsman."

Merrick surrendered a pleading smile. He was more than tired.

"I have to teach you how to summon the bird this night," the master continued. "For tomorrow, you fly."

CHAPTER TWENTY-TWO

POWER OF A WICKED TONGUE

Pernden ran a brush along the back of his griffin. Rocktail's sleek muscles were damp with sweat, and his feathers were particularly oily after flying all day. The griffin smelled as though he'd been cooking in the heat of the day. Pernden sniffed at himself and realized he needed to bathe himself later too.

He rested his forehead on Rocktail's back and squeezed his eyes shut in an attempt to ward off the welling tears. Since High Commander Danner Kane had returned to Clawstone, the Talon Squadron's secret base, and told him of Master Melkis's death, Pernden had been prone to short but piercing waves of grief.

The old master had been like a father to Pernden and his brothers when their own parents died long ago. The master's sage wisdom and compassion had helped the young captain grow into one of the finest knights in all the Guard.

Now, faced with the burden of the throne and its title, Pernden needed Melkis more than ever. The rule of Whitestone fell to Pernden, as next blood heir after his mind-bent cousin.

He didn't want it.

A crunch in the woods nearby jolted him upright. Rocktail stamped his feet, obviously sensing the guardian's discomfort.

"I'm sorry to startle you," Danner Kane apologized.

Pernden sighed and shook his head. "It's alright." He patted Rocktail and stepped toward Kane. "What can I do for you, High Commander?"

Kane carried a haunt with him. His usually clean, trimmed face was dirty and scruffy. He'd been laboring at plans for the past several days. He looked exhausted, and in fact, he was.

"My Lord."

Pernden winced. "High Commander, I've asked you not to call me that."

"It seems as though you're having trouble letting my title go," Kane said with a hint of teasing. Though a sadness swept over his visage. "I'm almost certain, it no longer applies."

Pernden laughed and found it unsettling to hear mirth come out of himself. "I'll make you a deal. I'll call you Danner if you call me Pernden again."

Danner Kane looked to the forest floor and huffed out an amused chuckle before turning serious. "None have left our ranks to be with their families in Whitestone. The consensus seems to be that our best chance at protecting our families and the people of Whitestone is to retake the city. And we'll need every guardian we have."

"Did you expect anything less from the Talon Squadron?" Pernden asked with a hint of pride.

He tossed Rocktail's brush into a wooden bucket and pulled out a rag. "Come here," he said to the griffin as he began the process of wiping away gunk around the creature's eyes.

Kane saw grief pressing down the young man's shoulders and said softly, "Pernden."

The burdened man stopped, his head fell forward, and he gripped the rag, wringing it in his hands. "Why would he do it?"

Danner Kane took a few steps closer. "Your cousin is not well. The sorcerer has some spell over him."

"What kind of darkness must he wield that's strong enough for Garron to betray his own people?" Pernden whirled on the older man.

Kane shook his head. "The orc was unlike any I've ever seen."

"What darkness exists that could twist him to kill Melkis?" Pernden shook with emotions.

"It is a wicked power I do not understand."

"How are we supposed to fight that?"

"I don't know," Kane said honestly. "But we'll find a way."

Pernden snickered. "How can you be so sure?"

"I have hope."

Pernden's facial contortions revealed his skepticism.

Kane pressed his lips into a tight smile and added, "Hope in the Talon Squadron, the best of our order. Hope that goodness will prevail. Hope in you."

The younger man shifted uneasily, tossing the rag back into the bucket. "That's a lot of hope."

"Exactly," Kane said. "Hope is a powerful ally. Battles have been won and lost on the razor's edge of hope and hopelessness; even before blades clashed."

"I get your meaning."

"Though I am sorry to see the burden fall to you, I do have hope in you. I have known you for much of your life. You are a natural leader. Whether you like it or not, you will make an honorable king."

Pernden winced again.

"Do you think I would have made you the captain of the Talon Squadron if I didn't believe you are an exceptional leader?" Kane asked.

When the younger man hesitated, Danner Kane recoiled in mock offense. "You think that poorly of my leadership that I would choose an unworthy officer to lead our elite force?"

Pernden hastened to defend his hesitation but noted the wide grin on the older man's face. "I just," he paused. The words caught in his throat. "I didn't want any of this."

Danner Kane moved toward him and placed a hand on his shoulder. "No one wants such things in their lives. Like so many guardians in the long lineage that came before us, I have no doubt you are capable of overcoming any challenge that arises. Even one so strange as this."

The younger man brushed at his cheek as though it would push back the tears that glassed his eyes.

"And besides," Kane continued. "You're not alone. You never have been."

The older guardian reached to his side and untied a sheath. He lifted it before him. Pernden recognized it immediately. Wintertide.

Kane took the weapon in both hands and pulled the hilt so part of the blade was visible. A runic marking glinted in the light as the tree leaves rustled, shifting dancing shadows all around. Pernden reached out and touched the white gemstone embedded in the hilt. A sudden wave of energy flooded him, and he pulled away in shock.

Danner Kane returned the sword to its sheath and held it out to Pernden. His pressed smile widened, and his eyebrow cocked. "I think this belongs to you."

The stench of goblin made Commander Jolan's nose twitch. Goblin foot soldiers were scattered in various inner chambers throughout Whitestone Castle where they hid from the sun. It would be setting soon enough, and their activity would resume.

Jolan was thankful for the brightness of the day that sent them scuttling for shade. It was the only time he could walk through the castle without their leering eyes on him. He surveyed the state of the castle as he walked freely.

Gear lined the hallways with clutter.

The castle was so well kept before, Jolan thought to himself. *What future do we build for ourselves?* He'd been asking the same question over and over for the last several days, but *we'll survive* was the only answer he could find.

As he weaved around a pile of shields, he thought back to the day that changed it all. Everything had happened so fast—the mirror-turned-magic doorway, the king's slaying of Master Melkis, Jaernok Tur's arrival, and Danner Kane's flight. Everything had changed.

Everything.

He shuddered at the thought of the sorcerer orc. Jolan, bigger than most men he knew, still stood short of the shrouded orc who seemed to be bathed in darkness. The commander did not like being in the sorcerer's presence and experienced continuous crawling sensations when near him, like a thousand spider legs creeping across his skin.

Regardless of his feelings toward the orc, Jolan had witnessed power in the sorcerer unlike any he'd ever seen. With such a powerful enemy, certainly they would have fallen to Drelek eventually. At least they would survive by Jaernok Tur's side if the sorcerer could be held at his word. The goblins hadn't killed any of the citizens of Whitestone, which Jaernok Tur threatened them not to do.

A shiver ran up Jolan's spine as he rounded the corner and saw the king's chamber at the end of the hallway.

Several days ago, in that same room, the sorcerer had grabbed his tongue and spoken some evil curse over it. Or was it a spell?

Maybe a blessing or a gift? Jolan had moments where everything made sense, but others when he wasn't sure what was going on. There was no question, though, that whatever the sorcerer had done to him had made easy work of convincing the rest of the Guard to fall in line behind Jolan. They were confused when he'd initially turned up at the Grand Corral with an edict from King Garron declaring him the new High Commander of the Griffin Guard. He explained to them the situation as best he could, and his words that day carried an eerily persuasive power, one he did not understand.

Some of the guardians had been less than happy about the arrangement with the incoming Drelek forces, but they had been dealt with. Those that argued were thrown into the dungeons until they could see the error of their ways.

Since then, it seemed better to keep the Griffin Guard on mission in search of the traitors. Danner Kane had obviously convinced his elusive Talon Squadron to take up his hopeless cause, for none of them had returned from the elite group's secret location.

A twinge of sadness struck him at the thought of his old friend. *Fool. What hope did we have against such dark forces? Do you really think your small band can fight this magic?*

Jaernok Tur had brought goblin foot soldiers and orc commanders through the Alkhoren Mirror. It was deliberate work and required much effort from the powerful sorcerer. That power alone made Jolan believe resistance was hopeless.

He stopped at the doorway to the king's chamber. The door was still broken and hung lazily on its hinges. Jolan took a deep breath and pushed into the room. King Garron sat in a chair next to the table, pouring over scrolls. His wretched body shook as he studied the contents feverishly. He looked like a sack of bones.

Jolan glanced about the room, initially relieved to not see the shrouded orc but almost immediately filled with a chilling dread. He could sense the sorcerer. He didn't know how, but the commander knew the orc was somewhere beyond the curtains that had sectioned off part of the chamber. The curtains were strangely adorned with markings Jolan didn't recognize. A scratchy, ugly language of a bygone era.

"It seems so simple ..." Garron muttered to himself.

"What's that?" Jolan asked, drawing nearer to the malnourished king.

Garron's eyes flicked up as he emerged from the scroll he studied. "What?"

"You said something," Jolan replied. When Garron stared at him as though he were crazy, Jolan said, "Never mind."

Garron stared toward Jolan, but his eyes looked far off.

"What spell did he use on you?" the massive commander asked the shriveled king.

"He showed me," Garron whispered.

"Showed you what?"

"Showed me the shadow. The coming wave. The end of our time."

The creepiness with which Garron said the words made Jolan step backward and uttered the response that he'd reasoned to himself over and over, "But he said that if we join him our people will survive."

King Garron tilted his head and muttered, "A ship is as a plaything to the sea. It might survive the waves, but there are storms—terrible storms—that can crush them."

Jolan blinked at the king. "If we are just going to get crushed in the end, why did you listen to him?"

"The same as you," Garron said, waving an absent hand. "Fear blinds. This was the only option visible that could potentially lead us through the storm. Some ships survive the storm and reach land in the end."

Without another word, Garron returned to his scroll.

Jolan stared at him for a long time. He wondered whether fear was the reason he was still here. Admittedly, he was afraid, but the power of the sorcerer had shattered his reality. He'd never experienced anything like it. As he thought about it, he was unsure whether he was impressed by the sorcerer's power. He also didn't know if his thoughts were his own anymore.

A flourish of the weirdly decorated curtains revealed Jaernok Tur. He looked tired. At least Jolan thought he looked tired. The orc's wicked grin appeared quickly at the sight of the commander. Jolan mustered all his strength to act unafraid. He was pretty sure the sorcerer could sense fear.

"Hello, High Commander," the orc said, whispers dancing off the ends of his words. "Do you bear good news?"

Jolan forced a step away from the weary king and toward the sorcerer, trying to prove his courage. "A report."

"Well, then. Do report."

Jaernok Tur turned away from the guardian, sizing up the Alkhoren Mirror for the next wave of troops and using his nonchalant attitude to remind Jolan how little power the man had against him.

"I have a griffin squadron en route to Dahrenport to inquire of the Talon Squadron and Danner Kane. It is possible they are holed up in the port city. Other squadrons are on rotation, taking shifts to scour Whitestone Forest. They've been working their way from east to west. The forest is dense, and the process is slow. We have covered only a quarter of the forest so far—"

Jaernok Tur growled.

Jolan gulped down the lump in his throat and continued, "I sent out a scout team to Hill Stop a couple days ago. They questioned the locals, but they said they hadn't seen anything."

"So, no news at all!" Jaernok Tur sneered, whirling around on the guardian.

Jolan took an involuntary step backward. "I am preparing another squadron to fly to Lakerun, farther south, in case they fled to—"

Jaernok Tur slithered into the man's face and loomed above him.

"Have I not given you power? Have I not ensured your people's survival? Have I not given you what you want?" The words echoed with whispers bouncing around the room. "I have been a benevolent master. Why won't you give me what I want?"

Jolan's chest wavered. "I-I am trying, Maste—"

The room grew suddenly darker, and Jaernok Tur's eyes turned the color of obsidian. Pressure squeezed at Jolan's heart, and his brain felt as though someone thrust their hand into his skull to grip it tight.

Jolan stammered, "If-if I had more men, I—"

Jaernok Tur's stare froze him.

As Jolan stood before the wicked sorcerer in total silence, it became apparent he wasn't staring at him, but to some distant realm.

The commander waved a cautious hand in front of him, utterly confused by the eerie development. A whimper from the king behind him jolted him from his thoughts, and Jolan saw another choice they hadn't been presented with before.

He reached his hand slowly to the hilt of his sword. Terror gripped the man. The metal slid against the sheath painfully slow.

"He's back …" King Garron whispered, giving Jolan the shivers.

And just like that, Jaernok Tur snapped. He looked tired. Or maybe frightened. Jolan couldn't tell which, but he had let his sword slide back into its sheath and moved his hands away just in time.

Jaernok Tur took a second to realign himself. When he spoke, his attitude was different. "I have more troops coming from Drelek, a wyvern squadron. But you need to accomplish the task I have given you."

Jolan shook away his confusion, suddenly and inexplicably inclined to help Jaernok Tur again. "I could possibly get it done faster by utilizing Whitestone citizens to search the forest on foot, as well. There is no guarantee Danner Kane is in the forest. He could be anywhere, really. If we can get some of the city's people out searching, I can send more griffin squadrons to the coast to search."

"Do it."

Jolan hesitated at the venom in the command, but he had more to offer.

Jaernok Tur noticed and softened his approach. "What is it, High Commander?"

"Well," Jolan looked back at the thin form of the king, still slumped over a scroll at the table. "The castle staff that was shooed out to make way for the goblins have spoken to others in the city. Word has gotten out about what is happening."

"That was never in doubt. The wave of the future is not easily missed by the ones in front of it." Jaernok Tur tried to dismiss the commander's concern.

The comment made Jolan pause. He felt as though he'd had a similar conversation recently. *Did I?* For some reason he couldn't remember.

"Yes, Master," he agreed. "However, it would do the people well to see their king." He checked himself. "Well, not like this."

Jaernok Tur's eyes flitted over to King Garron. The young man-kin had been wasting away. Since his arrival, the orc sorcerer had been focused on setting things into motion, getting goblins into the castle through the mirror doorway, and ensuring the prior High Commander of the Griffin Guard—and his special squadron—were found and killed before they were able to mount up any semblance of resistance. He had nearly forgotten the usefulness of the king.

"His father was a well-loved king. The people loved him as a prince and were pleased for him to be the new king," Jolan continued. "If my master would clean him up and give him strength once more, he could be very helpful. He could lean the people's hearts to your plans. With the people behind you, we could accompli—"

A stone clawed hand rested on the large commander's shoulder. It was heavy, as though the weight of the world fell on him with its touch. The sorcerer's features were softened though.

"It appears your wisdom was wasted before."

Jolan only stared back at the orc.

"He may have been loved," Jaernok Tur glanced over the man's shoulder toward the king and back. "And I will refresh him for these purposes."

"Thank you, Master."

"But when all this is over, I will reward *your* loyalty. And I will need to set up under-kings. Let us see how your wisdom plays out. Should it prove fruitful, who knows what riches I might bestow upon one so prudent?"

Jolan's heart tightened. He had no doubt the campaign would succeed. At the same time, he realized he had no idea how powerful Jaernok Tur was, but he intended to find out.

Pernden had spent the past hour sparring with Nera. Sweat matted his long blond hair and dripped into his eyes. Nera, as sweaty as he, simply glistened. How could he appear so rough while she looked radiant? Her heavy breathing, though, betrayed her exhaustion.

They smiled at each other as they lowered to the ground to catch their breath. Pernden was grateful she was willing to spar with him. To do something normal with him. Although their sparring session had been anything but normal.

Nera had been learning the magics of her spear, Santoralier, and Pernden understood clearly why it was called "Lightning Rider." For his part, Pernden was learning the magics of Wintertide, Melkis's weapon. Sadness enveloped him as he examined the sword in his hand.

The hilt was long enough to be used with both hands and was accented by a strange white crystalline stone. Pernden assumed the stone, combined with the ancient elven etchings, was the source of its magic. Its silvery blade shone as sunbeams poked through the trees waving in the wind. Somehow, even after the many battles it had seen, it still looked as though it were straight out of the forge.

Nera nudged Pernden with her elbow. "It's surreal to taste the familiar sting of Wintertide." She picked at some snowy ice stuck in the end of her long, thick braid. "You wield it with the fury of a blizzard!"

"I wish it were not I who wielded it."

Nera reached a sympathetic hand to his shoulder. "I know. Though, I also know he is in Kerathane right now, proud that you are the one who does. Melkis loved you like his own son."

"And I loved him like a father."

Nera let out a long exhale, trying to regulate her breathing. She leaned back, resting her body weight on her hands behind her and looking all around them. "I have always loved this place. Always thought it would be a wonderful place to build a cabin. Raise some children." She laughed at the notion.

Pernden nodded his agreement. "Thankfully, we have this haven. Imagine if the Talon Squadron had been somewhere else when the Drelek sorcerer broke into Whitestone."

"I'm not so worried about that."

"What?" Pernden was shocked by her words.

"I understand there is a battle before us," she reassured him. "But I have no power over that right now. When the battle comes, I'll be ready to fight. Until then, I'll fill my mind and heart with my reasons to fight and dreams of a future after victory. I'll think on hopes. It is better that than being consumed by worries. How can you fight if you are captive to worry?"

"You're the second one to mention the power of hope to me recently."

"Whoever it was must be incredibly wise," she said with a smirk.

Her dark skin glistened as the trees cast shadows and light waving around her. Pernden gazed into her eyes, no longer sparkling gold, since Santoralier rested beside her in the grass.

Nera's smile softened, and Pernden thought he could dream for a future as well. He leaned toward her, but a stick cracked under a heavy boot nearby, halting him and breaking their intimate silence.

Danner Kane approached them. His face teetered between the look of an approving father and an apologetic interrupter. The young captain stood to greet him.

"My Lord ..." Kane started.

"Danner, please." Pernden begged his mentor. "Please. My heart can't take the weight of the title."

The commander chewed on his response for a second and finally huffed out a laugh. "You are capable of far more than you know, Pernden. I am sorry I have not instilled in you the same confidence that I have in you."

Pernden realized the situation was not only awkward for him. He had been Danner Kane's protégé and had hung on to the older man's every word. Kane had led him through many challenges over the years. He'd taught the young man how to lead guardians well.

Suddenly, Pernden had become the leader. Why? Because of some blood relation to the crown? He didn't even want to be king. He'd never wanted to be king. He was happy flying around on griffin-back, worrying about nothing but his duty to the Guard.

"What can we do for you, High Commander?" Nera stepped in, recognizing the two men's internal struggles.

"Ah, yes," Danner Kane adjusted his stance. "I have been reaching out to my sources, gathering as much information as I can without us being detected. We could not risk being discovered before we are ready."

"And are we ready?" Pernden asked.

"Well, that's why I'm here," Kane continued. "It sounds like we will have to fight sooner than I'd hoped. I still do not understand the power of the orc sorcerer. Whatever power he wields enables him to twist the minds of others toward his will. It got me thinking since we are facing an enemy that thinks and works differently than us, we need to approach this in a different way."

"That's an understatement. It wasn't exactly a direct attack. The sorcerer has completely changed everything. We know Drelek's usual tactics have been shifting of late, but they still tend to lean on wyvern squadron raiding parties," Pernden added.

"Correct," Kane went on. "However, we were infiltrated by craftier means this time. More sinister, illusive means. Get into the heart of someone and you can turn them to your causes."

"Garron was clearly deceived into betraying Whitestone," Nera interrupted.

"That's what I believe," Kane admitted. "And I was thinking about how long Garron had been gone before his return. If I remember right, it was several weeks that he was away. It is possible the enemy could have captured him and twisted his mind then before sending him home to Whitestone. You remember when he came back?" he asked to Pernden.

The young captain wiped sweat from his brow. "Yes. He was ... different."

"He was," Danner Kane nodded solemnly.

"So, could the sorcerer do that to others as well?" Nera asked.

"Apparently, he's already doing so. My sources still in Whitestone tell me Commander Jolan has been decreed High Commander of the Guard. The sorcerer has been using Jolan as a mouthpiece to poison the Guard. The sorcerer has been bringing goblin soldiers into Whitestone through the Alkhoren Mirror and having Jolan manage the tensions between the incoming goblins and the Guard."

"That blasted mirror!" Pernden seethed.

"Goblins in Whitestone? The Guard would never allow that!" Nera protested.

"Again, we know not how wide the sorcerer's web of deceit can spread. It sounds like Commander Jolan's words have been ... persuasive. Any guardians that don't fall in line are locked up in the dungeons."

"Lock up any who would fight against them," Pernden visibly shook with rage.

"Yes. But also, the Guard has been kept away from the castle. Jolan has them running missions all over, looking for us. Keeping the squadrons separated in smaller groups may make it easier to control the guardians. Also, we don't know how deep his claws dig into people the longer he hexes them."

"Garron looked worse and worse as every day passed," Pernden put in.

"Which means we need to hurry. The more we delay, the worse the sorcerer's influence over the Guard will be," Nera reasoned.

"That's my thought as well," Kane said.

"Goblin foot soldiers we can manage. But the power of the sorcerer orc is unknown to us. If we fly in, we could be flying to our deaths," Pernden said gravely.

"Yes. However, the time for action is upon us. I've reached out to a source of mine in Ghun-Ra. She reports a wyvern squadron will be headed from there to Whitestone to solidify their hold."

"A source in Ghun-Ra?" Nera asked.

"A very old friend," Danner Kane said, with a reminiscent smirk. "A goblin's love of coin knows no bounds."

"So, foot soldiers, a sorcerer, and a wyvern squadron? Not to mention the rest of the guard is under the sorcerer's spell and hunting for us. Anything else we need to add?" Pernden quipped.

"Those are rough odds, even for the Talon Squadron, Commander," Nera pointed out.

"Exactly," Kane said. His eyes narrowed at Pernden.

"Oh, I see," Pernden said, his command brain taking control. "We must take them out separately. We can't fight them all at once. We go for the wyvern squadron and catch them as they crest the mountains. We never let them reach Whitestone in the first place."

"Exactly what I was thinking," the High Commander affirmed. "When we take them out, we will have to recover quickly. They will certainly send for another squadron. But we need to take Whitestone back before they arrive."

"So, we are agreed," Pernden concluded.

Danner Kane looked at the young man before him. Even in his exhaustion, he brimmed with fatherly pride. How much he had seen the young man grow. Kane longed to see him grow into the man that would lead their people into the future. He hoped he would be able to witness it.

"The lead is yours," he said.

Pernden nodded with determination.

"Prepare the squadron. We go to war."

Chapter Twenty-Three

Goodbye To A Dream

T he wizard Enkeli had been kind to them. He sent them with dried fish to sustain them along their journey. He had spoken fresh life into the companions, renewing their hope after such a difficult journey.

His talk with Coal had taken so long the others were almost finished preparing the *Lady Leila* for departure when he finally rejoined them.

Before they left, Enkeli handed a small hardened wooden token to Ezel without a word. As the gnome turned it over in his hands, he examined the markings and the design. The image was of an ornate tree surrounded by seven distinct runes the gnome did not recognize. He had never seen such markings and assumed they were of some ancient language.

Ezel signed his thanks for the gift, even though he was unsure of its purpose. The old wizard winked again and motioned for the gnome to rejoin his friends before they launched the boat without him. The wizard waved to the companions as they followed the Stranded Coast around the first bend north.

Before they disappeared, Ellaria yelled back to him, "Thank you, Enkeli! You have been a kind friend to us."

"And I will send another!" Enkeli hollered back with a wave of his hand, his burgundy and gold robes blowing in the sea breeze.

Ellaria's features scrunched. She did not know what he meant, but she was glad to have someone like the old wizard on their side.

They were on the water no more than an hour before they spotted Crossdin in the distance.

"No, no, no. This isn't right!" Coal paced the boat quickly, his confusion turning to laughter as he did. "How did ..."

"I thought you said it would be several days?" Orin asked. He worked the levers to steadily propel them up the coastline.

"It was supposed to."

The dwarf shook his head in amazement. Ezel signed to him, and Coal's face shone with realization.

"Ezel thinks Enkeli's tunnel through the storm took us farther than we thought," the dwarf translated. "Who am I to argue? The gnome knows more of magic than I!" He laughed heartily.

The gnome's hands moved fluidly as he insisted he did not understand the magic of the wizard but guessed based on their current circumstance. The friends shared a synchronized shrug, and Ellaria laughed at their display. Even Orin smiled at the joy in his friends. The surprise put all the friends in a jovial mood. Orin worked the levers faster, feeling a renewed sense of urgency. They had made up some time, and he cared only that they had, no matter how.

Coal smiled to himself. Wizard magic was strange magic, but maybe wizard magic wasn't so bad.

As they drew nearer to Crossdin, they began to pass larger fishing ships bustling with activity. Fishermen moved along like ants on a hill, working in a seemingly chaotic rhythm but wasting no effort.

One crew gawked at the sight of the *Lady Leila*, dwarfed by the much larger fishing vessels.

What a strange sight we must be, Orin thought to himself. Two bedraggled humans, and an equally ragged dwarf and a gnome. Their tiny boat coming in from the sea. *A strange sight, indeed.*

Coal took control as they entered port. He deftly maneuvered the boat through the traffic. They pulled alongside a long dock where a small boy stood, holding a rope. A little girl sat on a crate next to him, closely watching his every move.

"Hello sirs!" He called to them. "Got a rope for you here, sirs!"

"There's a lady, too," the little girl corrected him.

"Shush, you!"

"Alls I'm sayin' is that all you said was 'sirs,'" she poked at him.

"And my lady," he acknowledged Ellaria and shot a scowl at the girl next to him.

Ezel moved to the bow of the boat and reached for the rope. The boy looked quizzically at him. The bald gnome covered in tattoo runes must have been quite the surprise, for he looked to Orin for an answer.

"He'll take the rope," Orin smiled and nodded for the boy to pass it to Ezel.

The deep gnome recognized the boy's tentativeness, and the runes on his hand flared to lift the rope through the air. Ezel swirled his hands, and the rope danced in the air, forming shapes. He made a horse, then a ship, then a tree, and finally a castle. The little girl laughed and clapped with glee. The boy stood, astonished, his mouth wide. Ezel used his magic to tie an easy knot onto the *Lady Leila,* securing her to the dock.

Coal flicked a coin over to the gnome, who caught it midair with magical blue swirls and floated it to the boy, landing it in his hand.

"Wow!" the girl said to him. Jumping off the crate and looking over his shoulder at the coin.

The boy recoiled at how the girl hung on his shoulder and held the coin tight in both hands as though it were some far greater treasure. He turned to Ezel and said, "Thank you, sir!" Ezel signed back with his hands that he was very welcome, and the boy ran off, trailed closely by his little admirer.

"That was very kind, Ezel," Ellaria said.

Ezel shrugged a laugh.

"Folks don't see many gnomes about these days. Even fewer see grey gnomes like Ezel. Most of them live underground now. In all my travels, I have met few like him. Well, none like him!" Coal said fondly.

Ezel nodded his thanks to the dwarf for his kind words.

"You're the only gnome I've met, and I am thankful for you. Me life is better for knowing you," Ellaria said.

Ezel signed something to her. She thought she caught some of it. They had spent a lot of time together, and she had made special effort to learn some of his sign language during weary hours in the boat. Nonetheless, Coal translated for her, "This has been a surprising journey for us so far. And we've shared some difficulties along the way. But Ezel ..."—Coal interjected himself into the sentiment—"Ezel and I are glad to be with you, as well."

Ellaria smiled, leaned down, and kissed the top of the little gnome's head. For the first time since they had met, Orin thought he saw some color blush on Ezel's grey face. Their journey had been full of surprises thus far, least of which was the fair woman who beamed at the guardian. Her red hair flickered like fire in the breeze coming off the sea.

"I'll speak with the dockmaster," Coal said. "You lot should gather up what we have. We'll need to find transport to Galium.

I've been thinking it might be better to get our horses there. There are plenty of wagoners that travel between Crossdin and Galium. Once there, we can take the northern road all the way to Whitestone."

It was the best plan he could come up with and the fastest route to Whitestone.

It still sounded like a long journey to Orin, but he had also run through the scenarios and accepted Coal's plan as the most viable. "Agreed," he said. "I'll join you with the dockmaster if these two can handle the gear."

"We can handle it," Ellaria assured them with her smile.

Ezel nodded his agreement.

"Very good," Coal said. The dwarf paused and tugged at the bottom of his black braid. He inhaled deeply and shot a discouraged glance at Ezel, who regarded his oldest friend and pondered the root of his worry. Without further delay, Coal hopped on the edge of the boat, stepped to the dock, and strode off. Orin hustled out as well and fell in step with the dwarf's determined stride.

"Shall we?" Ellaria asked Ezel.

The gnome clapped his hands and rubbed them together. Then he signed, *"Let's get to work."*

Orin and Coal had been gone a long while, and Ellaria and Ezel completed the work of moving their supplies and repacking for the next leg of their journey across land. They sat on some crates at the end of the dock, enjoying the sights and sounds of the port. Massive ships moved along the water easily, defying their immense weight.

282

Footsteps along the dock behind them caught their attention, and the pair looked back in hopes their companions had returned. Instead, two sailors approached. Ezel shrugged to Ellaria, and they turned back to watch the water.

"This the one?" one of the men asked the other.

"Think so," the other replied.

Ellaria had the strange feeling they were closer than expected and turned around just as one of the men hopped into the *Lady Leila*.

"Hey!" she hollered.

The man looked up in surprise.

Ezel whirled around, blue faery fire in his eyes. He flourished his hands, and ribbons of blue power swirled around the man, lifting him into the air and flipping him into the murky port waters.

"Whoa!" the other man screamed, holding his hands out as Ellaria drew her bow on him.

"There'll be no thieving of our boat today!" Ellaria warned him. "Me friend and I will be seeing to that."

"We're not thieving anything!" the man wailed.

The man who had been thrown into the water sputtered as he broke the surface. He hacked, trying to clear the water out of his lungs, and grabbed onto the side of the boat for support.

Over the man's shoulder, Ellaria spied Orin and Coal running down the dock.

"What are you doing?" Coal hollered.

"These two were trying to thieve our boat," Ellaria explained, holding her bow steady.

Orin slipped past the man and put his hand gently on the bow. "These men are from the dockmaster."

"What?"

"We went to speak to the dockmaster," Coal said, placing a calming hand on the terrified man's back. "We needed to sell the boat to have enough money for our transport to Galium."

Ezel's fiery lights went out, and his hands dropped to his side. He understood the discouraged look Coal had given him earlier. Owning his own boat had been the dwarf's dream since their experiences on the Gant Sea long ago.

"You didn't think to ask me?" Ezel signed to him.

"What would you have me do?" Coal signed back, not wanting to burden the other two with the argument. *"We didn't have enough coin to pay our way. We're going on land from here. And when all this is done, how would we have gotten it back to the Palori River, anyway? We barely survived the Tandal Sea the first time."*

Ezel couldn't argue with his friend. All of Coal's points were valid. They wouldn't leave Orin and Ellaria on their own. What could they do with the *Lady Leila* here? They had no connections, and attempting to traverse the Tandal Sea to find a riverway to get them back would almost certainly mean their deaths. No, none of that would do, but he was sad for his friend. His dream was lost.

"I am sorry," he signed to the dwarf.

"I am, too."

The dockmaster's man slowly pulled his sopping friend back onto the *Lady Leila*. The two untied the boat and worked the levers to maneuver it away from the dock, weaving it away until the companions lost sight of it.

"Well," Coal cleared the lump in his throat. "Onward then."

They found where the wagoners gathered. Various workers—dwarves, men, elves, halflings, and more—loaded wagons. The group even ran into a female surface gnome with golden ringlet hair. Her skin was almost as golden as her hair, and her eyes were a vibrant blue-green, like the sea.

Coal nudged Ezel, who was staring, and encouraged him to talk to the she-gnome.

Ezel quickly stopped staring, and she giggled at his embarrassment. Ezel shoved Coal, who laughed as well.

Amid the various peoples, the travelers met a halfling named Tobin. The crew loading the plump halfling's wagon was quick with their work. Tobin was shorter than Coal but taller than Ezel by a hair, that is, his wild curly hair edged him just taller than the gnome. He gnawed at his pipe happily as he blew swirling rings of smoke.

The dockmaster had recommended Tobin as a quality wagoner with fair prices and a kindly way about him. As the dockmaster had been fair to them, they had taken his recommendation without a second thought. And thus far, his words had proved faithful.

"Are we ready then?" Tobin asked Coal.

"That we are."

"Good, good. You lot can climb into the back here. You should be plenty comfortable! I pride myself on making your riding experience the most comfortable of any wagon you've taken before. Really, it's all a part of the journey experience for folks who ride with me. If you're a happy rider, I'm a happy wagoner!"

Orin, Ellaria, and Ezel looked into the back of the wagon and found all the supplies had been pushed to the front and the sides. A couple of pillows and furs sat in the middle, creating a cozy little nest.

"Well, go on now," the halfling waved and pointed his pipe. "Plenty of room for all of you. Best wagon in all of Crossdin. Or Galium. Or probably Tarrine, if I dare guess. What can I say? I try to run a hospitable wagon. You know, there are others who cart you along with no consideration for comfort. Not me! If you're a comfortable rider, I'm a comfortable wagoner!"

The three climbed into the wagon, more than happy with the accommodations.

"What has you traveling to Galium?" He asked Coal as they strode around to the front of the wagon, Tobin inspecting it as they rounded.

"We bear grave news."

Tobin stopped, furrowed his brow, and asked, "Messengers? You know Georl runs letters, don't you? Mind you, he's probably not as fast as me. I would take you to Galium to hand deliver your message quicker than his letter cart."

Coal shook his head. "This news we must carry ourselves," he said sullenly.

"Grave, indeed," Tobin mused, popping his pipe back in his mouth. "Well, I'll get you to Galium as quickly as I can. I'm looking forward to seeing my sweet little Button."

"Button?"

"My daughter. She's only a tyke, but as beautiful as her mother, she is. Married the most beautiful dwarf woman you've ever laid eyes on, I did." He grinned, his teeth clamped hard on the end of his pipe. "Some of the dwarf men weren't so happy. Borgan even wanted to throw fists, you know. But my wife reminded him, Galium's been my home just as long as his.

Then she tells him her love for me is greater than any he has ever known or maybe ever will! You believe that? Firecracker, that woman!"

Tobin snapped the reins, and his two horses lurched the wagon into motion. They rolled along the path that wound through the rest of Crossdin. Tobin continued to narrate the whole way.

"You ever been to Galium?" He didn't wait for an answer. "Beautiful place, it is. One of the most impressive dwarf fiefdoms, I'd care to wager. Lots of activity from surrounding places. The castle is built right into the mountain—what a sight in the early morning twilight. Been my home my whole life. Well, not the castle, you see." He laughed. "Live in the hillside community, of course. Lots of beautiful rolling hills out that way ..."

The halfling wagoner didn't seem to breathe between his words, and if he did, it was to puff a few rings of smoke from his pipe. The dwarf wasn't sure how the halfling had enough air to keep talking, but Tobin's words didn't cease.

Coal peered back over his shoulder. Ellaria's eyes met his. Her wide grin told him she found his pain to be quite humorous. He tried to see Orin and Ezel, but they were hidden behind supplies. Coal imagined they were already being rocked to peaceful sleep by the wagon. The wagoner continued to talk, not distracted in the least by Coal's shifting. The dwarf rolled his eyes at Ellaria and looked forward again. He was going to have a long trip.

CHAPTER TWENTY-FOUR

REBELLION & CONQUEST

The return flight to Ghun-Ra was a solemn affair for Karnak. He initially flew near the front with the other orc gars but eventually hung back to get away from their prattling glee. They spoke of the power and might of the dragon with such joy and excitement, Karnak was certain they hadn't been affected by the massacre at Renjak. Klentja, for his part, was quiet too but flew near enough to continue listening.

They had left Gar Nargoh and his wyvern squadron in Renjak. The dragon had proved itself to Gar Jergahn's satisfaction, and the next phase in the plan was approved for launch. Nargoh, along with the dragon and his wyvern forces, would rest and regroup in the nearby fort of Porak, while gathering and preparing ground forces. Once they were rested and the ground forces were ready, they would make way for Galium, and everything would really begin.

When they returned to Ghun-Ra, the gars met to discuss their individual parts in the next phase. Gar Dahno would take his squadron immediately to Whitestone. A mixture of confusion and excited whispers broke out among the gars and their commanders.

"The command is issued. When we first arrived, it was reported to me that our forces are now in control of Whitestone and that your squadron will be going there to shore up our hold on the city of our longtime nemesis, the Griffin Guard," Jergahn explained.

"And where are the Griffin Guard?" Gar Dahno's commander asked. Around the room, heads nodded. It was a fair question.

"Jaernok Tur ensures they are falling in line with King Sahr's plan," Jergahn said shortly.

"They turn against their own people?" The commander asked.

A snarl rose up in Karnak at the notion. Had he and the other gars not just witnessed a slaughter of their people at their own hands?

"Jaernok Tur is working with the king of Whitestone, and the Griffin Guard follows him blindly."

"Fools," the commander cackled, and others laughed with him.

"Gar Karnak and Gar Klentja will head to Lakjo to wipe out the remaining rebel forces," Jergahn went on.

Karnak rebutted, quicker than he intended, "We won't."

Silence fell in the chamber. Klentja glared at him, trying to relay something with his eyes.

"The Scar Squadron is weary from travel to and from Renjak," Karnak quickly added. "We've had no rest, save today. We can't be expected to head straight into battle after such a trip."

His quick recovery made sense to the others in the room.

"That is why the Borok wyvern squadron will lead the way. They will be first contact, while the Scar Squadron flanks the enemy. Borok will already have engaged the enemy rebels, and your squadron will come in to finish them," Jergahn explained, confident in his plan.

Karnak could not argue with him, and to say more in that setting would certainly land suspicion upon his head and the heads of his orcs. He would not do that.

"I will be by your side, young gar," Klentja added comfortingly. Everyone nodded at the plan. For some reason, Karnak felt he was the only one who really heard the words the rotund gar said to him.

Gar Jergahn handed out a few other orders, but Karnak heard next to nothing. The Scar Squadron would rest the night and be on the move in the morning, flying with Klentja and his Borok squadron.

Belguv arrived later that evening. The gruff orc was greeted with a hug from his large gar. Karnak was happy to see him. Belguv, however, bore a weight upon his countenance, which quickly shifted the joyous reunion into deep conversation.

"Tell me of Reglese," Karnak said, concerned for the goblin.

Belguv laughed. "The goblin does well for himself. His tavern booms. I was able to find him among the caverns of Ruk quickly enough. Word of his glorb wine has spread with great haste. The tavern was full, though he said the leaders from upper tunnels were only just beginning to frequent his place."

"Well, his glorb wine will speak for itself. It must take great effort to set up a new tavern," Smarlo suggested. Karnak nodded along with his friend.

"Yes," Belguv replied. "But the journey bore more fruit than we could have hoped. While I was there, King Sahr himself appeared at the tavern."

Karnak stopped mid-stretch, hanging on Belguv's every word. Smarlo doled out three tankards of glorb wine from the barrel the gruff orc had brought back. "The king was at the tavern?" Smarlo sounded surprised.

"Yes. I tabled with him and bought him drinks. He was very willing to share his sentiments about many things." Belguv grabbed his mug and took a swig.

Karnak was thrilled that his plan to send Reglese to Ruk had worked—perhaps not as he had expected, but possibly more fruitful than he had anticipated.

Belguv's casual tone transformed to a grave timbre. "The king wants to see the rebels destroyed. He spoke of burning generations. He spoke of tearing down old honor."

"We've seen this." Karnak said, hardly able to look at Belguv as he explained. "Renjak was a slaughter. The dragon and its fire consumed the mountaintop. Women. Children .... It did not matter."

"I am sorry, my Gar. I flew as fast as I could but knew I would miss Renjak. King Sahr plans to smash the rebels at Lakjo next."

"Those are our orders," Smarlo confirmed.

Belguv looked as though he were trapped between thoughts. His unease was apparent to Karnak, for the young gar had felt the same tension many times over the past several days.

"I do not yet have all the answers," he assured Belguv. He leaned in closer. Looking around and lowering his voice, he added. "But I do not intend to slay generations."

Belguv visibly relaxed, clearly satisfied with the words, whether he knew what they entailed or not. Smarlo's lips pursed, however, for he understood what was at stake. "Karnak," he started, more as a friend than a commander in the moment. "Do you intend to let Klentja destroy the rebels' women and children?"

Karnak leaned back and took a long sip of his glorb wine. He thought on the question for a significant amount of time while the other two watched their gar. He swished the glorb wine in his mouth before he downed it. And then, the answer came to him clearer than he expected.

"No. No, I do not."

The flight north to Lakjo from Ghun-Ra was easier for the wyverns, as they weren't flying at the clipping pace of a larger dragon wingspan. Ker easily soared through the air, happier with the speed of the trip. She hadn't gotten much rest before they set out but managed the pace without trouble or complaint. Karnak was grateful for her good attitude.

They flew in the front with Gar Klentja, whose large face had been set like flint all day. He'd said almost nothing to the younger gar. Smarlo shot curious looks at his gar on occasion, but Karnak had no idea what was going through Klentja's mind. He had not gotten the chance to speak with him privately in Ghun-Ra before they left. He would have liked the chance to read the older gar in a conversation.

The Borok squadron followed them, and Belguv led the Scar Squadron behind them. On long flights, there was no need to fly in formation. It only stressed the wyverns to remain in proper sequence. Letting them fly freely in clumps and lazy lines kept them loose and efficient. They would arrive at their destination with more energy that way.

After flying most of the day, they took a break near an alpine lake that rested in a remote valley. Pines swayed all around them in the mountain breeze, and the orcs watered their wyverns before setting up cooking fires. Food would restore them before battle. Karnak expected they would gather their forces and go over the plan before they flew onward, but Klentja still had not approached the younger gar. He seemed to be avoiding Karnak. While that suited the large orc fine, Smarlo's nervous glances started to make him anxious as well.

Before Karnak could tumble down the rabbit trail of worry, he noticed a falcon flying above the temporary camp. He thought back to the huntsman.

Strange, he thought to himself. *I do wonder where the man-kin is and if he survived the perils of Elderwood Forest.*

And then it dawned on him, men were not the only race to practice falconry. Though the bird could very well be a wild falcon, it was also entirely possible they were being watched.

"Find Gar Klentja," he spoke with authority and fervor to Tark, the youngest among their ranks.

The young orc ran off through the pines, looking side to side. Karnak quickly retrieved a seeing glass from one of his orcs to monitor the falcon. He watched it for a minute and then scanned ridges in the area for any movement that might betray a scout.

Tark ran back with Klentja in tow.

"What is it, Karnak?" the older gar huffed.

"I'm not sure yet."

Tark looked nervously between them. Karnak continued to scan. "Ah," Klentja noticed the falcon. "A scout?"

"I can't spot any on the ridges."

Karnak handed over the seeing glass, and Klentja began to scan. The young gar from Calrok turned to his oldest friend. Smarlo shook his head, not liking the situation at all.

"It's moving away," Tark pointed to the falcon high above, moving off to the north.

"In the direction of Lakjo," Smarlo added.

"We must move on, now," Karnak said.

Klentja fiddled with the seeing glass for a minute. He was visibly thinking of the proper course of action. Though Karnak was a gar as well, in that situation, Klentja held seniority and would be the final decision maker.

"Clean it up. We fly on," he said without a look in Karnak's direction.

Smarlo barked orders at all around. Orcs that were leisurely spread around the area lurched into motion, cleaning up what little they had unpacked.

Karnak followed Klentja. He needed a minute with the older gar. "Klentja!" he yelled.

Gar Klentja stopped in his tracks, not turning to meet the younger gar's gaze. The pines swayed above them in the mountain breeze. If the circumstances were different, their location might have been a beautiful place to visit.

"You won't even look at me!" Karnak accused. "What are we doing?"

Klentja tensed as though he were about to turn around, but he only said, "We must fly on, Plak." They both winced at the older gar's mistake. Finally, he did turn around to face him. "Karnak. I meant Karnak. I'm sorry. We must fly on."

The large orc saw sorrow in Klentja's features, deeply etched, rooted somewhere far within him. The old gar spun on his heel and traipsed through the pines toward his wyvern. Karnak watched him disappear around a bend in the path.

They flew on to Lakjo, not having the cover of night. The Borok and Calrok squadrons' approach to the rebel stronghold of Lakjo in the early evening, while the sun still shone, could prove to be an advantage. The Lakjo orcs would have to adjust to the brightness in contrast to the interior of their mountain fort.

There was no advantage to be had, though. There had clearly been a scout. As Karnak and Klentja led their squadrons near to Lakjo, a singular figure wearing a long fur cloak about his armor rose through the air on the back of his wyvern. Klentja raised a hand signal and stayed the two squadrons, who were several leagues behind them. The wyvern squadrons began to circle in the air, holding their position, looking very much like buzzards awaiting some near-death meal.

The fur-cloaked orc rose to meet the two gars, not getting close enough to aggravate the already tense wyverns. Ker's reptilian skin shook on her neck, her small spikes and horns bristling.

"Klentja, it is good to see you, my dear friend!" he yelled over the mountain winds.

Klentja did not reply. Karnak wondered what he was thinking, but the round gar's face betrayed no emotion. The fur-cloaked orc nodded, also unsure of Klentja's thoughts. He turned to Karnak and gave him a genuinely amused smile.

"If I did not know better, my eyes would have seen my old friend, Plak. You must be Karnak, all grown. You look so much like him," the fur-cloaked orc continued.

Karnak looked to Klentja, hoping for some sign of what was to come from him. But finally, he could take it no more. "You must be Zotar?" Karnak asked more than stated.

"I am."

"Then you must know why we were sent here."

"I do," he replied calmly.

How can he be so calm if he knows why we're here? Where are his forces? What are you doing, Klentja? Karnak's mind raced. None of their situation sat right within him.

"Do *you* know why you were sent here, young Gar?" Zotar asked.

Klentja suddenly shifted himself in his saddle so he could also look upon the young gar. Both of the old orc warriors waited for him to answer.

"We were sent to end the rebel threat," Karnak replied with the obvious.

"On the surface, this is true. But why were you really sent here? Think of the sorcerer." Zotar pressed.

All of a sudden, it was as if the words Belguv had shared about King Sahr's thoughts lined up with the story Jaernok Tur had told him when they had first met. "I was sent to exterminate the ones that would stand against Jaernok Tur." It was curious how raw the words were when they came out of his mouth.

"Now, why would King Sahr want that? What does the sorcerer offer him?"

"Whatever it is, he no longer cares for his own people." Karnak surprised himself at how easily the statement came out. He may have said too much.

"Doesn't sound like a king worth following to me," Zotar gave a sideways shrug.

Karnak shook his head in confusion. He understood that, in order to accomplish a mission, a leader needed his followers to be in unity behind him. That was true of king or gar. It was also true some would not follow and would need to be cut out of the ranks for more effectiveness. He struggled as he teetered at the edge of treason against Drelek, the same Drelek for which his father had died. He shot a pleading look to Klentja, who watched the young gar with great compassion.

"Please ..." Karnak barely uttered.

"Karnak," Zotar broke him from his internal wrestle. "The Scar Squadron is of great renown. If you are willing to slay the people here, I will be the first to lay out before you. Take your axe and end me now. You would cut through us with ease. I have seen that axe in action many times when your father wielded it. I always knew your father to be an orc of honor. Not only big in stature, but in character as well.

"But Karnak, you are your own orc. You must forge your own path, your own legacy. We do not rest on the laurels of our fathers. Out of the great respect I had for yours, I will gladly lay down my life for what you think is best, for I knew well the orc that raised you."

Karnak's chin quivered as he looked between the two old warriors who had fought side by side with his father. He was not his father and could not live up to his father's memory. But, Zotar was asking him to be Karnak, not Plak. Klentja only waited for his response, taking neither side.

"And you?" Karnak asked the rotund old warrior. "You give me nothing. Is this some test of loyalty? As you were a friend to my father, I thought you were becoming one to me."

"Oh, but I am!" Klentja choked out. It was as though he had endeavored to be emotionless all day and wall up his words as securely as he could, but that wall had cracked. "I see in you a future for our people, unlike any we have known. I am old. And old orcs speak of honor and legacy. As the After draws near to us, we no longer think of what we have but what we leave behind.

"I won't be able to carry our future. It does not matter whether the threat comes from within or from Tarrine or even from Kelvur. Things are in motion we do not yet understand. Greater battles wait ahead that we do not yet see. But I have seen how you care first. I have seen compassion. Sympathy. Character. And regardless of what you choose now, young Gar,

I will stand beside you. I will hope for a legacy greater than myself."

Karnak gripped Dalkeri in his great hand. He felt the power of the axe vibrate through his fingers. The orange stone glinted, and magic flame burned bright around Fire Storm. And in that fire flashed a memory in his mind. Or was it a prophecy? He did not know.

He saw the young orc boy standing in the collapsing square of Renjak, flames all around. The young orc's devastation was as clear as when Karnak had seen it that horrible night. But something strange happened in the vision, and the boy's face morphed into another. One he knew. One he loved. The face of his son, Gernot.

Karnak slammed Dalkeri back into the saddle loop, recoiling his hand to erase the image from his mind as quickly as possible. But the phantom thought was seared into place. He thought of Tanessa and Gernot at home in Calrok, playing in the field of flowers that sloped behind their cozy home. They would be out there, enjoying the last bit of sunshine before the night covered the coastal orc city.

Tears flowed freely from his eyes. All the while, the old orc warriors watched him.

"You would slay your oldest friend? And his people? The women and children? To stand with me?"

Not knowing exactly what the young gar was thinking, Klentja let out a heavy sigh and visibly slumped into his saddle. With a quiver and a hint of exasperation, he replied, "I would not prefer it."

"And you," Karnak turned his tear-streaked face toward Zotar. "You would just lay down your life?"

"As my old friend has said, I would not prefer it. But," Zotar chose his words carefully. "I want to see Drelek thrive again. If the only way for you to get close to the king is through my death, then so be it. What kingdom can thrive with a king who does not care for his people?"

Everything had changed so much since his visit to Ruk. Jaernok Tur, the sorcerer from Kelvur, had brought war upon them. Karnak wondered for a fleeting moment what Kelvur looked like. How had that land fared under the march of Jaernok Tur? Regardless, Drelek was Karnak's land—the land and the peoples he was responsible to protect—and he could not deny the threat was from within.

At the end of the day, though, his decision would change much. The worst part was, he could not see how. All he could see was the decision before him, and he knew in his heart there was only one option that was right.

Tanessa, forgive me.

"Zotar," the tension between them balanced on a dagger's edge. "I hope you have a good plan. For now, you have the orcs to carry it out. But I will give account for how they are treated. Make no mistake, I will not let them be thrown into the mire. I will fight for them like a storm fights the flower. I will be a relentless fury."

Karnak placed a large orc finger to his brow and bowed slightly in the customary action to signify honor toward another.

Zotar returned the gesture. "I have no doubt you will. And I would expect nothing less."

"Thank you," Klentja said aloud, grateful for the outcome.

"Don't thank me yet," Karnak replied. "If Zotar can't lead us to victory, we march straight to our own deaths. Even worse, our families become traitors to the king."

"I have a plan already in motion," Zotar said, assuring them both. Suddenly he laughed as he remembered something rather funny to him. "I also have a letter for you."

Karnak's features scrunched in confusion.

Zotar enjoyed the look and the playful suspense but continued, "Perhaps you know of a Reglese from Ruk?"

Karnak, Son of Plak, Gar of Calrok,

I write to you with all haste, My Gar. I learned that you would be moving our brave Scar Cliffs warriors to Lakjo and needed to get this message to you.

King Sahr has quickly become a frequent visitor to my tavern here in Ruk. Better than we could have hoped for! I, of course, have shown him great hospitality and have engaged him in many conversations. As you no doubt know, Belguv and I were able to learn much from our interaction with him.

But I write this letter and seal it, hoping it finds you alone. I have learned of another part of the king's grand plan for conquest.

The sorcerer orc from Kelvur has promised many things to King Sahr, who seems to be wildly excited about his new friendship. The sorcerer's promises come with tasks to complete.

I have learned that once the king wipes out the rebellion, Jaernok Tur—I think that is the sorcerer's name—will bring soldiers over from Kelvur. Those soldiers will be at King Sahr's command. I hear they even have giants! Worst of all, King Sahr said he planned to give Calrok over to the incoming troops! He wants them to have a home that is easy to reach from Kelvur. He wants them to bring more and more troops.

He is mad with conquest. I think back to the stories of Torak the Terrible. I don't think the king knows what gift he opens with this Jaernok Tur. I fear it's not a gift at all but rather a curse.

I do not know what you would have me do next. My first thought was to run back to Calrok, to defend our home. Which, of course, you know, is a strange notion and against my nature. But I realize I am our only source here at Ruk. I will stand firm. I hope you do not destroy the rebellion before we are able to come up with a solution to this new problem.

This is the third copy of this letter. The pigeon keeper here in Ruk assures me his birds know the way to Lakjo, but I wanted to make sure you received this terrible news.

Save our home, My Gar. We are all counting on you.

With all honor,

Reglese

CHAPTER TWENTY-FIVE

AN AMBUSH

The Talon Squadron lay in wait for their prey. They had perched in rocky outcroppings spread out before the mountain range.

Tozer barreled over the rocky ridge, swooping down the slope in a mad dash. His old griffin lost some feathers in the great effort for speed. The grizzled old guardian signaled that the wyvern squadron from Ghun-Ra would crest the ridge soon.

The squadron was well hidden, and if the orcs came from the direction Tozer had, the guardians would easily get the jump on the wyvern squadron. It was the best advantage they had.

Tozer landed his griffin behind a large rock and shot a look over to Pernden. The young captain nodded to his friend. Seeing the dependable guardian's confident smile before the thick of battle always calmed him. Pernden made eye contact with Danner Kane, who signaled to the guardians on his side, then with Nera, who mimicked the action on her side.

Their chance approached. If they weren't able to halt the wyvern squadron, Drelek would solidify its hold on Whitestone, and the war would be lost. Pernden shook the thought from his mind. Defeat was not an option.

Long minutes passed like an eternity. Every guardian was on edge, and the tension was sensed by their griffins. Man and beast connected through the anticipation.

And then it happened.

The orcs crested the ridge before them. First one. Then another. Then even more. They flew in no recognizable formation.

Good, Pernden thought. *They don't expect a thing.*

The wyverns' membranous wings fluttered in the wind as they soared easily over the ridge toward the rocky outcroppings. The guardians would have to time it right. Pernden lifted a gloved hand to stay them. On his signal, they would attack.

Closer and closer the wyverns swooped, until one of the horned creatures sent out a bloodcurdling screech. It had spotted one of the griffins farther up the long slope. Pernden swung his arm forward, and the entire Talon Squadron launched into the air, each targeting a wyvern rider of its own and racing directly toward its prey.

The orcs yelled out at each other, noticing the ambush. The wyverns scattered without organization, preferring their chances one on one with the guardians. But the unwary orcs did not know they faced the Talon Squadron.

Wyverns and griffins collided in a furious battle of claw and talon, maw and beak. Guardians sliced and stabbed at orcs with swords and spears, while the orcs returned the violence with axes and lances.

Pernden and Rocktail hurtled toward a particularly foul orc, but before they could engage, a javelin blasted the orc from his mount and sent him falling to the earth.

Rocktail spun and dipped around the wyvern as Pernden sliced through the air with Wintertide, sending a blade of ice flying at the riderless creature. The magical ice blade connected with the unsuspecting wyvern's long neck, severing its head and sending it plummeting to the ground below.

Pernden looked in the direction from which the javelin had come and saw Danner Kane shifting his attention to a nearby orc.

Focus on your own fight, he mentally scolded his mentor.

The initial surprise of the ambush and its advantage had worn off. Orc and man clashed mid-sky. Pernden saw a flash of lightning smash against an orc and his wyvern, splattering and sparking onto another nearby. Other orcs in the vicinity scattered to gain more separation from their allies. Pernden smiled at Nera's ferocity. Those orcs did not know what they had unleashed upon themselves. His smile was short-lived as he caught, out of the corner of his eye, one of his own guardians careening into a rocky outcropping.

He shifted his focus to another orc and kicked his feet, spurring Rocktail into action once more. They flew directly at the rider, who glared at them crazily and sped toward them—an aerial showdown. The orc raised a throwing axe above his head, and his greenish-grey muscular arms hurled the axe end over end at the young captain. Rocktail whirled into a barrel roll, saving his rider. The axe missed by only inches. The griffin flourished out of the roll, swooping just outside of the wyvern's biting reach. Rocktail swung around in a wide loop to face them, again.

It was Pernden's turn. The orc held a long pike in his grasp, ready to chop at Pernden on the next pass. The young man was not going to give him the chance. He held Wintertide poised in both hands. Energy rumbled through his body. In the fury of real battle, Pernden felt the weight of its power for the first time. He had not known it in his sparring with Nera. In war, he intuited more about the sword than he had previously imagined.

Pernden swung the sword, the energy welling up a battle cry within him. Ice swirled ahead of the blade, forming into a massive lance. Pernden's muscles tightened in his arms as he leaned into the power. The more he let out the cry within, the more the power rose. He saw the eyes of his opponent widen just before the frigid lance impaled him and removed him from his mount.

Rocktail's razor sharp talons and beak scraped and slashed at the wyvern. Pernden quickly chopped the creature's long neck, finishing it as well.

Their plan had worked to near perfection, and it seemed as though they would decimate the Ghun-Ra wyvern squadron. That is, until Tozer yelled, "More! There's another squadron!"

Pernden turned toward the ridge to the north as the last orc wyvern in another squadron crested. The guardians stood at a disadvantage.

Nera struck down another rider with a blast of electric energy from Santoralier, which returned almost instantly to her hands.

She flew near to Pernden, and some of the other nearby guardians joined them. Their best chance was to form up and meet these new riders head-on while the others finished the first squadron. Unfortunately, they were outnumbered and already growing battle-weary.

Pernden looked quickly to Nera. He regretted not telling her what his heart had held for so long. Her golden eyes locked onto his, and he knew she already knew.

He faced the oncoming wyvern squadron and raised Wintertide high in the air. He released another battle cry that was joined by the small group of Griffin Guardians that rode with him. They flew with a speed and ferocity that would strike the bravest of hearts with fear, directly at the charging wyvern riders.

Before they could engage, a violet blast of magical energy launched the lead orc right off his wyvern, spinning him away awkwardly through the air. A massive falcon, almost as large as a griffin and speckled like the stars, collided with the confused wyvern, as a man on top of the creature loosed arrow after arrow at the other orcs.

The squad of Talon guardians halted in surprise as a host of pegasi riders engaged the orcs. The equine creatures flew with a beauty and grace that was stunning to behold. The shimmering armor of their riders danced in the sunlight. An orc axe slammed into one of the riders, sending him toppling. Pernden spurred his stunned group back into action.

They flew into the chaos of the aerial battle, weaving and dodging until they could connect their weapons with an orc or wyvern.

A nastily wounded orc turned his attention to Pernden while the young leader finished off another with the aid of an elf. The orc charged him, hoping for another kill before he succumbed to his mortal wounds.

Tozer intercepted the wide-open maw of the savage wyvern. It clamped its teeth into the veteran's armor, piercing it easily. Its savage hind claws tore at the old griffin, killing it quickly. Tozer screamed in pain as the jaws crushed the life out of him.

A lavender fire blast smashed into the side of the wyvern and the wounded orc, ending his lingering nuisance. The wyvern relinquished its hold on the man. He fell alongside the old griffin. They came to rest on the ground below with their deceased enemies.

The magic-wielding elf with flowing silver hair flew up next to Pernden. Her lavender eyes were filled with compassion, and she examined him to ensure his health. Satisfied that the guardian was alright, she spun an intricate staff, glowing purple, from one hand to her other and rode off to find another orc.

Pernden stole a glance at Tozer, far below. Another mentor and friend was gone.

King Garron, if one could still call him a king, looked like a sack of bones to Jolan. The aide that was brought in to spruce him up had done her best to make him look presentable. She had bathed him, and the new High Commander admitted the king smelled better, even if he didn't look it. She had dressed him in kingly garb, though none of it fit well, and she insisted Jolan get him to a tailor soon. She had even brushed his mop of hair and his beard. By all accounts, he would appear normal to those who did not know him well. But Jolan knew.

He could see it in the way the dark circles ringed the young king's eyes. He could see the thinness in his cheeks and the shakiness of his now slender limbs. Jolan remembered the strong muscles of a young warrior prince, but this Garron had withered to half the man he was before.

"Take him to the dining hall and put some food in his belly," Jolan commanded the aide, squeezing Garron's scrawny arm. "Meat. Put meat back onto his bones."

The aide agreed and slipped under one of the king's arms, ushering him down the corridor. It struck Jolan that he couldn't be sure the last time Garron had been out of the king's chambers. Certainly, he hadn't been seen by the people since shortly after the rite ceremony of King Farrin.

When it was completely quiet in the king's chamber, he heard Jaernok Tur speaking in some foreign orc language behind the unusual curtains where the orc retreated. Jolan assumed it was of some magical skew, as it did not sound like the language orcs used in regular conversation. Jaernok Tur's words were ... unsettling. That was the best way Jolan could describe them. The effect was amplified by the way the sorcerer's voice echoed in eerie whispers.

Jolan did not want to listen in, but he could not help himself. He found himself drawn toward the curtained area. The strange markings in the weavings came from some language he did not recognize. His fingers ran along the weave, feeling the unusual raised lines. One in particular looked of ancient origin, as if it were from some lost language rather than any spoken among the races of his day. He studied it with great intent until the hair on the back of his neck raised in revulsion.

"You are of curious mind, High Commander."

He felt the breath of the whisper on his neck. He froze, unsure whether to turn and face the dark sorcerer. He had been so caught up by the markings, he hadn't realized the orc had stopped speaking behind the curtains.

How did he get behind me? Jolan wondered, terrified at the notion.

"You wonder at my power," Jaernok Tur stated, more than asked.

"Yes," Jolan responded, still not turning to face the orc.

"Ask what you would."

Jolan took the invitation and converted it to courage. He faced the shrouded orc, who stood inches from him. His gnarled skin, almost reptilian, was pocked and shaded. His wicked tusks yellowed at the bottom. The sight of the sorcerer was terrifying. Though, his eyes of fire gold, not currently marred by the blackness of his magic, were normal enough to spur Jolan into the question that had nagged at him.

"Could you bring back my son?"

"Oh, Commander," Jaernok Tur's features softened, and he clicked his tongue at the commander like a father to a toddler. "The power you ask is great."

"I-I just ..." Jolan struggled to find his words. "I thought, if you could raise the dead ... Maybe ..."

Jaernok Tur gave the commander a rather wicked smile, though Jolan thought it was the orc's attempt at a sympathetic one. "The power to give life back to the dead is a great power, indeed. I have heard tell of very few magicians, sorcerers, or even wizards to have ever accomplished the feat. And even those claims are questioned among the learned."

"So ... you can't?" Jolan asked cautiously, trying not to insult the sorcerer.

"I cannot," he replied with a hint of disappointment. Clearly, it was an ability he wished to possess. "But I know of one who might be able to."

Suddenly, Jolan wanted to know everything. "The one you speak to when you retreat behind the curtains?"

Another wicked smile spread at Jaernok Tur's amusement. "You are a curious man-kin."

For the first time, Jolan was not afraid in the sorcerer's presence. The man had a renewed determination. If there was any chance whatsoever that Jaernok Tur could lead him to a place where he could get his son back, he would follow. He no longer doubted or hesitated. He thought only of how he could accomplish the mission so he might see his son again.

As if Jaernok Tur could read his mind—though Jolan wasn't sure the orc could—the sorcerer continued, "I can show you ways of mystery and magic of an ancient variety. With you by my side, we can be invincible. And maybe, just maybe, together we could bring back your son."

After the battle, the warriors gathered their fallen. They brought all the elf-kin and guardians back to Clawstone, where they set up rite stands for each. The elves were grateful for their compatriots' inclusion in the ceremonies, content with the means by which the guardians honored their dead.

Initially, the guardians intended to leave their orc foes out for the buzzards and scavengers. The elf-kin insisted they honor the orc warriors the way that Drelek peoples would. They made short work of it, though, as the silver-haired mage utilized her magical abilities to bury them among the rocky outcroppings where the battle had taken place.

The help of the elf-kin had been instrumental in the battle earlier that day, and Pernden had invited them to Clawstone without hesitation. He knew, and was affirmed by Danner Kane's wisdom, that they would be vital allies for the next phase of their plans. Taking back Whitestone from the sorcerer's grasp would be difficult, to say the least. They would welcome all the help they could get.

When the rite stands were lit ablaze in Clawstone, hidden deep within Whitestone Forest, a celebration ensued for their victory and new allies. They would celebrate the brave sacrifices of their brethren and their entries into Kerathane. Though the battle had seen losses, the leaders recognized the importance of the festivities. They needed to encourage their people to move forward.

Man and elf intermingled seamlessly, as though they'd been friends for decades. There was great food and laughter. A table of honor had been set up at the head of the long feast table. There sat the leaders of the two groups, finally getting to sit and speak with each other.

Danner Kane presented a stern elf, Commander Fario, to Pernden. The elf commander quickly introduced the other three with him: Ralowyn and Lanryn of Loralith and Merrick, son of Grell, the huntsman of Tamaria. Pernden acquainted them with Nera, who sat by his side.

"I must say, I am surprised to see a man with this band of elves," Pernden spoke directly to Merrick. "Of course, it's no complaint, I assure you. Your bird of prey was a spectacle, to be sure."

"Valurwind," Merrick explained. Ralowyn touched his elbow, though, as if he had said too much. "We are among friends," he comforted her but took note of her suggestion not to share the mystical bird's name with just anyone.

"Valurwind?" Pernden asked.

"An astral falcon of great mystery," Merrick continued. "I am still forging our bond."

"Where is the falcon now?"

"Well, that I do not quite understand yet."

"Valurwind returns to her own plane of reality among the stars," Ralowyn explained. "She comes at the call of the one who knows her name."

"So, anyone could call upon this magnificent creature?" Nera asked.

"No. Not without this," Merrick produced the beautiful crystal and stone bird from his cloak. It glimmered in the firelight. "There is some sort of connection with this carving that helps her hear me wherever I am."

"To be able to bond with the falcon is no small feat," Ralowyn added. "It requires more than the knowledge of her name."

"A gift to be sure," Kane nodded at the thought of such a powerful ally.

"Yes," Merrick agreed, nodding at the crystalline falcon in his hand. He had grown fond of her quickly and hoped the bond was not only forming on his end. He also recognized he might run into people with ill intentions regarding Valurwind. He did not sense lustful gazes at the bird here, but Ralowyn's warning alerted him that he must protect Valurwind from those that might long for her power.

"I am thankful for your involvement today. But I admit, I still do not know the purpose of your timely arrival," Pernden brought the group of leaders back to their present concerns.

Merrick pocketed the statuette and turned to Pernden with heaviness. "I bear bad news."

"I believe our hearts are well prepared for any more bad news that might come. We've had much of late," Pernden replied with a resolved sigh and a weak smile.

A dragon in Tarrine, however, was a greater surprise than any of them had imagined. Merrick told them about the battle near Tamaria, the closest recorded in as long as any could recount. He told them of the surviving guardian nursed back to health by his sister. He told them of their trip up the Palori River to the farmhouse. He told them of the encounter with the orcs at the Palori Ruins. And he described, with the best detail he could recall, the dragon.

The stunning news of the dragon impressed upon them the ever-increasing need for haste in their plan. Should Drelek decide to use the dragon to fortify Whitestone before they could win it back from the orc sorcerer, their odds of ever retaking their city would be slim.

Recognizing the increased pressure, Pernden quickly filled their new allies in on the situation in Whitestone. He told them of the mission to the Gant Sea Narrows to retrieve the Alkhoren Mirror. He told them of the mirror's terrible purpose, which brought a tinge of increased curiosity from Lanryn.

"The mirror is a doorway?" the elf mage asked.

"Yes, I have seen the magic myself," Danner Kane affirmed.

"How did it work?"

"I do not know."

"Describe it to me," he pressed.

"It has rune markings along the frame that glowed. Then the light flowed like a river around the mirror. It was like all the sound in the room was sucked away, and the walls began to bend. Suddenly, we were thrown backward by the power. We saw smoke, and then the sorcerer stepped through it. One of my sources back in Whitestone says that the sorcerer uses great power to open the door and bring soldiers through."

"So, it takes great effort for him to accomplish such a feat?" Ralowyn pondered out loud.

"I can't say for sure," Danner Kane admitted.

Commander Fario asked them questions about Whitestone's guard situation so he could put together a tactical plan. Unfortunately, they had few answers to his questions, as their information about the forces hiding within the walls of the castle was limited.

They did, however, have very accurate knowledge of the layout of the castle, and Fario seemed glad for it. They knew Jaernok Tur and the mirror were holed up in the king's chambers, and they knew all the routes that led to it, including balcony doorways. Commander Fario's highly experienced tactical wheels spun inside his head. He ordered one of his elf-kin to bring him parchment and a quill.

"Where is this guardian now? Certainly, he would have seen you back to Whitestone ..." Nera's words stalled as the thought of a guardian returning to Whitestone in its current state horrified her. Danner Kane and Pernden both caught on to her thought.

Before any of them could inquire further, Merrick answered their question. "I don't know. As I said, we were separated at the Macintroh farm. I had to help them get away. And we've not been able to reunite. In all honesty, I had hoped they would be at Whitestone already."

"I would have heard of such an arrival from one of my sources," Danner Kane assured everyone.

"Who was the guardian?" Nera asked.

Pernden was struck with the same curiosity. They had lost so many guardians over the past several months, it could have been anyone.

"His name was Orin."

"Orin lives?" Pernden shot up in his chair. Pools formed in his eyes, and his face was a mixture of confused emotions. Nera placed her hand on his back, a tear streaking down her own cheek, rolling to the side of a wide smile across her face.

"I pray it so," Merrick said. "In our short time together, he became to me as close a friend as one can have. Almost like a brother. I found him to be of high quality. If my sister must be out in the world facing dangers, I would want her to be with him. And Coal and Ezel, of course. They would make quite the formidable group, I'd say."

Merrick smiled at the thought of the group's abilities. He had grown more comfortable with the idea that they could handle anything thrown their way. On the other hand, he was concerned they hadn't yet made it to Whitestone. He wondered what they might have encountered to delay them.

"He still lived when you separated, though?" Pernden asked, through streams of tears.

"As far as I could see. And I have hope in them," Merrick assured him, glad he could bring some semblance of good tidings to his new allies. "Who is he to you?"

"He's not *like* a brother to me," Pernden replied, his smile shining in the firelight. "He *is* my brother."

Chapter Twenty-Six

Garvawk Warriors

O rin pressed back against one of the heavy barrels and twisted, stretching out some of the aches he still felt. He was careful not to go too far, as he didn't want to reinjure his ribs. The stretch felt good and helped him breathe easier.

The wagon ride had been quite pleasant. The cozy nest that Tobin, the halfling wagoner, had created for them was more than comfortable enough for the weary travelers. Orin had only awoken from his long rest a few minutes previously. Little Ezel snored next to him, cuddled up in a fur. Ellaria had fallen asleep at some point along the way, as well.

Occasionally, the wagon bumped hard on a rock and startled the nappers, but those rocks were few and far between. The road from Crossdin to Galium was well traveled and maintained by the two cities. They had wisely removed most of the dangerous rocks over the centuries people had been traveling the road.

Overall, they'd had a relatively smooth trip, or as Tobin had put it, "a wonderful journey experience." Amidst the rocking of the wagon, the cozy comforts of the nest, the smell of fresh air mixed with the sweet pipe weed Tobin puffed, and the wagoner's unending storytelling—for he had a soothing and kindly voice—they all experienced perfect conditions for rest.

Everyone, that is, except Coal.

The sun was setting low in the west behind them as they rolled into the outer hills of Galium. Tobin had apparently had a pleasant time with Coal in the front of the wagon and offered to bring the group to his own home to stay the night. He even offered some of his wife's famous cooking, or at least he claimed it to be famous.

"It's the best cooking you'll have had your whole trip. I promise you that. And then you could meet Button!" He added, realizing the fortunate bonus.

"No. No," Coal said as gently as he could muster. "We couldn't impose on your family. They must be missing you terribly."

"It would be no imposition! No, none at all," Tobin assured him. "Anyways, you can't go on to Whitestone this late. It's a long road, and you'll need the markets to be opened so you can prepare provisions for the trip."

"Too true," Orin added from the back.

Coal whirled in his seat, looking at Orin as though he were crazy. "No. Tobin has been all too kind to us. We couldn't take more of his kindness. We can stay at the nearest inn."

"Nonsense. Nonsense! You stay with me and mine, and you save your coin for your supplies. As you said, your mission is of great importance. It is the least my family can do."

"He does have wonderful hospitality," Orin chimed.

Coal glared at the man, who buttoned his lips tight together, hiding a wry smile as he sunk behind a crate and out of view.

"It's settled then!" Tobin brimmed. "Oh boy, I can't wait for you to meet Button. She is the pride of her daddy's eye, of course. And maybe Lenor is making lamb stew. Oooh, we'd be in for a treat. A real treat, I'll tell you! I'd wager it's the best lamb stew in all Tarrine. Certainly, in Galium. It's savory, but also ..."

Coal stole another glance toward the back but only glimpsed Orin's amused eyes peeking over the crate he hid behind. The dwarf said nothing, but Orin could read the question on his face: *Why would you do this to me?*

Tobin had been right. Lenor was making lamb stew, and it most certainly was a treat. Whether Coal wanted to admit it or not, he had thoroughly enjoyed roughhousing with tiny Button before she was off to bed for tuck-ins, a task Tobin gladly took upon himself.

Lenor was a handsome dwarf woman with long brunette hair braided like a net with stone beads accenting where the hairs crossed. She was also a wonderful hostess, kind and humble, quick to serve her guests. Her hospitality matched that of her generous husband's.

While Tobin was doing story time with Button, Lenor led the group into the sitting room, a cozy spot toward the front of their house, which was half-built into the side of the hill. There were several other houses carved slightly into the same hill, protecting them from weather and, of course, helping keep the homes warm during the winter.

The sitting room was cozy enough, though Orin and Ellaria had to duck under a beam to enter and found it more comfortable to sit on the floor near the fireplace than to squeeze awkwardly into one of the small chairs. Coal and Ezel gladly found two wingbacks with subtle floral patterns that suited them just fine.

Lenor brought in some tea and served it from a small side table, making sure to serve everyone before making a cup of her own and plopping into a seat next to Ezel.

The little grey gnome bobbed his head and signed to her pleasantly. She looked at him curiously but didn't lose her jovial smile.

"He says, 'Thank you for your kindness,'" Coal said after a hot sip of his tea.

"Oh. Well, yer very welcome now, aren't ye," Lenor replied to Ezel. "Er, he can hear me, then, yeah?"

Ezel nodded the answer and disappeared behind his teacup. Somehow, he had gotten the biggest one.

"We are grateful," Ellaria said. "We have had a long journey and have longer still."

"Aye," Lenor said. "On yer way to Whitestone, is it? Some terrible mission, Tobin said to me. But he's been known to get a little excited with a story or two," she giggled into her cup.

"He certainly likes telling stories," Coal half-grumbled.

His statement made Lenor laugh harder. "There is no shortage of words from my husband," she agreed. "But his words are more sweet than bitter, and his heart is sweeter than honey."

"I can see that," Ellaria agreed with the dwarf. "He was quite adamant about us staying with you. Surely, you would let us pay you something for the hospitality. We would have spent the coin at an inn, if not for your generosity."

Lenor raised a hand while she finished her sip. "No, no. That wouldn't do at all."

Orin shook his head as the steam from his tea swirled in front of his face. He smelled the scent of chamomile and something else but only barely over the fragrant wood in the low crackling fire. "I have been so very surprised by the kindness of the people of Tarrine."

"Why's that?" Tobin asked, having just entered the sitting room. He poured himself a cup of tea, brushed the hair away from Lenor's face so he could give her a kiss, and settled into the last seat, next to Coal. "I thought you were a guardian of Whitestone."

"I am," Orin confirmed. "But much of my life has been spent in or around Whitestone or along the front range of the Drelek Mountains. I've had very little time with others in Tarrine."

"You need to get out more, my boy!" Tobin corrected him, without scolding.

"I see that, now."

"It hasn't all been roses," Ellaria pointed out, remembering their encounter with King Hugen in Tamaria. Or their encounter with the faery king.

"That's true," Orin agreed. "I was thinking about something my commander had been saying a while back. He wondered why we would send our people to fight the forces of Drelek. Why wouldn't the rest of Tarrine rally and send fighters from their cities? He wondered why it was only Whitestone sacrificing for everyone else."

"It is a noble thing the Griffin Guard does," Lenor answered. "But ye can't believe ye do it all alone, can ye? There's the stone garvawks here in Galium, of course."

"Garvawks?" Ellaria asked.

"Vicious creatures," Coal explained. "Beautiful, but terrible. Beautiful at first ... When they are statues, that is. Like a beautiful winged panther, they are."

"Like a gargoyle—" Tobin began.

"No," Coal corrected. "Gargoyles are ugly creatures. Always stone, even when they attack. Garvawks are more like cats.

Impossibly clever. Darker than the deepest shadows of far-flung caverns. They hunt their prey, creeping among the stalactites. You don't even know they're upon you until they swoop down on you with their bat-like wings. They haunt the mines and caverns surrounding Kalimandir, as well."

Ezel shuddered, trying to keep his large teacup steady in his little hands.

"How does Galium husband them if they're so dangerous?" Ellaria asked, intrigued.

"Ha!" Coal laughed. "No one could grow such beasts. It's an ancient spell, you see."

"For some reason, the garvawks have a connection to the magic that thrives in the stone, just like our people do," Lenor added. "For some reason, which we do not understand, only dwarfs have been able to tame the beasts."

"Tame!" Coal blurted. "Far from tame, the monsters. First, you have to catch them, and only a mage can turn them to stone with the ancient spell. Then you have to carve the proper rune into its shoulder."

"Wouldn't that be painful?" Ellaria asked.

"They don't seem to feel the cuts they take while stone," Lenor said. "Though it is strange how they are always scarred over when they are awoken."

"Awoken?"

"Aye," Coal said. "Once a garvawk is caught ... turned to stone, I mean, the mark is etched. Then, a dwarven warrior is assigned to that garvawk. They are given the proper command to awaken the beast, and for some reason I don't understand, the beast listens to the warrior."

"I think, perhaps, it is because the warrior wakes the beast from its stone prison. Though I'm not sure they think it to be a prison. They are cats, after all. Surely, they don't mind the nap," Lenor finished cheerily.

"And these garvawk warriors are the ones that fight the Drelek wyvern squadrons here in Galium?" Ellaria concluded.

"That's it. And there are griffins trained to defend us, as well," Tobin added.

"And if ye don't forget the Riders of Loralith, certainly ye must know ye aren't alone in this fight, Orin?" Lenor asked.

"Oh, I don't think that, now. And I don't think I ever really believed that," Orin assured her. "Though I worry for my commander. He already struggled with our sacrifices and losses. By now, he must know his son, Anlon, was lost. I can't imagine how Commander Jolan has taken the news. I fear that bitterness could consume him."

"Then it shall be yer duty to tell him yer story," Lenor encouraged him.

"Maybe he needs to get out more, too," Tobin added, stealing a tea biscuit from the cookie jar on the side table. The halfling's hunger seemed insatiable. He sank back into his chair, realizing his comment had gotten him caught in the act. He smiled sheepishly at his dwarven wife, who feigned disapproval.

"I think that might be an important thing for the whole Griffin Guard," Orin said. "We should take rotations among the cities. Perhaps it will help us remember what we are fighting for. Or rather for whom."

"Seems wise to me, young guardian," Lenor said, pouring more tea into Orin's cup.

"Right now, it's most important for the Guard to know what we fight against," Orin said thoughtfully.

"Ah, the bad news, right?" Tobin asked, lighting his pipe and puffing small clouds of smoke.

"Yes. What is this bad news?" Lenor asked over her shoulder, refilling Ezel's cup before sitting again.

"A dragon," Coal said, and the whole room went silent.

Tobin laughed nervously at the silence. "A dragon? There hasn't been a dragon in Tarrine for generations. You can't mean a real-life dragon," he said incredulously.

"Aye, that's what I mean."

"Here? In Tarrine? Where? How far away was it?" Tobin's pipe drooped, limp in his teeth. For the first time, the group saw an emotion other than joy on the face of the plump halfling.

"We came across the monster at Palori Ruins. It was under the charge of Drelek orcs," Ellaria explained.

"Palori Ruins?"

"Calm, my dear husband," Lenor said.

"That's why we must get to Whitestone as quickly as possible. We have to warn the Guard," Orin explained.

"I think maybe ye don't."

The whole room went silent again, and everyone stared at the dwarven woman who took another sip of her tea.

"What do you mean?" Coal asked.

"Well, I think ye'll be needing to talk to one of those garvawk warriors in the morn," Lenor spoke with a calm consistency, and her voice comforted them even with the lack of explanation. Then she added, "My brother."

Lotmeag Kandersaw was a barrel of a dwarf. His armor was heavy and of obvious dwarven design. His helmet had a singular horn on the top with long, dyed red hairs attached to the point. When Tobin arrived at the castle with the ragtag group,

Lotmeag grimaced as he watched them ascend the stairs. He stood at the top of the steps leading to the castle's main entrance, and his long brunette beard wagged in the wind.

"What is it ye have here, Tobin?" Lotmeag asked. He nodded to the dispersing garvawk warriors to let them know he would be right behind them as they went inside the castle.

Galium's castle was impressive. Much like the houses built halfway into the hills surrounding the city, the castle jutted in precise angles at the front and melded into the mountain seamlessly. The renown of dwarven stonecraft was on full display in the majestic architecture.

"Travelers with important news, Lotmeag," Tobin replied.

The sturdy dwarf released a prolonged sigh. It wasn't as though he disliked halflings. In fact, there were many whose company he enjoyed. Many worked in the castle, and he knew more around the city. His problem was his sister had chosen Tobin as her husband. The plump halfling had a jovial way about him, but Lotmeag's duties were serious. He wished Tobin would be more serious once in a while. The dwarf doubted the halfling would be able to defend his sister if something were to happen.

At the end of the day, it was Lenor's love for Tobin that encouraged Lotmeag to be cordial. That, and of course, his favorite niece, Button.

Lotmeag scanned the strange company. A man and a woman, a deep gnome, and a dwarf. "What is all this about?" he shook his head wearily.

"Well, you see, I picked these fine folk up in Crossdin as I had space in the wagon. And you know I like to help travelers. Enjoy the company, I do. And well, Coal here was such a joy to converse with on the trip ..."

Coal looked awkwardly at Lotmeag. He had hardly gotten a word in edgewise during their trip. More importantly, he could sense the tension between the garvawk warrior and the halfling and didn't want the dwarf to extend the same frustration onto him by association.

"And anyways, Lenor was making lamb stew. Which you know is a treat. Truly, a treat! But as we were having tea last night, your sister said they should speak with you about the news they bear. And of course, I thought—"

"And what news do ye bear?" Lotmeag finally interrupted the halfling and asked the group, tilting his head in curiosity.

"News of a powerful enemy," Coal started.

"A powerful enemy? And who bears this news?"

Orin watched as Coal unraveled the linen wrappings from his calloused dwarven hand for the first time since they'd met. Coal rubbed at the palm of his sweaty left hand with the thumb of his right. He raised his left hand before him to bear a tattooed dwarven crest on his palm. "Corahl, Prince of Kalimandir, a son of clan Carraignyk."

"Clan Carraignyk?" Lotmeag muttered, taking a step back in surprise. Tobin gasped. The only one not surprised was Ezel. Though Orin and Ellaria knew very little of dwarven history, the surprise on the others' faces was enough to give them pause. The little gnome stood next to Coal with his arms crossed, as if the dwarf had not just revealed a great secret.

"Carraignyk?" Tobin sputtered. "I would have asked Lenor to make a feast!"

When the initial shock had worn off, Lotmeag's mind immediately shifted. "Come with me."

He led them straight through the main entrance into the castle. They hurried after the garvawk warrior, who walked with great determination. They turned a corner and flew past the kitchen filled with halflings and dwarves, preparing what must have been brunch. Tobin's nose nearly carried him away at the aroma of fresh bread, but Ellaria shooed him along.

They turned another corner onto a hallway that moved them into a long, high corridor with high ceilings. Orin guessed they were under the mountain. A set of stairs before them at the end of the corridor rose and split to a second level on either side. As Orin followed, he noted the stone garvawks perched in uniform fashion at the edges of the floor above them. They climbed the stairs to a door at the top that Lotmeag pulled open and entered.

Before Orin followed, he stole a look at the nearest garvawk. It did seem a terrible creature. But it also had a sleek elegance to its frame. He had seen mountain lions before, but even in their stone form, the garvawks looked to have more muscle packed onto their limbs. Their wings gave them a shadowy ominous feel. Behind the garvawk was a smaller door. Orin noticed a door behind each of the garvawks lining the outside of the corridor.

Tobin grabbed at Orin's tunic and ushered him into the room.

"What is this, Lotmeag?" asked a gruff-looking dwarf with a hideous scar over his milky left eye.

"A prince of Kalimandir from clan Carraignyk," he answered hurriedly.

Whispers broke out among the warriors gathered in the room.

"Clan Carraignyk?" The gruff dwarf repeated. "Why bring a prince of Kalimandir to the hall of garvawk warriors? Why not take him to the king?"

"He bears news of a powerful enemy."

"Ah, does he?" The dwarf looked Coal over with his one good eye. "Does he also have a voice of his own? Or did Kalimandir send us a lame prince?"

A ripple of laughter sounded around the room from the gathered warriors.

"Aye, he does have a voice," Coal growled. He moved past the other dwarves in the room until he stood before the gruff dwarf leader. "And he doesn't like the tone of yours."

Orin instinctively placed a hand on the hilt of his sword. He did not know much of dwarven politics, and Coal's recent revelation as a prince of Kalimandir had been news to him. He was not sure if his title was a benefit or a hindrance to their mission.

"And what ye going to do about it, laddy?" The gruff dwarf's grey beard waggled as he leaned into Coal's face.

"I intend to change your mind."

"Oh, is that so?"

For a long moment, they stared at each other, neither revealing anything that would give the other an upper hand. Orin and Ellaria watched in worry.

Suddenly, Coal grabbed the gruff dwarf by the shoulders and slammed his forehead against the older dwarf's forehead.

A raucous cheer erupted from the other dwarfs in the room. One of the dwarves started filling flagons from a nearby barrel of mead, as hearty laughter broke out. Tobin was more than happy to aid in the filling of mugs, especially at the one to three ratio he poured for himself.

The gruff leader was boasting to a nearby dwarf with his arm slung over Coal's shoulder like they were the best of friends.

Orin and Ellaria looked to Ezel for an explanation, but the grey gnome just replied with a grin and a shrug and signed, *"Dwarves."*

As they enjoyed general merriment and fellowship, Coal explained what the group had endured since departing from Tamaria. Ezel used his magic to float mugs and other items into the air to reenact some of the scenes, to the great amusement of the garvawk warriors. And of course, Coal came back to their encounter with the dragon, the primary news they bore. He explained how they needed to get to Whitestone so Orin could rally the Griffin Guard to fight against the Drelek dragon.

When Coal had finished, the gruff dwarf leader, whom they came to learn was Bendur Clagstack, the commander of the garvawk warriors, stood from his stool and stepped away. He looked as though in deep thought. When he turned back toward the group sitting around the table, he said, "We have much to catch ye up on, Son of Clan Carraignyk."

CHAPTER TWENTY-SEVEN

AN ORC GAR'S PATH

K arnak held the crinkled letter from Reglese in his large green hand as he sat near an exterior building high upon the mountain slope of Lakjo. The paper blew awkwardly over itself in the mountain wind, in the same direction the long black hair on Karnak's head waved. The letter had confirmed nearly all his concerns about King Sahr's new friend Jaernok Tur of Kelvur. The letter also gave him much-needed clarity. He was thankful he had chosen not to slay Zotar and his rebels. It was the decision he had felt in his gut to be right. Reglese's letter affirmed that decision.

When his and Gar Klentja's squadrons had landed in Lakjo without any resistance, several of the orcs had been confused. Karnak was not sure all of them would take the news of their shifted allegiance positively. To his surprise, as he explained his concerns regarding the sorcerer of Kelvur and his twisting of their king, his squadron trusted his judgment, and none raised any noise against the change. There were a couple of questions, as orcs worried for their families back in Calrok. Karnak was able to share Reglese's letter and Jaernok Tur's plan to take Calrok away, which ignited greater zeal from the Scar Cliffs Squadron. They would not let the sorcerer take their home so easily.

As he leaned against the building, Karnak stared over the range before him. The sun was setting in the west. The sky's oranges and pinks gave the mountains a warm hue, even against the biting chill of the wind. Smarlo rounded the corner of the stone structure and perched beside his gar. He sat for a minute, enjoying the view.

"I think they're all settled now. Zotar's people are quick to show hospitality. I think they're glad not to be fighting a battle they would not have won," Smarlo said, giving Karnak an update as well as his assessment of the situation. "The wyvern riders have opened their homes for our squadron. Their barracks is far too small to add all of us and Gar Klentja's orcs."

"Good. It will be good for them to see the families of those they will fight beside. It's not just our home at stake but theirs as well. We fight for the same things, even if they are far apart."

"I am glad you chose this path for us."

Karnak paused at the comment. He knew he had chosen the right path for his people, but there were still many details to work out. Whatever the plan was, they needed to make sure Jaernok Tur couldn't bring his troops from Kelvur into Calrok. He did not know how long they would have to fight. What sacrifices would they have to make to endure the war? The path ahead was anything but certain.

"Zotar and Klentja are ready to meet with us," Smarlo said, recognizing he wasn't going to get a response.

"Well, I hope they have a plan, for I can't see the path ahead of us," Karnak admitted.

Smarlo caught the hint of defeat in his oldest friend. "You saved the lives of a whole orc city. You saved the lives of the children and the generations to come in Lakjo. Do you see that as wrong?"

"No. That was right. But we do not know what challenges lie ahead of us now."

"Whatever they are, we'll fight together. As we always have," Smarlo smiled and clapped a thin hand on his friend's muscular shoulder. "You've been my best friend for far longer than you've been my gar."

"Ha! Not always for the better," Karnak joked.

"Remember that time we went hunting for treasure?"

"Yes. And we were gone so long my mother had my father rally the squadron to search for us?"

"Yes! We wandered the Northern Caves for hours looking for the 'Lost Chamber.' You listened to Glorto's story and thought for sure you could find it."

"Glorto," Karnak shook his head at the far-off memory of the orc.

"You were so certain you could find it, and I believed you could too! So, of course, I followed you as we weaved through those tunnels and got lost."

"Exactly. What did we get for it?"

"We never found the treasure. Gar Plak was more than upset, and we got our hides whipped, of course." Karnak bobbed his head at Smarlo's words; he could almost feel the sting on his rear. "I think we found something more valuable than treasure."

"Oh?"

"We found adventure. We found friendship. We found we could rely on each other even when we were scared. When you were scared," Smarlo shot him a wink. "When we thought we heard a rinont down that side corridor! I wouldn't trade that memory for anything."

"Maybe not the trouble after."

Smarlo laughed. He could agree with that part. "We had no idea what the path looked like in front of us, but I followed you then and never regretted it. You weren't even my gar yet."

Karnak could see Smarlo's point, not that he totally agreed with the reflection, as they had been children, then. He was thankful for his friend's confidence in him.

"I'll follow you now, even if we don't know what the path ahead looks like." Smarlo jumped to his feet and extended a long skinny hand to Karnak. The big orc accepted it, and his friend hoisted him up. "Now, let's go see the map these old gars are drawing up for us. Maybe there'll be treasure!"

Zotar resembled a large bear under his fur cloak that was, indeed, made from a Drelek silver mountain bear pelt. He sat in a large chair near the fire. The room appeared to be designed more for comfort than tactical deliberations, but Zotar didn't think it necessary to discuss their strategies hunched over a planning table. The chamber had high ceilings, and the torches cast enough light for their orc eyes to make out every detail of the room.

There were plenty of chairs, and all were placed cozily around a large pelt rug of what looked to be a northern white elk. The creature must have been a monster, as the rug covered a large swath of the floor. Zotar and Klentja sat conversing but greeted Karnak and Smarlo as they took up two of the other chairs.

"Please, have some tea," Zotar offered, swiping a tray from a small table next to him. "It's of particularly good spice, this batch."

Karnak politely declined but passed the tray to Smarlo, knowing he would want some.

"Deklahn will join us shortly," Zotar continued. "He is retrieving some things from the war room. I thought it would be more comfortable for us to meet in the den."

"It is very comfortable," Karnak remarked, settling into the soft chair.

"Genjak won't be joining us," Klentja added. "He's busy getting the squadron settled into the homes your people have graciously opened to them."

"The least we could do," Zotar answered.

"Gar Zotar, I don't mean to be rude, but I am not here for pleasantries," Karnak started. "I know I am coming into this party late, but Reglese's letter has spurred a sense of urgency for the Scar Squadron."

"Straight to it, then," Zotar answered. He let out a disappointed grunt as he sat up in his chair. "I had hoped we would be able to wait for Deklahn to return, but he will be here shortly.

"It was a rather bold move for you to insert the goblin Reglese into Ruk. Bold, but clever. What brought you to that decision?"

"When I met Jaernok Tur, I was left with a sense of ... unease. I didn't care for our first encounter, and I knew within me there was more at work than the sorcerer let on," Karnak replied.

"On pure instinct," Klentja noted.

"It appears the sorcerer leaves a rather lasting first impression. Either one of awe or one of unease," Zotar pointed out. "Our first meeting with the sorcerer was the spark to our doubts, as well. Maktom and I immediately discussed different paths. Jaernok Tur is shrouded in evil."

"As though it follows wherever he goes," Karnak affirmed.

"Unfortunately, as soon as Maktom brought it up to some of the others, we were marked as traitors. And here we are now. Rebels. Or at least, here *we* are." Zotar's voice wavered, and

Klentja's eyes fell into his mug. Karnak looked away, trying to fight back the searing image of the orc boy surrounded by fire.

"It seems you also saw through the sorcerer's illusions," Zotar got back on track. "And made some clever moves."

"Reglese runs the tavern in Calrok, and his glorb wine is the best," Karnak said.

"Yes, if you don't believe us, he'll be sure to let you know," Smarlo added with a chuckle. The whole group was glad for the drop of humor.

"Again, very clever. But I've got a concern," Zotar said.

"And what's that?" Karnak asked.

"We only received two letters from him. In his letter, he said he sent three copies."

"You think someone else got their hands on the third," Karnak stated bluntly.

"The thought has crossed our minds. The flight between Lakjo and Ruk is quite easy. Pigeon carriers usually have no troubles. I discussed the matter with our own pigeon keeper here in Lakjo, and she said it would be unusual for a pigeon to be lost between our two forts."

"So, Reglese could be in some trouble."

"I said 'unusual,' not impossible. But if someone were to think him a traitor, he could be in grave danger."

Karnak looked around the room as if trying to find a solution in the dim of the chamber. His jaw clenched, and his lips fidgeted around his short tusks. He was frustrated.

Why did I put him in that position? he thought.

"We must make haste with our plans," Karnak growled, not at the orcs in the room, more at the general situation.

"That's why we will fly this night," Zotar assured him.

"We fly for Ruk this night?" Karnak started to raise his voice. "What do we know of the sorcerer? What powers does he wield?"

"We know Jaernok Tur isn't in Ruk," Zotar answered him calmly.

Karnak's confusion grew. "What? How do we know that?"

Suddenly, the door to the chamber swung open and slammed against the wall. Deklahn, a tall, thin, strange-looking orc, shuffled into the room, trying to close the door with his foot. He balanced a load of scrolls and maps in his arms, but one fell to the ground as he attempted to sweep the door closed. Smarlo set his tea to the side and ran to aid the struggling orc.

"Uh, thanks," he said to Smarlo, who picked up the wayward scroll and closed the door. "Can you grab that table?"

Smarlo grabbed the short table, no higher than his knee, and followed Deklahn. He swung around him and placed it in the middle of the great rug. Deklahn unloaded his arms, unfurling some of the maps.

"Very good," Zotar said. "Deklahn, do you have the shell?"

"Uh, yes, my Gar."

The quirky orc mage patted his robes, looking for the right pocket, and produced from one of them a beautiful green abalone seashell. Karnak and Smarlo leaned in to see the strange item, as Deklahn delicately laid it on the center of the table.

"This, my young Gar, is how we know Jaernok Tur is in Whitestone," Zotar said.

"Whitestone?" Smarlo asked. Karnak did not take his eyes off the shimmering shell.

"Yes. The treachery of Jaernok Tur's plans is not limited to our people alone, it would seem," Zotar stated.

"What magic does this hold?" Smarlo asked Deklahn, one mage to another.

"Well," Deklahn blinked uncomfortably, but Zotar nodded for him to explain. "Argus calls them Shells of Callencia."

"Argus?" Smarlo asked. The name was unknown to him, which was quite unusual. The mage community among the orcs was rather small, and they all knew of each other, even if they had never met in person.

"Argus Azulekor, of Galium."

"An orc in Galium?"

"A dwarf, actually," Deklahn corrected.

"A dwarf?" Smarlo blurted.

The revelation snapped Karnak upright. "You dabble with dwarven magic?"

Zotar also stood. Though he was smaller than Karnak, his armor and fur cloak gave him bulk to match. He raised pleading hands to the young gar.

"When we were first marked as traitors, Maktom thought it would be wise for us to seek aid in uncommon ways. We sent Deklahn with a couple of guards as an emissary to the dwarves in Galium. We are fortunate they had a rather unusual mage there by the name of Argus Azulekor. Where others were suspicious, he saw an opportunity for our peoples to cooperate."

Karnak's mind reeled. None of it made sense. Dwarves and orcs had been enemies for centuries. Though the divide between them and elves was deeper, the dwarves were a close runner-up. "I don't understand."

"Understand this. We may not be able to fight Jaernok Tur's forces from Kelvur without the help of the other peoples of Tarrine."

Zotar's statement hung on the silence of the dim chamber. Only the crackle of the fire made any noise. None in the room had an argument against his words. For really, they knew little of the sorcerer's power. They only knew hearsay about his forces in Kelvur. They did know how crafty the sorcerer was and the fact that he was in Whitestone was an unheard-of feat.

"How has he taken Whitestone?" Karnak asked, not overly enthusiastic about the new developments but not wanting to be in discord with the other gars. They would need to be on the same page against their crafty adversary.

"Apparently, by manipulation," Deklahn said. "The king of Whitestone was captured during a skirmish a while back. Jaernok Tur went to work twisting the king's mind."

"King Farrin was captured? Why didn't news of that spread through all of Drelek?" Smarlo asked.

"Not Farrin. His son Garron," Deklahn corrected. "King Farrin was gravely ill and died shortly after his son returned to Whitestone. Jaernok Tur has taken over Whitestone with the use of a magic mirror that turns into a doorway."

"What?" Smarlo was intrigued by the magics he was hearing about. His curiosity led his thoughts to all sorts of imagined possibilities, which was the same intrigue that had gotten him into magical arts.

Deklahn continued, "The she-elf reported that their pegasi squadron arrived at a secret Griffin Guard location somewhere in Whitestone Forest, and they—"

"She-elf?" Smarlo snarled.

Karnak placed a large hand in front of his friend, silencing him. The young gar patiently listened, trying to put everything together.

"Y-yes," Deklahn said, nervously eying Karnak's unpleasant demeanor. "They have gone to aid the members of the Griffin Guard that are going to fight against Jaernok Tur. They reported the sorcerer has been bringing troops through the mirror into Whitestone."

"With Jaernok Tur in Whitestone and the dragon with Gar Nargoh in Porak preparing for their siege on Galium, this is our best chance to take Ruk and take the throne," Zotar said plainly.

"How old are these reports?" Gar Klentja asked.

"They are from today."

"If they are from today, who knows how accurate they are," Smarlo pointed out.

"I think you misunderstand," Zotar said. "The elves arrived in Whitestone Forest today, and the report came today."

Smarlo's scrunched features mirrored the thoughts of Karnak and Klentja.

"How?" Karnak asked.

"Ah, yes. Well," Deklahn knelt next to the low table, placing his elbows on top. He reached both hands together under the Shell of Callencia and lifted it just off the table. "Let me show you."

He mumbled a few words under his breath, and a small ball of light appeared as though it were a pearl floating above the shell. The light shimmered off the variety of green and blue hues.

"Argus!" Deklahn called out.

The orb of light flickered as a voice came back in response, *"Deklahn, I am here."*

"It is good to hear your voice, old mage."

"And yours," Argus laughed. *"I was worried for you. I wondered how you would fare in the battle."*

"We were fortunate enough not to battle today."

"Ah, so the young gar from Calrok saw the reason behind your actions?" Argus replied excitedly.

"He stands in this very room. There was little argument. He chose to join us out of his own convictions," Deklahn explained.

Karnak stood, awestruck. He had never seen such magic, and judging by the looks on Klentja and Smarlo's faces, neither had they.

"Are you prepared for the siege coming your way?" Deklahn asked.

"We are preparing," Argus said. *"We'll be ready when they come."*

"Do not underestimate the dragon," Karnak said. His words startled the others in the room, who were enraptured by the spectacle before them.

Deklahn quickly relayed the sentiment. "Gar Karnak says to beware the might of the dragon. Do not underestimate its power."

"Wise counsel," Argus agreed. *"Pride often comes before one falls."*

It was clear the dwarven mage could only hear Deklahn, whether because the orc mage held the shell or because of the magic he used, Karnak could not say.

"We will try to take the throne at Ruk tomorrow," Deklahn reported.

"Hmm." The orb of light flickered as Argus hummed through his thoughts. *"A bold move. But if the Riders of Loralith and the remaining Griffin Guard attack Whitestone tomorrow as planned, then the sorcerer will be divided. Certainly, he couldn't defend both or be in both places at once."*

"Our thoughts exactly," Deklahn replied.

"Good then. I wish you the best of luck. We will continue to prepare for the coming battle here. You win yours there. And at the end of all this, we can share a barrel of mead in celebration," Argus encouraged.

"I prefer glorb," Deklahn ribbed back.

"As any good orc," Argus laughed.

"To a future hope."

"To a future hope."

The orb of light dissipated, and the room fell silent. They looked around at each other, Zotar waiting for anyone's thoughts. Karnak wasn't sure what to think, but the revelations had all been much more than he anticipated.

Suddenly he laughed, a rolling laugh from deep within him. The others started to laugh along with him, though none of them knew why. The sheer inability to understand everything that was going on sent them into laughter. It seemed if the energy did not come out as laughter, it could have come out as crying.

As they settled down, Karnak shook his head and said, "So, I suppose we'll even be allying ourselves with the likes of man-kin then."

"Well," Zotar shrugged helplessly. He didn't need to finish the thought, for Karnak had already figured it out.

Karnak pulled back the black hair on his head and tightened it into a knot, took a long deep breath, and said, "To a future hope."

CHAPTER TWENTY-EIGHT

THE TALON FIGHTS BACK

M errick soared high above the rolling emerald hills peppered with monumental marble stones rising at odd angles toward the sky. The view was breathtaking. He'd only heard of Whitestone's strange beauty in stories. He'd never been to the city of the Griffin Guard. While the circumstance was not ideal, the view was quite the treat for him. He was still getting used to flying, though.

Valurwind glided on the air effortlessly. The massive falcon easily bore the weight of the huntsman. The great bird's speckled feathers fluttered in the wind, and her wide yellow eyes darted about, taking in their surroundings. She was not used to such vibrant greens, for she flew amongst the stars when not called to this plane, and it had been some years since she soared over their world.

Merrick caught Ralowyn staring from her pegasus not far away. She had expressed to him her complete astonishment at his ability to connect so easily with the astral bird. She looked at him curiously.

He laughed to himself and thought. *I am a falconer, after all. Wouldn't be a very good one if I couldn't work well with falcons, now would I?*

On his other side, Pernden floated, riding his griffin, Rocktail. Merrick was humored by all the new things he had experienced on their trip. Even Rocktail and the other griffins were of some awe to him. The only griffin he'd seen prior was the recovering Silverwing back in Tamaria, as Ellaria had been mending him back to health.

The memory raised thoughts of home. How was his mother doing? And his father? Certainly, his brothers had been picking up the slack in his absence. Grell was a master hunter who had taught Merrick everything he knew. He didn't doubt his brothers' skills were growing, and they'd be fine hunters to help the family.

He found it strange that in the calm before the storm, he thought of home. He thought of his brother Greggo and wondered if he were sitting up in Kerathane, looking down on him with pride. Did Greggo know his sacrifice kept Merrick safe for this purpose? He nodded his head.

Greggo knows.

Rocktail let out a brief caw, which made Valurwind roil slightly. Merrick gripped a little tighter. In the heat of battle, he hadn't thought twice about the height. He merely trusted Valurwind and aimed his bow, sometimes nearly doubling over to loose an effective shot. But without the fires of battle raging in his belly, any unknown movement or noise from the great bird ruffled Merrick's nerves. The moment passed, and the huntsman settled back into rhythm with the calmed falcon.

Merrick readied himself and floated higher to keep Ralowyn in his view. The three of them watched Whitestone from far off, waiting for the signal.

Danner Kane and the rest of the Talon Squadron emerged from the forest edge just outside of Whitestone, walking directly toward the Grand Corral. They were only halfway across the field before they heard the horns sounding the alarm. The approach was clever, as they were able to get close to the Corral without being spotted. Obviously, Commander Jolan had the guards watching the skies, not the ground.

The horns continued to blow, and the guardians spurred the griffins into a quick lope. Once the other guardians began to rise out of the Grand Corral like a swarm of bees from their hive, the Talon Squadron took to the air to meet them. By Danner Kane's count, only two squadrons were in front of them. Jolan must have the rest out searching for them. The ones that were present moved themselves into formation. While they were doing so, Danner Kane took the opportunity to approach the forming squadrons alone.

As he neared, a wave of murmuring side conversations erupted. He did not know what lies had been spewed about his demise or defection and could not hear their hurried words to each other. Many looked at him in utter shock. He wondered if they had all thought him dead. But then, why would they be searching so vigorously for him and the Talon Squadron? He thought himself close enough to yell out to them but dared to fly nearer to ensure they heard his words.

Suddenly, Commander Jolan shot out from the Grand Corral, racing past the forming squadrons. Danner Kane stopped. He wanted to be far enough away from the formed guardians that he could have private words with Jolan but close enough that if he raised his voice, they would be able to hear. Jolan zipped past the other guardians and pulled his griffin into a stationary flapping.

"I have been looking for you," Jolan said, seething.

"I can see that," Danner Kane made his movements obvious as he scanned the two squadrons before him. "Where are the other squadrons?"

"Some are on the coast of the Gant Sea. Some are scanning the forest. We even have one in Lakerun looking for you. And yet, here you are."

"Here I am," Danner Kane raised his arms and turned side to side, showing he held no weapon in his hands. Murmurs ran through the squadrons again.

"Would you like to turn yourself in? Or, though I would not prefer it, would you rather die in this field?"

What a curious question, Danner Kane thought to himself.

He would gladly die defending Whitestone, but it seemed odd Jolan would ask such a question. "What do you gain from my demise?" he asked Jolan.

"What?" Jolan looked confused.

"What do you gain from my demise?" Danner Kane repeated, a little louder, to make sure the others watching heard.

Jolan's griffin stirred in obvious protest to the commander's increasing tension. "It is only the first step toward the future!" he snapped, frustrated with his griffin and the old High Commander.

"And what future is that? A future where goblins rule the halls of Whitestone?"

More conversation rolled in a wave through the watchers. Jolan caught Kane's purpose.

"You seek to turn them against me!"

"I do not. Don't you see the sorcerer twists us against each other? Divided, it makes the Guard weak. That's what he wants. He wants us weak, so he can work his evil conquest."

"You just want your command back!" Jolan spat.

"No," Kane said calmly. "No, I want my home back. I want Whitestone to rise to its former glory, untainted by the poison that has cast shadow over us."

"No! Jaernok Tur is the only one who can make things right!" Jolan's words were hoarse. "He's the only one who can ..."

Jolan seemed to fade away with his words. His mind had gone to another place, but it was his eyes that struck Danner Kane's heart with terror. Jolan's eyes had turned an abyssal black. His stare far off, as he sat silently on the back of his griffin.

Danner Kane took the opportunity to address the formed squadrons. "Brothers and sisters! Guardians! Our home has been invaded, and we posture against each other while the real threat stands unopposed. The future of Whitestone is in its people, not under the thumb of a corrupt sorcerer, but united with purpose. To think that the orc's plans will end within the walls of the castle and spread no further is folly.

"We must stand together and take back our home. Think of your brothers and sisters out there, right now, who are on a fool's errand. They have been tricked. They have been lied to, as you have. We must take back our home, so they have a home to come back to.

"I am proud to call you all frien—"

The dagger that struck Danner Kane's ribs knocked the wind from his chest in a sudden burst. His griffin reeled at the slumping master on its back, trying with great effort to get to the ground without throwing Kane from its back. The onlookers were stunned as they watched him float to the field below.

345

The act was a jolt to their senses. Commander Mattness, who had been positioned at the point of the closer formation, suddenly ached with sadness. She looked to the seething High Commander Jolan, his shoulders rocking up and down with deep vengeful breaths. And then she looked at all those around her, none sure how to react.

"We are the Guard ..." she said to herself, but others around her heard the words. She repeated them. "We are the Guard. Is it not our duty to guard? And if we cannot even guard our own home, we would be a pretty sorry guard, indeed."

Those around her nodded. Some even cheered, "That's right!" and "Yeah!"

"We have been led astray!" she yelled.

Commander Jolan turned his griffin to face her. He floated there, one against two whole squadrons with the Talon Squadron to his rear. The elite squadron had flown in closer after seeing their leader grounded. Jolan was completely outmatched.

He bolted.

"Get him and bring him back to the Grand Corral!" Commander Mattness barked to a handful of guardians who sped off in pursuit of the fleeing Jolan.

Mattness flew to meet the Talon Squadron before they could engage. Her action slowed them as they approached, and Mattness held her hands out wide to stay them.

"You two," she pointed to a pair near the front. "Go and see to High Commander Kane."

The two guardians didn't hesitate. They hurtled toward the ground, each swooping on wide wings near the bottom to avoid a collision. They dismounted quickly and ran to the side of the High Commander.

Mattness turned to the rest of the Talon Squadron. "Deception has been plucked from our eyes like sleep. We must head to the castle and take back our home!"

Commander Fario's Loralith elves looked nothing of the sort. The Talon Squadron members had given them their own cloaks and garments to conceal their elven heritage. The naturally taller elves looked like teenage boys outgrowing their sleeves and pant legs. The hoods and hats covered their pointed ears and fairer features to complete the ensembles. They had infiltrated the greater town of Whitestone before the dawn and had made their way to the castle square. They had loitered around the square in nooks and crannies that hid them in complete shadow and, one by one, immersed themselves in the crowds as the market stalls opened.

One of Fario's elves climbed to the top of the wall surrounding the square to watch for any sign from the direction of the Grand Corral. Elf eyes are particularly adept at seeing at long range, and his young eyes, only three hundred years old, would see things others' might not.

Lanryn walked through the crowd, doing his best to fit in and go unnoticed. He stopped every once in a while at busy stalls where people were too engaged in bartering to recognize the odd figure. To his elf eyes, it was easy to pinpoint all the other elves around the square. But thus far, no man-kin had stopped long enough to catch one of them. He looked over to the castle at the end of the square and followed the straight edges up until he spotted what he thought was the king's tower. He would stand in that tower before the day was done.

Two human guards stood at the top of the square stairs leading to the castle entrance. Lanryn wondered if they knew what they were guarding. Did they know they defended a castle full of goblin foot soldiers? He didn't think so, or they were adequately charmed by the dark magic of the sorcerer. Either way, he was confident his squad would disarm the two without killing them.

The elf on top of the wall with his leg dangling like a bored adolescent whistled like a bird. The whistle was echoed by several other bird calls across the square, which would have been noted as strange if the square hadn't been so preoccupied with business.

Two of Fario's elves acting as boys playing a game with a sack of beans lobbed it just past the guards. One of the guards was kind enough to turn around and pick it up for them. The elves, however, weren't there for the toy. They quickly subdued the guards with choking lock maneuvers that put them to sleep. Most people in the square were too busy to notice—most.

"Oy!" a man yelled across the square. "What er you boys doin'?" He scolded them. Several others looked in the direction he was yelling. Seeing the two boys where the guards had stood a moment before struck them as odd, and they began to look on in curiosity.

The two elves ran to the castle doors, mighty and tall. They tried with all their strength to rend them open. One hooted the appropriate call they had designated to indicate the doors were locked.

Lanryn strode through the crowd with purpose. More people looked in the direction of the door; and one man, also walking up the stairs, looked as though he meant to bring trouble down on the mischievous youths. Lanryn's wand slipped from his sleeve and into his grip. He raised it toward the massive doors, muttered an incantation, and let loose a blast of magical energy that smashed the doors in on themselves with a blinding light and explosive force.

People in the square screamed as goblins poured from the doorway. Fario and the rest of the elves ran in, smoothly navigating the chaos with weapons drawn.

Nera, who had been significantly disguised so she wouldn't be recognized by the citizens who knew her, threw off her cloak and hurled Santoralier at the swarm of goblins attempting to guard the entrance. A loud deafening *crack!* rang out, and it was as if lightning struck. The spear dematerialized into a line of pure electric energy colliding with the unlucky goblin at the front of the group, killing him instantly and scattering like a spiderweb onto nearby goblins. Searing arcs of energy snapped at them like whips, downing some and wounding others. The goblins hollered in outrage.

Lanryn let out another blast of his wand that sent half a dozen goblins flying in all directions. He paused on the stairs to help the man who had scolded the youths. He lifted the man-kin to his feet and said to him, "We're here to help. Get your family to safety."

The man could say nothing, but his fear-etched face nodded in understanding as he ran off.

Pernden and Rocktail shot off like an arrow. Nera's lightning strike with Santoralier was their signal. Ralowyn kicked her pegasus into action and sped after the guardian. Merrick took a deep breath, uttered a quick prayer, patted Valurwind on the neck, and set them in motion. They caught the others quickly and took the lead. Valurwind's speed and ability were unmatched by the other creatures. She and Merrick flew with all haste toward Whitestone Castle. He knew which tower was the king's, as Pernden had made sure to inform him and Ralowyn, in case something should happen to the young captain.

As they approached, they heard the screams of goblins fighting below and the clanging of metal on metal as some of them parried deft blades once, and occasionally twice, before being cut down by the swift elven warriors. The sheer numbers, however, were in the favor of the goblins, and eventually, the elves would tire. Merrick and the other two needed to accomplish their task before then.

Out of the corner of his eye, Pernden saw a speeding griffin rider being chased by a handful of others. A mass group of Griffin Guard in the distance seemed to be heading toward the castle as well. For a fleeting moment, he wondered how the encounter had gone at the Grand Corral. He worried for Danner Kane and the Talon Squadron—his squadron. He had to let it go and learn their fate later. First, they must get into the king's chamber. He spurred Rocktail on, as Merrick's great falcon gained distance from them.

A pair of goblins emerged onto the balcony of the king's chamber. They appeared to be trying to see the commotion. The surprise on their faces at the incoming falcon and huntsman was genuine. Merrick loosed an arrow that met its mark, downing one of them before Valurwind swooped in to rip the other from the balcony and throw him. The goblin toppled headlong to the ground, far below. The great falcon grabbed at the balcony railing, spreading her wings wide to balance long enough for Merrick to dismount.

When he entered the room, he stopped instantly. The great orc sorcerer Jaernok Tur stood in the middle of the room, staring directly at him. Strangely, though, Merrick sensed the sorcerer was not seeing him, but something else entirely. A curious chill came over Merrick as he looked at the orc. The sorcerer was much taller than him. The orc's stone arm moved as he spoke in a strange language unknown to the huntsman. The orc's other hand firmly gripped a long staff with a black stone at the peak. His eyes seemed even more black, if that were possible. He seemed to be pleading, but not to Merrick. To someone ... else.

The huntsman braved a few steps forward, his bow nocked and drawn.

"Merrick, shoot!" Pernden yelled from the balcony. The guardian had just arrived with Ralowyn in tow.

Pernden's sudden shout startled him, and he loosed the arrow. Time slowed. The arrow moved with sluggish speed through the air. Merrick heard his own heartbeat.

There was a sudden flourish from the sorcerer. His stone arm reached out to deflect the arrow, but his return to the present was late. The arrow scraped and redirected off the stone arm, sinking into the flesh of the sorcerer's side.

"Arghh!" Jaernok Tur roared.

He brandished his staff, sending a wave of slithering black energy flying at the trio. Ralowyn slammed her staff to the ground, and a purple barrier erupted from the stone floor, blocking the sorcerer's attack.

Upon hearing the commotion, goblins flooded into the room.

Jolan's griffin dipped and flapped furiously, dodging arrow after arrow from the pursuers. They flew at breakneck speeds, gaining on the traitor, even as he changed directions often to avoid being an easy target. He flew as direct a course as he thought was safe toward the castle. He had thrown his dagger into the side of the man he used to follow. Unfortunately for him, that had turned the others against him, so his only chance was to make it to Jaernok Tur's side. He had underestimated the love of the guardians for the old High Commander, and it was possible he had overestimated the charm magic of the Kelvurian sorcerer.

He couldn't think that way, though. Jaernok Tur was the only being he had ever met who knew some way to bring back his son. If there was any chance at all to see his Anlon again, Jolan would take it. First he had to get himself out of his predicament. He banked suddenly to avoid another arrow that zipped past his ear. He shook his head, trying to keep himself out of his own thoughts and on the task at hand.

That was too close.

As they neared the castle, loud noises of battle rang from the square. The air sizzled with magic as explosions of energy blasted at the forces streaming from the castle. Jolan thought he saw lightning. The scene struck him, as a javelin from one of his chasers struck his griffin.

His griffin died instantly with his wings half unfurled. They careened into the castle, crashing through a window on a higher level into a long hallway and slamming into several goblin soldiers there. The scene was a mangled mess of feathers and shattered glass.

The battle raged at the castle's entrance. The Loralith elves cut down goblin after goblin with a symphonic and lethal dance. Their superior training and dexterity outmatched the goblins, but the continuous flow of goblin soldiers wearied the elves.

Commander Fario, not one to lead from the rear, sliced down another goblin with his sword, which tangled in the sharp armor. He struggled to free it. He turned toward a laughing goblin, brandishing a jagged sword and even more jagged grin. Fario pulled his dagger from his belt and sighed. If he was going to die, so would the goblin.

An arrow struck the goblin, and his wicked grin shifted to a look of confusion. He hobbled a step toward the elf commander before a frying pan clanged against the side of his head, dropping him instantly. Fario's face was almost as confused as the goblin's had been, but then he realized what had happened.

The citizens of Whitestone—men, women, and even teenagers—were hurtling articles at the goblins. They hollered insults at their invaders and brandished lackluster weapons of all kinds: pitchforks, scythes, frying pans, hunting bows, even broomsticks. Their heart gave Fario much encouragement.

He gripped his sword and, with a mighty tug and flick, plucked it away from the dead goblin's armor. As he faced the goblins once more, he caught the terror on their faces. Many tried to push their way back into the castle, toppling over others that were trying to join the battle. The goblins screamed as they fell over each other. Some pointed to the sky. Fario turned his head to see what horrified them.

The Griffin Guard was coming.

Pernden spun around a jabbing pike, bringing Wintertide down in a flash. The trio in the king's chamber fought tooth and nail against the goblins pouring into the room. Merrick loosed a few arrows but resorted to close combat, taking up a fallen goblin's spear. He twirled it like he used to do with his walking stick on so many hunts in his lifetime. Though he was an untrained warrior, he fought with ferocity and wit, following Pernden's movements and allowing Ralowyn to strike down opponents he didn't think he could take with ease.

Angry bickering arose from the hallway as goblins pushed each other out of the way. The huntsman had tried to get a clear shot at the sorcerer from Kelvur again, but the wave of goblins had been too great a challenge. The entire time they had been distracted with the goblin foot soldiers, the sorcerer had been conjuring some magical incantation, and the corners of the room began to bend and shift at odd angles.

Boom!

A blast of energy sent goblins skittering in all directions. Merrick clambered back to his knees and nocked an arrow, as all the others in the room regained their faculties. He took aim at the sorcerer, who was lifting himself from his knees, having also been affected by the power of the mirror. Merrick wobbled for a second, steadied himself, and loosed the arrow.

"Nooo!" Jolan screamed as he dove over the shrouded orc. The arrowhead pierced the guardian's shoulder, between the layered plates of armor.

Jolan looked quite a mess. He had feathers pinned between layers of his armor, though several layers seemed to be missing. The crash he'd endured was a bad one, but the goblins that his hurtling griffin had hit gave him a softer landing than a stone wall. When he'd composed himself enough to move, pure will and determination drove him through the corridors to the king's chamber. He'd finally pushed his way through hordes of goblins to the doorway, when the room exploded. As he stepped through the door, he saw the huntsman taking aim and hurled himself in front of the sorcerer.

Jaernok Tur turned a wicked eye toward the huntsman. He raised his staff and shot an orb of black magic at the man-kin. The Staff of Anvelorian, however, was swift in the elf mage's hands, and ribbons of lavender magic swept the black orb safely away.

Ralowyn spun the staff and sent a return volley toward the sorcerer, who batted it away with his own magic staff. The injured Jolan, looking quite like death, pressed the orc toward the smoky portal, and the wounded pair stumbled through.

The goblins in the room were regaining their faculties and picking up arms once more.

Pernden saw their opportunity slipping away. As he raised Wintertide to send a mystic blade flying after the sorcerer, a wretched figure tackled him from the side, screaming, "Nooo!"

The figure beat at Pernden, sitting on him and whaling with his fists. The face was of a man the captain once knew. Then again, he seemed more a wretched, vile creature than a man. He was so thin and pale, Pernden nearly didn't recognize his cousin Garron.

The butt of a spear struck the side of Garron's head, knocking him unconscious and allowing Pernden to get to his feet.

"Hurry," Merrick yelled as he jabbed the spear into the belly of another goblin.

"We must get through the doorway before it closes!" Ralowyn added. "I do not know how to reopen it. If it closes, it could be months before we figure it out."

She swirled the staff, and a wave of mystical purple force sent a group of goblins skittering into each other. Merrick grabbed Pernden's arm and hoisted him to his feet as the three hacked and batted at goblins between them and the Alkhoren Mirror.

Screams erupted from the corridor outside the king's chamber, which halted several goblins by the door. Onward, the trio pushed until finally they reached the smoky portal, took a deep breath, and plunged into the mysterious mirror.

The Griffin Guard had infiltrated the castle through windows and balconies on different levels and sides. The Loralith elves easily sliced through the goblins that filled the corridor to the king's chamber. The goblin foot soldiers didn't stand a chance, and they knew it. Many gave up the fight and climbed over others, seeking safety, only to fall on their allies' swords or axes. In the pandemonium, some were trampled. Many others were slain at the hand of the skilled guardians and their savage griffins.

That sudden shift in the battle gave the elven warriors renewed vigor and speed. Their intent had been to get to the king's chamber. When the Griffin Guard had arrived and demanded much of the goblins' attention, they had paved the way for the elves. Commander Fario flagged down the lead guardian, Commander Mattness, and the two conversed briefly, the elf bringing her up to speed on the plan. She barked orders to several guardians that hovered nearby, waiting for their turn to enter the fray. She led several of them toward windows and balconies at higher levels and preceded a group heading toward the king's room.

In Nera's capable hands, Santoralier did significant damage in the crowded corridor of the king's chamber. Goblins screamed in horror as arcs of searing energy bounced off their compatriots and struck them. As Nera and Lanryn led the charge into the king's chamber, goblins pushed each other and scurried toward the magic mirror. Others looked for things to hide behind in the royal room but were petrified by the three guardians who jumped into the room from the balcony behind them.

Nera and Lanryn turned toward the mirror, the source of the goblins' escape. Nera looked determined. Lanryn, curious. Goblins shoved each other, each trying to get through the smoky portal first.

Pop!

The room went still for only a second. The energy river that had been circling the smoky doorway had vanished, and the mirror appeared to be just that, a mirror. One unfortunate goblin had tried to dive through and left half of himself in the king's chamber as the mysterious mirror closed its portal.

The hopeless goblins threw down their weapons and raised their hands above their heads. They cried pitifully, begging for mercy. The elves gathered them and lined them up in the hallway.

Commander Mattness knelt near a limp body on the floor near the king's bed. She inspected it tenderly. Nera went to greet her, glad to see one of her fellow guardians. She stopped short when she saw the body the commander had been inspecting was human, not goblin.

"King Garron," Mattness said.

"Is he ...?" Nera asked, feeling a little guilty about her relief that it wasn't Pernden.

"He lives," she said solemnly.

"Your king lives. Is this not good news?" Lanryn asked, not looking in their direction but studying the Alkhoren Mirror with great interest.

Nera and Mattness looked at each other. Neither said a word. Neither had to.

Their silence at his question drew Lanryn's curiosity away from the mirror. He looked from Nera to Mattness and back again. He could not read minds but decided it better he did not ask. They had accomplished their mission.

Out of his pocket, Lanryn retrieved a shell with mother-of-pearl markings. He muttered a low incantation, and a small orb of light appeared, floating above the shell, reflecting the light with dancing shimmers.

"Whitestone has been reclaimed!" he stated clearly. "The city is secure. The king lives, though the sorcerer has escaped through the mirror."

Nera stared at the elf, watching him speak into the floating orb of light.

Lanryn paused and then repeated, "The sorcerer has fled through the mirror."

CHAPTER TWENTY-NINE

DWARVEN COUNCIL

The meeting chamber where Coal and his companions waited for the king of Galium was much larger than the one in the garvawk warriors' barracks. The room also had windows and was at the top of a wide tower built up the front of the mountain. Out the east window, Orin saw the rolling hills and the front range of the Drelek mountains. From the south window, the view showed the greater city of Galium.

To the west, a beautifully manicured rooftop courtyard sat atop the great castle. It was surrounded by stone walls and the mountainside. But it was open to the sky to give the trees much-needed sunlight for the few hours a day the beams bathed the courtyard. Ellaria noticed a halfling gardener picking at one of the beds of plants, whistling joyfully to himself.

Tobin had Ezel pinned in the corner, talking the gnome's ear off. He spoke with nervous anticipation, for it was not often he got a chance to see the king. Occasionally, Ezel would try to sign that he needed to remove himself from the corner of the room or go talk to Coal or Ellaria or anyone else. But the halfling, who did not understand the grey gnome's gestures, took them as agreements with his own thoughts and continued at a blissful pace.

Coal smirked at the grey gnome's pleading face but did nothing to save his poor friend. Instead, he conversed with

Bendur Clagstack and Lotmeag Kandersaw, rather glad to be in the company of dwarven warriors again. He hadn't realized he missed it while he was working the Palori River on the *Lady Leila*, but he was enjoying their exaggerated tales.

The door to the meeting chamber slammed open, and everyone inside moved closer to the short table in the center of the room. An old dwarf with a long, white, wispy beard shuffled into their midst. His blue hooded cloak fluttered behind him, and the silver stars embroidered into his garment sparkled. He muttered to himself, not looking at anyone in the room, and moved straight to the table where he deposited a stack of parchment.

He paused, finished his audible thoughts, and nodded to himself, seeming quite pleased with his conclusion. He looked up and smiled.

"Corahl," he acknowledged Coal.

"Argus?" Coal said, recognizing the old dwarf. "Argus Azulekor, you old coot. Is that you?"

"One and the same, my Prince!" he beamed.

"You must be three hundred years old by now!"

"Two seventy-one this summer, thank you," the old dwarf corrected, feigning offense. "I've got lots of life in me still. Too many magics still a mystery. Too many things to discover."

Coal moved around the short table to embrace the old mage but was halted by another dwarf entering the room. King Thygram Markensteel's boots clanked with every step on the stone floor. His golden armor was regal and embedded with gems from Galium's famous Deep Mines. He walked with the swagger of a king and strode to the table as all the others gave a slight bow. Orin and Ellaria joined in, not wanting to be disrespectful to their royal host.

Thygram stopped and looked curiously at the two humans before he asked, "And what do we have here?"

"Travelers," Bendur Clagstack answered. "They've encountered the Drelek dragon."

"The Kelvurian dragon," Argus corrected.

Orin looked over to Coal, surprised by the way they spoke of the dragon. Clearly, Galium knew more than their group had expected.

"And ye managed to survive," Thygram nodded to them approvingly. "Where did ye encounter the dragon?"

"At the Palori Ruins. A farmer from Tamaria had suffered at the hands of the orcs and taken his grievances to King Hugen. I was asked to look into it before returning to Whitestone," Orin explained. "We found more than we expected."

"I imagine so," the king laughed.

"Testing the dragon's breath on the elven architecture, like Deklahn said," Argus pointed out to the king.

"It seems so."

"They have given us no reason to question their word," the old mage added.

"So far," Thygram replied airily. "Have I not gotten our army started on preparations for the battle to come?"

Argus lifted his hands in resignation. "I do not mean to offend."

"You don't," Thygram assured him. He turned toward Orin. "Tell me of the creature's might."

Orin described everything they had seen to the best of his recollection, and Ellaria added details where she saw fit.

"That matches Deklahn's account of the dragon," Argus said, again speaking aside to the king.

"Excuse me," Coal butted in. "But it seems you know more of the dragon than even we do. How'd you come by this knowledge?"

"And who inquires?" King Thygram asked, giving Coal a once-over.

"This is Corahl, Prince of Kalimandir, Son of Onik, a son of Clan Carraignyk," the mage answered for him.

"Ah, an old friend, Argus?"

"I have known him in the past. He has always been a good, if not brash, dwarf," Argus replied.

Coal's cheeks flushed. When he'd left Kalimandir years earlier, he'd been a young dwarf lacking the wisdom of grey hairs. He still had no grey hairs in his jet-black beard, but he had gained life experience on his travels. He believed himself to be a better dwarf than the one who had left so long ago.

"I have ... grown," Coal replied.

"I see that in you," Argus affirmed.

"A touching reunion," the king said, reinserting himself into the conversation. "I welcome you, young prince of Kalimandir."

"I am grateful," Coal said in the customary dwarven response.

"We have much to discuss," King Thygram Markensteel said. "But I think it would be better on a full stomach. Segin!"

A round halfling scuttled into the room from the hallway. His hair was matted with sweat, and Orin had a tinge of sympathy for the poor fellow. Many stairs led to the meeting chamber, and though the guardian did not know how long the halfling had been standing in the hallway, it appeared he was still recovering from the climb.

"We'll take lunch here today," the king instructed.

Tobin sucked in an audible breath of excitement as he straightened, looking around at his new friends. Certainly, he wasn't the only one who was hungry. Segin, for his part, was less than enthused about returning to the stairs but hurried off to make preparations, nonetheless.

"It is always easier to hear bad news with a happy belly," the king said.

"And what bad news is that?" Coal asked, an eyebrow shooting up.

"Ye'll not be going to Whitestone just yet."

After the initial shock and uproar at the king's declaration that the group would not be continuing to Whitestone, there had been much debate. Orin, in particular, felt strongly that they must continue onward. When Argus explained that Whitestone already knew of the dragon and Orin's skills would be needed in Galium over the next week, the guardian recalled the words of Enkeli the wizard, *"You will be where you are needed soon."* Orin wondered if the situation before him might be what the wizard had meant.

When Orin's arguments fell silent and Coal and Ezel continued with fervor, the old mage produced a beautiful shell from inside his robes.

"This is one of the Shells of Callencia. My own creation. And a rather clever magic, if I do say so myself." Argus Azulekor seemed tickled with his own brilliance. "It allows a mage the ability to speak to others at vast distances. This is how we have been able to get the word to Whitestone. It's also how we know that the dragon, at least one wyvern squadron, and an army of foot soldiers are on their way to Galium, as we speak."

Much to Tobin's delight—for the halfling was quite tired of all the arguing that had stressed him to so great a hunger—Segin and several others spilled into the room carrying platters of lunch. There was bread and fruits. Vegetables and dips. A nice bowl of steaming mutton stew. The spread was a royal one, to say the least.

The dwarf mage had stopped talking when the servants had come in with the meal, and the others wisely held their questions, recognizing the need for discretion.

One particularly small halfling shuffled into the room, far behind the others. Orin guessed his shorter legs had slowed him on the climb up the stairs. The halfling cheerfully served up a platter of cheeses that made Tobin's eyes light up. And then, as quickly as they had arrived, the servants disappeared through the doorway.

"I should like to hear more of Whitestone," Orin said plainly. "Are they preparing for the attack? Have they set squadrons in motion to come to Galium's aid?"

Argus glanced to King Thygram, who was filling a bowl of stew for himself. The king shrugged, as though to tell the old mage that his response would ultimately change nothing.

"Well ... Whitestone is currently under the control of a sorcerer orc from Kelvur," Argus said as gently as he could muster.

"What?" Orin, Coal, and Ellaria said at once.

"Whitestone has fallen? I was too late to warn them?"

"No ..." Argus started but then corrected himself. "Well, yes. The Griffin Guard knows of the dragon. The Riders of Loralith have grouped up with the Talon Squadron of the Guard to mount a counterattack, and they plan to retake Whitestone this very day."

Orin's mind reeled. The revelation that his home had been captured by some orc sorcerer from across the Gant Sea was more than he could have imagined. Everything in his being wanted to run down to the garvawk barracks and try every magical utterance he had ever heard to wake one of the panther-like creatures and fly off to Whitestone. But the notion was foolish. Orin had never once been able to do any magic. He knew no word that would wake a garvawk. And even if he did, if the battle were today, he would never make it in time to help.

Ezel sensed the confusion and restlessness in the guardian and grabbed Orin's hand. The little gnome's hand grounded Orin back to the present. The man looked at the gnome's eyes—blue even without the faery fires burning—and the compassion on his tiny face nearly broke the guardian.

"This must be a lot to stomach, young guardian," Argus continued. "I assure you, the Riders of Loralith have sent a couple of mages along to aid in the battle for Whitestone. I have no doubt they will be victorious."

"Talon Squadron is the Guard's best unit. They will fight with a fury unseen in ages," Orin said, trying to comfort himself as much as agree with the old mage's hopes.

The old mage brightened, as though he remembered something. It was a strange coincidence of sorts, and he felt compelled to share. "They tell me of a human huntsman who rides with the elves to Whitestone's aid, as well. Now, remembering the details relayed to me, I cannot help but wonder if you might know of him."

Tears poured from Ellaria's eyes, though her face was a picture of pure joy. Coal looped his arm around the young woman's waist and pulled her in for an excited hug. Ezel and Orin exchanged bewildered but relieved looks.

"With all the bad news going around, I don't think you could have given us better news than this!" Coal said graciously.

"I am happy to share it then," Argus replied.

"The battle for Whitestone is not the only battle happening today, though," King Thygram cut in, having finished a bowl of stew.

"You said earlier that we have a couple of days before the army of Drelek arrives here," Orin said, confused by the king's words.

"Ah yes. But our friends from Lakjo fly to take Ruk today, as well," Argus explained.

"Friends from Lakjo?" Coal retorted.

"Yes," the old mage continued. "The ones who warned us of the coming army. They are in rebellion against King Sahr of Drelek, who allied himself with Jaernok Tur, the sorcerer of Kelvur."

As the puzzle began to piece together in his mind, Coal still couldn't reconcile the fact that they were calling orcs of Drelek, "friends."

"And the orcs are working with us?" Coal asked.

"Yes," Argus said. He understood the dwarf would need more explanation. "Deklahn is a mage among their people. They sent him and a pair of guards here as emissaries to Galium. We imprisoned them immediately, of course. Orcs extending an olive branch was the last thing we ever thought we'd see. But as they explained the situation they found themselves in as rebels against the king and his new ally, I sensed no deception on their part. And Deklahn used no magic to veil their intentions.

"After days with them, I could find no malice and had to conclude that they, indeed, wanted to extend friendship. I spent another couple of days with Deklahn and decided they could be great allies in the war to come. Before they went home to Lakjo, I gave Deklahn one of the Shells of Callencia. A risk, to be sure. But one I felt we had to take. At the very least, if we sensed them using it against our combined efforts with the elves, we would stop using it immediately."

"And they have been speaking to you through this ... this shell?" Coal asked incredulously.

"Yes," the old mage replied. "They have given us reports to keep us informed, and they have given us no reason for distrust."

Coal squirmed, still not comfortable with the idea. He had a sense that the union could come back to bite them. But then again, he had no experience trusting orcs.

All of a sudden, the shell sitting on the table in front of Argus sparked to life. A bright orb of light appeared above it and flickered with a voice from far away.

"Whitestone has been reclaimed!" the voice said. *"The city is secure. The king lives, though the sorcerer has escaped through the mirror."*

"Lanryn," Argus said to the others, who watched in absolute amazement. "A mage from Loralith."

Their hearts soared. Whitestone was reclaimed! Orin could hardly contain his joy. He was overwhelmed with the news. That is, until the voice came through the shell once more, and he heard the part he dismissed the first time.

"The sorcerer has fled through the mirror."

CHAPTER THIRTY

THE ORC & THE HUNTSMAN

The orc warriors of Calrok, Borok, and Lakjo only got a few hours' rest before they were awoken in the middle of the night. All of the orcs gathered in the center of an open area on the side of Lakjo mountain. A large fire roared in the middle of the gathering, and the gars walked up on top of a flat rock so the orc squadrons could see them. Smarlo, Deklahn, and Genjak stood behind their respective gars, holding huge bowls in front of them.

"Our home has been infiltrated by a crafty enemy," Gar Zotar shouted over the surging fire. "An enemy that walks under a cloud of evil. He has twisted our own king against us. King Sahr has traded his birthright for a bowl of elk stew. He no longer thinks of the welfare of the Drelek peoples—orc, troll, or even goblin. No. He only wishes to satisfy his own gluttonous desires. He has chosen a Kelvurian sorcerer's false promises over his own people. But we will take back our home!"

The orcs erupted in a raucous roar. They cheered their leaders and cursed the wicked king. Zotar raised a wide hand high above his head to settle them down.

"We ride for Ruk this night, for tomorrow we battle. Tomorrow will be the dawn of a new day for Drelek. As such, we mark ourselves for battle with the colors of Calrok. Calrok is the first of our great cities to taste the sun each morning, and it will be the first to taste it in the new dawn of Drelek."

Gar Zotar dropped his wide hand into the bowl that Deklahn held. He lifted his hand, covered in orange paint, and raised it high. All watched in reverent silence as Zotar drew his hand down Karnak's face, leaving jagged lines of orange war paint all the way to his chin. "For great wisdom and sight as you fight and lead ..."

The older gar swiped his hand from Karnak's shoulder over his large pectoral to the center of his chest. "That your fight would always be in line with your heart."

Karnak put a finger to his brow and gave Zotar a slight bow of respect. He turned and put his hand into the bowl Smarlo held, and Karnak blessed Klentja the same way. Klentja dipped from Genjak's bowl and blessed Zotar to finish the ritual.

When the three gars were finished, their commanders carried the bowls throughout the crowds of orcs. Each orc dipped their hands and partnered up to ensure every orc had been covered. The voices were low, and most could not be heard over the raging fire in their midst.

Once the three commanders returned to the front, having decorated one another, Gar Zotar overlooked the gathered squadrons, with pride in his brothers. "We do not know what greatness the future holds for us, but neither does Jaernok Tur!"

"Yargh!!" The orcs cheered.

"Let us fly to a new dawn for Drelek and to a future hope!"

The orcs scattered to their wyverns. The fire burned in their bellies. They were fueled for war.

When the two soldier orcs entered Reglese's tavern wearing full armor and bearing their weapons, he knew something was wrong.

Not that other orc soldiers didn't frequent his establishment, but they usually came half-armored and never brandished weapons. Orcs and goblins, and even a couple of trolls, had found Reglese's tavern to be a great getaway in the capital city of Ruk.

When the soldiers entered, they asked about the proprietor of the establishment. Reglese made himself scarce behind the bar, but there was no place to hide. As Getta came behind the bar to grab a tray of more tankards, an idea sparked. Perhaps he could make himself too busy for the soldiers to engage. He grabbed the tray Getta was about to pick up, confirmed the table number, and hustled off to deliver it to the regulars.

The two soldiers spotted and cornered him, trying to pull him aside for a conversation.

"So sorry, fellas. I 'ave lots of customers, you see. Find some seats at the bar and relax. I can pour you a couple mugs of my famous glorb wine," Reglese suggested.

They didn't bite.

Instead, they pressed him further into the corner. Others in the tavern watched as the orcs towered over the barkeep. One of the orcs grabbed him by the arm, and the other punched him in the gut. Reglese cried out as the wind left his lungs.

"You are going to the dungeons for treason against Drelek," the punchy orc said.

Reglese heaved, still catching his breath. "But ..." he sputtered. "I ... *Gulp* ... I've done nothing wrong."

"A letter has been found with your name on it, suggesting you stand against King Sahr and Drelek. You will be punished for your treachery and tortured for years to come."

Reglese started to cry. All he wanted to do was make glorb wine and lots of gold. Was that too much to ask? He wanted to help his home too, of course. He never thought he would spend the rest of his life on the torture racks in the dungeons of Ruk to do so.

Getta and Kig had both drawn close to the encounter, neither sure what was going on. Reglese had been a good partner and a kind boss. Neither of them understood what was happening, but neither of them wanted to lose him, either.

Suddenly, the caverns and tunnels echoed a low rumbling, as if there was a far-off collapse somewhere along the mountain network. When that one ceased, another started a few seconds later. Everyone in the tavern sat statue still, listening.

And then they sounded.

Horns of alarm blew and echoed throughout the tunnels under the great mountain, bouncing off stone walls and ceilings, rounding corners, even reaching the deepest depths of the mountain city. All the orc soldiers in the tavern, except the two holding Reglese, jumped into action, running out the tavern door.

In the chaos, as other regulars ran for the exit—likely headed to care for their families or defend their shops—Getta made her move. She swung a mighty fist, connecting with the punchy orc's jaw, sending spittle flinging from the ends of his tusks. His body crashed hard to the ground. The other soldier spun on her and shook his jagged sword in front of him. He took two steps forward but then took a cast iron frying pan to the head.

The orc's dazed gaze turned to see Kig standing on top of a table next to him, frying pan held high. He dropped to the floor and slipped into unconsciousness.

Reglese looked at his friends with surprise and gratitude and a dash of fear. Several goblins and a couple of orcs remained in the tavern, all too terrified to leave.

"Let's watch over these ones," Reglese said to his friends, pointing to the scared patrons. "I 'ave a feeling this could be a long day."

The combined forces of wyvern squadrons from three different cities descended upon Ruk like a swarm of locusts. The surface forces had obviously been warned by a spotter as wyvern riders of Ruk poured out of two holes in the side of the mountain. The Lakjo orcs flew in formation, guarding the biggest of their wyverns, who carried an immense boulder between its clawed feet.

The attacking orcs collided with the resistance forces of Ruk, peeling away to engage, as more emerged against them.

Enough riders were in place, however, to escort the big boulder carrier all the way to the barracks hole, as wyvern troops spilled out in spurts. The large wyvern released its massive boulder, which crashed down on the exit, collapsing it. Orcs and wyverns screamed in agony until they were silenced by the collapsing tunnel.

To Karnak's great pleasure, Klentja's Borok squadron accomplished the same task at the other barracks exit. Their plan was working perfectly so far. He would have liked fewer wyvern riders to fight off, but all things considered, they had trapped probably half of Ruk's wyvern riders in the tunnels. Should all things continue to go according to plan, they would dig them out later and give the survivors the option to join their new dawn.

As the squadrons from Lakjo and Borok engaged the riders of Ruk, the Scar Squadron barreled in for the king's landing. Goblin soldiers poured out in formation from the corridor leading into the mountain. Several trolls joined their ranks as the goblins nocked bows to launch arrows at the incoming orcs.

Karnak raised Dalkeri. The axe blazed with magical fury, as if it were excited to taste battle again. Ker dipped to the right and flourished her membranous wings wide, leveling them out after dodging a pair of arrows. Karnak heaved back and hurled Dalkeri, which flew through the air, blazing like a storm of fire.

The axe crashed into an unfortunate goblin in the center of the ranks, spouting flame on others around him. Even with no axe in his hand, the wild smile on Karnak's orange war-painted face sent chills down the spines of the goblins toward the front.

Ker tore one of the goblins with her jaws and batted others with her wings, sending them soaring off the landing into the crevasse below. The other Scar warriors landed in similar fashion, sending half the goblin forces into a terrified frenzy.

The orcs quickly dismounted, and the wyverns took off to avoid the goblin arrows. Though, not one of them managed to do so unscathed. One unfortunate wyvern took more than her fair share of arrows, tearing holes in her wings. That slowed her escape, and a large troll skewered her with a well-aimed javelin. She toppled and fell into the ravine.

One goblin thought himself rather fortunate to face Karnak without a weapon and raised his spear with glee. Karnak's malicious grin made the goblin waver just before Dalkeri blasted through the goblin, back into Karnak's open hand. The large gar turned his attention to several other goblins who thought they would take the orc together. He slammed his axe down hard on one of them and sliced sideways at another. The fury of Dalkeri's hunger for battle would be satisfied.

The day would not be a good one for the goblins.

High above them, Deklahn pulled himself away from the fight as he felt the magic of the Shell of Callencia in his pocket. He pulled out the shell, and the little light orb was flickering above it saying, *"—king lives, though the sorcerer has escaped through the mirror."*

He slid his scepter into a saddle loop and patted around himself, looking for his horn.

The orb flickered again, *"The sorcerer has fled through the mirror."*

Deklahn finally found his horn and sounded it in a quick burst of three blows. He did that repeatedly to be sure all of the forces heard his warning.

The sorcerer was coming.

Pernden and Merrick stumbled in opposite directions as they emerged from the smoky portal. Ralowyn was the only one unaffected by the disorientation caused by the Alkhoren Mirror. She stepped quickly from the shadows and into the light next to the throne in the large chamber.

"We are in Ruk," she said quietly to the men with her. "We must hurry."

She turned toward a side door that was flung wide open and heard loud battle cries and clanging metal. They had arrived in the midst of a battle. Though it was relatively dark in the massive chamber, her elven eyes easily picked up a trail of blood drops headed in the direction of the open door.

The other two joined her near the doorway. "He went this way?" Merrick asked, noticing the spots of blood on the stone floor.

"So, it would appear," Ralowyn said, unsure. She sensed something wasn't right.

"What are we waiting for?" Pernden asked. "We have the sorcerer injured. We should finish him while he's weak!"

"I concur, but it seems as thoug—"

Ralowyn's thought was cut off as a wave of magical energy slammed into their backs and sent them sliding across the stone floor into the long hallway. The doors creaked and slammed behind them. Merrick saw the wicked grin of Jaernok Tur just before they closed.

"No!" Merrick jumped to his feet and banged on the door. "Help me get it open!"

Pernden ran up next to him, and the two slammed the door in unison.

"Wait!" Ralowyn said, but the men did not hear her. "Wait! Be quiet!"

When they stopped and looked at her, they saw her visage turn to fear.

"What is it?" Merrick asked.

"I can hear his mystical mutterings ..."

"What is he doing?" Pernden asked. "We can't let him get a spell on us."

"Oh, no," she said under her breath, looking around.

"What is it Ral—"

Merrick caught sight of the gargoyles sitting on podiums lining the hallway. They were no longer statues, immobile and lifeless. They were shaking off the dust of long years of sitting, their stone bodies crackling as they stretched. As one, they spotted the intruders. The gargoyles screeched and flew into the air. The hallway became a mess of stone bodies flying in a chaotic flurry.

Ralowyn launched a purple orbed magic missile and blasted one of the gargoyles into the hallway wall. It was dazed by the attack but shook it off quickly. The trio would not survive in the narrow hallway with the rampaging gargoyles. They had to reach open air.

"Run!" Ralowyn shouted. She used her magic to lob a spell that sucked several of the gargoyles together midair. They roiled angrily, kicking and scratching at each other, trying to separate themselves. It wasn't much, and the spell would only hold for a moment. It was enough for them to start their escape. They bolted down the hallway as a dozen hideous stone gargoyles chased them.

Pernden took a swing at them from the rear. Wintertide sent a frozen blade slicing at them. Some of the gargoyles grew streaking icicles, but they remained undeterred by the half-hearted attack.

The chase was on.

Karnak met a troll that loomed high over his large frame. The troll was particularly nasty. His face was marred and covered with piercings. Karnak wondered if the troll was chosen for his role because he was an adept fighter or because he boasted a particularly scary demeanor. Neither answer mattered to the gar. He would slay the troll either way.

The troll bellowed as he heaved his massive mace. The wicked weapon whirred past Karnak's head as the gar dodged its path. He rolled to one knee and poised himself for a counterstrike. A nearby goblin rushed him but was blasted away by a powerful magic missile from Smarlo. Karnak nodded to his friend before Smarlo sought his own troll to battle.

Swiftly, the troll was on Karnak again. The brute came down with a heavy slam of his mace. The orc gar rolled away again, but that time caught his momentum and turned it for a counterattack. He leaped into the air and hammered Dalkeri into the shoulder of the great troll. The troll hollered in pain as the axe seared his flesh. He writhed in agony, catching Karnak with a massive elbow to the face, sending the orc sprawling to the ground. Dalkeri blazed, stuck in the shoulder blade of the monstrous troll.

Smarlo was fully engaged with another troll on the large platform. As Karnak recovered to his knees, he let the ringing in his head work itself out. His vision was unclear but strangely focused at the same time, a disorienting feeling. He looked around and saw his Scar Squadron warriors battling the Ruk soldiers in blurry sequence. His clarity of vision unfortunately landed on the warriors who had fallen. Goblins and trolls of Ruk. But not only them ... Orange war-painted orcs of the Scar Squadron and several from Borok who had joined them lay sprawled across the platform. It was a disheartening sight.

As his faculties returned and the ringing faded, Karnak realized he was surrounded. Three goblins took measured steps toward him, each with their weapons leveled at him. The troll, Dalkeri wavering and burning in his shoulder, stalked near with rage in his hideous face that convinced Karnak it would be the last face he saw.

"Tanessa, I'm sorry," he whispered.

Merrick batted at another gargoyle that swooped in to scratch at the huntsman. The three companions bolted out of the hallway into a great entry corridor that opened to fresh mountain air. As they entered the corridor, the gargoyles scattered from the trio and flew to attack other intruders. The scene playing out before the companions was a shock. They did not stop running, but their pace slowed so their minds could make some sense of what they saw. Ruk was experiencing some sort of civil war. Orcs, goblins, and trolls fought one another.

"Wait, the gargoyles chase after new prey." Pernden shouted to his friends over the noise of the battle. "We must get through the door to Jaernok Tur."

"No! Wait," Ralowyn said. "The orcs with the war paint—they fight for the rebellion."

"Good for them. Let's go!" Pernden shouted back.

"No! We must help them push through," Ralowyn insisted. "They will aid us against Jaernok Tur. Lanryn told me of the rebellion. They are our allies!"

"Orc allies?"

"Yes!"

Pernden looked at Ralowyn as though she were crazy and turned to Merrick for support. Merrick shot a glance at the tunnel and then to the battle scene on the great landing area before them. He knew nothing of these allies, but he trusted Ralowyn greatly.

"If she says they are our allies, then we must aid them," Merrick stated plainly.

Pernden hesitated. He was pretty sure they were both crazy, but he had to trust them. He would need their aid against the sorcerer, anyway.

"Well then, let's help our allies," Pernden said. He rolled his eyes incredulously, set his stance, and charged toward the fray.

Ralowyn and Merrick charged in behind him. The elf mage lobbed a magic missile from her staff that exploded into the side of a massive troll dragging a mace. Merrick hurtled his spear into the back of a goblin next to two others. He flipped his bow around and shot an arrow into the one staring at his dead goblin friend in surprise. But Merrick was out of arrows, having lost a few during their escape from the gargoyles. He ran at the other goblin with his bow in his hands as though he meant to bludgeon the goblin with it. The goblin waited in hungry anticipation, his sword at the ready.

Before Merrick could engage him, a blazing axe flew in from the side and swatted the goblin like a bug. He flew through the air and bashed against a troll farther away, the axe searing through him and into the troll's thick hide.

Merrick immediately grabbed the spear he'd thrown and pulled it from the dead goblin. He raised it in a defensive posture, ready to fight, but then he saw who had taken out the goblin. A large orc was kneeling on one knee, his dark black hair was tied in a knot on the back of his head, and his face and chest were covered in smeared orange war paint. Merrick recognized that orc face, even behind the war paint.

"This is some twist of fate, Huntsman," Karnak said, baffled and exhausted. Dalkeri had been loosed from the massive troll when the explosive lavender spear had erupted in the monster's side. The axe had immediately flown back to Karnak, who was then able to bat away the remaining goblin to protect his rescuer, the huntsman.

A slew of emotions welled within Merrick. He stood before the orc who had killed Rora, his beloved falcon, and the orc was defenseless. He gripped the spear in his hands. His knuckles turned white. Merrick could skewer the orc and avenge Rora. Something aside from vengeance brewed within him.

"I am sorry, Huntsman. I didn't know we were of like mind," Karnak said with all sincerity. "I wish our first meeting had been different."

Merrick's chin quivered. He walked to the kneeling orc slowly, never taking his eyes off him. His spear pointed directly at the orc's heart.

Karnak nodded solemnly. "I was foolish to believe in a future hope where orc and man might walk as friends. There is too much past for us to overcome. I understand if you need vengeance. Even now, the others are pushing through the last of the king's forces. They will accomplish the mission without me. I only wish you to know this warrior's heart is one of sorrow before I die."

Merrick glared at him as he spoke. His eyes brimmed with tears at the memory of Rora. Karnak closed his eyes, ready to accept his fate.

"My name is Merrick."

Karnak opened his eyes and stared at the man-kin in surprise. He'd loosened his tense stance and stood with the spear at his side. His hand extended to the large orc.

"You don't have to call me 'huntsman.' My name is Merrick."

"Karnak," the orc gar replied and took the man's hand. Merrick heaved with all his might to help the great orc to his feet. Karnak gave a slight chuckle. "Perhaps there is a future for us to hope toward yet."

"I believe we have to hope for something greater than ourselves. You and I should still have words when this is all done. But I want to hope for something greater than vengeance."

Karnak looked down at the man-kin, though he thought him large and mighty. The orc gar placed a finger to his brow and gave a slight bow to the man.

The huntsman had surprised him yet again.

The battle for Ruk ended quickly when the wyvern riders of both Lakjo and Borok finished off the riders of Ruk and joined the fight on the king's landing. Only a few trolls remained standing, and perhaps fifteen goblins. They threw down their weapons and surrendered as soon as the other squadrons joined in. The battle was already lost, and goblins didn't tend to be particularly brave to begin with, save for a few notable exceptions.

Some of the wyverns' wings had been torn by the pesky gargoyles. Those steeds would be grounded for life. Thankfully, Smarlo and Deklahn were able to wrangle the stone monsters back into their statuesque rest. Though, some of them were rather ornery and plummeted into the ravine when they were put to sleep.

The gars set up guards and put together teams to dig out the riders of Ruk, so their wyverns would not suffocate in the collapsed tunnels. The surviving orcs would certainly have gotten out through doorways into the inner tunnels. The gars sent teams to go through the inner tunnels and pass along the news to all the occupants of the city.

"Let the people know King Sahr is no longer king of Drelek," Zotar instructed.

Gar Zotar and Gar Klentja joined Karnak and the three companions from outside of Drelek in the hallway to the throne chamber. Karnak threw Dalkeri into the doors, and the axe blazed into an inferno as it wedged itself into the magic-imbued wood. Ralowyn, who made several of the orcs uncomfortable with her elven magic, flourished the Staff of Anvelorian and sent forth a streak of lavender fury that connected with the blazing magic of Fire Storm. The combined power exploded the doors wide open.

They immediately turned toward the mirror in the corner of the chamber, but it was too late. The mystic river of energy faded just as they entered the room.

A crazy laugh rang out and echoed in the large chamber. "They've gone! They've gone," the voice sang. Then came a loud hacking, as though someone were coughing up their lung. "Who do you think you are, entering my throne room without being summoned?"

"Where is the sorcerer?!" Zotar yelled at the mad king.

"Through the mirror he goes!" the king laughed wickedly. "Took his pet, the man-kin, with him! But I couldn't go. No, no, no, no, no ..." His voice trailed off.

"Jolan went with him ..." Pernden growled under his breath, to no one but himself. "Wait, did he go back to Whitestone?" The sudden realization that the sorcerer could have returned to Whitestone made his heart sink into his stomach.

"You let this dog speak to your king!" Sahr screamed. With every word, his head waggled crazily.

"You are no king to anyone. Not anymore!" Zotar spat back at him.

"What? What?"

382

King Sahr grabbed a sword he clearly did not know how to use and dashed like a rabid animal at Zotar. Before anyone else could move, the king ran himself through on the spear of the huntsman, who had positioned himself quickly between the mad king and the gar. The king's head waggled one more time as he tried to get a good look at the man-kin who had ended him.

"You don't know what fury you have unleashed, man-kin. This is only the beginning ..." He laughed and coughed, choking on his own blood. Then, he slumped into a grotesque heap on the floor.

Deklahn and Smarlo entered the room from the hallway as the king breathed his last.

"Deklahn, we must know if the sorcerer has returned to Whitestone. Quickly!" Zotar barked.

Though confused, Deklahn quickly produced the Shell of Callencia from his robes. He muttered the magic commands to it, and the shell glowed. "Lanryn! Lanryn!"

Everyone waited without a word. The silence seemed greater in the dark cavernous chamber.

The orb suddenly flickered to life, *"Yes? Sorry, we've been cleaning up, and I was helping to carry a dead goblin into the hallway."*

"Has Jaernok Tur returned to Whitestone?" Deklahn asked quickly.

"No. We've covered the mirror. It hasn't made a peep."

Deklahn looked toward the others. No one had a response for him, save for Ralowyn.

"There must be another mirror," she concluded.

Deklahn nodded to her, but he could hardly believe it himself.

"Wait! Did he escape through the mirror in Ruk?" Lanryn asked.

Deklahn shook out the shock of the new revelation. "Yes, sorry. We think there must be another mirror."

"Then we must make sure to secure them well. We don't know where the other might be," Lanryn warned.

"Agreed," Ralowyn said to the others. "It is most likely in Kelvur."

"The mirrors are of greater power than we knew." Deklahn said, directing his thought to Zotar.

"We will have to convene on the mirrors after all this is done," Gar Zotar instructed.

"Lanryn, we will need to convene on the mirrors when all this is done," Deklahn relayed to the elf through the shell.

"Very good, then," Lanryn replied.

The illuminated orb that floated above the shell flickered and vanished.

The fact that the sorcerer was still out there, somewhere, left the group feeling uneasy.

While the day was a victory, they worried the war may have just begun.

Merrick sat above the world at the edge of the king's landing. There had been much to do, and they had aided in the process of cleaning up after the great battle that had taken place. Evening drew near. He watched to the west as the sun streaked its colors across the expanse. The mountain breeze made the evening quite comfortable.

While the others discussed the next move in the throne room, Merrick had found it dark and constricting. And frankly, he was no strategist. He barely considered himself a warrior. Perhaps he would have to change that mentality. Somehow, he'd not only survived one battle, but three. Regardless, his words would be of little value compared to the seasoned warriors, so he had decided to enjoy the view from Ruk, since he did not know when he would get the chance again.

Footsteps behind him caused him to glance over his shoulder. He heaved a long sigh but stayed seated where he was. Karnak approached the seated huntsman and asked, "May I join you?"

"Please," Merrick replied. Though he was happy to be alone, he knew the orc was trying to build a bridge between them.

"I have always loved the way the sun paints the sky over the mountains," Karnak offered as he sat next to the huntsman.

Merrick laughed. "It was a little dark in there for me."

Karnak laughed along. "Me too. Believe it or not, that is a rather well-lit chamber for a Drelek fort. That's why I love Calrok."

"Calrok, near the Scar Cliffs on the Gant Sea?" Merrick asked, sorting it out on the map in his memory.

"You know of it!" the orc said, excitedly.

"Only from maps," the huntsman admitted.

"Ah then, you do not know of its beauty. It sits where the mountains meet the sea. I can gaze upon the beauty of my wife as the sea breeze blows through her dark hair. And on the same evening, climb rocks with my son, Gernot. He is a rambunctious tyke."

Merrick smiled at the thought of the large orc playing with a child. It seemed an odd notion to him.

"In Calrok, we love the sun," Karnak continued. "We enjoy the warmth and life of it. The sea glitters in its light. The mountains and cliffs wear different shadows every day. It is a beautiful place to call home—a home worth defending."

The two fell silent, neither knew how to address their previous encounter. Honestly, neither really wanted to do so.

After a long silence, Merrick spoke again. "I have seen many wondrous things on this wild journey, and I think I should like to see Calrok as well."

Karnak smiled at the huntsman. "And, I think I should like to welcome you."

The two sat, quite content in their silence, as the sun continued to set. They watched over the mountain range, a truly inspiring sight, and one Merrick had never seen the like. They sat in each other's presence, neither harboring hard feelings. Both were ready to let go of the past. They would take the moment of peace, for they knew that soon enough, the others would summon them. There was more work to be done.

For the moment, they enjoyed the beauty of the painted sky.

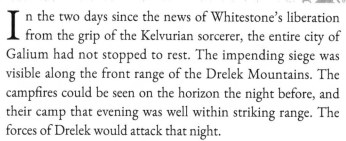

CHAPTER THIRTY-ONE

AN EMERALD ARROW

In the two days since the news of Whitestone's liberation from the grip of the Kelvurian sorcerer, the entire city of Galium had not stopped to rest. The impending siege was visible along the front range of the Drelek Mountains. The campfires could be seen on the horizon the night before, and their camp that evening was well within striking range. The forces of Drelek would attack that night.

Galium had made preparations. The wagoners had carried as many families as possible out of the city and its surrounding hills. Tobin was of great help. He gathered the others and organized them to take as many families as they could out to Crossdin. Should Galium's defenses fall, at least the innocents would be safely away from the city.

Any of the families that couldn't leave were brought within the great stone walls of the city, where they could be better protected. Though King Thygram Markensteel was rather direct in his communication with people, his compassion for them was evident. He gave short directions to anyone and everyone, but always for their benefit. The soldiers were another story. He would speak to them of glory unknown and the tales that the bards would tell of their valiant battle. He spoke to them with encouragement and a fervor that even inspired Orin and his companions.

The defense plan was rather simple. Orin and Coal would ride with the hog cavalry. They did equip Orin with a horse, for war-hogs are better suited to dwarves. Coal would ride a great hog named Grub, a rather shaggy beast with mighty tusks.

Ellaria and Ezel would remain atop the wall to aid from there. With Ezel's magic and Ellaria's bow, they would be able to defend at a distance. They would try to keep the wyvern riders distracted, along with the rest of the Galium archers. And finally, Bendur Clagstack and Lotmeag Kandersaw would lead two teams of garvawk warriors to fight the dragon.

It was as solid a plan as could be made for the circumstances. And though the nerves of the entire city were on edge, they waited in the calm before the storm, knowing they had done all they could to prepare.

The first horns sounded in the middle of the night while the moon was high and illuminated the battlefield. Among the goblin foot soldiers stood tall orcs and even taller trolls. The orcs seemed to be commanding the goblins and keeping them in order. The brutish trolls, however, maneuvered through the lines without regard to the formation the orcs tried to keep, sending goblins skittering in bunches to avoid large troll feet.

Argus Azulekor laughed at the disarray but restrained himself quickly. Even though he found their lack of discipline humorous, he recognized the graveness of the situation. They had seen no sign of the dragon or the wyvern riders, but they knew the beast would show itself before the battle was through. King Thygram, standing next to him, gave a long sigh. The moment had arrived.

He turned to look behind him where the war-hog riders were standing, ready. His eyes fell upon the stranger in their midst. Orin looked odd, saddled on a horse, tall above the others. Though the king was thankful to have the guardian with them. The Griffin Guard trained expert warriors, and he had no doubt Orin would fight a good fight to defend his kin.

"The hour is here!" The king spoke over them. "We have seen no sign of the dragon, but surely our enemy thinks the dragon to be a surprise for us. The beast is almost certainly looming in the shadows of the mountains. But we know he is there. Even with this knowledge, we bear hearts of steel. Galium has never wavered, and it never shall. It shall be as the stone of the bedrock that our ancestors built it upon.

"So, take heart, brothers and sisters. Be strong as the mountain that stands as a beacon for all we are here. They think we do not know what they bring against us. Truly, they do not know what they have unleashed against themselves!"

"Yeah!!" a particularly excited war-hog rider hollered. The dwarves all around laughed. Even King Thygram let out an amused chuckle before he turned back to look over the battlefield.

"This has turned into quite the adventure, hasn't it?" Coal said to Orin, gazing up at him and smiling.

"Not at all what I expected," Orin nodded, finding the scene surreal.

"Life doesn't always give us what we expect, but what we do with the unexpected tells the tale of who we are." The sentiment from the dwarf surprised the man, but he said nothing to ruin it. Coal continued, "I am glad to ride alongside you. I did not expect to make such a sure friend."

"Nor did I," Orin agreed. "Let's finish this well, so we might enjoy more fellowship together."

"Aye," Coal said. "That was my plan."

Coal straightened the helmet on his head and adjusted himself in the saddle on top of the war-hog. Grub grunted at the motion, and Coal patted the creature on its shaggy shoulder. He gripped the mighty war hammer in the saddle loop, admiring its craftsmanship. It had been a gift from King Thygram's own collection. It was a finely crafted dwarven war hammer, as fine as any the dwarf prince had ever seen. The metal shimmered in the moonlight, and the golden accents and runic markings brought the whole piece together with a beautiful elegance. It was equal parts art and tool of destruction. And Coal was ready to use it for the latter.

Atop the wall, Ellaria shrugged in the light armor the dwarves had put together for her. It was not uncomfortable; she merely was not used to it. And admittedly, she shifted in her nervousness. She was no warrior, but here she stood at the edge of battle, surrounded by warriors depending on her. A slender hand pressed against her palm, wrapping around hers, giving a gentle and comforting squeeze. She looked down at Ezel. Even though the wall-walk had a low battlement for their protection, Ezel stood in between them for visibility.

He didn't look over the battlefield. He looked at the young woman next to him. His kind eyes smiled at her; and though she was nervous, she realized she was not alone.

Suddenly, an arrow struck the little gnome, sending him toppling over on the wall-walk. He still held Ellaria's hand, so he didn't tumble off the back of the wall. She released a terrified scream that sent shivers down Orin's spine. She gathered up the little gnome, who blinked at her curiously as though he had no idea what just happened. The hardwood medallion he wore around his neck glowed with an auburn tint; even stranger, the arrow was nowhere to be found.

Argus Azulekor rushed to the side of the gnome and stared at the token. "What is that?" the old mage asked hurriedly.

Ezel looked at it with surprise, as well. He had not learned anything about the medallion yet, but somehow it was imbued with a magic that had just saved him.

"I don't know," Ellaria answered the mage. "The wizard Enkeli gave it to him."

"A wizard?" Argus restated, stunned. He inspected the little grey gnome, and finding no wounds on him, declared, "I think that wizard just saved your friend's life."

"Is he able to stand?" King Thygram asked.

"Oh, he is quite fine, my King," the old mage replied. "I should very much like to inspect that token later, though," he said to Ezel.

The gnome nodded his agreement. Perhaps the dwarf mage would be able to help him understand the gift.

"Good," the king said. He turned back to look out over their enemy's formations. "It appears our enemies think they are ready to face us."

King Thygram Markensteel waved his hand above his head to signal the war-hogs into action.

"Let us show them how wrong they are!" The king shouted.

With those words, the battle for Galium began.

Dwarven arrows fell like rain upon the Drelek forces. For their part, the goblin archers had moved into position to return fire, but the superior height advantage went to the dwarves atop the wall of Galium.

The war-hog riders burst forth from the gates and charged ahead to meet the warriors of Drelek. The boars' large tusks met ill-fated goblin bellies. Though, the ones that took the brunt of dwarven steel might have argued themselves as less fortunate. As the dwarven warriors barreled through the first line of goblins, the clanging of steel on steel erupted. The goblins fought back with all they had.

Lotmeag Kandersaw itched to join the battle, but Bendur Clagstack stayed the younger warrior with a steely look. They sat hunched in the dark spots of the mountains, hiding in crags as if they were the shadows themselves. The garvawks waited silently, totally obedient to their dwarven riders. The sky was still unplagued by wyvern riders, and they'd seen no sign of the dragon, yet.

As the intensity of the battle far below raged more and more, so did the fire in the warriors' bellies. Lotmeag knew they had to wait. For Drelek would not so carelessly attack Galium.

The dragon would come.

Coal's mighty battle hammer slammed into a goblin's face as his war-hog greeted another with its vicious tusks. Coal laughed, happy that Grub had turned out to be such a fierce battle companion.

Orin had become quite the target as the largest member of the cavalry. His height upon the horse made him easy to pick out. The horse, however, was rather set on surviving the battle and moved swiftly as Orin cut down the foes that came against them.

Several goblins with spears rallied together to surround the war horse. They inched ever closer as the horse bucked uncomfortably. Orin turned it side to side, looking for an out but saw nothing. As he was preparing to dismount and fight them on foot so the horse could get away, a blazing green arrow pierced one of the goblins right through the neck, dropping him instantly. A blue bolt of faery fire blasted into another, just before another arrow whizzed by. Orin looked up to his friends on the wall and gave them a nod as the surrounding goblins panicked. He was not sure they would see his gratitude from the distance, but he felt it still. He would have to make sure to show it when they celebrated later.

Coal rode in behind one of the spear-wielding goblins and heaved his hammer into its back. A loud crack sounded, and the goblin dropped. Orin noted that the dwarf looked as though he were having fun. Though a fire burned within him and adrenaline coursed through his veins, the man wouldn't say he was having fun. The guardian was optimistic, and he would keep that attitude. A hopeless warrior sees no future and shrivels in battle. Orin would fight for his friends and their new allies. There was a lot more at stake than just his life.

"Take down the troll!" Orin shouted to Coal over the clanging of weapons.

Coal nodded to him, and the two rode straight at a nearby troll who was causing havoc among some of the other hog riders. Grub ran straight for the troll's legs, cutting the monster's thick hide with its razor-sharp tusks. The troll squealed at the pain in its leg as Coal laid a hammer blow right into its knee. The massive troll reacted and swung down hard with his mace. It slammed into Grub, sending the war-hog and the dwarf flying off to the side.

Two other war-hog riders started beating at the troll's injured leg as Orin rode past, slicing at the troll's middle. The troll swung wildly, not sure which enemy to go for first, feeling as though it were being swarmed. A haphazard swing caught Orin right in the chest, sending him flying to the ground. Fortunately for him, he had been close to the troll and taken the extended handle of the mace rather than its spiked head.

Orin coughed as he tried to breathe. He'd gotten the wind knocked clean out of him, and it took everything he had just to suck air back into his lungs. He rolled over in the dirt, heaving. He looked up at the troll as it moved toward him with rage in its eyes, lifting its mace high. It stumbled as one of the riders dug his axe deep into the troll's already ripped leg. The troll wailed as he fell to his good knee and turned to attack the rider.

As he turned, Coal's mighty war hammer came in like an avalanche, smashing into the troll's lowered head. In his dazed state, Orin watched with amazement as the dwarf seemed to fly through the air to hit the troll.

Orin coughed a couple more times as Coal heaved the guardian to his feet. "You alright there?" the dwarf asked, concerned. He looked the man over for any punctures Orin's armor might have taken from the spiked mace.

"Hit ... with the handle ... A wild swing," Orin assured him.

"Good!" Coal slapped him on the back. "Can't have you dying already. We haven't even seen the dr—"

And before the word left the dwarf's lips, a sudden roar from above the peaks rattled the entire valley.

Dwarf and goblin alike paused at the arrival of the dragon of Drelek. The beast soared over the ridge, bathed in moonlight and followed by a squadron of wyvern riders. Loud cheers rolled out from the goblins on the battlefield, which spurred the dwarves back into action. The battle raged anew.

The dragon swooped low over the battlefield and released a burst of flames, scattering warriors from both sides. It wafted high into the air once more and charged toward Galium. Orin watched in awe.

"Come on, then," Coal said to the guardian. "That one is for the garvawks. These ones are for us." He turned toward the goblin army and squeezed the mighty war hammer in both hands.

"Then let us have them!" Orin agreed. And the two ran back into the fray.

Argus Azulekor swirled his hands in a well-practiced but seemingly aimless way. He chanted some ancient illusion spell that crackled and sparked magic energy in the air around him. Sparks turned to flame, and suddenly the magic blazed to life in a red and orange symphony of lights. The flames flew up into the air and unfurled mighty wings, taking on the shape and size of a dragon, which flew across the front of the ridge.

Much to their delight, the Drelek dragon immediately changed course to chase after the mage's illusion. The dragon flew with the fury of hurricane winds. It had never seen such an opponent, and the dragon raged to destroy it. When its great maw took on only sparks and flame with no flesh to sink its teeth into, the beast flapped in great fury. The wind from its wings split the illusion into pieces, sending sparks flying in every direction. The distraction had done its job.

Bendur, Lotmeag, and the rest of the garvawk warriors appeared suddenly through the sparks and flames and attacked the great dragon's underbelly with their piercing panther claws.

The dragon writhed in confusion, and the waves of wind from its massive wings sent several of the garvawks spinning away.

The dragon launched itself high into the air to get away from them and scratched and kicked at the ones still clinging to his underbelly. One poor dwarf got scraped right off his garvawk and flung to the mountainside below. His garvawk didn't fare any better as the dragon's great claws clamped around its body and crushed it.

It took a minute for the wyvern riders to realize the dragon's screeches and roars were a result of it being attacked. They had initially swooped in to aid the ground forces but were quite distracted with the archers on the wall. Half of them had been on their way to the wall when they swerved to aid Gar Nargoh and the dragon. The other half was too engaged with the ground forces to notice.

"No, no, no!" Argus cursed the situation.

When the wyverns arrived to aid the dragon, Lotmeag took his garvawk into a dive along the ridge. They couldn't fight the dragon and the wyverns. He whistled as loud as he could, and his team of garvawk riders fell into a dive behind him. The motion of the garvawks diving into the shadows of the ridge halted the wyvern riders as they lost sight of the warriors. The moon was high and bright, and the contrasted shadows made it difficult for the orcs to spot their opponents. A couple of the wyvern riders moved closer to the ridge, trying to find the dwarves in the shadows.

Suddenly, the garvawk warriors reappeared out of the shadows, overcoming the two wyvern riders who had ventured too close. The other orcs swooped in to engage the garvawk warriors while they were visible in the moonlight. Tooth and claw and maw and sword and axe and spear collided in mayhem.

With fewer garvawks to contend with, the Drelek dragon ripped through the warriors quickly. Bendur Clagstack's face ran with tears as he did everything he could to fight the dragon, while his brothers fell left and right. He was the last of his team remaining and came face to face with the dragon. He looked past the great maw of the dragon to lock eyes with the orc that rode the vile beast.

Bendur's great grey beard flew sideways in the mountain breeze. He wiped his face with his sleeve, took his last throwing axe in his hand, and settled himself in the saddle. "I'm sorry, love," he patted his garvawk's sleek fur and kicked hard.

The garvawk shot off, and the two charged at the massive dragon. Bendur let out a primal war cry as they flew. The dragon's neck began to glow as it worked up the fire from its belly. It opened its great jaws and unleashed a blast of fire, but not before Bendur Clagstack loosed his last throwing axe. The dragon turned its body ever so slightly as it crunched its teeth down on the cooked snack.

The throwing axe flew harmlessly by the orc rider, ringing with a clang off the hardened scales of the dragon's tail.

"Our garvawk warriors have failed," King Thygram said to Argus. He turned his attention to the archers. "Focus all of your arrows on the wyverns over the battlefield!"

Argus looked up into the sky at the mighty dragon. It was coming their way.

Ellaria grew more in tune with the magic of the green stone around her neck as she loosed arrow after arrow. In fact, she had run out of physical arrows and had not replenished her quiver from the arrow barrels. Instead, she simply nocked and drew her bowstring with arrows made of pure green magical energy with seamless, fluid motions.

As she stole a look up at the dragon and saw the beast burn and eat one of the garvawk warriors, she realized their original plan was failing. She loosed another green arrow toward a wyvern rider, and at that exact moment, one of Ezel's blasts struck the same wyvern. The green and blue mystical forces came together and erupted into a massive explosion against the unlucky wyvern and its orc rider. Both hit the ground, unmoving.

A sudden idea came to her, and judging by the similar look in Ezel's eyes, it was in line with his own thoughts.

"Argus!" she yelled.

"What is it, my lady?" the mage asked as he lobbed a fireball from his short silver and blue scepter.

"I have an idea!" she yelled before loosing another blazing emerald arrow. "Ezel and I need to get to the tower! Can you get the dragon to come this way once we're there?"

"The beast comes this way now!" Argus replied.

Ellaria and Ezel turned, and sure enough, the dragon was on its way. They bolted along the wall-walk, running behind dwarven archers and hopping over the fallen, wishing for more time to proceed past them with reverence. They ran with the urgency of active battle. The pair slipped through a doorway and turned down the hall toward the stairs, which they ascended rapidly. They heaved through the door at the top and tried to catch their breaths.

But the dragon was upon them.

The dragon of Drelek swooped low over Galium and unleashed a shower of fire. The archers that didn't dive and scatter away from the fire shot arrows feverishly. The hardened scales of the dragon rejected entry to the bee stings, and arrows fell dangerously back at the dwarven archers.

"We're going to need a better shot," Ellaria said to Ezel, looking out one of the great windows.

She climbed out the window onto the ledge and used the cleverly smithed stonework on the outside of the tower to climb onto the roof. Ezel managed the climb as well, and they readied themselves for the dragon's next pass. The smell of smoke rose into the air, and the embers of reduced buildings inside Galium lit the city.

The dragon took a wide turn before settling on its next path of destruction over the dwarven city. And then it charged.

"We'll fire on three, yeah?" Ellaria said to Ezel. She didn't need to look at him to know he was with her. "One."

The dragon flew in with a madness in its great eyes, as though it were hungry for more devastation.

"Two."

Ellaria held her bow taut, the muscles in her arms shaking not out of weariness but with the power of the magical stone. Ezel swirled his hands in a holding pattern, waiting to unleash the blast. His eyes blazed with blue faery fire, and several of his runic tattoos were alight. Their faces were set like flint as they watched the incoming dragon.

The furious monster's neck glowed amber as the fires welled within him. Just as the dragon began to spew his vile flames, "Three."

Green and blue magic intersected in midair to become one bolt of ruin. The bolt landed a massive blow to the shoulder of the dragon, which instantly turned and spewed flame at the tower and slammed its wicked tail against the building. The beautiful stonework was undone, as the roof of the tower was smashed below them, sending the woman and the gnome toppling off the side.

They tumbled through the sky together. Ezel had grabbed Ellaria and combined his magic with the magic of the token to shield her from the fire. All seemed to slow down. Ellaria and Ezel had only a split second to think of the demise that raced toward them before a silvery griffin swooped in and caught the pair.

Stunned, Ellaria gripped the griffin tightly, tears flowing freely off her chin. She clung to the griffin as Ezel clung to her. Tied around the griffin's foot was a small banner of crimson cloth with golden stitching.

"Enkeli!" She joyfully shouted to Ezel. She had thought them dead, but here was the helper he'd promised to send.

When she regained some sense about her, she realized she knew the silvery feathers of the griffin. She shook herself upright on the creature to view him properly. "Silverwing!" She shouted with glee. "You silly boy!"

She could hardly contain the excitement within her, but Ezel tapped her firmly to grab her attention. The dragon had been dealt a blow it did not appreciate. It had flown up high into the air over the battlefield to compose itself. That, or the orc rider needed to regain control of the beast. Either way, the dragon roared furiously and shook its massive body as if to shake off the pain of the blow.

"Alright, silly boy, I hope you're ready to do some fancy flying, because we've got something to finish! You ready, Ezel?" She asked, looking over her shoulder at him. The gnome nodded, a new determination in his eyes, blazing blue again.

Ellaria kicked, and Silverwing shot off toward the dragon. She leaned into the speed, and her red hair flowed behind her like a banner in the wind. Ezel clung to the back of her light armor as they flew with all haste, directly at the dragon of Drelek.

The great monster saw them riding in and puffed up his chest, preparing to let out the greatest cascade of fire the creature had ever loosed. The dragon heaved his head high and his wings wide—exactly what the companions had hoped for.

Ellaria sat as straight as she could and nocked an emerald energy arrow that drew magic continually from the stone as they flew within range. Ezel pushed all the force of magic he could from his own body, flowing from the runic tattoos, through his arms, off his hands, and wrapping around the woman to join forces with the magic arrow poised in her bow. The thing became a spectacle of light in the sky as they drew closer.

The dragon drew its breath.

As if they were two chords of the same symphony, all their powers unleashed at the same time.

The javelin of pure energy was faster than the dragon's fire, and it erupted into the beast's chest. It pierced the hardened scales and struck the dragon's heart with an explosive force. The green and blue light overwhelmed the fiery amber within, only to be overtaken by darkness as the dragon plummeted to the ground far below. Goblins, orcs, and trolls ran screaming in all directions, trying to avoid the large falling mass. The dragon's final blow was against its own masters as it crashed hard to the ground, taking dozens of Drelek warriors with it into death.

When Ellaria looked up from the dragon on the ground, her emerald eyes landed on a face she knew, in an unexpected place. Not far off, Merrick, sitting atop a great spotted falcon, stared at her in awe, and behind him a great force of peoples from all over Tarrine gathered. He shook his head at her in disbelief, but his shaking soon turned to an impressed nod.

A young man decked in Whitestone armor hollered for a charge, and all the peoples that rode with him went into a dive over the battlefield. Griffin Guard, Loralith Riders, and even orange-painted Drelek orcs followed the man into the fray.

Pandemonium ran through the attacking Drelek forces when the dragon was felled. Those at the rear of the battlefield turned tail and ran. Others fought with renewed fervor, desperate for their lives. The wyvern riders fought tooth and claw but were overcome by the combined forces. Lotmeag and the few surviving garvawk warriors helped finish off the attacking wyvern riders.

Once the wyvern riders were gone and the host of flying warriors hovered over the battlefield with no aerial opponents to engage, the Drelek ground forces threw down their weapons in defeat. They begged their enemies to have mercy on their surrender. Karnak and Smarlo landed near a large group of surrendering goblins to help the dwarves, while the Scar Squadron and the Griffin Guard secured all the prisoners.

The Elves of Loralith went to the city to aid in suppressing the fires of the dragon and look for anyone who might have gotten caught in the rubble of some of the fallen buildings.

Ellaria and Ezel landed near Orin and Coal, who sat on a rock. Coal was ripping a piece of smoke-dried meat to share with the exhausted guardian. Orin laughed at the sight of Silverwing.

"Enkeli sent him," Ellaria said with a baffled shrug. She hugged the neck of the beautiful griffin, who nuzzled her, happy to be with her again. Orin shook his head in amazement.

Ezel climbed slowly onto the rock to join them. His little body was sore, but he was happy to see his friends unharmed and wanted to be near them. Orin and Coal extended hands and heaved the gnome onto the rock.

"Thanks," he signed and took the chunk of dried meat from Coal's other hand, which he munched happily.

Coal's confused expression revealed he had no idea what just happened or why he no longer had any jerky.

Then a great falcon swooped in and landed near Silverwing and Ellaria. Merrick hopped off the mighty bird and ran to his sister, taking her in his arms and squeezing her hard enough to make sure she wasn't an illusion.

"I knew it!" Coal yelled. "Never doubted your survival for a moment." Orin and Ezel shook their heads and grinned, as they took bites of the meat and watched the family reunion.

"It's good to see you," Orin shouted to Merrick.

"I thought I might never see you again. But then again, I have never known one as stubborn as you, little brother," came a familiar voice from the side of them.

Orin turned, and there stood Pernden. He hopped to his feet, tossed the meat to Coal, who happily accepted it, and climbed off the rock.

"I feared what had become of you," Orin said.

"It's been a rather busy season at Whitestone," Pernden shrugged. "I feared you dead."

Orin smiled at his brother, only a year and a half his elder. The two shared a brotherly hug, and Pernden grabbed at his brother's shoulders, taking stock of him.

"I'm fine," Orin assured him. "I'm fine." A quiver ran through his face, and he stepped back and pulled Rayin's sword from his sheath.

Pernden understood immediately. Their younger brother had died.

"I have had time to grieve for him. And you, as it happens," Pernden said comfortingly to his brother.

Orin bowed slightly and raised the sword up in front of him, offering it to Pernden, the head of their family. "This is for you. For memory and honor."

Pernden waved a hand to his younger brother and shifted. He revealed Wintertide from his own belt and shook his head. "I have already inherited one," he said sadly.

Orin recognized the blade immediately. "Melkis?" he asked, grief followed shock in his parade of expressions.

"We have much to discuss," Pernden said, pulling Orin into another embrace. "But I am glad to see you."

Coal and Ezel finished their jerky and watched their friends, completely content. It had been a long night, and dawn was birthing a new day.

The dwarf nudged the grey gnome with his elbow and signed, *"Well, see? We did it."*

Ezel tilted his head; the dwarf was right. They had done it. They had helped their new friends defeat the dragon of Drelek. And though there was much cleanup to do, they had won the battle.

"And what will we do now?" Ezel asked.

Coal laughed. *"I don't know. We have lots of new friends. Maybe it's time for a new adventure,"* he flourished with his hands.

Ezel smiled back as he twiddled the token that hung around his neck. *"This hasn't been adventure enough for you?"*

The dwarf laughed from deep within his belly and added, *"After some good rest, of course."*

"Of course," Ezel responded, exhausted but grateful.

CHAPTER THIRTY-TWO

A FUTURE HOPE

Three days had passed since the Battle of Galium. Everyone pitched in on the city's cleanup efforts. The elves organized the final rites for all the fallen. The orcs' large frames were particularly helpful in moving rubble. The dwarves quickly began stonecrafting to rebuild what had been lost. The Griffin Guard aided in corralling prisoners then helped the peoples of Galium get back to their homes or find new ones if theirs had been lost to dragon fire.

None could remember a time in their history books when all the peoples of Tarrine had worked together in such a way. The common cause of helping their neighbors inspired them, and through the days of working and intermingling, many formed new and unlikely friendships.

King Thygram Markensteel prepared a grand feast for the gathered peoples. The banquet hall of Galium was filled end to end with orc and elf and man and dwarf. Tables lined the length, with every square inch covered in amazing food that halflings and dwarves had prepared.

Tobin and Lenor had returned with Button and many of the other families that had fled to Crossdin for safety. Since Tobin had brought Orin and his companions to the castle, he and Lenor were invited to the great feast. Tobin piled food into his mouth and spoke almost unintelligibly between bites.

Lotmeag listened graciously to his brother-in-law as he played with his favorite niece. The garvawk warrior had a renewed perspective on life after losing so many of his compatriots and found the halfling's ramblings less annoying than before. He knew that even with his faults, the halfling loved him as a brother. He was happy to have loved ones. Though he'd lost many friends in the battle, he did not want to waste their sacrifice by wallowing in self-pity. That wouldn't do. He wanted to celebrate their entry into Kerathane and live the life he still had, enjoying the ones he loved.

General merriment filled the buzzing banquet hall. Despite their vast differences, the peoples gathered had one thing in common: they were warriors. And warriors know how to talk to warriors. There was laughing and joking. Some taught others games, while others discussed the beauty of their homes.

At the front of the banquet hall, leaders from the different groups spoke with ease.

Argus, Lanryn, and Deklahn huddled together while Smarlo, Ralowyn, and Ezel listened with great interest. The mages were excited to all be together for the first time. Before long, Argus produced from his blue robes another Shell of Callencia and handed it to Smarlo.

"This will allow *you* to speak with us as well," he said excitedly. "Think of all the mysteries we can uncover. All of us working together!"

Thygram, Pernden, and Karnak discussed the pressing needs in Drelek and Whitestone. As much as they would like to continue enjoying the generous hospitality of Galium's king, Ruk and Whitestone had been through their own battles and required their attention and presence.

Both needed to establish new kings. Though Garron had survived, the people of Whitestone would never trust him again.

Whatever Jaernok Tur had done to the king had damaged him greatly. Pernden would have to take over the throne in the guardian city. Though he was not fond of the notion.

Nera reminded Pernden, much to his chagrin, they would have a coronation for him in Whitestone soon. Of course, everyone at the table was invited.

Karnak promised he would make it to Whitestone for the coronation if Pernden did not think it too raw for the people to see an orc in the city after the ordeal they had endured.

"We sit together. We eat together. We speak together," Pernden pointed out. "Seems to me our peoples have had some false illusions of each other's qualities. It will be a sign to all that we embark on a new path."

"A future hope," Karnak put in.

"To a future hope!" the mages at the end of the table echoed joyfully, raising their mugs high. They were obviously having fun in one another's company.

Karnak shook his head at the mages' humorous display before turning back to Pernden. "It would be an honor."

The large orc looked across the table at Merrick, who had an approving look on his face.

"I wonder if I might be able to join you back to Drelek?" Merrick asked.

His question caught the attention of the women flanking him.

"Merrick, I … I just got you back …" Ellaria said with worry in her eyes.

"Gar Karnak and I have had time to speak before this. He tells me of the beauty of the city of Calrok by the sea. I should greatly like to see it."

"And I should like to join him, if the gar permits," Ralowyn nodded to Karnak.

"Then I should like to show you both," he smiled around his tusks. He assured Ellaria, "And fear not. I will bring him back to you in Whitestone for the coronation celebration."

Coal and Orin watched and listened, each happy just to be at the table. It had been a long journey, one with many twists and turns. Embarking on a future hope that saw all the peoples of Tarrine coming together would have no shortage of adventure. They looked forward to it.

Orin realized that in all the preparations and everything that had happened, he hadn't asked Coal about his clan in Kalimandir.

"So, clan prince, huh?" the guardian whispered to him.

"Ah! I don't want to talk about that. This is a celebration," the dwarf deflected.

"Alright," Orin nodded suspiciously. "But you will tell me at some point. I should very much like to hear that tale."

"Bah," Coal waved the man away.

King Thygram Markensteel climbed atop the table in front of the assembly and clanged his gauntlets together. Everyone paused their side conversations to give the dwarf king their attention.

"The merriment of this evening brings great joy to me grieving heart!" He yelled so all in the banquet hall could hear. "To see so many peoples gathered in one place is a sight unseen. Surely, this is a mark in history, where the peoples gather for a future hope.

"And I see that hope in ye. Look around! Elf sitting and laughing with orc-kin. And dwarf and man. Halfling and even our very own deep gnome," he nodded to Ezel. The gnome's eyes brimmed with tears, overwhelmed by the mention.

"We have lost much," Thygram went on. "But our loss is to their gain. Surely the fallen share a feast in the halls of Kerathane, celebrating our victory with us."

Quiet agreements resonated throughout the great banquet hall. A mixture of loss and pride in their fallen comrades rolled through all present.

"This is not the end of this triumph; it is only the beginning. That future hope is now. We will not let the spark that burst into flame here go out. The peoples of Tarrine will write a new history, starting from this point. The Battle of Galium will never be forgotten. It is truly the day we battled for the heart of Tarrine and will always be remembered as the day a new sun dawned.

"In memorial of this mark in history, we will paint the ceiling of this great hall with a mural that includes all the peoples that were part of this victory. But again, this is not the end—only the beginning.

"I encourage ye; drink, eat, and enjoy each other's company. Make friends and send pigeons and ravens to each other. Make future plans with one another. This is how we build our future: together!"

An unusual chilly fog hung over the next morning. The guardians of the Talon Squadron and the orcs of the Scar Squadron talked easily as they prepared to set off for their homes. They utilized the last moments together to joke and have more fun.

Up in one of Galium's towers, Argus, Lanryn, Deklahn, and Smarlo waited until the last possible moment to part. They had been up the whole night discussing different magics and learning from one another. They discussed, too, some of the more concerning matters. Lanryn told them of the foreboding warning of Seer Zelor in Loralith. Argus scrunched his face at the words but did not give away his initial thoughts.

"Does the elven witch think something else is coming?" Deklahn asked.

"She's not a witch. She's the current Seer of Loralith, a position of great tradition," Lanryn corrected the orc.

Deklahn looked at Smarlo. She sounded like a witch to them, but they weren't elves, so what did they know?

"It would be wise for us to be on guard," Argus cut in. "The Alkhoren Mirrors allowed Jaernok Tur to escape. And he was not found in Ruk or Whitestone. We should be very cautious with the artifacts. We don't know how many there might be."

The graveness in his tone put a damper on the attitudes of the gathered mages. They had enjoyed their time with one another and were optimistic about what they would be able to accomplish together in the years to come. The thought of something coming against that put them in a foul mood.

"We mustn't get down, my friends," the dwarf encouraged them. "We do not know what tomorrow will bring. But as far as it is up to us, we will live peaceably with one another. And we will be of one accord. Should something come against one of us, the others will rise to answer!"

His words raised their moods again, and they talked excitedly as they left the room. They made their way down the stairs and out to the stables where Smarlo and Deklahn needed to saddle their wyverns.

Argus and Lanryn offered their heartfelt goodbyes to the pair of orcs and walked back into the castle.

"I had hoped the Riders and I could stay until it was time to travel to Whitestone for the coronation of young Pernden," Lanryn said to the old dwarf.

"I would be glad to host you a little longer. In fact ..." Argus's thoughts trailed off, and then he continued. "I could very much use your help."

"With what?" The elf mage asked curiously.

"A wizard artifact."

"A wizard artifact?" he repeated.

"Yes, one given to our gnomish friend by a wizard."

"Ezel? I find him quite the curious creature."

"Yes ... very strange to see a grey gnome on the surface. I am intrigued by the magic he bears. It is of a source I do not understand. And strangest of all, he carries the trinket of a wizard," Argus mused.

"Did he say the wizard's name?"

"Ellaria said the wizard's name was Enkeli," Argus shared.

"Really?" Lanryn asked quietly.

"Do you know of him?" Argus asked. He thought it good Lanryn was staying, so he could employ the mage's help.

"I have read the name in ancient scrolls," Lanryn said, his face contorting as he searched his memory. "I think, though, we may need to spend some time with our gnomish friend."

"I think that might be wise, indeed."

CHAPTER THIRTY-THREE

CALROK BY THE SEA

They'd argued in circles for several days, but Karnak had finally hit the end of his patience.

"I won't take the throne, Zotar. I am no king," he said plainly. "You will have to raise another."

Before Gar Zotar could respond with another argument as to why Karnak should be the king of all Drelek, Gar Klentja, who had also heard enough of the debate, put in, "I, too, am disappointed. I also had hoped you would be the new king."

That truly was the reason Zotar argued with such fervor. He had hoped Karnak would be the new king as well. Maybe it was partially due to some continued loyalty to his old friend Plak, but he saw much in the young gar and believed his destiny was greater than Karnak realized for himself.

"I'm sorry," Karnak's hand engulfed the elder gar's shoulder. "But I belong under the sun, breathing in the mist of the windswept sea."

"A poet, too," Gar Zotar grumbled sarcastically.

"Perhaps you set up Deklahn as king. If Jaernok Tur were to return, at least he would be able to fight magic with magic and defend his own mind from being twisted," Karnak suggested.

Deklahn quickly shut the idea down. "I am engaged with the other mages south of the mountains. I would not have the focus to care for the peoples of Drelek."

"I still don't understand why you can't take it, Gar Zotar. You were the one who raised the rebellion when others followed blindly," Smarlo said, trying to help Karnak.

"Gar Klentja and I are too old. The peoples of Drelek need a younger face. A face that is unknown to them. A face that signals change and a new direction. It will be hard enough for the peoples of our nation to break down the barriers in their minds regarding our new allies," Zotar said, gesturing to Merrick and Ralowyn. The two had been listening to the debate in silence. They did not want to interfere with the discussion, for they were honored even to be in the room for such an important moment. "Right now is the time for change that holds the tradition of honor among our peoples in high regard but leads to greater honor as we grow into our world."

Zotar's explanation was well crafted, and they were inspired by the idea. Karnak still wanted nothing to do with the throne. He wanted his simple life back in Calrok.

"Then Genjak," Karnak said, trying anything to keep the attention off himself.

Everyone in the room turned to Gar Klentja's second-in-command. The younger orc stood there, not sure what to say. He'd said next to nothing during the proceedings, anyway. No one else knew what to say either. None of them had considered the idea. Once he was presented, none of them could think of a reason why he couldn't be raised up to lead.

Young Genjak looked at the throne with great hesitation. The facts that he did not jump at the opportunity and that the rest of them had no immediate arguments made Karnak feel as though he were on to something.

"He cares deeply for the people. When we were all meeting at Lakjo to discuss Jaernok Tur's movements and our engagement with the dwarves, Genjak was the one helping the soldiers settle into homes where they could get some rest before our departure," Karnak pressed. "And surely, Deklahn can serve as an adviser while he pursues the magical mysteries with the other mages. In fact, it would be of great value for him to be so near the new king, so the king knows the goings-on of our neighbors to the south."

"It would be my great honor to serve the new king," Deklahn offered, pleased with the compromise.

"I have always known him to be loyal and honorable," Gar Klentja added about Genjak. He couldn't help but agree with the proposal.

Certainly, Genjak had not lived a perfect life, for none had. There in the throne room, though, none could bring an accusation against him that would disqualify him from taking the throne. He stood under their staring eyes, not sure what to say.

"Well, what say you, Genjak, son of Pargo, Commander of Borok?" Zotar asked.

The young orc sighed, his face solemn. "I would not dare take the throne without the wisdom of elders surrounding me," he stated firmly.

"And you shall have it," Gar Zotar responded. "There is great wisdom, even in that request. That humbleness will serve you well."

"Much wisdom can be found in a multitude of counselors," Klentja added. A smile of fatherly pride spanned his wide face. "And we shall be glad to serve you in that role."

"Yes," Zotar continued. "We will set up a council to aid and guide you. You will not bear the weight alone."

Genjak glanced at each of the orcs in the room, all of whom watched him with encouraging looks on their faces. Even the man-kin and elf woman gave him sympathetic smiles. They did not understand the full weight of the responsibility the orc gars presented him, but they recognized it was a heavy matter for him.

Finally, his gaze landed on the empty throne. "To a future hope," he said.

With that, Genjak accepted his fate.

As Karnak, Smarlo, Merrick and Ralowyn walked through Ruk, curious orcs, trolls, and goblins stopped and stared at the company. Karnak's annoyed looks made many of them turn away quickly, baffled at what they'd witnessed.

Smarlo bombarded Ralowyn with questions. The orc mage's curiosity had been fanned into flame as they discussed the magic of the elves. Ralowyn would offer a question here and there as they walked through the corridors and weaved down the hallways that lanced through the mountain. Smarlo was especially excited to find the magic of the elves was not so different in nature from their own. The elves simply tapped into ancient knowledge the orcs had no access to. Knowing Ralowyn planned to travel to Calrok with them, Smarlo excitedly offered to show her their small mage library.

Merrick's human eyes struggled in the din of the tunnels, but with a little help from an incantation of Ralowyn's making, he was able to witness the massive corridor with a huge stalagmite in the center. He turned to the left when the clanging of a heavy hammer stopped. A troll stood with his hammer raised halfway, staring over his anvil toward the man-kin.

The puzzled look on the troll's face made him appear quite silly. Merrick raised a hand and gave the troll a slight wave and smile. The troll looked shocked and turned slowly to see if there was someone behind him. When he turned back, he seemed to realize the human was waving at him, and he returned the wave with a tentative hand in the air. Merrick nodded and turned back to his group, which was entering a tavern across from the blacksmith. The hammering didn't continue for a good long while, as the troll questioned the reality of what he thought he'd witnessed.

Gar Karnak was greeted with cheers inside the tavern. Half the patrons were his own Scar Squadron, having found Reglese's tavern while their gar was in his meetings. A table near the bar had been reserved specifically for the group. Reglese had looked forward to seeing his gar after all the trials they'd been through.

Karnak was relieved to see the goblin in one piece. When he had thought the goblin entrepreneur to be in harm's way, guilt weighed on him. He enveloped Reglese in his great arms, and more cheers rang out. Getta delivered a round of glorb wine for the group that sat at the table and swapped stories. Reglese told his story with more than a little embellishment, as goblins are prone to do. He recounted how the two orc guards were ready to kill him, the impeccable timing of the cave-ins in the tunnels high above, and the heroics of his friends Getta and Kig.

The excitement that filled the tavern was palpable, and it made Merrick think of the Flagkeep Tavern back in Tamaria. Perhaps all their peoples weren't so different, after all. Though admittedly, he wasn't sure his human stomach could handle any more glorb wine. He pretended to nurse his goblet out of politeness and enjoyed the goblins and orcs reminiscing.

They asked Merrick to share his part of the story. Every one of them watched, listened, and marveled at what he'd endured. They enjoyed his tale, and when he explained the last bit about wanting to experience more with the orcs, they all cheered. Many slapped large hands on his back with excitement. Ralowyn giggled as she took a second away from her and Smarlo's continued conversation to watch Merrick take all the encouraging, but rough, back pats.

"Reglese," Karnak started. "You've served Calrok with great honor. It will not be forgotten."

The goblin accepted the compliment from his gar, placed a finger to his brow, and gave a slight bow. "I would do it again in an 'eartbeat," he said. Since he thought it would not be necessary, he felt safe to be as noble as possible.

"Will you be returning with us to Calrok?" Karnak asked.

"Actually," the goblin hemmed. "It's as you 'ave said. Lox is good at 'is job, and 'e didn't run the tavern in Calrok to the ground. And Getta and Kig are very capable 'ere. I thought I might try to open another in Borok and then maybe Dak-Tahn. And then I can expand west to build a tavern on my glorb wine in every orc fort in Drelek."

"Great dreams you have." Karnak smiled. "I am happy to see you chase them. But I want you to know you are always welcome back home in Calrok."

Karnak stood and yelled. "Scar Squadron!" The entire place went silent as all the riders from Calrok stood and listened. "One for Reglese, honorary warrior of Calrok."

Karnak placed his finger to his brow and bowed. All around the tavern, Scar Squadron members did the same. Merrick and Ralowyn were moved by the scene, as others throughout the tavern stood and joined the Calrok warriors in honoring the goblin.

Reglese was overwhelmed with the display, and tears escaped his eyes.

Karnak looked at the goblin directly and said, "Thank you, my friend."

"My Gar," Reglese nodded through his tears.

Then Karnak raised his goblet high. "The next round's on me!"

Cheers rang out once more, and excited goblins and orcs clanged their tankards together, resuming their celebration.

Karnak had never been more excited to see the Gant Sea appear as they crested the mountains on the eastern edge of Drelek. He glanced over to Merrick, riding the marvelous astral falcon, and caught the man-kin's mouth agape in wonder. His response did not disappoint the orc, for the man-kin was in utter awe. Having talked with Merrick, the gar had learned the huntsman had never seen the sea and that seeing things from this altitude was also a new experience. Karnak had expected the moment would be quite the experience for the man. Indeed, it was.

Scar Squadron riders split off in multiple directions as they made their way to their individual homes. Even Smarlo nodded and waved his goodbye to Ralowyn and Merrick, who were to follow Karnak on his descent.

They landed in a field of wildflowers that sloped away from the rocky mountains with a graceful ease. Karnak slipped out of his saddle and removed it from Ker's back. He slid his hand along her neck and thanked her for her faithful service before releasing her to an evening of fishing. She would probably find some time to rest up on the Scar Cliffs at some point during the night, but she had been far from the coast for a long time and was excited to enjoy fresh fish.

Merrick and Ralowyn followed suit and dismounted. Merrick stroked Valurwind's speckled feathers, and the great astral bird clicked its tongue happily. They were getting along quite well, and Merrick found great comfort in knowing the bird would come whenever he called. In the meantime, the mighty bird would be off to the astral planes, soaring among the stars. Valurwind flapped her great wings and lifted herself away from the trio, who watched as a glittering black mist swirled about her before she vanished.

"Is there a place where this one will be safe?" Ralowyn asked Karnak as she unsaddled the grey spotted pegasus, whose name was Henry.

A rather ordinary name for a pegasus, Merrick had thought to himself. Having seen the pegasus in person, he did not think the creature to be ordinary in the least.

"Of course," Karnak said. "This paddock is my family's. That small barn over there is where we can hang our saddles. Come. I'll show you."

As Ralowyn followed the large orc to the structure, Merrick stretched his back and gazed over the city of Calrok. The Scar Cliffs stood with a mighty presence high above the city to his left, their ridges and face chiseled with shadow and light. The Gant Sea glinted in the evening sun that was trying to disappear over the mountains behind him. The view from the field was almost as incredible as the one he had enjoyed when they'd crested the mountain ridge. Karnak had not exaggerated the beauty of his home.

Henry nuzzled Merrick's shoulder, content as he munched on some wildflowers he'd found to be rather tasty. Karnak and Ralowyn came out of the barn, laughing with each other. As they did, a small green creature with wild black hair darted across the paddock to greet them.

"Dada!" he squealed, his hands waving above his head, out of control, as he ran.

"Gernot!" Karnak returned the call and scooped up the little tyke in his arms. He swung him through the air to make the little orc feel like he was flying. Karnak then tucked the chubby orc in close and hugged him for a long time. "I have missed you, my son."

"Save some of that affection for your wife, too, now!" A female orc called from the doorway of the cozy house at one end of the field.

Karnak's smile grew into a great grin. "Why don't you come and get it!" He called back.

Tanessa feigned offense but started walking through the field of flowers to meet her husband. Karnak couldn't help himself and met her halfway. They embraced each other with a kiss and a tight hug that made Gernot laugh as he was squished between them.

Ralowyn stepped next to Merrick as they watched the family's touching reunion. It seemed odd to Merrick that in all the stories he'd heard about orcs in years past, he had never heard one of orc families. He thought that peculiar, for it seemed to him so obvious that Karnak, as Merrick had come to know him, would be an orc who loved his family.

Tanessa prepared a fine meal for the weary travelers. The fish in the center of the table was larger than any Merrick had ever seen. The cooked creature was of the sea and made the river and brook fish he'd eaten before look like snacks. Tanessa had seasoned the fish with a mixture of herbs, some grown from her own garden and some acquired from Calrok's market square. She had also prepared a spicy grain rice and some form of purple cruciferous vegetable. Merrick was pleasantly surprised at how appetizing everything looked. The mix of spices and the crackling fire made for a warm and welcoming aroma.

Merrick insisted on helping clean up after dinner, even though Tanessa tried to shoo him away several times. When he proved himself adept at cleaning, the orc woman relaxed and embraced his help.

Merrick laughed with Tanessa as he brought more from the table. "My mother would have my neck if I didn't help tidy."

"I suppose mothers have that effect on their sons in many cultures," Tanessa smiled. "Karnak's mother used to live in the cottage when we first got married and his father had passed. She got on him all the time for chores around the paddock."

Merrick chuckled at the thought of the giant orc being scolded by his mom. "Mothers can be pretty good at pointing out what their sons should do."

"Nevertheless, she doted on him as though he were a treasure."

Tanessa looked into the sitting room where Karnak sat on the floor with Gernot, laughing and playing. Ralowyn used magic lights to create moving images in the middle of the room for the little tyke's entertainment. Gernot tried to grab a flying lavender pegasus, which spun and whirled into the form of a wyvern out of the little orc's grip. He laughed crazily at the game as Karnak spurred him on with encouragement. Ralowyn noticed the two watching from the kitchen and flashed them a joyful smile.

"It seems like a treasure to me," Merrick said to the orc wife and mother.

"I like them, alright," she teased. "I'll keep them around a while."

The night drew to a close after a riveting orc tale that put the wiped out Gernot to sleep. Tanessa walked Merrick and

Ralowyn to the cottage near the barn, while Karnak tucked his son in for the first time in weeks.

Tanessa opened the door to the small cottage and explained there was only one room with a proper bed. Karnak's mother had always run cold, though, so there were enough blankets to make up another sleeping spot in the small sitting room. Merrick pushed the pair of large weaved chairs to the walls and made room for the blankets Tanessa produced from the small bedroom.

"Thank you," Merrick said. "I have to admit your kindness surprises me."

"Perhaps you do not understand orcs as well as you thought you did," Tanessa said to him with a wry grin.

"No, I did not," he admitted. "But I'm learning."

"To be fair," the orc woman said. "I was not entirely sure about you two, either. But I trust my husband. And I do not believe there is anything in this world he wouldn't do to protect us. Because of that, I do not believe he would have brought you here if he thought any ill of you.

He is an honorable orc. He's not perfect—ask his wife," she winked to him playfully. "But in the end, he always tries to do the right thing."

Merrick nodded thoughtfully. He and Karnak's first meeting had resulted in the loss of his dear falcon Rora. Since then, he had come to know the large orc to be kind and generous. Forgiveness had not been his initial thought when he saw Karnak on his knees, high upon the king's landing at Ruk. They had been through much since, and he had forgiven the orc.

He chuckled slightly. "It seems he found himself a great woman to keep him grounded and fighting for what's right."

Tanessa took the compliment in stride and motioned her head in the direction of the small bedroom. "And seems to me you might have found one yourself?"

Merrick looked over to the bedroom and heard Ralowyn humming as she prepared for bed. The huntsman's cheeks flushed as he tried to deny the orc woman's notion. "No. I ... Uh, we're ... Well ..."

He shook his head, not knowing how to dissuade her, but Tanessa gave him a knowing look and shrugged her shoulders. "Karnak didn't realize I was the best thing for him at first either. Took him a while to see it, too."

Tanessa gave him a sideways glance and a mischievous smile as she bade him goodnight and closed the cottage door behind her. Merrick released a burst of amusement. He walked to the doorway where Ralowyn was standing the Staff of Anvelorian in the corner. The bed was without wrinkle as she had fixed it with different blankets. They had taken the thicker ones off the bed so Merrick could have them in the sitting room. He watched her for a moment as she hummed to herself.

She turned and caught him at the doorway, staring. Her bright grin added to her shimmering beauty, as flowing strands of silvery hair fell in front of her face. She shyly pulled them back behind her pointed ear.

Merrick smiled at her and said, "Goodnight, fair Ralowyn."

He turned away and returned to the sitting room where he would make his nest of blankets into a usable bed.

"Goodnight," he heard from the other room as the door closed quietly with a wind of magic.

He smiled as he gathered two blankets and a pillow. When he got comfortable, he put his hands behind his head and stared at the ceiling in the small cottage. The moonlight formed interesting shadows as it crept through the window.

Merrick thought of all the things that had happened since he left Tamaria. It had been quite the adventure, with highs and lows. As he lay in the cottage of an orc gar near the Gant Sea, he could hardly believe how it all had played out. Even in that strange scenario, he found a sense of peace and slipped into his dreams with ease.

Chapter Thirty-Four
A Gathering In Whitestone

C oronation day snuck up on them all. Everyone had been busy recovering from the various battles. Not only did they have repairs and preparations to make, they also had funerals and leadership changes that needed to take place.

Whitestone, in particular, had been in a mad scramble over the past couple of weeks. People worked together to clean up and prepare their city for visiting guests from all of Tarrine.

The Griffin Guard had taken some huge blows, and many of them had fallen prey to the deception magic of Jaernok Tur. Over the past two weeks, though, all of them had been able to shake off the residual effects of the dark magic. The guardians who had been thrown into the dungeons and tortured during the sorcerer's brief control were released and healed. Many of them had already returned to duty.

The Griffin Guard was being rebuilt and restructured. The loss of High Commander Danner Kane was particularly heavy for all of them. He had been well loved and regarded by the guardians with unwavering trust.

Pernden and Commander Mattness had many discussions, and she had accepted the call of her soon-to-be king and taken on the role of High Commander of the Griffin Guard. Pernden had always known her to be tough but fair. The fact she was able to shake the dark magic of the sorcerer at the perfect time and rally the rest of the guardians was a testament to her ability to lead. She was the obvious choice.

Nera had led beside him for a long time, so Pernden quickly chose her as his replacement for Captain of the Talon Squadron. The squadron knew her well. Not to mention, her new prowess with the magical spear Santoralier left none in doubt of her abilities. She would lead them well.

Plus, while Pernden would have many new responsibilities as king, he considered the close access he had to the king when he had been Captain of the Talon Squadron. Whether he would admit it or not, he wanted Nera near him. He greatly valued her advice and opinions, two assets he welcomed as he took on his weighty role.

Orin had lost his entire squadron, and diving into another was not at the forefront of his mind. Pernden thought better of it as well. As Orin had explained his experiences and the need for the guardians to remember who they fight for, Pernden could think of no one better to organize the initiative. Orin had spent more time among the peoples of Tarrine during his sojourn than most guardians had in years. There would be more to discuss on the matter, but Pernden saw the necessity of the guardians being part of the world they protected.

The coronation was a grand affair. Whitestone had not seen so many dignitaries in all its history. King Thygram Markensteel had brought a group of his people and a small regiment of war-hog warriors. The Loralith Riders who had stayed in Galium had traveled with them.

Coal and Ezel embraced Orin and Ellaria, who greeted them when they arrived. Argus and Lanryn looked around excitedly for Smarlo and Deklahn as the wyvern riders of Drelek flew into town.

The whole city took a collective breath as the orcs flew overhead. But Pernden, who was already doing a fine job at encouraging his people, was the first to greet the travelers from Drelek when they landed.

All said, they had four kings in the city. Genjak, the new king of Drelek, had come to show his support for their peoples' budding friendship. Even King Solorin and Queen Velari had made the journey from Loralith.

The ceremony was magnificent. Orin was granted the honor of placing the crown upon his brother's head in front of the great crowd of witnesses. In that moment, the brothers shared a look, recognizing the heaviness Orin placed on Pernden.

"We will visit our cousin tomorrow," Pernden said with a hint of sadness.

"Dona says he seems to have come back to himself, at least to the best of her ability to heal." Orin shrugged slightly. Sorrow filled his eyes.

"Perhaps after we visit him, we can bring Ellaria to see him. Who knows what her magic could do to help him?"

Orin's head dipped. He worried for a second but then shook it away. "That is a matter for tomorrow."

He hugged his brother close, took a step back, placed his fist on the Whitestone crest on his new armor, and bowed low.

The entire gathering bowed low to honor the new king. Even the other royals present gave him a slight bow, acknowledging his new position.

For the first time, as Pernden looked over the sea of peoples, intermingled—as many of them had found the friends they had made in Galium—the young king recognized the true weight of the event. He was among the leaders who would have to protect that newfound unity. They would have to nurture and grow the future hope for their peoples.

He had always been confident in his abilities. Not prideful, but certain he could handle anything. Melkis had trained him and his brothers well and instilled in them a solid foundation of confidence and faith. Pernden had been selected to serve in the Griffin Guard's elite Talon Squadron from a young age because of his abilities. He had led them through many difficult and sometimes seemingly impossible missions.

But the task ahead was different. For the first time in his life, his confidence wavered.

He had always led warriors on warrior tasks. The weight of responsibility over all these people and the challenges facing them all began to crush him.

A slender hand curled its fingers in a comforting grip with his. Nera's eyes peeked up at Pernden, and her smile brimmed with the confidence he needed. He took it and squeezed her hand in thanks.

"Thank you, all!" he shouted as the gathered peoples looked back up to him at the top of the stairs in Whitestone's main square. "I am honored to be called your king. And I will do my best to live up to that call."

The crowd watched him silently. He wasn't sure, but it seemed as though they waited for him to make some rousing speech. He looked to the leaders who stood nearby, and all of them beamed at him with pride. He looked out over the crowd again and decided it was much too quiet and he had no such speech.

"I'm pretty certain this is supposed to be a celebration." He paused again, as everyone looked at him in confusion. "So, let's celebrate!"

The crowd exploded in an uproar of applause and laughter. Musicians around the square played old songs of kings and new songs of heroism inspired by recent battles. People enjoyed food and drink, stories and jokes. Where there was hesitation about the orcs earlier, they now enjoyed great fellowship.

Many came to congratulate the new king with excited dreams about the future of Whitestone.

Merriment echoed around the city, reverberating off the white stone and reaching into the depths of the damp dungeon. A fallen king drew himself nearer to a high window so he might hear some of the joy he utterly lacked in his current state. Garron's mind had cleared to an extent, but he had spoken very little to anyone, including Dona. She had been nursing him back to health and had been kind to him.

A shuffling noise behind him shifted his attention into the darkness of the dungeon. His eyes had a difficult time adjusting to the pitch after staring at the brightness of the window. He peered hard into the darkness but saw nothing.

"Though blind, you have seen ..."

Garron's heart pounded as though it wanted to climb out of his chest. He shook his head and blinked his eyes, trying to see through the dim or shake the voice out of his mind. When the light of the window glinted off some flowing golden fabric beyond the bars of his cell, he realized he was not alone and hearing whispers.

"W-what?" Garron stammered. "Who's there?"

"Though blind, you have seen."

The figure groped at the bars with gangly fingers. She pressed her face between two bars, and Garron recoiled at the sight. It was a she-elf who wore a strange cloth over her eyes, and streaks ran down her face.

"Who are you?" he asked.

"I am like you. I am a seer," she responded. "You know the land is destined to be covered by shadow."

"No ..." Garron started to argue, but he could not.

"Yes. You know it to be so." Her voice came out in a hoarse whisper as she scolded him.

"No. My cousin has defeated him ..." Garron started again.

"Hahaha!" she cackled. "How does a man defeat one who walks among the shadows?"

"He is an orc. Orcs can be killed."

"And how did that work out for you, fallen king?"

"I—"

"You what?" she yelled. "The wave is coming. None will be saved from the flood of darkness."

"Then warn them." Garron yelled back, frustrated by her blasé tone. "If he intends to return, then you must help them."

"They do not listen to my ways anymore. The peoples of Tarrine have gotten arrogant. The old ways are forgotten," she spat. "The end draws nearer, and they cannot see. This war cannot be won."

"I don't believe you ..." Garron growled.

"You lie to yourself," she laughed. "For you have seen. You know it to be true."

A sudden noise of children running and playing a game outside the window startled Garron. When he turned back again from the window, the seer was gone. Tears streaked his own face, and pressure built up in his creased forehead. His sobs sent his body into a heaving fit as he curled into a ball in the corner of his cell.

While the whole of Whitestone celebrated, its fallen king wept.

The morning sun spilled through the high windows of the dungeon beneath Whitestone castle. In the mornings, the dungeon was well lit, which woke occupants early. Dona hummed as she entered, the same tune she'd hummed thousands of times. She caught herself, thinking it rude to hum while she led guests into the place.

When Garron saw her and the two men she escorted, a single tear rolled down the side of his face.

Pernden was struck with how much better his cousin looked, even in that wretched place. Garron had been eating again at Dona's constant nagging. He had filled back in a little, no longer looking like a bag of bones. Dona had also been adamant about cleaning him up. He was freshly shaved only a couple days ago, and his hair was trimmed, making him look less scraggly than he had before.

Garron approached the bars and stared in shock as Orin stepped to Pernden's side.

"Cousin!" Garron said, elated.

"Hello, Garron," Orin smiled. "It's good to see you again."

"You would not have said so only a few days ago. Dona has been taking very good care of me." He paused and looked over at the nurse, who waited with a raised eyebrow as if to let him know he should finish his thought with care. "Even if I'm not always happy about it."

They all shared amused looks, even Dona.

"How do you feel, cousin?" Pernden asked.

Garron shifted uncomfortably. There was a long pause. An uneasy tension filled the room.

"I am sorry," Garron said to Pernden. "I was out of my mind. I was not myself."

"I know," Pernden said. "This whole thing has been a mess."

"Yes," Garron's head drooped as he agreed.

After another brief silence, Orin laughed. "Do you remember that time when we were young boys, and Melkis had Garron spend the week with us at the Corral to give him a taste of what life would be like when he eventually came to train with us?"

The other two snickered at the memory.

"Garron was always getting us into trouble," Pernden added.

"I seem to remember a certain young Orin who climbed through the window of the war room to unlock the door for us," Garron said, feigning offense.

"Yeah? And who was it that said we should add tar to the feathers before we covered the whole room?" Orin asked.

"Yeah, who was that?" Garron echoed, giving Pernden a wry look.

"Okay, okay," Pernden surrendered with his hands up. "That was a sticky mess. I had tar on my hands for weeks. The only reason we even got caught."

"It felt like it took weeks to clean the war room," Orin said.

"It was only a few days," Garron shrugged, humorously. "And I took most of Melkis's—"

There it was. He hadn't said Melkis's name since ...

Orin noticed their flinches, and the awkward silence fell in the room again. He tried to recover the heartfelt moment.

"You know, no matter how much trouble you two got me tangled up in," he smirked at them both, "you always managed to fix it later."

Pernden and Garron looked at each other.

"I'm sorry for what I have taken from all of us," Garron said, tears welling.

"I am too," Pernden replied.

"I'm also sorry that the weight of the crown has fallen upon your shoulders. It was my responsibility. My duty. But I cannot be the people's king. I have killed the heart of their trust."

"No. You can't." Pernden sighed. He did not want to be the king of Whitestone. It had never been a thing he'd considered. But the duty had fallen to him, and here he was. "I will carry the burden the best I can."

"I will help in whatever way I can," Garron said, reaching his arm to Pernden through the bars.

Pernden took the extended arm. "We will get you better and get you out of here."

All of a sudden, Garron was caught in a difficult position. He heard the words of the elven seer in his mind. The doom she foretold. The devastation he knew was coming. He wanted to warn them. He wanted to tell his cousins what was coming. But he also realized how crazy he would sound, and he did not want to stay in the dungeons anymore. No. Perhaps if he waited for the right time ... If he waited until they could see he was sound of mind again. Then he could tell them, and they would listen.

Garron drew in a deep breath and tipped his chin. "I look forward to it."

Coal and Ezel happily munched on a couple of skewered meats they had acquired from a vendor in the Whitestone Market. They hurried along to keep up with their friends' longer strides.

The vendors of Whitestone had quite enjoyed the many visitors from out of town. Many of the orcs and elves and dwarves were eager to try all that Whitestone locals had to offer. It was great for business. And after everything that had happened, it revitalized many of the merchants.

Orin led the group onward, following the road through the city. He intended to show them the renowned Grand Corral, a place that had been his home for so many years. It was then, as they walked and laughed together, that he remembered their time at the beginning of their journey on the *Lady Leila*, rowing up the Palori River. Though Ralowyn had not been with them then, she and Merrick seemed to be growing closer. As she had spent more time with them, she fit right in with their ragtag group.

When they arrived at the Grand Corral, Orin took them inside and gave them a thorough tour. So thorough, Coal ribbed him about the tour being so long it was time for another meal. Orin paused for a moment. His muscle memory had him moving toward his old room. When another guardian emerged, it took a second for him to remember they had all thought him to be dead.

The thought that he would not get another room in the barracks, but rather, one at the castle, was still odd. He would miss being here with all the other guardians. Like the Griffin Guard, Whitestone, and the rest of Tarrine, Orin, too, was entering a new season.

Once the tour was over, Orin took them to the Corral's main dining hall but was redirected to the officer's dining hall by an adamant High Commander Mattness. Orin graciously accepted the redirect because of his guests but felt awkward about eating there. He'd spent so many years eating with the other guardians, it gave him an uncomfortable twinge not to do so. The rambunctious group that accompanied him distracted from the location, and he soon fell into the conversation with his friends.

"I'm thinking Ezel and I will stay here in Whitestone with you and Ellaria for a while if that's alright," Coal said.

"Of course," Orin replied. "In fact, I may need some help with a new mission from Pernden. That is, if you don't have other plans."

"I don't know ..." Coal trailed, tugging at the long black braid on the front of his big beard. "The last time we helped you, it caused us all sort of trouble."

"Of course, we'll help," Ezel signed.

"Of course," Coal waved him off. "I was only playing with him."

"I need a break from Galium for a while."

"Yeah, no kidding," Coal said. "Argus has always been a little bit pushy—"

"A little?"

Coal laughed. "Well ... maybe a little more than a little. But he and Lanryn ... ugh, you know the elf mage from Loralith?"

Coal shrugged a knowing hand toward Ralowyn, hoping she could chime in on the elf mage.

"I know him," she said, looking quite amused, while the rest of the group nodded.

"Well, anyway, those two have been asking Ezel questions about our time with the wizard, Enkeli. They want to know how the token works and what else it might do. I guess it's not every day you run into a wizard artifact. I also think they don't like that they don't understand Ezel's magic. I tried to explain to them it was a sea witch that saved his life. A monster of a pirate had nearly killed him, you know."

Everyone stared at the dwarf, no idea what he was talking about.

"Oh, I haven't told you that story yet?"

"Another time," Ezel waved him off the rabbit trail. *"Point is, I'm tired of all their prodding. So, yes. We can stay and help you."*

Orin had caught some of Ezel's signing. He was getting better at it. Coal translated anyway, so all knew what the deep gnome had said.

"And will you be staying for a while, Ralowyn?" Ellaria asked.

"Well ..." the elf started to reply and pulled some of her silvery hair out of her face. She tucked the strands behind her pointed ear.

"Actually, sister," Merrick cut in. "The people of Calrok have been rather good to us. They have been kind, and the city is so beautiful."

"You mean to stay in Calrok?" Ellaria asked.

She watched as Merrick looked to Ralowyn. They had been getting close. She saw something in her brother she hadn't seen in a very long time: hope. Though, Ellaria wasn't sure her brother realized yet what he and Ralowyn's relationship could bud into.

Boys, she shook her head humorously.

"Gar Karnak has graciously extended the invitation for us to stay longer," Merrick continued. "I've begun training with Valurwind on the Scar Cliffs with the wyvern squadron there. I'm learning so much. Valurwind and I are really starting to work as a team. And Ralowyn and I have spent a lot of time with Karnak's family."

Merrick laughed at a thought, and Ralowyn pursed her lips, knowing what he was thinking. She shared with the others. "Just the other day, I was playing in the field with Gernot, by their home, and he ran off to hide. I couldn't find him, and of course, I got worried that I lost our host's son. I was frantically looking everywhere for him, while Merrick sat on the steps to the cottage and watched me."

"She even grabbed her staff and tried to use magic to find him!" Merrick added to the story.

"Yes, but the whole time, Merrick had him hidden under a heavy cloak sitting in a pile right next to him on the step."

Merrick laughed again, and the others joined in his glee.

"I couldn't help it. Her face was so great!"

"I'm glad to see you like this, Merrick," Orin said. "It seems Calrok has been good for you."

"It has," Merrick said, as Ralowyn elbowed him playfully.

"It's funny, but you don't usually think of orc families," the she-elf said.

"You know, I had the same thought when we first arrived. But Gernot is great. And Tanessa is beautiful."

"Tanessa is absolutely lovely," Ralowyn agreed.

Ellaria teared up as she watched her brother. Merrick caught the look, stood, and walked around the table. He bent over to give his sister a big squeeze. "I love you, Ella," he said softly.

"I love you, too," she said. "I just love seeing you happy."

Merrick chuckled. "It's been some time since I've felt this way."

"Who would have thought I would find my brother again in an orc city?"

Merrick looked her straight in the eyes. He had no more words. He had tried to be a good brother, but he'd always felt he had let his entire family down when they'd lost his big brother Greggo. Here, with his sister and their new friends, he realized it had never been his fault, and he was never going to be Greggo. He didn't need to be; he could be Merrick.

"I think it'll be great for you to stay in Calrok and continue to grow there," Orin said. "Part of what Pernden wants me to do is help Whitestone and the Griffin Guard be more tightly knit within the fabric of the other peoples of Tarrine. If you can grow in an orc city, it gives me great hope we can do so, as well."

"Karnak and Smarlo have spoken often of this 'future hope' we are embarking on," Merrick added.

"Argus and Lanryn, as well," Coal put in.

"With everything we've seen," Orin said. "It seems Tarrine has a great future for us to build toward, together."

The friends raised their cups and took deep swigs. They laughed and ate and drank for a long time. Tomorrow, they would get to what the future held. Today, they were glad to be together.

EPILOGUE

O ne month later ...

The huntsman enjoyed sitting on the porch to the cottage, overlooking the city of Calrok. The great moon illuminated the city with a silvery glow and made the waves of the Gant Sea sparkle. The Scar Cliffs best lived up to their name in the glow: scarred silhouettes etching the night sky.

Merrick had embraced the evenings as his time for peace and quiet. Evenings had also become an opportunity for reflection with Ralowyn, sometimes Karnak, and even on occasion, Tanessa. He enjoyed the evenings so much they had moved the two chairs from the little cottage to its porch.

When Merrick first sat down that night, Karnak waved before heading inside for the evening. Everyone had turned in, and Merrick was grateful for his time of peace.

Once fatigue set in, he lifted himself out of the old chair and entered the small cottage.

They had seen fit to acquire a more proper bed for him, and the sitting room had been transformed into a bedroom for him. Merrick glanced at the door on the right and smiled at the thought of Ralowyn asleep there. He had learned that the slight elf could snore like a great plains bear. He grinned at the memory of a particularly loud night. But that night, all was quiet, and the stillness made for great sleeping conditions. He was in bed for only a moment before he was swept off into his dreams.

The night was quiet across the city of Calrok. Even the bells near the docks chimed almost inaudibly as the moored ships bobbed on calm waves. The orcs in the watchtowers that overlooked the docks were content to save their whispered conversations for another night.

Everything was quiet, including the deliberate and controlled paddling that cut through the water.

The small crew of the boat that crept around the bend, following the coastline northward, rowed in silent synchronization. They did not need to speak or whisper. They had reviewed their plan many times. They knew what to do and why they had come to Calrok.

As they beached their vessel among some reeds to the south of the city, they climbed out and hiked over the low ridge of a rocky outcropping. The moon's light touched them for only a second before they disappeared into the shadows again. One of them signaled to the others, and they spread out, each following a path of their own to the same destination. Their work would be painstakingly slow in order to make their way through the still city undetected.

They were there because they were the best. Each brandished their preferred weapon for the dastardly work they were well trained to do. They would swoop in like a shadow and vanish like smoke. If all went according to plan, none of the sleeping folk of Calrok would even know they had been there.

Someone would eventually find their prey. But by then, the team of assassins would be long gone. After all, they were the best Kelvur had to offer.

And even better, the huntsman did not know he had become the hunted.

ACKNOWLEDGEMENTS

Thank you for reading my book! I hope you had as much fun flying through the sky with the Griffin Guard as I did writing this adventure. If so, please leave a wonderful review. Reviews are the lifeblood of indie authors like me. The more positive reviews we have, the more likely it is that others will pick up the book as well.

A lot went into this book and I've had some great encouragement and love from folks along the way. But I would be remiss if I didn't thank a few very specific people for helping me on this journey.

First of all, Crystal. You were the first to dive into the world of Finlestia and explore the adventures within. Your suggestions and encouragement were instrumental in this process. More importantly, your friendship means the world to me.

Joy, thank you for joining me on this mission and helping me to grammar. I believe this book is absolutely better because of your guidance and magic touch. Looking forward to working together for a long time!

And finally, my wife Brittany and our kids, you encouraged and inspired me to chase after this crazy dream. You have sacrificed time on countless days to allow me to blaze trails through this fantasy world. I love you guys.

ABOUT THE AUTHOR

Z.S. Diamanti is an author, illustrator, and creator. His debut novel, *Stone & Sky,* is an epic fantasy adventure and the result of his great passion for fun and fantastical stories. He went to college forever and has too many pieces of paper on his wall. He is a USAF veteran of Operation Enduring Freedom and worked in ministry for over 10 years. He and his wife reside in Colorado with their four children where they enjoy hikes and tabletop games.

You can get the *Stone & Sky Preludes Series* of stories for FREE at zsdiamanti.com

Connect with him on social media: @zsdiamanti

CONNECT

CONTINUE THE ADVENTURE!

READ THE SECOND BOOK IN

THE STONE & SKY SERIES

AVAILABLE
EARLY 2024

ORDER NOW!

Good reviews are vital for Indie Authors. The importance of reviews in helping others find and take a chance on an indie author's book is impossible to overstate.

If you enjoyed this book, would you help me get it in front of more people by taking a minute to give it a good review? I can't tell you how thankful I'd be.

Check out this link for the best places to review this book and help me get it to more readers who love good books just like you and me!

Made in the USA
Middletown, DE
19 November 2023

42952110R00276